THE BEST SHORT PLAYS *1972*

BOOKS AND PLAYS *by Stanley Richards*

BOOKS:

The Best Short Plays 1971
The Best Short Plays 1970
The Best Short Plays 1969
The Best Short Plays 1968
Best Mystery and Suspense Plays of the Modern Theatre
Best Plays of the Sixties
Modern Short Comedies from Broadway and London
Best Short Plays of the World Theatre: 1958–1967
Canada on Stage

PLAYS:

Through a Glass, Darkly
August Heat
Sun Deck
Tunnel of Love
Journey to Bahia
O Distant Land
Mood Piece
Mr. Bell's Creation
The Proud Age
Once to Every Boy
Half-Hour, Please
Know Your Neighbor
Gin and Bitterness
The Hills of Bataan
District of Columbia

Chilton Book Company
PHILADELPHIA / NEW YORK

THE BEST SHORT PLAYS *1972*

edited and with an introduction by

STANLEY RICHARDS

First Edition

Published in Philadelphia by Chilton Book Company
and simultaneously in Ontario, Canada,
by Thomas Nelson & Sons, Ltd.

ISBN: 0-8019-5588-2
Library of Congress Catalog Card Number 38-8006
Manufactured in the United States of America
Designed by Adrianne Onderdonk Dudden

for Norman Holland

"I count myself in nothing else so happy
As in a soul remembering my good friends."
—William Shakespeare

CONTENTS

INTRODUCTION

Since this present collection marks the fifth anniversary of my editorship of *The Best Short Plays,* I felt that the occasion should be celebrated with a personal and generous measure of appreciation to those who have contributed to the success of the series as well as to the all-important audience without whom no theatre could possibly exist.

My gratitude to my contributors and our readers is immense, for without either there could not have been the record of achievement that has made the past five years so productive and rewarding. Thus, if I seem to be trumpeting a bit loudly this year, I sincerely beg forgiveness.

Beginning with *The Best Short Plays 1968,* these annuals have presented seventy-one plays; almost ninety percent of them receiving their first publication in these pages. The list of contributors include some of our foremost international dramatists, yet there is an almost equal representation of new and outstanding young talents, a number of whom have since gone on to their own prominence.

Plays from these collections have been widely produced on professional and amateur stages, in colleges and universities, community and summer stock theatres, and on network television.

Quite a few have successfully survived sea changes by being effectively produced in distant areas of the world ranging from Cairo to Rio de Janeiro. And this, to me, is one of the most significant tasks of an editor: the ability to select plays that can appeal widely and to various cultures.

One might well, and justifiably, ask: just how is this accomplished? The answers, of course, are numerous and dependent upon those questioned. Yet, a basic factor remains steadfast in spite of all the advances of theatrical techniques and increasing experimentation. Drama is rooted in humanity and, consequently, for a play to have audience appeal it must revolve about that most essential element, characterization; vivid, vibrant people from whom all else springs dramatically. When the legendary Sarah Siddons was queried about what she was looking for in plays, whether new or old, she is reported to have replied, "truth to nature." She did not mean naturalism but rather that the situations and the emotions expressed by the *characters* should be credible ones which both she and her audiences could accept as true to human nature, however extravagantly or in whatever form they might be expressed.

Undoubtedly, there will be some members of the esoteric brigade who will take a dim view of this theory. Yet, if they delve into theatrical history, beginning with ancient Greece through Shakespeare to modern times, they surely will concede that the most durable plays have been those that dealt first with characters, then ideas.

Too many of our younger and less experienced dramatists (at least those whose work I have read during the past several years) seemed to have reversed things: they started with ideas and tacked on their people, higgledy-piggledy. Often they dealt with worthy subjects, themes that lent themselves to dramatic exploration, but the plays were negated because there was little or no true involvement of characters: they merely were moveable figures in a mechanical game contrived by the author when they ought to have been the motivating factors in the development of the plays.

By coincidence, as this was being written, I had a telephone call from a representative of a new theatre magazine. In essence, the call was to gather information on how I compile my anthologies and what particular type of audience I intended to reach. My reply was candidly simple: "All types."

A perusal of the contents of the first five volumes of *The Best Short Plays* proves this, I believe, for there is a vast diversity in style and content, yet all the plays dramatically explore various facets of the human condition, the world that engulfs all of us.

Assuredly, not all of the selections will have appealed to everyone. But, just as assuredly, each play will have appealed to someone and, consequently, by diversifying my annual selections, hopefully we reach through to all types of audiences. And while each of us undeniably has personal predilections, I should like to take the liberty of quoting the Nobel Prize poet, Pablo Neruda: "And yet I dare think we agree on what we *all* want: a theatre that is simple without being simplistic, critical but not inhuman, advancing like a river of the Andes whose only limits are those it itself imposes."

Now, on to the next five years. . . .

STANLEY RICHARDS
New York
February, 1972

Clare Boothe Luce

SLAM THE DOOR SOFTLY

Clare Boothe Luce

Regardless of one's political proclivities, it can not be denied that Clare Boothe Luce is one of the most notable American women of the twentieth century. Indeed, in a Gallup poll conducted in the early 1950's, she was listed fourth among the world's "most admired women," after Mrs. Eleanor Roosevelt, Queen Elizabeth II, and Mrs. Dwight D. Eisenhower.

Born in New York City on April 10, 1903, she attended Clare Tree Major's School of the Theatre and as a child understudied Mary Pickford in David Belasco's production of *A Good Little Devil* and played a minor role in a motion picture. Her plans for a career in the theatre were interrupted, however, by a trip to Europe with her parents and later by marriage to George T. Brokaw.

When her marriage to Brokaw ended in divorce in 1929, she resumed her former name and as Clare Boothe joined the staff of *Vogue* as an editorial assistant in 1930. A year later she became associate editor of *Vanity Fair* and by 1933 she was its managing editor. But the theatre beckoned once again and in 1935 her first produced play *Abide With Me,* arrived on Broadway. Two days after the play opened, Miss Boothe married the publishing magnate, Henry Luce.

Though her first Broadway entry was not too well received, she enjoyed enormous success the following year (1936) with *The Women*. It ran for 657 performances in New York, toured extensively, and eventually was presented in eighteen foreign countries. In 1939, it was made into a vastly popular film with a gilded roster of stars headed by Norma Shearer, Joan Crawford, Rosalind Russell and Joan Fontaine.

Her next play was *Kiss the Boys Good-bye* (1938), a comedy suggested by the highly publicized search for an actress to play Scarlett O'Hara in the Hollywood version of *Gone With the Wind*. The comedy entertained New York audiences for 286 performances and later was filmed with Mary Martin. Her next contribution to the Broadway stage was *Margin for Error* (1939) and it was performed 264 times; two of its principals were Sam Levene and Otto Preminger.

Soon after the outbreak of World War II, Mrs. Luce went to Europe as a journalist for *Life* magazine and the account of her travels was published in a book, *Europe in the Spring* (1940). With the exception of an original film story, *Come to the Stable,* and *Child of the Morning* that closed during its pre-Broadway tryout tour, politics largely took up the succeeding years. She served for two terms as a Congresswoman from Connecticut and in 1953, President Dwight D. Eisenhower appointed her as the United States Ambassador to Italy. Mrs. Luce became the second woman Ambassador in American history and the first assigned to a major world power.

Slam the Door Softly, published here in an anthology for the first time, initially appeared in *Life* magazine under the title, *A Doll's House 1970.* Inspired by Ibsen's classic drama, which foreshadowed today's women's liberation movement, the present title relates to the then-electrifying denouement of the Ibsen play, of which it has been said that Nora's decision to leave home and husband was "the slam of the door that was heard around the world."

Characters:

THAW WALD

NORA WALD

Scene:

The Thaw Walds' cheerfully furnished middle-class living room in New York's suburbia. There are a front door and hall, a door to the kitchen area, and a staircase to the bedroom floor. Two easy chairs and two low hassocks with toys on them, grouped around a television set, indicate a family of four. Drinks are on a bar cart at one end of a comfortable sofa, and an end table at the other. There are slightly more than the average number of bookshelves. The lamps are on, but as we don't hear the children, we know it is the Parents' Hour.

Thaw Wald, a good-looking fellow, about thirty-five, is sitting in one of the easy chairs, smoking and watching TV. His back is to the sofa and staircase, so he does not see his wife coming down the stairs. Nora Wald is a rather pretty woman of about thirty-two. She is carrying a suitcase, handbag and an armful of books.

Thaw switches channels, and lands in the middle of a panel show. During the TV dialogue that follows, Nora somewhat furtively deposits her suitcase in the hall, takes her coat out of the hall closet, and comes back to the sofa carrying coat, purse and books. She lays her coat on the sofa and the books on the end table. The books are full of little paper slips—bookmarkers. All of the above actions are unobserved by Thaw. We cannot see the TV screen, but we hear the voices of four women, all talking excitedly at once.

THAW: (*To the screen and the world in general*) God, these Liberation gals! Still at it.

MALE MODERATOR'S VOICE: (*Full of paternal patience wear-*

ing a bit thin) Ladies! Lay-deez! Can't we switch now from the question of the sex-typing of jobs to what the Women's Liberation Movement thinks about . . .

OLDER WOMAN'S VOICE: May I finish! In the Soviet Union 83 percent of the dentists, 75 percent of the doctors and 37 percent of the lawyers are women. In Poland and Denmark . . .

MODERATOR: I think you have already amply made your point, Mrs. Epstein—anything men can do, women can do better!

YOUNG WOMAN'S VOICE: (*Angrily*) That was *not* her point and you know it! What she said was, there are very few professional jobs men are doing that women couldn't do, if only . . .

THAW: Well, for God's sake then, shuddup, and go do 'em!

BLACK WOMAN'S VOICE: What she's been saying, what we've all been saying, and you men just don't want to hear us, is things are the same for women as they are for us black people. We try to get up, you just sit down on us, like a big elephant sits down on a bunch of poor little mice.

MODERATOR: Well, sometimes moderators have to play the elephant and sit down on one subject in order to develop another. As I was about to say, ladies, there *is one thing* a woman can do, no man can do—(*In his best holy-night-all-is-bright voice*) give birth to a *child*.

YOUNG WOMAN'S VOICE: So what else is new?

THAW: One gets you ten, she's a Lesbo.

MODERATOR: (*Forcefully*) And *that* brings us to marriage! Now, if *I* may be permitted to get in just *one* statistic, edgewise: two thirds of all adult American females are married women. And now! (*At last he's got them where he wants them*) What *is* the Women's Lib view of Woman's Number One job—Occupation Housewife?

THAW: Ha! That's the one none of 'em can handle!

YOUNG WOMAN'S VOICE: (*Loud and clear*) Marriage, as

an institution, is as thoroughly corrupt as prostitution. It is, in fact, legalized and romanticized prostitution. A woman who marries is selling her sexual services and domestic services for permanent bed and board.

BLACK WOMAN'S VOICE: There's no human being a man can buy anymore—except a woman.

THAW: (*Snapping off the TV*) Crrr-ap! Boy, what a bunch of battle-axes! (*He goes back to studying his TV listings*)

NORA: (*Raising her voice*) Thaw! I'd like to say something about what they just said about marriage.

THAW: (*In a warning voice*) Uh-uh, Nora! We both agreed months ago, you'd lay off the feminist bit, if I'd lay off watching Saturday football.

NORA: And do something with the children. But Thaw, there's something, maybe, I ought to try to tell you myself. (*Thaw is not listening. Nora makes a "what's the use" gesture, then opens her purse, takes out three envelopes, carefully inserts two of them under the covers of the top two books*)

THAW: Like to hear Senators Smithers, Smethers and Smothers on "How Fast Can We Get Out of Vietnam?"

NORA: (*Cool mockery*) That bunch of potbellied, baldheaded old goats! Not one of them could get a woman—well, yes, maybe for two dollars.

THAW: You don't look at Senators, Nora. You listen to them.

NORA: (*Nodding*) Women are only to look at. Men are to listen to. Got it.

(*Thaw is now neither looking at her nor listening to her, as he methodically turns pages of the magazine he has picked up*)

THAW: Finished reading to the kids?

NORA: I haven't been reading to the children. I've been reading to myself—and talking to myself—for a long time now.

THAW: That's good. (*She passes him, carrying the third*

envelope, and goes into kitchen. Then, unenthusiastically) Want some help with the dishes?

NORA: (*From kitchen*) I'm not doing the dishes.

THAW: (*Enthusiastically*) Say, Nora, this is quite an ad we've got in *Life* for Stone Mountain Life Insurance.

NORA: Yes, I saw it. Great. (*She comes back and goes to sofa*)

THAW: It's the kind of ad that grabs you. This sad-faced, nice looking woman of fifty, sitting on a bench with a lot of discouraged old biddies, in an employment agency. Great caption!

NORA AND THAW: (*Together*) "Could this happen to *your* wife?"

NORA: I'll let you know the answer very shortly. (*A pause*) You really don't hear me anymore, do you? (*He really doesn't. She buttons herself into her coat, pulls on her gloves*) Well, there are enough groceries for a week. All the telephone numbers you'll need and menus for the children are in the envelope on the spindle. A girl will come in to take care of them after school—until your mother gets here.

THAW: Uh-huh . . .

NORA: (*Looks around sadly*) Well, goodby dear little doll house. Good-by dear husband. You've had the best ten years of my life. (*She goes to the staircase, blows two deep kisses upstairs just as Thaw glances up briefly at her, but returns automatically to his magazine. Nora picks up suitcase, opens the door, goes out, closing it quietly*)

THAW: (*Like a man suddenly snapping out of a hypnotic trance*) Nora? Nora? *Nor-ra!* (*He is out of the door in two seconds*)

THAW'S AND NORA'S VOICES: Nora, where're you going?—I'll miss my train—I don't understand—It's all in my letter—Let me go!—You come back! (*They return. He is pulling her by the arm. He yanks the suitcase away from her, drops it in the hall*)

NORA: Ouch! You're hurting me!

THAW: Now what is this all about? (*He shoves her into the room, then stands between her and door*) Why the hell . . . ? What're you sneaking out of the house . . . ? What's that suitcase for?

NORA: I wasn't sneaking. I told you. But you weren't listening.

THAW: I was listening—it just didn't register. You said you were reading to yourself. Then you started yakking about the kids and the groceries and the doll house mother sent . . . (*Flabbergasted*) Good-by? What do you mean, *good-by?*

NORA: Just that. I'm leaving you. (*Pointing to books*) My letter will explain everything.

THAW: Have you blown your mind?

NORA: Thaw, I've got to scoot, or I'll miss the eight-o-nine.

THAW: You'll miss it. (*He backs her to the sofa, pushes her onto it, goes and slams the door and strides back*) Now, my girl, explain this.

NORA: You mean what's just happened now?

THAW: Yes. What's happened now.

NORA: Oh, that's easy. Muscle. You've made with the muscle—like a typical male. The heavier musculature of the male is a secondary sexual characteristic. Although that's not certain. It could be just the result of selective breeding. In primitive times, of course, the heavier musculature of the male was necessary to protect the pregnant female and the immobile young.

THAW: (*His anger evaporates*) Nora, are you sick?

NORA: But what's just happened now shows that nothing has changed—I mean, fundamentally changed—in centuries, in the relations between the sexes. *You* still Tarzan, *me* still Jane.

THAW: (*Sits on sofa beside her, feels her head*) I've noticed you've been, well, acting funny lately.

NORA: Funny?

THAW: Like there was something on your mind. Tell me, what's wrong, sweetheart? Where does it hurt?

NORA: It hurts (*Taps head*) here. Isn't that where thinking hurts *you?* No. You're used to it. I was, too, when I was at Wellesley. But I sort of stopped when I left. It's really hard to think of anything else when you're having babies.

THAW: Nora, isn't it about time for your period?

NORA: But if God had wanted us to think just with our wombs, why did He give us a brain? No matter what men say, Thaw, the female brain is not a vestigial organ, like a vermiform appendix.

THAW: Nora . . .

NORA: Thaw, I can just about make my train. I'll leave the car and keys in the usual place at the station. Now, I have a very important appointment in the morning. (*She starts to rise*)

THAW: Appointment? (*Grabs her shoulders*) Nora, look at me! You weren't sneaking out of the house to . . . get an abortion?

NORA: When a man can't explain a woman's actions, the first thing he thinks about is the condition of her uterus. Thaw, if you were leaving me and I didn't know why, would I ask, first thing, if you were having prostate trouble?

THAW: Don't try to throw me off the track, sweetie! Now, if you want another baby . . .

NORA: Thaw, don't you remember, we both agreed about the overpopulation problem.

THAW: To hell with the overpopulation problem. Let Nixon solve that. Nora, I can swing another baby.

NORA: Maybe you can. I can't. For me there are no more splendid, new truths to be learned from scanning the contents of babies' diapers. Thaw, I *am* pregnant. But not in a feminine way. In the way only men are supposed to get pregnant.

THAW: Men, pregnant?

NORA: (*Nodding*) With ideas. Pregnancies there (*Taps*

his head) are masculine. And a very superior form of labor. Pregnancies here (*Taps her tummy*) are feminine—a very inferior form of labor. That's an example of male linguistic chauvinism. Mary Ellmann is *great* on that. You'll enjoy her *Thinking about Women.*

THAW: (*Going to telephone near bookshelf*) I'm getting the doctor. (*Nora makes a dash for the door, he drops the phone*) Oh, no, you don't! (*He reaches for her as she passes, misses. Grabs her ponytail and hauls her back by it and shoves her into the easy chair*)

NORA: Brother, Millett sure had you taped.

THAW: Milly *who?* (*A new thought comes to him*) Has one of your goddam gossipy female friends been trying to break up our marriage? (*He suddenly checks his conscience. It is not altogether pure*) What did she tell you? That she saw me having lunch, uh, dinner, with some girl?

NORA: (*Nodding to herself*) Right on the button!

THAW: Now, Nora, I can explain about that girl!

NORA: You don't have to. Let's face it. Monogamy is not natural to the male.

THAW: You know I'm not in love with anybody but you.

NORA: Monogamy is not natural to the female, either. Making women think it is, is the man's most successful form of brainwashing the female.

THAW: Nora, I swear, that girl means nothing to me . . .

NORA: And you probably mean nothing to her. So whose skin is off whose nose?

THAW: (*Relieved, but puzzled*) Well, uh, I'm glad you feel that way about—uh—things.

NORA: Oh, it's not the way I *feel.* It's the way things really are. What with the general collapse of the mores, and now the Pill, women are becoming as promiscuous as men. It figures. We're educated from birth to think of ourselves just as man-traps. Of course, in my mother's day, good women thought of themselves as private man-traps. Only bad women were public man-traps. Now we've all gone public. (*Looks at watch*) I'll have to take the eight-forty. (*She gets out of her coat, lays it, ready to slip into, on back of sofa*)

THAW: (*A gathering suspicion*) Nora, are you trying to tell me that *you* . . .

NORA: Of course, a lot of it, today, is the fault of the advertising industry. Making women think they're failures in life if they don't make like sex pots around the clock. We're even supposed to wear false eyelashes when we're vacuuming. Betty Friedan's great on that. She says many lonely suburban housewives, unable to identify their real problem, think more sex is the answer. So they sleep with the milkman, or the delivery boy. If I felt like sleeping with anybody like that, I'd pick the plumber. When you need *him,* boy, you *need* him!

THAW: (*The unpleasant thought he has been wrestling with has now jelled*) Nora . . . are you . . . trying to tell me you are leaving me for someone else?

NORA: Why, Thaw Wald! How could you even *think* such a thing? (*To herself*) Now, how naïve can I be? What else do men think about, in connection with women, *but* sex? He is saying to himself, she's not having her period, she's not pregnant, she's not jealous: it's *got* to be another man.

THAW: Stop muttering to yourself, and answer my question.

NORA: I forgot what it was. Oh, yes. *No.*

THAW: No what?

NORA: No, I'm not in love with anybody else. I was a virgin when I married you. And intacta. And that wasn't par for the course—even at Wellesley. And I've never slept with anybody else, partly because I never wanted to. And partly because, I suppose, of our family's Presbyterian hangup. So, now that all the vital statistics are out of the way, I'll just drive around until . . . (*Begins to slip her arms into coat. He grabs coat, throws it on easy chair*)

THAW: You're not leaving until you tell me *why.*

NORA: But it's all in my letter. (*Points*) The fat one sticking out of Simone de Beauvoir's *Second Sex*.

THAW: If you have a bill of particulars against me, I want it *straight*. From you.

NORA: Oh, darling, I have no bill of particulars. By all the standards of our present-day society, you are a very good husband. And, mark me, you'll be president of Stone Mountain Life Insurance Company before you're fifty. The point is, what will I be when I'm fifty?

THAW: You'll be my wife, if I have anything to say. Okay. So you're not leaving me because I'm a bad husband, or because my financial future is dim.

NORA: No. Oh, Thaw, you just wouldn't understand.

THAW: (*Patiently*) I might, if you would try, for just one minute, to talk logically.

NORA: Thaw, women aren't trained to talk logically. Men don't like women who talk logically. They find them unfeminine—aggressive.

THAW: Dammit, Nora, will you talk sense!

NORA: But boy! does a man get sore when a woman won't talk logically when *he* wants her to, and (*Snaps fingers*) like that! And *that* isn't illogical? What women men are! Now, if you will step aside . . .

THAW: (*Grabbing her and shaking her*) You're going to tell me why you're walking out on me, if I have to *sock* you!

NORA: Thaw, eyeball to eyeball, *I am leaving you*—and not for a man. For reasons of my own I just don't think you *can* understand. And if you mean to stop me, you'll have to beat me to a pulp. But I'm black and blue already.

THAW: (*Seizes her tenderly in his arms, kisses her*) Nora, sweetheart! You know I couldn't really hurt you. (*Kisses, kisses*) Ba-aaby, what do you say we call it a night? (*Scoops her up in his arms*) You can tell me *all* about it in bed.

NORA: The classical male one-two. Sock 'em and screw 'em.

THAW: (*Dumping her on sofa*) Well, it's been known to work on a lot of occasions. Something tells me this isn't one of them. (*Pours a drink*)

NORA: I guess I need one, too. (*He mixes them*) Thaw?

THAW: Yes.

NORA: I couldn't help being a *little* pleased when you made like a caveman. It shows you really do value my sexual services.

THAW: Geez!

NORA: Well, it can't be my domestic services—you don't realize, yet, what they're worth. (*Drinks*) Thaw, you do have a problem with me. But you can't solve it with force. And *I* do have a problem. But I can't solve it with sex.

THAW: Could you, would you, *try* to tell me what my-your-our problem is?

NORA: Friedan's *Feminine Mystique* is very good on The Problem. I've marked all the relevant passages. And I've personalized them in my letter. (*He goes to book. Yanks out letter, starts to tear it up. Nora groans. He changes his mind, and stuffs it in his pocket*)

THAW: Look, Nora, there's one thing I've always said about you. For a woman, you're pretty damn honest. Don't you think you owe it to me to level and give me a chance to defend myself?

NORA: The trouble is, *you* would have to listen to *me*. And that's hard for you. I *understand why!* Not listening to women is a habit that's been passed on from father to son for generations. You could almost say, tuning out on women is another secondary sexual male characteristic.

THAW: So our problem is that *I* don't listen?

NORA: Thaw, you always go on talking, no matter how hard I'm interrupting.

THAW: Okay. You have the floor.

NORA: Well, let's begin where this started tonight. When you oppressed me and treated me as an inferior.

THAW: I oppressed . . . (*Hesitates*) Lay on, MacDuff.

NORA: You honestly don't think that yanking me around by my hair and threatening to sock me are not the oppressive gestures of a superior male toward an inferior female?

THAW: For Chrissake, Nora, a man isn't going to let the woman he loves leave him if he can stop her!

NORA: Exactly. Domination of the insubordinate female is an almost instinctive male reflex. *In extremis,* Thaw, it is *rape.* Now, would I like it if you should say you were going to leave me? No. But could I drag you back?

THAW: You'd just have to crook your little finger.

NORA: Flattery will get you nowhere this evening. So, where was I?

THAW: I am a born rapist.

NORA: Wasn't that what you had in mind when you tried to adjourn this to our bedroom? But that's just your primitive side. There's your civilized side, too. You are a patriarchal *paterfamilias.*

THAW: What am I now?

NORA: Thaw, you do realize we all live in a patriarchy, where men govern women by playing sexual politics?

THAW: Look, you're not still sore because I talked you into voting for Nixon? (*She gives him a withering look*) Okay. So we all live in a patriarchy.

NORA: Our little family, the Walds, are just one nuclear patriarchal unit among the millions in our patriarchal male-dominated civilization, which is worldwide. It's all in that book.

THAW: Look, Nora, I promise I'll read the damn book —but . . .

NORA: So who's interrupting? Well, Thaw, all history shows that the hand that cradles the *rock* has ruled the world, *not* the hand that rocks the cradle! Do you know what brutal things men have done to women? Bought and sold them like cattle. Bound their feet at birth to deform them—so they couldn't run away—like in China. Made widows throw themselves on the funeral pyres of their husbands, like in India. And men who committed adultery were almost never punished. But women were always brutally punished. Why, in many countries unfaithful wives were *stoned* to death!

THAW: This is America, 1970, Nora. And here, when wives are unfaithful, *husbands* get stoned. (*Drinks*) Mind if *I* do?

NORA: Be your guest. Oh, there's no doubt that relations between the sexes have been greatly ameliorated.

THAW: Now, about *our* relations, Nora. You're not holding it against *me* that men, the dirty bastards, have done a lot of foul things to women in the past?

NORA: (*Indignant*) What do you mean, in the *past?*

THAW: (*Determined to be patient*) Past, present, future —what has what other men have done to other women got to do with us?

NORA: Quite a lot. We *are* a male and a female.

THAW: That's the supposition I've always gone on. But Nora, we are a *particular* male and a *particular* female: Thaw Wald and his wife, Nora.

NORA: Yes. That's why it's so shattering when you find out you are such a typical husband and . . .

THAW: (*A new effort to take command*) Nora, how many men do you know who are still in love with their wives after ten years?

NORA: Not many. And, Thaw, listen, maybe the reason is . . .

THAW: So you agree that's not typical? Okay. Now, do I ever grumble about paying the bills? So that's not typical. I liked my mother-in-law, even when she was alive. And God knows that's not typical. And don't I do every damn thing I can to keep *my* mother off your back? And that's not typical. I'm even thoughtful about the little things. You said so yourself, remember, when I bought you that black see-through nightgown for Mother's Day. That I went out and chose myself. And which *you* never wear.

NORA: I had to return it. It was too small. And do you know what the saleswoman said? She said, "Men who buy their wives things in this department are in love with them. But why do they all seem to think they are married to midgets?" That's it, Thaw, that's *it!* Men "think little"—like "thinking thin"—even about women they love. They don't think at all about women they don't love or want to sleep with. Now, I can't help it if you think of me as a midget. But don't you see, I've got to stop thinking of myself as one. Thaw, *listen* . . .

THAW: Why the devil should *you* think of yourself as a midget? *I* think you're a great woman. A *real* woman! Why, you're the dearest, sweetest, most understanding little wife—most of the time—a man ever had. And the most intelligent and wonderful little mother! Dammit, those kids are the smartest, best-behaved, most self-reliant little kids . . .

NORA: Oh, I've been pretty good at Occupation Housewife, if I do say so myself. But, Thaw, *listen*. Can't you even imagine that there might be something *more* a woman needs and wants?

THAW: My God, Nora, what more can a woman want than a nice home, fine children and a husband who adores her?

NORA: (*Discouraged*) You sound like old Dr. Freud, in person.

THAW: I sound like Freud? I wish I were. Then I'd know why you're so uptight.

NORA: Oh, no you wouldn't. Know what Freud wrote in his diary when he was seventy-seven? "What do women want? My God, what do they want?" Fifty years this giant brain spends analyzing women. And he still can't find out what they want. So this makes him the world's greatest expert on feminine psychology? (*She starts to look at her watch*) To think I bought him, in college.

THAW: You've got plenty of time. You were saying about Freud . . . (*He lights a cigarette, hands it to her, determined to stick with it to the end*)

NORA: History is full of ironies! Freud was the foremost exponent of the theory of the natural inferiority of women. You know, "anatomy is destiny"?

THAW: I was in the School of Business, remember?

NORA: Well, old Freud died in 1939. He didn't live to see what happened when Hitler adopted his theory that "anatomy is destiny." Six millions of his own people went to the gas chambers. One reason, Hitler said, that the Jews were *naturally* inferior was because they were effeminate people with a slave mentality. He said they were full of those vices which men always identify with women—when they're feeling hostile. You know, sneakiness and deception, scheming and wheedling, whining and pushiness, oh, and materialism, sensuousness and sexuality. Thaw, what's *your* favorite feminine vice?

THAW: At this moment, feminine monologues.

NORA: I didn't think you'd have the nerve to say sneakiness. I saw you sneak a look at your watch and egg me on to talk about Freud, hoping I'll miss my train. I won't.

THAW: So nothing I've said—what little I've had a chance to say . . . (*She shakes her head*) You still intend to divorce me?

NORA: Oh, I never said I was divorcing you. I'm deserting you. So you can divorce me.

THAW: You do realize, Nora, that if a wife deserts her husband he doesn't have to pay her alimony?

NORA: I don't want alimony. But I do want severance pay. (*Points to books*) There's my bill, rendered for ten years of domestic services—the thing sticking in *Woman's Place* by Cynthia Fuchs Epstein. I figured it at the going agency rates for a full-time cook, cleaning woman, handyman, laundress, seamstress, and part-time gardener and chauffeur. I've worked an average ten-hour day. So I've charged for overtime. Of course, you've paid my rent, taxes, clothing, medical expenses and food. So I've deducted those. Even though as a housewife I've had no fringe benefits. Just the same, the bill . . . well, I'm afraid you're going to be staggered. I was. It comes to over $53,000. I'd like to be paid in ten installments.

THAW: (*He is staggered*) Mathematics isn't really your bag, Nora.

NORA: I did it on that little calculating machine you gave

me at Christmas. If you think it's not really fair, I'll be glad to negotiate. And, please notice, I haven't charged anything for sleeping with you!

THAW: Wow! (*He is really punch drunk*)

NORA: I'm not a prostitute. And *this* is what I wanted to say about the Lib girls. They're right about women who marry *just* for money. But they're wrong about women who marry for love. It's love makes all the difference.

THAW: (*Dispirited*) Well, *vive la différence.*

NORA: And, of course, I haven't charged anything for being a nurse. I've adored taking care of the children, especially when they were babies. I'm going to miss them—*awfully.*

THAW: (*On his feet, with outrage*) You're deserting the children, too? My God, Nora, what kind of woman *are* you? You're going to leave those poor little kids alone in this house . . .

NORA: You're here. And I told you, your mother is coming. I wired her that her son needed her. She'll be happy again—and be needed again—for the first time in years.

THAW: (*This is a real blow*) My *mother!* Oh, migod, you *can't,* Nora. You know how she—*swarms* over me! She thinks I'm still twelve years old! (*His head is now in his hands*) You know she drives me out of my cotton-picking mind.

NORA: Yes. But you never said so before.

THAW: I love my mother. She's been a good mother and wife. But, Nora, she's a *very* limited woman! Yak, yak—food, shopping, the kids . . .

NORA: Thaw, the children love this house, and I don't want to take them out of school. And I can't give them another home. Women, you know, can't borrow money to buy a house. Besides, legally this house and everything in it, except my mother's few things and my wedding presents, are yours. All the worldly goods with which thou didst me endow seem to be in that suitcase.

THAW: Nora, you know damn well that all my life insurance is in your name. If I died tomorrow—and I'll probably blow my brains out tonight—everything would go to you and the kids.

NORA: Widowhood is one of the few fringe benefits of marriage. But, today, all the money I have is what I've saved in the past year out of my clothes allowance—$260.33. But I hope you will give me my severance pay.

THAW: And if I don't—you know legally I don't have to—how do you propose to support yourself?

NORA: Well, if I can't get a job right away—sell my engagement ring. That's why they say diamonds are a gal's best friend. What else do most women *have* they can turn into ready cash—except their bodies?

THAW: What kind of job do you figure on getting?

NORA: Well, I do have a Master's in English. So I'm going to try for a spot in *Time* research. That's the intellectual harem kept by the Time, Inc. editors. The starting pay is good.

THAW: How do you know that?

NORA: From your own research assistant, Molly Peapack. We're both Wellesley, you know. She's a friend of the chief researcher at *Time,* Marylois Vega. Also, Molly says, computer programming is a field that may open to women.

THAW: (*Indignant*) You told Peapack you were leaving me? Before you even told *me?* How do you like *that* for treating a mate like an inferior!

NORA: Thaw, I've told you at least three times a week for the last year that with the kids both in school, I'd like to get a job. You always laughed at me. You said I was too old to be a Playboy Bunny and that the only job an inexperienced woman my age could get would be as a saleswoman.

THAW: Okay. Where are you going to live?

NORA: Peapack's offered to let me stay with her until I find something.

THAW: I'm going to have a word with Miss Molly Peapack tomorrow. She's been too damned aggressive lately, anyway!

NORA: She's going to have a word with you, too. *She's* leaving.

THAW: Peapack is leaving? Leaving *me?*

NORA: When you got her from Prudential, you promised her, remember, you'd recommend her for promotion to office manager. So, last week you took on a man. A new man. Now she's got a job offer where she's sure she's got a forty to sixty chance for advancement to management. So you've lost your home wife and your office wife, too.

THAW: And *this* is a male-dominated world?

NORA: Thaw, I've got just five minutes.

THAW: You've still not told me *why*—

NORA: Oh, Thaw darling! You poor—*man*. I have told you why. I'm leaving because I want a job. I want to do some share, however small, of the world's work and be paid for it. Isn't the work you do in the world—and the salary *you* get—what makes you respect yourself, and other men respect *you?* Women have begun to want to respect themselves a little, too!

THAW: You mean, the real reason you are leaving is that you want a *paying* job?

NORA: Yes.

THAW: God, Nora, why didn't you say that in the beginning? All right, go get a job, if it's that important to you. But that doesn't mean you have to leave me and the kids.

NORA: I'm afraid it does. Otherwise, I'd have to do two jobs. Out there. And here.

THAW: Look, Nora, I heard some of the Lib gals say there are millions of working wives and mothers who are doing two jobs. Housework can't be all that rough.

NORA: Scrubbing floors, walls. Cleaning pots, pans, windows, ovens. Messes—dog messes, toilet messes, children's messes. Garbage. Laundry. Shopping for pounds of stuff. Loading them into the car, out of the car—(*A pause*) Not all of it hard. But all of it routine. All of it *boring*.

THAW: Listen, Nora, what say, you work, I work. And we split the housework? How's that for a deal?

NORA: It's a deal you are not quite free to make, Thaw. You sometimes *can't* get home until very late. And you have to travel a lot, you know. Oh, it might work for a little while.

But not for long. After ten years, you still won't empty an ashtray or pick up after yourself in the bathroom. No. I don't have the physical or moral strength to swing two jobs. So I've got to choose the one, before it's too late, that's most important for me—oh, not for me just now, but for when *I'm* fifty—

THAW: When you're fifty, Nora, if you don't leave me, you'll be the wife of the president of Stone Mountain Life Insurance Company. Sharing my wealth, sharing whatever status I have in the community. And with servants of your own. Now you listen to *me,* Nora. It's a man's world out there. It's a man's world where there are a lot of women working. I see them every day. What are most of them really doing? Marking time and looking, always looking, for a man who will offer them a woman's world—the world you have here. Marriage is still the best deal that the world has to offer women. And most women know it. It's always been like that. And it's going to be like that for a long, long time.

NORA: Just now I feel that the best deal I, Nora Wald, can hope to get out of life is to learn to esteem myself as a person—to stop feeling that every day a little bit more of my mind—and heart—is being washed down the drain with the soapsuds. Thaw—listen. If I don't stop shrinking, I'll end up secretly hating you and trying to cut you—and *your* son—down to my size. The way your swarmy mommie does you and your dad. And you'll become like your father, the typical henpecked husband. Thinking of his old wife as the Ball and Chain. You know he has a mistress? (*Thaw knows. He belts down a stiff drink*) A smart gal who owns her own shop—a woman who doesn't bore him.

THAW: Well, Nora . . . (*Pours another drink*) One for the road?

NORA: Right. For the road.

THAW: Nora . . . I'll wait. But I don't know how long.

NORA: I've thought of that, too . . . that you might remarry . . . that girl, maybe, who means nothing. . .

THAW: Dammit, a man needs a woman of his own.

NORA: (*Nodding*) I know. A sleep-in, sleep-with body servant of his very own. Well, that's your problem. Just now, I have to wrestle with my problem. (*Goes to door, picks up suitcase*) I'm not bursting with self-confidence, Thaw. I do love you. And I also need . . . a man. So I'm not slamming the door. I'm closing it . . . very . . . softly. (*She leaves*)

Curtain

Ted Shine

CONTRIBUTION

Ted Shine

Although Ted Shine has been actively involved with the theatre for a number of years, it wasn't until 1969 that he moved into the vanguard of contemporary black playwrights. The activator was the Negro Ensemble Company's Off-Broadway presentation of *Contribution,* which appears in an anthology for the first time in *The Best Short Plays 1972.* Produced on a bill of three short plays by a trio of black playwrights whose work had not previously been presented by the resourceful company, *Contribution* was accorded the major honors of the evening. Clive Barnes described it in *The New York Times* as "bright and funny . . . the humor is at least as much in the situation as in Mr. Shine's writing, but there is no doubt at all about the ingenuity of the idea." The play also evoked praise from Walter Kerr who reported that "Mr. Shine has written a tight, quiet, uproariously plausible fantasy." He much admired the author's "low-key sauciness, together with an uncanny knack for being simultaneously warm-hearted and blood-curdling."

In 1970, *Contribution* once again dominated an Off-Broadway stage when it was presented at Tambellini's Gate Theatre with two other plays by Mr. Shine, *Plantation* and *Shoes,* under the blanket title of *Contributions.* The production was directed by Moses Gunn, starred Claudia McNeil, and brought further adulation to the author. Clive Barnes termed him "a new black playwright with a great eye for a funny situation," one "who writes from the heart with a brash and bitter humor," while Walter Kerr was impressed with "the gentle skill with which he uncoils his snake-charming plot."

A delightful comedy about rapidly changing black attitudes and the approach of two different generations in the cause of civil rights, *Contribution* expresses the playwright's view that "the young of today have more in common with the old than those who are in the middle."

Ted Shine was born in Baton Rouge, Louisiana, but lived most of his early years in Dallas, Texas. He attended Howard University, where he studied playwriting under Owen Dodson, then spent two years at the Karamu Playhouse, Cleveland. After serving in the U.S. Army, he resumed his education at the State University of Iowa and received his Master's in 1959. At present, he is working toward a Ph.D. at the University of California at Santa Barbara.

The author's other produced plays include: *Epitaph for a Bluebird; Morning, Noon and Night; Sho Is Hot in the Cotton Patch; Miss Weaver; Comeback, After the Fire; Idabel's Fortune; Hamburgers Are Impersonal;* and *Flora's Kisses.* He also has written an all-black television soap opera dealing with urban problems which was produced by the Maryland Center for Public Broadcasting in Baltimore, Maryland.

A recipient of many honors and awards, Mr. Shine has taught and lectured at a number of colleges and universities.

Characters:

MRS. GRACE LOVE
EUGENE LOVE
KATY JONES

Scene:

A small southern town. Early 1960's. Mrs. Love's kitchen. Clean, neatly furnished. A door upstage center leads into the backyard. A door right, leads into the hall. In the center of the room is an ironing board with a white shirt resting on it to be ironed.

Mrs. Love, a Negro woman in her late seventies, stands at the table mixing cornbread dough. Now and then she takes a drink of beer from the bottle resting on the table. Her neighbor, Katy Jones, thirty-eight, sits at the table drinking coffee. She is ill-at-ease.

MRS. LOVE: (*Singing*)
Where He leads me
IIIIII shall follow!
Where He leads me
IIIIII shall follow!
WWWWWWhere He leads me
IIIIII shall follow!
IIIIIII'lllll go with Him . . .

EUGENE: (*Offstage*) Grandma, please! You'll wake the dead!

MRS LOVE: I called you half an hour ago. You dressed?

EUGENE: I can't find my pants.

MRS. LOVE: I pressed them. They're out here. (*Eugene, twenty-one, enters in shorts and undershirt, unaware that Katy is present*)

EUGENE: I just got those trousers out of the cleaners and they didn't need pressing! I'll bet you scorched them! (*He sees Katy and conceals himself with his hands*)

MRS. LOVE: You should wear a robe around the house,

boy. You never know when I'm having company. (*She tosses him the pants*)

EUGENE: I'm . . . sorry. 'Mornin', Miss Katy. (*He exits quickly*)

KATY: 'Mornin', Eugene. (*To Mrs. Love*) He ran out of here like a skint cat. Like I ain't never seen a man in his drawers before.

MRS. LOVE: (*Pouring cornbread into pan*) There. I'll put this bread in the oven and it'll be ready in no time. I appreciate your taking it down to the sheriff for me. He'd bust a gut if he didn't have my cornbread for breakfast. (*Sings*)

I sing because I'm happy,
I sing because I'm free . . .

KATY: I'm only doing it because I don't want to see a woman your age out on the streets today.

MRS. LOVE: (*Singing*)

His eye is on the sparrow
And I know He watches me!

KATY: Just the same I'm glad you decided to take off. White folks have been coming into town since sun up by the truck loads. Mean white folks who're out for blood!

MRS. LOVE: They're just as scared as you, Katy Jones.

KATY: Ain't no sin to be scared. Ain't you scared for Eugene?

MRS. LOVE: Scared of what?

KATY: That lunch counter has been white for as long as I can remember—and the folks around here aim to keep it that way.

MRS. LOVE: Let'em *aim* all they want to! The thing that tees me off is they won't let me march.

KATY: Mrs. Love, your heart couldn't take it!

MRS. LOVE: You'd be amazed at what my heart's done took all these years, baby.

EUGENE: (*Entering*) Where's my sport shirt? The green one?

MRS. LOVE: In the drawer where it belongs. I'm ironing this white shirt for you to wear.

EUGENE: A white shirt? I'm not going to a formal dance.

MRS. LOVE: I want you neat when you sit down at that counter. Newspaper men from all over the country'll be there, and if they put your picture in the papers, I want folks to say, "My, ain't that a nice looking, neat, young man."

EUGENE: You ask your boss how long he'll let me stay neat?

MRS. LOVE: I ain't asked Sheriff Morrison nothin'.

EUGENE: He let you off today so you could nurse my wounds when I get back, huh?

MRS. LOVE: You ain't gonna get no wounds, son, and you ain't gonna get this nice white shirt ruined either. What's wrong with you anyway? You tryin' to—what y'all say—"chicken out"?

EUGENE: No, I'm not going to chicken out, but I *am* nervous.

KATY: I'm nervous, too—for myself and for all you young folks. Like the mayor said on TV last night the whites and the colored always got on well here.

MRS. LOVE: So long as "we" stayed in our respective places.

KATY: He said if we want to eat in a drugstore we ought to build our own.

EUGENE: Then why don't you build a drugstore on Main Street with a lunch counter in it?

KATY: Where am I gonna get the money?

MRS. LOVE: Where is any colored person in this town gonna get the money? Even if we got it, you think they'd let us lease a building—let alone buy property on Main Street?

KATY: I know, Mrs. Love, but . . .

MRS. LOVE: But nothin'! If I was a woman your age I'd be joinin' them children!

KATY: I'm with y'all, Eugene, in mind if not in body.

EUGENE: Um-huh.

KATY: But I have children to raise, and I have to think about my job.

MRS. LOVE: Why don't you think about your children's future? Them few pennies you make ain't shit! And if things stay the same it'll be the same way for those children, too, but Lord knows, if they're like the rest of the young folks today, they're gonna put you down real soon!

KATY: I provide for my children by myself—and they love me for it! We have food on our table each and every day!

MRS. LOVE: Beans and greens! When's the last time you had steaks?

KATY: Well . . . at least we ain't starvin'!

EUGENE: Neither is your boss lady!

KATY: Mrs. Comfort says y'all are—*communists!*

MRS. LOVE: I'll be damned! How come every time a black person speaks up for himself he's got to be a communist?

KATY: That's what the white folks think!

MRS. LOVE: Well, ain't that somethin'! Here I am—old black me—trying to get this democracy to working like it oughta be working, and the democratic white folks say wait. Now tell me, why the hell would I want to join another bunch of white folks that I don't know nothin' about and expect them to put me straight? (*To Eugene*) Here's your shirt, son. Wear a tie and comb that natural! Put a part in your hair!

EUGENE: Good gracious! (*He exits*)

KATY: Militant! That's what Mrs. Comfort calls us—militants!

MRS. LOVE: (*Removing bread from oven*) What does that mean?

KATY: Bad! That's what it means—bad folks!

MRS. LOVE: I hope you love your children as much as you seem to love Miz Comfort.

KATY: I hate that woman!

MRS. LOVE: Why?

KATY: I hate all white folks—don't you?

MRS. LOVE: Katy Jones, I don't hate nobody. I get disgusted with 'em, but I don't hate 'em.

KATY: Well, you're different from me.

MRS. LOVE: Ummmmmm, just look at my cornbread!

KATY: It smells good!

MRS. LOVE: (*Butters bread and wraps it*) Don't you dare pinch off it either!

KATY: I don't want that white man's food! I hope it chokes the hell outta that mean bastard!

MRS. LOVE: I see how come your boss lady is calling you militant, Katy.

KATY: Well, I don't like him! Patting me on the behind like I'm a dog. He's got that habit bad.

MRS. LOVE: You make haste with this bread. He likes it hot.

KATY: Yes'm. I ain't gonna be caught dead in the midst of all that ruckus.

MRS. LOVE: You hurry along now. (*Gives her the bread and Katy exits. Mrs. Love watches her from the back door*) And don't you dare pinch off it! You'll turn to stone! (*She laughs to herself, turns and moves to the hall door*) You about ready, son?

EUGENE: I guess so.

MRS. LOVE: Come out here and let me look at you.

EUGENE: Since when do I have to stand inspection?

MRS. LOVE: Since *now!* (*Eugene enters*) You look right smart. And I want you to stay that way.

EUGENE: How? You know the sheriff ain't gonna stop at nothing to keep us out of that drugstore.

MRS. LOVE: Stop worrying about Sheriff Morrison.

EUGENE: He's the one who's raisin' all the hell! The mayor was all set to integrate until the sheriff got wind of it.

MRS. LOVE: Yes, I know, but—don't worry about him. Try to relax.

EUGENE: How can I relax?

MRS. LOVE: I thought most of you young cats had nerve today.

EUGENE: And I wish you'd stop embarrassing me using all that slang!

MRS. LOVE: I'm just tryin' to talk your talk, baby.

EUGENE: There's something wrong with a woman almost eighty years old trying to act like a teenager!

MRS. LOVE: What was it you was telling me the other day? 'Bout that gap—how young folks and old folks can't talk together?

EUGENE: The generation gap!

MRS. LOVE: Well, I done bridged it, baby! You dig?

EUGENE: You are ludicrous!

MRS. LOVE: Well, that's one up on me, but I'll cop it sooner or later.

EUGENE: I know you'll try!

MRS. LOVE: Damned right!

EUGENE: That's another thing—all this swearing you've been doing lately.

MRS. LOVE: Picked it up from you and your friends sitting right there in my living room under the picture of Jesus!

EUGENE: I . . .

MRS. LOVE: Don't explain. Now you know how it sounds to me.

EUGENE: Why did you have to bring this up at a time like this?

MRS. LOVE: You brought it up, baby.

EUGENE: I wish you wouldn't call me baby—I'm a grown man.

MRS. LOVE: Ain't I heard you grown men callin' each other baby?

EUGENE: Well . . . that's different. And stop usin' "ain't" so much. You know better.

MRS. LOVE: I wish I was educated like you, Eugene, but I *aren't!*

EUGENE: Good gracious!

MRS. LOVE: Let me fix that tie.

EUGENE: My tie is all right.

MRS. LOVE: It's crooked.

EUGENE: Just like that phoney sheriff that you'd get up at six in the mornin' to cook cornbread for.

MRS. LOVE: The sheriff means well, son, in his fashion.

EUGENE: That bastard is one dimensional—all black!

MRS. LOVE: Don't let him hear you call him black!

EUGENE: What would he do? Beat me with his billy club like he does the rest of us around here?

MRS. LOVE: You have to try to understand folks like Mr. Morrison.

EUGENE: Turn the other cheek, huh?

MRS. LOVE: That's what the Bible says.

EUGENE: (*Mockingly*) That's what the Bible says!

MRS. LOVE: I sure do wish I could go with y'all!

EUGENE: To eyewitness the slaughter?

MRS. LOVE: You young folks ain't the only militant ones, you know!

EUGENE: You work for the meanest paddy in town—and to hear you tell it, he adores the ground you walk on! Now you're a big militant!

MRS. LOVE: I try to get along with folks, son.

EUGENE: You don't have to work for trash like Sheriff Morrison! You don't have to work at all! You own this house. Daddy sends you checks which you tear up. You could get a pension if you weren't so stubborn—you don't have to work at your age! And you surely don't have to embarrass the family by working for trash!

MRS. LOVE: What am I suppose to do? Sit here and rot like an old apple? The minute a woman's hair turns gray, folks want her to take to a rockin' chair and sit it out. Not this chick, baby. I'm keepin' active. I've got a long time to go and much more to do before I go to meet my maker.

EUGENE: Listen to you!

MRS. LOVE: I mean it! I want to be a part of this "rights" thing—but no, y'all say I'm too old!

EUGENE: That's right, you are! Your generation and my generation are complete contrasts—we don't think alike at all! The grin and shuffle school is dead!

MRS. LOVE: (*Slaps him*) That's for calling me a "Tom"!

EUGENE: I didn't call you a "Tom." But I have seen you grinning and bowing to white folks, and it made me sick at the stomach!

MRS. LOVE: And it put your daddy through college so

he could raise you with comfort like he raised you—Northern comfort which you wasn't satisfied with. No, you had to come down here and "free" us soul brothers from bondage as if we can't do for ourselves! Now don't try to tell me that your world was perfect up there—I've been there and I've seen! Sick to your stomach! I'm sick to my stomach whenever I pick up a paper or turn on the news and see where young folks is being washed down with hoses or being bitten by dogs—even killed! I get sick to my stomach when I realize how hungry some folks are —and how disrespectful the world's gotten! I get sick to my stomach, baby, because the world is more messed up now than it ever was! You lookin' at me like that 'cause I shock you? *You* shock me! You know why? Your little secure ass is down here to make hist'ry in your own way. And you are scared shitless! I had dreams when I was your age, too!

EUGENE: Times were different then. I know that . . .

MRS. LOVE: Maybe so, but in our hearts we knowed what was right and what was wrong. We knowed what this country was suppose to be and we knowed that we was a part of it—for better or for worse—like a marriage. We prayed for a better tomorrow—and that's why that picture of Jesus got dust on it in my front room right now—'cause the harder we prayed, the worser it got!

EUGENE: Things are better now, you always say.

MRS. LOVE: Let's hope they don't get no worse.

EUGENE: Thanks to *us*.

MRS. LOVE: If you don't take that chip off your shoulder I'm gonna blister your behind, boy! Sit down there and eat your breakfast!

EUGENE: I'm not hungry.

MRS. LOVE: Drink some juice then.

EUGENE: I don't want anything!

MRS. LOVE: Look at you—a nervous wreck at twenty-one —just because you've got to walk through a bunch of poor white trash and sit at a lunch counter in a musty old drugstore!

EUGENE: I may be a little tense—it's only natural. You'd be too!

MRS. LOVE: I do my bit, baby, and it don't affect me in the least! I've seen the blazing cross and the hooded faces in my day. I've smelled black flesh burning with tar and necks stretched like taffy.

EUGENE: Seeing those things was your contribution, I guess?

MRS. LOVE: You'd be surprised at *my* contribution!

EUGENE: *Nothing* that you did would surprise me at all! You're a hard-headed old woman!

MRS. LOVE: And I'm *justified*—justified in whatever I do. (*Sits*) Life ain't been pretty for me, son. Oh, I suppose I had some happiness like when I married your granddaddy or when I gave birth to your daddy, but as I watched him grow up I got meaner and meaner.

EUGENE: You may be evil, but not mean.

MRS. LOVE: I worked to feed and clothe him like Katy's doin' for her children, but I had a goal in mind. Katy's just doin' it to eat. I wanted something better for my son. They used to call me "nigger" one minute and swear that they loved me the next. I grinned and bore it like you said. Sometimes I even had to scratch my head and bow, but I got your daddy through college.

EUGENE: I know and I'm grateful—he's grateful. Why don't you go and live with him like he wants you to?

MRS. LOVE: 'Cause I'm stubborn and independent! And I want to see me some more colored mens around here with pride and dignity!

EUGENE: So that Sheriff Morrison can pound the hell out of it every Saturday night with his billy club?

MRS. LOVE: I've always worked for folks like that. I worked for a white doctor once, who refused to treat your granddaddy. Let him die because he hated black folks. I worked for him and his family and they grew to love me like one of the family.

EUGENE: You are the *true* Christian lady!

MRS. LOVE: I reckon I turned the other cheek some—grinned and bowed, you call it. Held them white folks' hand when they was sick. Nursed their babies—and I sat back and watched 'em all die out year by year. Old Dr. Fulton was the last to go. He had worked around death all his life and death frightened him. He asked me—black me—to sit with him during his last hours.

EUGENE: Of course you did.

MRS. LOVE: Indeed! And loved every minute of it! Remind me sometimes to tell you about it. It's getting late. I don't want you to be tardy.

EUGENE: I bet you hope they put me under the jail so that you can "Tom" up to your boss and say, "I tried to tell him, but you know how . . ."

MRS. LOVE: (*Sharply*) I don't want to have to hit you again, boy!

EUGENE: I'm sorry.

MRS. LOVE: I've got my ace in the hole—and I ain't nervous about it either. You doin' all that huffin' and puffin'—the white folks are apt to blow you down with a hard stare. Now you scoot. Us Loves is known for our promptness.

EUGENE: If I die, remember I'm dying for Negroes like Miss Katy.

MRS. LOVE: You musta got that inferior blood from your mama's side of the family. You ain't gonna die, boy. You're coming back here to me just as pretty as you left.

EUGENE: Have you and the sheriff reached a compromise?

MRS. LOVE: Just you go on.

EUGENE: (*Starts to the door, stops*) I'll be back home, grandma.

MRS. LOVE: I know it, hon. (*He turns to leave again*) Son!

EUGENE: Ma'am?

MRS. LOVE: The Bible says love and I does. I turns the other cheek and I loves 'til I can't love no more. (*Eugene nods*) Well . . . I reckon I ain't perfect. I ain't like Jesus was; I can only bear a cross so long. I guess I've "had it" as you young folks say. Done been spit on, insulted, but I grinned and bore my cross for a while. Then there was peace—satisfaction. Sweet satisfaction. (*Eugene turns to go again*) Son, you've been a comfort to me. When you get to be my age you want someone to talk to who loves you, and I loves you from the bottom of my heart.

EUGENE: (*Embarrassed*) Ahhh, granny . . . I know . . . (*He embraces her tightly for a moment. She kisses him*) I'm sorry I said those things. I understand how you feel and I understand why you . . .

MRS. LOVE: Don't try to understand me, son, 'cause you don't even understand yourself yet. G'on out there and get yourself some dignity. Be a man, then we can talk.

EUGENE: I'll be damned, old lady . . .

MRS. LOVE: Now git!

EUGENE: (*Exiting*) I'll be damned! (*Mrs. Love watches him go. She stands in the doorway for a moment, turns and takes the dishes to the sink. She takes another beer from her refrigerator and sits at the table and composes a letter*)

MRS. LOVE: (*Writing slowly*) "Dear Eugene, your son has made me right proud today. You ought to have seen him leaving here to sit-in at the drugstore with them other fine young colored children." Lord, letter writin' can tire a body out! I'll let the boy finish it when he gets back.

KATY: (*Offstage*) Mrs. Love! Mrs. Love!

MRS. LOVE: (*Rising*) Katy? (*Katy enters. She has been running and stops beside the door to catch her breath*) What's wrong with you, child? They ain't riotin', are they? (*Katy shakes her head*) Then what's the matter? You give the sheriff his bread? (*She nods, yes*)

KATY: I poked my head in through the door and he says: "What you want, gal?" I told him I brought him his breakfast. He says, "All right, bring it here." His eyes lit up when he looked at your cornbread!

MRS. LOVE: Didn't they!

KATY: He told me to go get him a quart of buttermilk from the icebox, then he started eatin' that bread and he yelled at me—"Hurry up, gal, 'fore I finish!"

MRS. LOVE: Then what happened?

KATY: I got his milk and when I got back he was half-standin' and half-sittin' at his desk holding that big stomach of his'n and cussin' to high heaven. "Gimme that goddamned milk! Can't you see these ulcers is killin' the hell outta me?"

MRS. LOVE: He ain't got no ulcers.

KATY: He had somethin' all right. His ol' blue eyes was just dartin' about in what looked to be little pools of blood. His face was red as a beet.

MRS. LOVE: Go on, child!

KATY: He was pantin' and breathin' hard! He drank all that milk in one long gulp, then he belched and told me to get my black ass outta his face. He said to tell all the Negroes that today is the be-all and end-all day!

MRS. LOVE: Indeed!

KATY: And he flung that plate at me! I ran across the street. The street was full of white folks with sticks and rocks and things—old white folks and young 'em—even children. *My* white folks was even there!

MRS. LOVE: What was they doin'?

KATY: Just standin', that's all. They wasn't sayin' nothin', just starin' and watchin'. They'd look down the street towards the drugstore, then turn and look towards the sheriff's office. Then old Sheriff Morrison come out. He was sort of bent over in the middle. He belched and his stomach growled! I could hear it clear across the street.

MRS. LOVE: Oh, I've seen it before, child! I've seen it! First Dr. Fulton a medical man who didn't know his liver from his kidney. He sat and watched his entire family die out—one by one—then let hisself die because he was dumb! Called me to his deathbed and asked me to hold his hand. "I ain't got nobody else to turn to now, Auntie." I asted him, "You related to me in some way?" He laughed and the pain hit him like an axe. "Sing me a spiritual," he told me. I told him I didn't know no spiritual. "Sing something holy for me, I'm dyin'!" he says. (*She sings*) I'll be glad when you're dead, you rascal, you!

I'll be glad when you're dead, you rascal, you . . .
Then I told him how come he was dyin'.

KATY: He was a doctor, didn't he know?

MRS. LOVE: Shoot! "Dr. Fulton, how come you didn't treat my husband? How come you let him die out there in the alley like an animal?" When I got through openin' his nose with what was happenin', he raised up—red like the sheriff with his hands outstretched toward me and he fell right square off that bed onto the floor—dead. I spit on his body! Went downstairs, cooked me a steak, got my belongings and left.

KATY: You didn't call the undertaker?

MRS. LOVE: I left that bastard for the maggots. I wasn't his "auntie"! The neighbors found him a week later stinking to hell. Oh, they came by to question me, but I was grieved, chile, and they left me alone. "You know how nigras is scared of death," they said. And now the sheriff. Oh, I have great peace of mind, chile, 'cause I'm like my grandson in my own fashion. I'm too old to be hit and wet up, they say, but I votes and does my bit.

KATY: I reckon I'll get on. You think you oughta stay here by yourself?

MRS. LOVE: I'll be all right. You run along now. Go tend to your children before they get away from you.

KATY: Ma'am?

MRS. LOVE: Them kids got eyes, Katy, and they know what's happenin' and they ain't gonna be likin' their mama's attitude that much longer. You're a young woman, Katy. There ain't no sense in your continuing to be a fool for the rest of your life.

KATY: I don't know what you're talkin' about, Mrs. Love!

MRS. LOVE: You'll find out one day—I just hope it ain't too late. I thank you for that favor.

KATY: Yes'm. (*She exits*)

EUGENE: (*Entering. He is dressed the same, but seems eager and excited now*) Grandma! They served us and didn't a soul do a thing! We've integrated!

MRS. LOVE: Tell me about it.

EUGENE: When I got there every white person in the county was on that street! They had clubs and iron pipes. There were dogs and fire trucks with hoses. When we reached the drugstore, old man Thomas was standing in the doorway. "What y'all want?" he asked. "Service," someone said. That's when the crowd started yelling and making nasty remarks. None of us moved an inch. Then the sheriff came down the street from his office. He walked slowly like he was sick . . .

MRS. LOVE: Didn't he cuss none?

EUGENE: He swore up and down! He walked up to me and said, "Boy, what you and them other niggers want here?" "Freedom, baby!" I told him. "Freedom my ass," he said. "Y'all get on back where you belong and stop actin' up before I sic the dogs on you." "We're not leaving until we've been served!" I told him. He looked at me in complete amazement.

MRS. LOVE: Then he belched and started to foam at the mouth.

EUGENE: He was *mad,* grandma! He said he'd die before a nigger sat where a white woman's ass had been. "God is my witness!" he shouted. "May I die before I see this place integrated!" Then he took out his whistle . . .

MRS. LOVE: Put it to his lips and before he could get up the breath to blow, he fell on the ground.

EUGENE: He rolled himself into a tight ball, holding his stomach. Cussing and moaning and thrashing around.

MRS. LOVE: And the foaming at the mouth got worse! He puked—a bloody puke, and his eyes looked like they'd popped right out of their sockets. He opened his mouth and gasped for breath.

EUGENE: In the excitement some of the kids went inside the drugstore and the girl at the counter says, "Y'all can have anything you want—just don't put a curse on *me!*" While black faces were filling that counter, someone outside yelled . . . .

MRS. LOVE: "Sheriff Morrison is *dead!*"

EUGENE: How do you know so much? You weren't there.

MRS. LOVE: No, son, I wasn't there, but I've seen it before. I've seen . . .

EUGENE: What?

MRS. LOVE: Death in the raw. Dr. Crawford's entire family went that away.

EUGENE: Grandma . . . ?

MRS. LOVE: Some of them had it easier and quicker than the rest—dependin'.

EUGENE: Dependin' on what?

MRS. LOVE: How they had loved and treated their neighbor—namely *me. (Unconsciously she fumbles with the bag dangling from around her neck, which she removes from her bosom)*

EUGENE: What's in that bag you're fumbling with?

MRS. LOVE: Spice.

EUGENE: You're lying to me. What is it?

MRS. LOVE: The spice of life, baby.

EUGENE: Did you . . . did you do something to Sheriff Morrison?

MRS. LOVE: *(Singing)*

In the sweet bye and bye
We shallllllll meet . . .

EUGENE: What did you do to Sheriff Morrison?

MRS. LOVE: I helped y'all integrate—in my own fashion.

EUGENE: What did you do to that man?

MRS. LOVE: I gave him peace! Sent him to meet his maker! And I sent him in grand style, too. Tore his very guts out with my special seasoning! Degrading me! Callin' me "nigger"! Beating my men folks!

EUGENE: *(Sinks into chair)* Why?

MRS. LOVE: Because I'm a tired old black woman who's been tired and who ain't got no place and never had no place in this country. You talk about a "new Negro." Hell, I was a new Negro seventy-six years ago. Don't you think I wanted to sip me a coke-cola in a store when I went out shopping? Don't you think I wanted to have a decent job that would have given me some respect and enough money to feed my family and clothe them decently? I resented being called "girl" and "Auntie" by folks who weren't even as good as me. I worked for nigger haters, made 'em love me, and I put my boy through school—and then I sent *them* to eternity with flying colors. I got no regrets, boy, just peace of mind and satisfaction. And I don't need no psychiatrist! I done vented my pent-up emotions! Ain't that what you're always saying?

EUGENE: You can be sent to the electric chair!

MRS. LOVE: Who? Aunt Grace Love? Good old black auntie? Shoot! I know white folks, son, and I've been at this business for a long time now, and they know I know my place.

EUGENE: Oh, grandma . . .

MRS. LOVE: Cheer up! I done what I did for all y'all, but if you don't appreciate it, ask some of the colored boys who ain't been to college and who's felt ol' man Morrison's stick against their heads—they'd appreciate it. *Liberation!* Just like the underground railroad—Harriett Tubman—that's me. Only difference is I ain't goin' down in history. Now you take off them clothes before you get them wrinkled.

EUGENE: Where're you going?

MRS. LOVE: To shed a tear for the deceased and get me a train ticket.

EUGENE: You're going home to daddy?

MRS. LOVE: Your daddy don't need me no more, son. He's got your mama. No, I ain't going to your daddy.

EUGENE: Then where're you going?

MRS. LOVE: Ain't you said them college students is sittin'-in in Mississippi and they ain't makin' much headway 'cause of the governor? (*Eugene nods*) Well . . . I think I'll take me a little trip to Mississippi and see what's happenin'. You wouldn't by chance know the governor's name, would you?

EUGENE: What?

MRS. LOVE: I have a feeling he just might be needing a good cook.

EUGENE: Grandma!

MRS. LOVE: Get out of those clothes now. (*She starts for the door*) And while I'm downtown, I think I'll have me a cold ice cream soda at Mr. Thomas'! Ain't much left, Lord . . . I wonder who'll be next? I'll put me an ad in the paper. Who knows, it may be you . . . or you . . . or you . . . (*Sings as she exits*)

Where He leads me
I shallllll follow . . .
Where He leads me
I shallllll follow . . .

(*Eugene sits stunned as the old woman's voice fades*)

Curtain

Lanford Wilson

THE GREAT NEBULA IN ORION

Lanford Wilson

Within a single decade, Lanford Wilson has climbed the theatrical ladder from Off-Off-Broadway to the stage of a major opera house. The Missouri-born (1937) author, who started to write plays while a student at the University of Chicago, inaugurated his professional career at the now defunct Caffe Cino in Greenwich Village. After having had ten productions at this pioneer Off-Off-Broadway café-theatre and six at the Café La Mama, he moved to Off-Broadway in 1965 with the presentation of *Home Free!* at the Cherry Lane Theatre. In 1966, Mr. Wilson again was represented Off-Broadway, this time with a double bill, *The Madness of Lady Bright* and *Ludlow Fair,* at the uptown Theatre East. *This Is the Rill Speaking,* another of his short plays, was seen during that same season at the Martinique Theatre in a series of six works originally done at the Café La Mama.

In 1967, Mr. Wilson won a Vernon Rice-Drama Desk Award for his play, *The Rimers of Eldritch,* a haunting dramatic study of life in a small town in the Middle West. This was followed by another full-length play, *The Gingham Dog,* which opened in 1968 at the Washington Theatre Club, Washington, D.C. In the following year, it was presented on Broadway with Diana Sands and George Grizzard as stars and Alan Schneider as director. The author returned to Broadway in May, 1970, with *Lemon Sky,* a work that prompted the following comment from Clive Barnes: "Mr. Wilson can write; his characters spring alive on stage; he holds our attention, he engages our heart."

The climb upward continued and in 1971, Mr. Wilson received considerable praise for his libretto for the operatic version of Tennessee Williams' *Summer and Smoke,* which had its world premiere in June in St. Paul, Minnesota. The opera, with music by Lee Hoiby, is to be given its New York premiere in March, 1972, by the New York City Opera at Lincoln Center.

From the maskeshift intimacy of the Caffe Cino to the splendorous ambiance of the New York State Theatre is no mean achievement. Lanford Wilson has made the transition with accompanying honors, including a Rockefeller Foundation grant and an ABC-Yale Fellowship.

Among the author's other works for the theatre are: *Balm in Gilead; Wandering; So Long At the Fair; No Trespassing; Serenading Louie;* and *The Great Nebula In Orion,* which appears in print for the first time anywhere in this anthology.

Characters:

LOUISE

CARRIE

Scene:

An apartment overlooking Central Park West and Eighty-first Street, New York City.

Living room, doors to bathroom and bedroom; bedroom door ajar. The set need not be represented completely, but can be sketched and properties can be minimal. The play would benefit from being set as close to the audience as possible in, perhaps, a three-quarter round area. There is a minimal kitchenette in the living room, and the apartment should convey the feeling of a woman with good taste.

The apartment is empty. After a moment, a voice off says: "Oh, wow, I hope you don't mind . . ." There is the sound of a key in the lock. Louise, carrying several packages, bustles in. She is a smart woman in her early thirties and rather direct. Carrie, a slightly plumpish and attractive woman of the same age and somewhat woolly, enters rather tentatively behind Louise. Both are extremely well dressed, Carrie in a Chanel suit.

LOUISE: Man, oh, wow, have I ever got to go to the . . . make yourself comfortable. The john? The can? What did . . . to the loo? What did we call . . . ?

CARRIE: I don't really . . .

LOUISE: (*Overlapping*) When we had to pee. We had a cutsie-pie, prim-assed euphemism.

CARRIE: I'm not quite . . . (*Louise has managed to set the packages down in several places and throw her coat across a chair*)

LOUISE: Well, in any case, I've got to!

CARRIE: (*Who tends to cling to her purse*) It's a lovely . . .

LOUISE: Make yourself comfortable, I'll only be a sec. (*She flies off to the bathroom door, closing it*)

CARRIE: (*Alone. Looks to the audience, smiles, embarrassed, looks out the window. Calls*) Is this the park?

LOUISE: (*Off*) What's that?

CARRIE: (*Calling*) I said was that the park? Is that Central Park? (*A pause as she listens, waits, smiling. The smile fades. To the audience*) Well, obviously it is the park. This is a terrible mistake. I knew it was, coming up here. I have no idea why I . . .

LOUISE: (*Off*) What? I'll be with you in a jiff.

CARRIE: Nothing. Fine. (*Quietly, whispering to the audience*) It's rather like being sent up in one of those balloons—like—well, not a balloon, maybe, but a rocket or—in any case there's a theory about time being at a different wavelength or some such, you know. And if you go to Mars, say, though you might return only two months older the trip would take several years and things on earth would be completely altered—or some such thing. You know. Relativity. And here I am. It's all rather disquieting. (*Shrugs, making do*) In any case.

LOUISE: (*Re-entering*) What's that, sweet?

CARRIE: I said bumping into you like this.

LOUISE: Yes, a lot of catching up. You look super, by the way, and I won't hear anything except that I'm more ravishing than ever. You look a lot thinner.

CARRIE: Thank you.

LOUISE: (*To the audience*) It's a girdle, right? In this day and age, do you believe it? Oh, well. (*She turns back to Carrie, smiling*)

CARRIE: You do, you look wonderful. (*To the audience*) It's almost tra . . .

LOUISE: What is?

CARRIE: No, darling—I was . . .

LOUISE: (*Realizing this was said to the audience and not

her) Oh, I'm sorry. (*She has measured water into a sauce pan and set it on the stove, preparatory to making a chemex of coffee*)

CARRIE: Quite all right. (*Continuing to the audience*) Almost tragic to see someone whom you remember as so unusually striking and realize that . . .

LOUISE: (*Pouring the boiling water into the chemex*) Coffee we decided, didn't we?

CARRIE: . . . that special . . . (*To Louise*) Yes, please—just black, no sugar. (*Back to the audience, almost in a whisper*) . . . thing that they had was a vitality and youthful bloom, and then that's gone . . .

LOUISE: This will drip through and we can talk. (*To the audience*) Black no sugar, could you die?

CARRIE: (*To the audience, still whispering*) What you really feel of course, because you don't feel time passing, you know, minute by minute—you don't feel as though you're ageing, and then you see someone with whom you were young, and you see the age in them and feel sorry, not so much for them as for yourself.

LOUISE: Yes, well, I think I've finally gotten over that pretty much. Remember the trauma when we turned twenty?

CARRIE: Oh, yes. Blank many years ago.

LOUISE: Just fourteen.

CARRIE: Oh, God!

LOUISE: The coffee is going to be swill. I'm lousy in the kitchen.

CARRIE: You want help?

LOUISE: Lord, no! Nothing is organized. The place is a wreck, what kitchen there is. I have a larger space for my filing cabinets. You wouldn't be able to find anything.

CARRIE: (*To the audience*) I used to wait on her hand and foot.

LOUISE: Of course, you know what a klutz I am in the kitchen anyway. I've never been able to understand how I could be so relatively organized professionally and the reverse—(*Burns herself—not badly—she doesn't want to be in the kitchen anyway*) Damn! Tell me about the children—(*To the audience*) I can't. Just can not imagine Carrie—Carolyn Brown nee Smith, class of nineteen fifty-beep—I think even that gives away too much; make that nineteen beep-beep—can not imagine her with children. Well, you know how it is. It's marvelous. She showed me their pictures. You know—*that* scene? In Bergdorf's, yet. Where I never go. And I thought "Oh, my God, she isn't going to whip out photographs is she?" And as I'm watching everyone watch us and trying to smile and look interested. . . . You know we've had the big scene: "Carrie, darling! Louise, baby! It's been ages!" And throwing our arms around each other and everybody smiling on, saying, "Look, how sweet!" She says you've got to see my two kids! And whips out these practically eight-by-ten color photographs and wouldn't you know they're gorgeous! They're beautiful. I almost burst into tears right in the middle of Mme. Greis' god-awful autumn. . . . If ever you could just *wish* children into being without all the bother, they're what you'd wish for. A dark boy, very straight and serious and an angel girl as blond as. . . . Demure, long thin hands and a knowing look at about age seven. . . .

CARRIE: They're angels. They really are. Five and seven.

LOUISE: Five and seven . . . (*They smile, amazed at the years, the moment turns first into a musing pause, then an awkward silence. Carrie takes a drink of coffee, smiles to Louise*)

CARRIE: (*To the audience*) The coffee's swill.

LOUISE: Would you rather have a drink? Let's lace it up a bit. I can't really make anything—and this is supposed to be so simple.

CARRIE: That's not a bad idea. (*To the audience*) She said at work she's organized and I'm sure she is—that's . . . (*Louise is pouring brandy into her cup*) That's fine. Oh, my!

LOUISE: (*She has poured rather a lot*) What the hell!

CARRIE: (*Quickly*) Yes, it's after twelve.

LOUISE: What's that got to do . . . Oh, well.

CARRIE: (*Immediately back to the audience*) She has

really a marvelous position with—well, no names—one of the better dressmakers. Her own line. Really very successful. Beautiful clothes. She's always had a wonderful feeling for fabrics. Weight, drape, and all that.

LOUISE: Yes. It's nice. (*She has poured herself a straight brandy*) It's work—it's . . .

CARRIE: I mean she's really becoming rather a name.

LOUISE: Exhilarating sometimes and fun.

CARRIE: It makes me feel rather proud in a way, I suppose.

LOUISE: (*Taking a sip, proudly*) Hmmmm.

CARRIE: (*To the audience*) And then of course, well, I don't know . . . it's sad.

LOUISE: Sometimes I feel my clothes are rags. I mean, I say that. No one else had better! Then other times I'm really quite proud. I sometimes feel like more of a businesswoman than a designer. I can't think of any other reason why I succeeded in such a dog-eat-dog business when so many other people. . . . Oh, well, hash. What are you watching?

CARRIE: (*By the window*) What's the building?

LOUISE: The green one? It's the Planetarium.

CARRIE: Have you ever been?

LOUISE: Not actually. I understand it's quite ordinary.

CARRIE: Damn.

LOUISE: Beg pardon?

CARRIE: Oh, nothing. I don't think I like it. Could I have a brandy, darling? I don't much . . . (*She sets down the cup*)

LOUISE: Of course, of course. It's better than anything to take the chill off. The coffee's awful, isn't it?

CARRIE: No, no, it's quite good. I . . . (*To the audience*) Why is that, I wonder? I guess it's just so absurdly simple to make good coffee. Of course, I couldn't cut a dress.

LOUISE: (*Handing her the glass*) Cheers. Is that OK or do you want rocks?

CARRIE: No, this is fine. (*To the audience*) That's funny. Are you ever a little proud when someone—well, this isn't a good example, but some slang like "rocks" for "ice" and you know what they mean? I mean it isn't my word for it. Of course, I don't usually drink. I mean I'm not a drinker, so my first thought when someone says "rocks" is rocks! But, well, if I happen to answer immediately like that—"No, this is fine," I'm always just a little proud. I mean when we were in school we didn't say rocks. We said—I don't know—up?

LOUISE: No, up is without.

CARRIE: Salt? It was . . .

LOUISE: I'll think of it. We used it all the time.

CARRIE: Well, no matter.

LOUISE: I'll think of it.

CARRIE: (*She has managed to drink the pony of brandy by now*) The way we talked. All that slang—you know, I dread the kids growing up, because I know I won't understand a word they're saying. Remember the way *we* talked? (*To the audience*) My, that's warm—I shouldn't have—well, that damn Planetarium.

LOUISE: Another?

CARRIE: Just a bit. (*She shrugs to the audience*)

LOUISE: (*To the audience*) Drinks like a sieve. Always has. Wouldn't admit it on a stack of Bibles. Always was a prig. Good family and all that, you understand—churchmouse poor, but lineage out the ass.

CARRIE: (*Lifting the glass*) Where on earth did you get . . . ?

LOUISE: I don't know. They're not really good—Victorian.

CARRIE: They're lovely though.

LOUISE: Aren't they? A little musty shop down in the Village. I've had them for . . . (*Biting her lip, blinking, remembering the circumstances, suddenly almost in tears*) Golly.

CARRIE: (*Not noticing*) It's a beautiful rug.

LOUISE: Needs a good cleaning. How's David doing?

CARRIE: (*Surprised*) Oh! Marvelously. (*At a loss*) He's . . . just built himself a workroom out from the house.

LOUISE: (*Trying to be interested*) Workroom?

CARRIE: Shop. He does woodwork.

LOUISE: God!

CARRIE: Makes toys and things.

LOUISE: Oh, God!

CARRIE: No, he's very good at it. I don't know, it's a hobby. He had it in the basement, but you can't imagine. . . .

LOUISE: I *can* imagine!

CARRIE: I mean, aside from the noise, the sawdust. . . . It's much better away from the house.

LOUISE: You have land then?

CARRIE: We have three acres—not land.

LOUISE: (*To the audience*) He's rolling in money, it's absurd. (*To Carrie*) It must be wonderful for the kids.

CARRIE: Oh, yes it . . . there are trees to climb and David's got David junior a base-softball diamond, I suppose it is, and a tree house. And Alice has a doll house and garden house. He's really marvelous with them.

LOUISE: They're such angels.

CARRIE: Do you hear from your brother?

LOUISE: Sam? He's not one to write all that much. Neither am I for that matter. From time to time. Twice a year. I can always count on him to send me something embarrassing for Christmas. He was here a year ago.

CARRIE: Has he ever mentioned a Richard Roth?

LOUISE: Richard Roth; R.R.; Roth. I don't think, but then I never pay any attention to what he tells me. I don't know how he's remained single. I guess no one would have him.

CARRIE: I thought he was nice.

LOUISE: Sam? Oh, he's great. It really delights him that every woman comes equipped—and he thinks they're made that way especially for his own personal enjoyment. I think he's marvelous.

CARRIE: Yes, I . . . ah . . . (*To the audience, embarrassed*) I really don't think Louise has changed a bit. I . . . ah . . .

LOUISE: (*Continuing*) Of course he's damn good at it. Practice makes perfect!

CARRIE: Ah-ha.

LOUISE: I know he taught me everything *I* know about sex.

CARRIE: (*Exasperated, to the audience*) Now, I mean *that* sort of thing. Even if it's true, you don't . . .

LOUISE: (*Pouring another*) Who's Roth?

CARRIE: (*Stopped short*) Oh. A friend. Of Sam's. One of his friends.

LOUISE: (*To the audience*) I'm a year older than Carrie and the year I left Bryn Mawr was the same year Sam came to Haverford, which is just a long goodnight walk away. And Carrie had met Sam, so they saw each other. They didn't date, God knows. Of course, all Sam's friends were older. (*To Carrie, suddenly*) Oh! I've got to tell you. (*Pleased and delighted with this story*) We were having lunch—a bunch of us girls—no one you know, I don't think. I mean, we meet nearly every Friday. We have a table reserved for us. And the conversation never is rough, exactly, but we didn't really notice that we had a new busboy. A very young kid with his hair shaved off. It couldn't have been more than a quarter-inch long and big old ears sticking out from the side of his face. Maybe fourteen years old. And the girls were talking while he's sitting water and butter around. No one's paying any attention to him, and someone asked Berilla what she'd been up to, and she said she'd been going to night school. Of course nobody was listening, really. (*Aside to the audience*) This is an old joke, it's not going to be funny, particularly. (*Back to Carrie*) But after about half an hour, someone turned to Berilla and said whatever are you doing in night school? And the kid's taking off plates by now and Berilla said, "Oh, I'm just taking a course in intercourse. All you have to do is come." And. We laughed, a little. But this kid had never heard it before. I don't imagine he'd ever heard a woman . . . well, he bit his lip and set the dish back . . . (*Laughing*) . . . on the table and made a beeline for the kitchen. The ears—those big old ears—just burning. He thought it was the funniest thing he'd. . . . He was so funny and sweet. We just collapsed. He came back flushed and biting his tongue, with tears in his eyes. Such a dear.

CARRIE: He was probably as shocked as anything.

LOUISE: Oh, yes! Shocked and surprised and so endearing. With those big old ears.

CARRIE: He sounds sweet.

LOUISE: Really wonderful. (*A long pause. Carrie gets up and walks a few steps away. To the audience*) Well, she's shocked. I suppose with kids of her own. Well, crap.

CARRIE: Humm? Oh, no. Not at all. I'm abstracted. I'm not really good company today. It's wonderful seeing . . . (*Breaking off, to the audience*) I'm not shocked. I've had a few drinks and I'm pleasantly high. I've decided whatever it was I was shopping for can wait until. . . . (*Back to Louise*) Is it warm in here?

LOUISE: It is a little, I can . . .

CARRIE: No, no, I'll just take off my jacket. (*She does, and in a minute, her shoes*)

LOUISE: That's a beautiful suit. Chanel?

CARRIE: Umm.

LOUISE: (*To the audience*) I loathe it, right? But then I would. It's a beautiful suit. It's not the sort of thing I do. I drape, Chanel cuts. It's a very complicated pattern. You take it apart the jacket alone is in about fifty pieces. I mean she's been making the same damn suit for about fifty years, but what the hell, right?

CARRIE: Oooh. That's better.

LOUISE: Actually I love the damn suit but it's all wrong for her. That's real, you understand. Notice the fabric; that's no rack copy. Money, my dears . . .

CARRIE: I have one of yours.

LOUISE: Do you? Which?

CARRIE: Well, I would, wouldn't I? A black wool with white piping.

LOUISE: (*To the audience*) Oh, God. Well, she could do worse. Actually it should look rather nice on her.

CARRIE: Oh, I love it. I didn't bring it with me.

LOUISE: (*To change the subject*) Who's Roth?

CARRIE: Oh, well, if you don't know him . . .

LOUISE: I might. I never listen to Sam.

CARRIE: I don't think they were that close. I didn't really know him at school. I met him there with your brother, but after I went out to California.

LOUISE: (*Fishing neatly*) Wait, is this the guy you wrote me . . . ? God, that's years ago.

CARRIE: I thought I had. The poet.

LOUISE: A poet, right.

CARRIE: Or he was when he was at Haverford, but I met him again in California.

LOUISE: With David?

CARRIE: No, no, David doesn't know him. *Before* David. He was a really exceptional poet but with. . . . One of those very intelligent guys with enormous gaps. Like he spoke Greek and Latin. Actually spoke! Well, I mean he didn't go around speaking it, but he could, and one time I remember I mentioned the Secretary of State and he'd never heard of him. Didn't know any of the cabinet. And on art, painting at least, he was absolutely blank. Never heard of the most obvious—Magritte, Gris . . .

LOUISE: Mmmm.

CARRIE: But he was one of the most independent and impulsive and masculine and I don't know, one of . . .

LOUISE: Probably what you mean to say is he laid you.

CARRIE: Well, I don't mean . . .

LOUISE: Without so much as a will-you-waltz. I know the type.

CARRIE: Well, as a matter of fact, but it wasn't that. That's neither here nor . . . oh, well, it's silly.

LOUISE: (*To the audience*) She's a little tight-assed, but she loosens up. Not such a bad egg really. We had some great times.

CARRIE: (*Loosely*) I *am* feeling easier. I don't know. I'm only in town for two days. I have a list as long as my arm, I run into Louise in Bergdorf's, of all places. I mean I haven't seen her in what?

LOUISE: Six.

CARRIE: Six, nearly seven years. We were really close in school. But I thought—oh, my God—scratch that! Oh, my gosh, I don't like that kind of talk when I go out.

LOUISE: Right, I couldn't agree more. (*To the audience*) Bombed, right?

CARRIE: I hear enough of that kind of talk on the street. But I ran into her and thought . . .

LOUISE: "Oh, my God!"

CARRIE: Right. No, and I'm not bombed either. (*Straightens*) It just needs a little concentration.

LOUISE: You want another?

CARRIE: Ummm. And I thought I hope it goes all right, you know? You run into a great friend after a while, and you find you have nothing to talk about. It's embarrassing. You feel like a fool. So I said it was a mistake to come up for a bit, and here I am relaxing when I've got a thousand things to be doing. Have you kept up?

LOUISE: Pardon?

CARRIE: With the girls?

LOUISE: Oh, I get the . . . No, I haven't really. I get the paper. You're in a better position than . . .

CARRIE: I don't know why you think that.

LOUISE: Well, I . . . perhaps not.

CARRIE: No, of course I am, but—no. I haven't. I don't really. I mean, I read about *you* from time to time, and Ruth.

LOUISE: (*To the audience*) An actress.

CARRIE: (*To the audience*) Films. (*Suddenly dizzy*) Oh . . . Oh, I don't think . . .

LOUISE: What's wrong?

CARRIE: I had a chicken thing . . . for lunch. I'm all right.

LOUISE: Sure? So how do you like Boston?

CARRIE: Well, we're outside Boston some. It's really lovely. A little—well, you know I *move* well in those. I was going to say I don't think *you* would like it much. It's all rather provincial; Garden Party; or you'd feel it was. It's really very sweet. You don't want me to tell you about my bridge club and . . .

LOUISE: Oh, you don't . . .

CARRIE: What? Of course. What else? And they'd never forgive me if I didn't bring back some juicy gossip about the fashions for the fall.

LOUISE: Oh, I'll tell you, you won't like it.

CARRIE: Oh, no?

LOUISE: I know it must seem glamorous. I'm not very damn glamorous, but everyone seems to feel I must be. There have been some really wonderful times. There's an award. Probably you don't even know about it—it's in the trade—that I've managed to win. Twice actually. And that was a thrill. There's a presentation luncheon and I don't know—I never . . . (*Full stop, thinking*) Well. It wasn't that I never got along with mom, she's very—well, I should say that I'm quite like her. There was never any question of family pride or any such thing. We all of us—Sam, too—all of us took each other for granted. It was a very casual sort of family. We weren't like families. I mean, I had left home by the time I was eighteen which isn't really terribly shocking anymore, but, well, the first time she came to see me—she didn't call or anything and I was having this torrid three-day affair with a what-was-he-a-writer—Oh, God—I mean for the newspaper. Worse, he wrote those daily horoscope things. Well, he was a Pisces and they're into that—and mom comes to the door. Pisces is in bed naked. Mom comes to the door with a little overnight bag and a hat with feathers or a feather, and I answer the door. I've not seen her in a year. And she was broadminded, you know, but I said, "Oh, mom, sweet, how wonderful, darling, but there isn't a cube of ice in the house, could you run down to the deli? It's just on the corner." And mom said, "Oh, sure, of course." She didn't think a thing of it. I mean we got along. And she's a teetotaler. But really, at bottom, she wanted me to be different from what we had been. To have a family and not mess with a career. She didn't see much use in it, or why I was so caught up. Well, I had two smashing seasons in a row and was pretty much the toast of the town that spring, and I guess everyone knew I was going to win this award. I know *I* did. But you can't really know it until you . . . I mean what it's like until you do. And all my friends were there, who have been of—well, they've been wonderful. And I was very young, the youngest designer ever. I still was, the second year I won—and—everyone *stood.* (*She is very moved*) They were . . . I just didn't expect it. I know I—I—got the award and everyone cheered and they all stood and all I could think . . . Stupid—all I could think of, standing there with this award (*Crying suddenly, covering her face*) was: If mother could be here, if she could see. She could . . . (*Out of it*) Silly! It was the last thing I expected to think at a time like that. I mean, we weren't even close. She didn't even like me all that much. Well, this is silly. You're right. (*Gets up*) It isn't a good idea. (*Walking around*) No, it's wonderful, it is. It's good to see you. I need . . . Yes, Central Park. Fifth Avenue on the other side. Whyever do you hate the Planetarium? I think it's kind of lovely.

CARRIE: (*Beat*) That's very . . .

LOUISE: Oh, we weren't even close. It's such a silly thing. At a time like that what comes over you. What you *think*. (*Beat*) We haven't talked about school.

CARRIE: No.

LOUISE: Thank God. Whatever (*Undecided*) happened to Phyllis Trahaunt?

CARRIE: (*But interested*) I haven't a clue.

LOUISE: (*At random*) She was going with someone I think.

CARRIE: Oh, no. No! You knew.

LOUISE: I've wondered. She's one of the few women I've wanted to dress; she carried herself so well.

CARRIE: (*In a hush-hush tone, implying scandal*) Oh, she was beautiful. For all the good. But she wasn't *going* with anyone. Never.

LOUISE: I heard she was.

CARRIE: I don't much think so from what I heard.

LOUISE: No?

CARRIE: She didn't much like the boys, I hear.

LOUISE: Oh, really?

CARRIE: I'm surprised you didn't know. She was in your class.

LOUISE: I guess I never really thought. We had a few classes together.

CARRIE: But she never dated. She was always in Philadelphia.

LOUISE: I just assumed she had family there.

CARRIE: I haven't heard a word of her.

LOUISE: Huh? Nor I. (*She pours another drink*)

CARRIE: None for me. (*Louise looks to the audience as if to say something serious, decides against it, corks the bottle. Carrie is looking away, deep in troubled thought. The tone of her voice, serious and troubled, comes from the blue*) Louise . . . ?

LOUISE: (*Startled, seriously in return*) What, darling?

CARRIE: Oh.

LOUISE: I'm sorry, that sounded so odd. I'm hearing oddly today.

CARRIE: Well, I've joined practically everything there is to join. I mean, I know you aren't interested in politics or anything like that . . .

LOUISE: Well, more than I was, actually.

CARRIE: Oh, darling, I am glad. But I know I have my children and they are . . . well, I won't show you again.

LOUISE: (*To the audience*) Small favor. No, they're lovely.

CARRIE: And I have a wonderful home and David and the kids . . .

LOUISE: And you've joined everything.

CARRIE: I've even taken some night courses. Not like your friend . . .

LOUISE: Berilla? No. I'm sure. I don't mean . . .

CARRIE: I know. I really, in spite of that, envy you. You're like some of the girls, and I don't know how they do it. I know it's just an attitude, I mean a state of mind, but knowing that doesn't help, does it?

LOUISE: It might, if I knew what the hell we were talking about!

CARRIE: Well . . .

LOUISE: I mean, they say the first thing an alcoholic has to do is admit he's hooked.

CARRIE: Well, then, what I've got to admit is that I'm not. Hooked. Even with all my activities, I really envy you. You're . . .

LOUISE: Darling, I'll trade anytime.

CARRIE: Well, see, though, that's . . . You wouldn't really, would you?

LOUISE: Well, no, not really. But then, really, neither would you.

CARRIE: But I would. When I first saw you, I thought you looked all of six years older and probably so did I, and I didn't really want to think about it. And of course I know you're a wonderful success and that's probably never easy but you seem—engaged.

LOUISE: Oh, I'm engaged.

CARRIE: Well, I'm not much.

LOUISE: What is it, David?

CARRIE: No, I don't really think it's David. I'm afraid it's more *me*. David is the happiest married man I know of. (*Count six*) Well, that's silly. It's not really anything. It's just seeing you again after all this time. You start thinking back about the times we had and those times. It's silly.

LOUISE: Is there anything . . . ?

CARRIE: (*Irritated. Almost uppity*) Oh, don't be ridiculous. That's ridiculous!

LOUISE: What is?

CARRIE: Well, weren't you going to ask me if I need help or something? What I need is about two less drinks.

LOUISE: Or two more.

CARRIE: I don't think. (*To the audience*) Well, now I *am* uncomfortable and I thought . . .

LOUISE: Have another drink then.

CARRIE: No! Thank you.

LOUISE: Have you been trying to solve the world's problems again?

CARRIE: No, I don't crusade anymore. It would look rather hypocritical. David has so many very rich friends.

LOUISE: And is no pauper himself.

CARRIE: Oh, dear. I really had no idea when we were married. I mean I knew he had money, but I'd no idea. It's just that being around them you realize that actually the country isn't run quite the way you thought it . . . I mean, they're really very powerful people.

LOUISE: I'm sure they are.

CARRIE: And, well, the country *isn't* run quite the way you think it is. The way people are led to believe it is.

LOUISE: I don't really think people believe it is.

CARRIE: I mean it's worse than that.

LOUISE: How?

CARRIE: Well, it's all a sham. I don't actually think I should say anything. It's just things I sense. The way they talk. I only meant that I decided crusading wouldn't have much effect. I don't mean I drift and mope. I diet and run about from this to that. You should see my schedule, but I'm just not . . .

LOUISE: Engaged?

CARRIE: Well, my mind isn't. Or I'm losing it or something. I'm not all there, is all. This brandy is something else.

LOUISE: A present. Isn't it great?

CARRIE: I'm not so sure. (*She finishes it off as Louise looks at her*)

LOUISE: (*Not too obviously*) Richard Roth.

CARRIE: Huh?

LOUISE: I don't know. I think you may have written about him.

CARRIE: I thought I must have. (*To the audience*) We

used to write years ago. But you know, we slacked off and finally just dwindled down to exchanging Christmas cards. (*To Louise*) Dick never wrote a letter in his life.

LOUISE: Dick Roth. What's he up to now?

CARRIE: Oh, now, who knows? Removed to Australia, the last I heard. That was years ago. I wouldn't have any idea now.

LOUISE: I don't know about poets.

CARRIE: Oh, he was great but he was a nut. Everyone reviewed his work, if that means anything. I didn't really know him when he wrote, I really met him in California. I've probably told you: he had these enormous gaps and he knew practically nothing about astronomy or any of that, so I guess it came as a shock to him. He read somewhere that the sun—you know, our sun—would burn up in about a billion years or two. Or whatever it's supposed to do: burn out or blow up, and he never wrote a word after that. I suppose he reasoned that anything that was written would simply always be around somewhere, and if there was going to be an end to it all one day, he didn't see any point. As I said he was a nut. So he left school and came out to California.

LOUISE: Why California?

CARRIE: Astronomy. Mount Palomar. I guess he got very interested in cosmology or something. He was really crazy about it for a while. You know he was one of those types that's never interested in any one thing for any length of time. I think for about a month he was even interested in me. His sister was ecstatic. Apparently he'd never been interested in a *person* before.

LOUISE: (*To the audience*) After Carrie left school she went for a year out . . .

CARRIE: A little less.

LOUISE: Out to California.

CARRIE: We used to sit out on the beach at night. It was incredible. You've never seen skies like they have. And the nights aren't really cold but you need a sweater. We used to build up a bonfire. There's tons of driftwood around on the beach that washes up, and we dragged it in from everywhere. You could have seen it for miles out to sea. You aren't supposed to, but no one says anything. There was a group of probably twenty of us. Dick and I used to wander out down the beach —you couldn't get lost—and you could see the fire with little people running off and dragging up more wood all the time. I even learned a few of the constellations. They're really easy. I mean, at first they're just stars, but once you start getting them placed in your mind, the whole sky starts dividing up into patterns like a quilt. And you can't look up without seeing, recognizing, Andromeda and Orion and the bears and the Seven Sisters. It's amazing.

LOUISE: I can't even find the big dipper.

CARRIE: Oh, you could. There's a way. You just have to find Polaris. Well, I mean, I couldn't either but you learn. Orion is the one though; you've seen him, you just didn't know what he was.

LOUISE: I don't imagine.

CARRIE: No, you had to. He's the one that you say, I'll bet anything that's some damn constellation. This is Orion. See, there are three stars . . . (*On the table, with her finger—dot, dot, dot*) Big ones across. That's the belt. And here. (*To the audience*) Do you know this? (*Back to Louise*) Perpendicular to the belt there are three more, closer together and fainter. (*On the table*) And that's his sword. And this—the center star in the sword is the Great Nebula in Orion.

LOUISE: The Great Nebula in Orion.

CARRIE: Or of Orion, whichever. Which isn't a star at all.

LOUISE: Of course not.

CARRIE: Do you know this?

LOUISE: No. (*To the audience*) Crocked, right? Plastered!

CARRIE: Well, it's very interesting. The Great Nebula is a lot of hydrogen gas that's lit up by a couple of stars behind it somewhere, and some by it's own heat, because it's condensing. It's moving, like a whirlpool, all the time and getting tighter and tighter—what was that?

LOUISE: (*Who has uttered a polite "umm" at "tighter"*) Nothing.

CARRIE: And hotter and hotter. And it will keep getting more and more compact and hotter and smaller. I mean it's vast! And tighter and smaller until it's so hot and compact—just a ball of fire, burning by itself—that it will be a star. And we could actually see that. I mean the center star. We could see that it was fuzzy, a big fuzzy spot. And Dick said that would be a star someday.

LOUISE: A star is born.

CARRIE: Oh, come on. I though it was interesting.

LOUISE: I think you had to be there.

CARRIE: Well, in any case you can't see it in Boston. The sky is so hazy you can't even find the sword.

LOUISE: In New York you're damn lucky to find the sky.

CARRIE: Well, we can usually see the belt, but no more. I kept wishing you'd come out there. I wrote you, didn't I?

LOUISE: I was working, darling, I couldn't.

CARRIE: But you'd have loved it.

LOUISE: I went to California once and I didn't love it. I wasn't having a whirlwind courtship and marrying a catch.

CARRIE: (*Brief pause*) It was kind of a whirlwind, wasn't it? More whirlwind than courtship. We had two dates, David said will you and I said where's Boston and we were having breakfast with his mother.

LOUISE: And you forgot about astronomy.

CARRIE: Well, Roth had pulled his remove to Australia, just a few . . .

LOUISE: Weeks?

CARRIE: Days . . . days.

LOUISE: Well, he sounds kind of silly anyway.

CARRIE: But he was fun though. You really would have loved it. You weren't working at anything important.

LOUISE: No, I suppose not actually, but it was nice. It was a good year all around. You should have asked Roth what sign the moon was in.

CARRIE: Oh, he didn't know anything about astrology; he hated it. Of course by now he's probably gone totally occult.

LOUISE: And New York at the time was—different. Charmed or something. I'd never been here and the girl I roomed with—here, this very apartment; we found it—she was new to the city, too.

CARRIE: She was Bryn Mawr?

LOUISE: Yes. But I don't think you knew her.

CARRIE: It's a very exciting city. I don't know though, with all the crime. Of course it's just as bad in Boston, but somehow anything that happens in New York is glamorized or something. Maybe more *does* happen here.

LOUISE: (*Who has been adrift. Waking up, after a beat*) What? I'm sorry, darling. What?

CARRIE: Nothing, I was just rattling on. Listen, it's late . . .

LOUISE: (*Longish pause. Waking again*) What? Oh, God, I'm sorry. (*To the audience*) Have you ever done that? God, that's embarrassing.

CARRIE: (*Fishing into-her shoes*) That's all right, I should go. Oooh.

LOUISE: Have another drink.

CARRIE: Well, I guess. I don't really want to shop. I'm out of the mood. There's nothing I can't really get in Boston.

LOUISE: You're here another day.

CARRIE: (*Standing, walking about*) It's really a lovely apartment. You have another room. It's bigger than I . . . (*She opens the door*)

LOUISE: Oh, don't go in there, darling. It's a mess. You know me. (*Carrie retreats, rather startled, just a little*) It's just the bedroom.

CARRIE: It's large.

LOUISE: It's such a mess. Here. Cheers.

CARRIE: Yes.

(*They sip. Carrie sits back down, looking puzzled*)

LOUISE: I really am a terrible housekeeper. We're both going to be stone drunk in the middle of the afternoon and create a scandal. Boston society Girl and Famed Designer arrested for etc., etc.

CARRIE: I know. Think of the ladies' clubs. Well, I suppose Boston has the best fish markets in the country, that's something. There and Maine and we have a place in Maine. I really . . . I really hate fish, I . . .

LOUISE: That's funny.

CARRIE: I can't even walk down half the streets.

LOUISE: Listen, *I* want to appear sometimes at work in overalls!

CARRIE: What?

LOUISE: I don't know, I think I'm a little fuzzy. What did you call that? The great fuzz in Orion?

CARRIE: (*Away*) Belt. Er, uh, nebula. The Great Nebula.

LOUISE: I'd like to be there.

CARRIE: Yes. (*Pause*) David is very chowder; a chowder person.

LOUISE: (*Reviving*) Listen, why don't you write for a change, now that I've . . . that *we've* re-established some kind of . . . now . . . (*Laughing*) I don't know what I'm saying!

CARRIE: I know I'm going to be very popular, having—I'll tell them lunch—with my famous alumnus.

LOUISE: Tell them to buy something!

CARRIE: Oh, they will, they'll have to.

LOUISE: I want to do a whole line for little girls. Your little girl is so adorable. Women overdress their little girls, I'd love that. Call it the . . . what's her name?

CARRIE: Alice.

LOUISE: The Alice Line.

CARRIE: She'd be very proud. (*She has on her jacket; she stands now*)

LOUISE: (*Superficially, phony*) It's really been fun, Carrie.

CARRIE: (*The same*) Hasn't it? I'm so glad I . . . (*Stops, biting her lip. Covers her eyes with her hand. Louise looks at her, painfully, Carrie sits down. Louise sits down beside her. Carrie is trying very hard not to cry*)

LOUISE: Carrie. Can I get . . . what?

CARRIE: (*Shaking her head, not looking up. Weakly*) No, nothing. (*Now looking at her*) Louise, I saw her picture, Phyllis' picture in your . . . I'm sorry, I didn't mean . . . I didn't know. I had no idea. I'd . . .

LOUISE: (*Looking away*) Well, we all have our . . . (*Biting her lip, Carrie begins to cry openly*) You *don't* want to go back, do you?

CARRIE: (*Breaking down completely*) No. (*Sobbing openly, audibly, shaking her head*) No, no, I can't. No.

(*Louise begins to cry now, too. They sit at opposite ends of the sofa. Carrie reaches out her hand, Louise takes it, grasping hard, tightly. They continue crying openly. Not looking at one another. Carrie withdraws her hand, opens her purse, blows her nose*)

CARRIE: Ma-maybe . . . (*They look at each other now, their faces bathed in tears, both with the same thought, trying to laugh, shaking their heads up and down in agreement*) Maybe Richard Roth ran off with Phyllis Trahaunt.

LOUISE: (*Who has said "Phyllis" with her*) Yes, yes! (*Wiping her face*) Damn my face!

CARRIE: What are we going to do?

LOUISE: I don't know, Carrie. I don't know. I've not known for six goddamned years!

CARRIE: I know.

LOUISE: Maybe David'll build us a little rocket ship in his workshop, huh? We'll fly off to your . . . (*A motion with her hand, crying again*)

CARRIE: (*Crying, trying to laugh*) Nebula.

LOUISE: Do you think he could?

CARRIE: No. No. (*They laugh*) He's a terrible carpenter. He is!

LOUISE: I suspected as much.

CARRIE: (*Blowing her nose again*) Oh, he only spends

his time out there because he can't understand why I'm always in such a foul mood. I look like hell! Oh, I don't care. (*She stares off*)

LOUISE: You could ask his sister where . . .

CARRIE: No, I couldn't. She's married, I don't really know her. I couldn't anyway.

LOUISE: I guess . . .

CARRIE: Where did Phyllis . . . ?

LOUISE: Thin air, darling.

CARRIE: I'd forgotten how lovely . . .

LOUISE: Oh, don't. Her parents wouldn't answer my "enquiries." She was very honest with them, so they didn't think much of me. I stay in the apartment because if . . .

CARRIE: (*A long pause. Finally picking up her gloves*) Well.

LOUISE: Oh, don't go.

CARRIE: The thought of that hotel room is a bit . . .

LOUISE: Stay. We'll fix ourselves up and go out to a film. Have some great fattening dinner. You can have the sofa bed; it's miles better than mine. They floodlight the Planetarium at night, it makes a great nightlight coming through the window.

CARRIE: (*With some humor*) I don't know if I need that.

LOUISE: Take your pick. (*Carrie smiles*) Good.

CARRIE: The thought of that hotel . . .

LOUISE: Darling, the thought of *anything*.

CARRIE: (*Neither moves*) I had such great ideas of changing the world. You remember? I always thought . . .

LOUISE: We're better off than most.

CARRIE: They keep telling us.

LOUISE: Umm.

CARRIE: I worked so diligently, and believed so . . .

LOUISE: Yes, didn't we?

CARRIE: (*With a sigh*) Oh, God, Louise . . .

LOUISE: It's all just a great . . .

(*They sit, huddled in their separate corners of the sofa*)

CARRIE: (*Pause*) The ironic thing . . .

LOUISE: (*Pause*) Of course, it's all . . .

CARRIE: Any other woman would be . . .

LOUISE: Yes . . .

CARRIE: (*A long pause. The lights begin to fade, very slowly. They hardly move, staring off, lost in mixed images*) It's all such a . . .

LOUISE: (*A long pause. With just a touch of humor*) The terribly . . . ironic . . . thing. . . .

(*A long pause. The lights fade out completely*)

Curtain

N. F. Simpson

WE'RE DUE IN EASTBOURNE IN TEN MINUTES

N. F. Simpson

The work of N. F. Simpson, one of England's best-known modern humorists, frequently has been likened to Lewis Carroll and even, upon occasion, to Eugène Ionesco. A member of the new wave of British dramatists that flourished in the late 1950's, following in the wake of John Osborne's success with *Look Back in Anger,* Mr. Simpson (who worked in a bank before World War II and later as an adult-education lecturer) basically is a serious writer, but his mood is absurdist. While he satirizes, however, he is taking direct jabs at society and his criticism is no less sharp for it. As theatre essayist and historian Frederick Lumley has pointed out, "Simpson loves logic and like Lewis Carroll he tries to stand it on its head; inverted logic is the key to his dramatic method. His feeling for inversion extends to making the ordinary appear extraordinary and the extraordinary appear ordinary; the world he gives us is one of carefully worked out topsy-turvydom." As the author himself has stated, "The retreat from reason means precious little to anyone who has never caught up with reason in the first place; it takes a trained mind to relish a *non sequitur.*"

Norman Frederick Simpson was born in London on January 29, 1919, and was educated at London University. He first came to public notice in 1956 when his comedy, *A Resounding Tinkle,* won a prize in *The Observer's* play competition and subsequently was seen at the Royal Court, London, "as a play without decor." In 1958, a shortened version of the comedy, with full production accoutrements, was presented at the same theatre on a double bill with Mr. Simpson's second play, *The Hole.* The distinguished cast included Nigel Davenport, Robert Stephens, Wendy Craig and Sheila Ballantine and was staged by William Gaskill.

A Resounding Tinkle was the first of Mr. Simpson's comedies to involve his two favorite characters, Bro and Middie Paradock, and it was described in the press as "a devastating and extremely funny analysis of suburban inanity." In the initial work, the Paradocks nonchalantly harbor an elephant in their suburban garden while in *We're Due in Eastbourne in Ten*

Minutes, published here for the first time in the United States, the couple casually contend with an antique compost in their living room.

In addition to the aforementioned, Mr. Simpson is the author of *One Way Pendulum,* produced in London, 1959, in New York, 1961, and made into a film in 1965; *The Form;* and *The Cresta Run.* He also has contributed to a number of popular London revues.

We're Due in Eastbourne in Ten Minutes was written for television presentation on the B.B.C., but the author believes it lends itself "most readily to being produced in the theatre, even though originally written for a different medium." This was proven eminently correct when the comedy was given a highly successful stage production in a London playhouse in 1971.

In an offstage philosophical moment, Mr. Simpson has commented on the moral tone of the play: "I would like to think it was set by the attitude to life of the two main characters, Bro and Middie Paradock. For them, there is nothing so outrageous but what it may well have happened somewhere only last week; and nothing so preposterous that it may not happen here before the day's out—in all probability at a moment's notice and ringing a handbell. Consequently, they treat life very much like the weather, and organize themselves around its vagaries as best they can with such means as come to hand. And in doing so, let me say, they are to my mind on far solider ground than those who succumb to the ludicrous delusion that life is something they have some kind of edge on. It makes for cautious resignation—and a simple faith in the axiom that for those to whom life is an exercise in survival, the secret is in knowing how to ride with the punch."

Characters:

MIDDIE PARADOCK
BRO PARADOCK
MARTHA
HUMPHREY
DELIVERY MAN
LAURENCE GRIMSBY
PARSON

Scene:

With the exception of a few scenes, the action takes place in the home of Bro and Middie Paradock. This is an ordinary suburban semi-detached house. The front door opens onto a small hall, where the telephone is kept and where coats are hung up. The stairs are immediately opposite, and to the right of the stairs is a passage leading through to the kitchen, which is at the back of the house and has a door leading into the garden. On the right of the hall and passage are two doors. The first opens into the living room and the second into the dining room. The living room has a fireplace opposite the door, and bay windows looking out onto the small front garden. It is divided by curtains from the dining room, which has french windows onto the garden at the back and a hatch through to the kitchen. The television set is kept in the dining room.

Early evening, living room. (Bro, in casual clothes, is reading the paper. Middie is giving the room a final going over)

MIDDIE: You're not going to sit there too long, are you, Bro?

BRO: What?

MIDDIE: They'll be here in half an hour or so.

BRO: Oh. (*Back to paper, then afterthought*) Who will?

MIDDIE: You *know* who, Bro. Martha and Humphrey. You can't have forgotten.

BRO: Is that tonight?

MIDDIE: You know it's tonight.

BRO: (*Making no move*) I'd better get ready, then.

Bedroom of Martha and Humphrey

(*Humphrey is standing in front of a mirror and taking his time about doing up his shirt*)

MARTHA: (*In the doorway, with her hat and coat on*) We haven't got all night, you know. They're expecting us in twenty minutes.

HUMPHREY: Get dressed in haste, repent at leisure, Martha.

MARTHA: Yes. And better a clean shirt under a pile of freshly ironed handkerchiefs in the top left-hand drawer than a cartload of old beige cardigans on their way to a rummage sale. But it's not going to get us to Bro and Middies's.

HUMPHREY: All in good time, Martha.

MARTHA: And another thing. Just in case she gives us nuts again, we'll take our own nutcrackers.

HUMPHREY: I always carry a pair, Martha.

MARTHA: Not last time you didn't. We were cracking them with the heel of an old army boot they'd dug up from somewhere.

Kitchen

(*Table covered with various kinds of nuts. A large bowl almost full. Middie is carefully arranging the topmost layer of assorted nuts, choosing and discarding them nut by nut, as if decorating a cake*)

MIDDIE: You might look for the nutcrackers, Bro. I've been looking everywhere for them. (*Bro is now dressed for the evening*)

BRO: We're not giving them nuts again!

MIDDIE: Martha likes nuts. So does Humphrey. All I want to know is, what's happened to the nutcrackers.

(*Bro starts looking for them*)

BRO: They'll be where you put them, Middie, I haven't touched them. (*Phone rings in the hall*)

MIDDIE: Oh, no! (*She goes*)

Hall

MIDDIE: (*Going to phone*) This'll be Nora with some tale of woe again. (*She picks up phone*) Pestalozzi 0411 . . . Oh, hello, Nora . . . Yes, I can't stop long, though, Nora, because . . . (*Eyes to heaven*) Oh, dear, I *am* sorry, Nora . . . I'm sure . . . It must be, Nora . . . Yes . . . I can well imagine . . .

Kitchen

(*Bro, still looking for nutcrackers, pauses at the mixer and looks at it. It is a very large electric one. He picks it up and carries it to the table, looks at it again, ponders, and then crosses to a shelf where there is an equally large, bulbous, genial-looking mincer attachment. He comes back to the table with it*)

Hall

MIDDIE: (*On phone*) Yes, well, as a matter of fact he's out in the kitchen, Nora. I'll go and . . . Yes, I'll go and ask him. Hold on a moment, Nora. (*She puts the phone down*)

Kitchen. (*Bro has fixed on the mincer attachment, as Middie enters*)

MIDDIE: Nora.

BRO: What is it this time?

MIDDIE: Would we care to go half and half with them in a compost heap.

BRO: In a *what?*

MIDDIE: She's waiting.

BRO: Well . . . I don't know, Middie. I think I should want to see it first.

MIDDIE: What's this lot out for?

BRO: It's . . . I was just trying something out, Middie. I thought in a pinch we could use it instead of the nutcrackers, that's all.

MIDDIE: You can't crack a nut with a thing like that.

BRO: Well . . .

MIDDIE: It's like using a steamroller to boil an egg.

BRO: If we can't find the nutcrackers, Middie . . . !

MIDDIE: You know it's got no plug on it, don't you?

BRO: (*Taking up the plugless cord*) That won't take a minute. I can soon put a plug on it. (*He goes to a drawer for a plug, pliers, and screwdriver*)

MIDDIE: Anyway, what do I say to Nora? Do we, or don't we?

BRO: It depends what it's like, Middie. What condition it's in.

MIDDIE: It's just an ordinary compost heap. Sliced down the middle.

BRO: And what are we supposed to use it for?

MIDDIE: There are plenty of uses it can be put to.

BRO: I can't think what. Except as a doorstopper.

MIDDIE: In any case, we don't have to keep it. We can always get rid of it, if we don't like the look of it. There's bound to be somebody who'd be glad to have it.

BRO: Who?

MIDDIE: Somebody with half a garden. It might be just the thing he's looking for.

BRO: Yes.

MIDDIE: So I'll say we'll have it, shall I?

BRO: I suppose so.

MIDDIE: (*Going*) She'll only be offended or something if we refuse. You know what she is. (*Middie goes out*)

BRO: I hope we shan't regret it, that's all.

Hall

MIDDIE: (*Picks up phone*) Yes, Nora, we'd love to have it.

Kitchen. (*Bro is at mixer, preparing to fix plug on cord*)

BRO: (*To himself*) Something else they've picked up cheap and then changed their minds about.

Hall

MIDDIE: (*Looking ever so slightly apprehensive*) That's very kind of you, Nora . . . Yes. We'd be delighted . . . Thank you very much, Nora . . . Yes, we will . . . Goodbye, Nora.

Kitchen. (*Bro busy with screwdriver, pliers, plug. Middie enters*)

MIDDIE: Apparently it's an indoor one.

BRO: What is?

MIDDIE: Are you going to be long with that, because . . .

BRO: It's only a minute or two's job, Middie. I've been finding the pliers.

MIDDIE: They're in the drawer.

BRO: I've got them.

MIDDIE: And I think we'd better have the cart for that, as well. To take it in on. (*She goes to the door and out. She comes back in with the cart*) Then we can wheel it 'round to whoever wants it. (*She gets a duster*) We can hardly ask them to have it on their laps. (*She starts rubbing the trolley over with the duster*)

BRO: When you say "indoor", Middie . . .

MIDDIE: What?

BRO: I mean . . . is it . . . ?

MIDDIE: I don't know, Bro, do I? I haven't seen it. (*Bro says nothing*) She's sending it in one piece, by the way.

BRO: You mean the whole thing?

MIDDIE: Rather than cut into it. And then find we're not really smitten with it after all.

BRO: You realize how much room it's going to take up?

MIDDIE: Yes—well . . . (*She has finished with the duster on the cart, and is waiting for Bro*) It's something they've had up in the attic. An heirloom or something.

BRO: Yes. I've met some of Nora's heirlooms before. If you ask me, it's more likely something they've picked up at a church bazaar and then had second thoughts.

MIDDIE: It's always possible it might be worth something.

BRO: What might?

MIDDIE: If it's genuine.

BRO: Genuine in what way, Middie?

MIDDIE: Well, what about that Rembrandt? That somebody found. That was found in an attic, and it turned out to be worth a fortune.

BRO: In the first place, Middie, it wasn't a Rembrandt.

MIDDIE: What was it, then?

BRO: It was a Rubens.

MIDDIE: It's the same thing.

BRO: Not as a compost heap, Middie. (*Bro has finished*)

MIDDIE: Is it finished?

BRO: I'll just plug it in. (*Bro plugs in and switches on. Sound of a car starter ineffectually whooping. Cut to next scene*)

Car Interior. (*Humphrey and Martha sitting side by side*)

MARTHA: If we'd started out in time, we could have got there before it happened. (*Humphrey tries the starter again. Same noise*) Instead of which, we shall have to trot out some excuse again.

HUMPHREY: It's just a minor mishap, Martha, that's all.

Kitchen. (*Bro and Middie as before*)

MIDDIE: We shall have them here. They're late as it is. (*Bro switches on. A gentle hum*)

BRO: That's better.

Car. (*Humphrey and Martha as before. Engine running sweetly, and car moving*)

HUMPHREY: We can simply say we tripped over a bunch of grapes and fell headfirst into a bucket of whitewash.

MARTHA: We said that last time.

Kitchen. (Bro and Middie as before)

BRO: We'd better try it out with an almond, I think. *(Middie picks one out of the dish)*

MIDDIE: Where do I . . . ?

BRO: Let me do it. *(Doorbell, as Bro is about to drop the nut into the mincer)*

MIDDIE: I told you they'd be here. Give it to me. You go and let them in. I'll get the things on the cart.

BRO: *(Going)* Be careful how you put it in.

MIDDIE: Tell them I'm in the kitchen. *(She starts arranging things on the cart)*

Hall. (Bro to door. He opens it. Delivery Man in white overall)

MAN: Mr. Paradock? Compost heap.

BRO: Oh. That's very quick. We weren't expecting it just yet. Middie! *(Middie coming from kitchen)*

BRO: It's the . . .

MIDDIE: *(To man)* Oh, yes. We were expecting it. Would you . . . ?

MAN: Bring it in? Right.

(Middie leads the way into the living room)

Living Room. (Bro is already inside. Middie enters, with Delivery Man following)

MIDDIE: If you could just . . .

MAN: Over here?

MIDDIE: Yes, anywhere there.

(We see the compost heap for the first time. It is sitting rather primly in the middle of a large round low coffee table, quietly steaming. It is surrounded by an ornamental brass flange about an inch high, which imparts a kind of

discreet dignity to the thing. They put the table down on the floor, roughly in the middle of the room. Middie looks at it, as though not quite sure what to make of it)

MAN: (*To Bro, taking out order book and pen*) Not sorry to see the back of that.

BRO: No. I can imagine.

MAN: If you'd just . . . (*Bro takes the book and signs*) Yes. It's a tidy old weight. (*Bro hands back the book and pen*) Thank you very much. Don't bother to . . . (*He goes out, with a nod at Bro and Middie*)

BRO: (*To Middie*) I'd better . . .

MIDDIE: Yes. (*Bro goes out*)

Hall. (Man to door. Bro comes out, reaches behind the telephone, as from habit, and brings out a small plastic cruet)

MAN: (*At door*) Right. Well . . . (*Bro puts cruet in his hand, as though it were a tip*) Oh. That's very kind of you. (*Opening door*) Any time you . . . (*He goes out*) Did I . . . ? (*Feeling in pocket*) No, I didn't. (*He brings out a brochure and comes back with it to Bro*) Nearly went off with it in my pocket. That's the brochure that goes with it.

BRO: Oh. Thank you.

MAN: You'll need that. Guarantee on the back.

BRO: Ah, yes.

MAN: Cheerio, then. (*He goes*)

BRO: Goodbye. (*Bro closes the door and goes into the living room*)

Living Room. (Middie is looking down at compost heap. Bro enters)

MIDDIE: I suppose we've done the right thing.

BRO: Well, it's done now, Middie. Whether we have or not.

MIDDIE: If I'd known it was going to take up quite so much room . . .

BRO: Well . . .

MIDDIE: It's not the thing itself, it's the table or whatever it is it's on. There's no room for anything else in the room. We shall have to rearrange everything around that.

BRO: I did try to warn you, Middie. (*Bro is looking at the brochure*)

MIDDIE: What's that?

BRO: It's the guarantee. That came with it. "You are now the owner of a Pearson-Bennett Garden of England Patent Old World Compost Heap." (*Middie looks at it*) "The Pearson-Bennett Garden of England Patent Old World Compost Heap, mounted on a best quality mahogany coffee table and with pleasing brass surround, is an authentic replica of a centuries-old piece of traditional furniture, designed originally by craftsmen to bring a country garden atmosphere into the stuffy drawing rooms of well-to-do town houses."

MIDDIE: (*Bends forward and sniffs*) It's past its best, if you ask me.

BRO: (*Sniffs too*) That's what they call the "nose," Middie. They all have that. It's how you tell a good compost heap.

MIDDIE: How long's that going on for, then?

BRO: Well, for as long as . . .

MIDDIE: It's dreadful. I can smell it from here.

BRO: It's the heat of the room bringing it out.

MIDDIE: (*With brochure*) No wonder.

BRO: What?

MIDDIE: (*Handing brochure to Bro*) At the bottom.

BRO: "Every Pearson-Bennett Garden of England Patent Old World Compost Heap was laid down at least two hundred years ago . . ."

MIDDIE: I thought it couldn't be any too fresh.

BRO: They're not meant to be fresh, Middie. The older they are the better. It's like wine. They need time to mature. It tells you here, amongst other things. (*He reads*) Oh. (*He looks at the compost heap*) Perhaps that explains it.

MIDDIE: Explains what?

BRO: "Every Pearson-Bennett Garden of England Patent Old World Compost Heap is guaranteed fortified with real farmyard manure."

MIDDIE: I could smell that without being told. Go and close the door. We shall have it all over the house. I'll open the window. (*Bro closes the door, as Middie opens the window*)

BRO: It's certainly a bit on the strong side.

MIDDIE: A whiff of the country's one thing. (*She comes back to compost heap*) Isn't there anything we can do? It's terrible, Bro.

BRO: I don't know what, Middie.

MIDDIE: Sprinkle it with lavender water. Anything.

BRO: I suppose we could try a deodorant.

MIDDIE: It needs something, Bro, really.

BRO: (*Going*) If I can find one that'll stand up to the strain.

MIDDIE: It's impossible as it is. (*Bro goes out*) Close the door.

BRO: Oh.

(*Door closes. Middie moves a chair by way of regrouping the furniture in relation to the compost heap. Bro comes back in with an aerosol tin*)

BRO: See what this does.

MIDDIE: Close the door.

BRO: Oh. (*He closes the door, and then squirts the compost heap with deodorant. Middie's mind is on the furniture*) I suppose a connoisseur would look on this as sheer sacrilege. (*He sniffs and squirts some more*)

MIDDIE: (*Moving a chair*) If I'd known she was going to send it 'round tonight, I'd have said leave it till the morning. Just as you've got people coming, to have something like this landing on you.

BRO: I think that's better, Middie. What do you think?

MIDDIE: (*Sniffing*) Oh, yes. That's a lot better.

BRO: I think we can probably close the window.

MIDDIE: Yes. (*She closes the window*) If it were in a farmyard, I wouldn't have said so much, but when you've got to live with it.

BRO: All I hope is that we haven't put it out of commission for good and all.

MIDDIE: You don't think by putting it there it looks as if we're trying to draw attention to it?

BRO: There's nowhere else for it, Middie, is there?

MIDDIE: We could put it over there, I suppose.

BRO: No. Leave it where it is. It's all right.

MIDDIE: They're late.

BRO: It's just as well they are, or we should have had it arriving while they were here.

MIDDIE: I shall be happier when we've had somebody in to look at that.

BRO: Look at what?

MIDDIE: Who knows something about them. Make sure we haven't got hold of some dreadful eyesore. (*Doorbell; going*) At last.

Hall. (*Middie opens front door. Martha and Humphrey. Bro behind Middie*)

MIDDIE: Martha! Humphrey! Come in.

MARTHA: You must have thought we were never going to get here. How are you, Middie?

HUMPHREY: Co-opted onto a road safety committee just as we were turning the corner.

MARTHA: We'd have been here half an hour ago.

MIDDIE: Never mind. You're here now. Let me take your coat, Martha.

MARTHA: Well, we can't really stay long, can we, Humphrey? We're due in Eastbourne in ten minutes.

MIDDIE: Oh, dear.

HUMPHREY: Dip in the briny.

MARTHA: And see what we can find in the way of pebbles.

HUMPHREY: For the back bedroom.

MIDDIE: You can stay for an hour or so, surely? Long enough to have a nut.

MARTHA: Well . . .

MIDDIE: When's your train?

MARTHA: When's our train, Humphrey?

HUMPHREY: Thursday.

MIDDIE: Oh, well—you've got plenty of time. (*She glances at calendar on wall*) It's only Monday morning.

BRO: (*Consulting pocket diary*) I think you'll find that's slow, Middie.

MIDDIE: Is it?

BRO: It's Tuesday evening.

MIDDIE: They've still got plenty of time.

MARTHA: Oh, yes . . .

MIDDIE: If they're not going till Thursday.

MARTHA: We've got longer than we thought, Humphrey.

MIDDIE: Of course you have. Give Bro your coat, Humphrey. (*To Martha*) We'll go upstairs.

MARTHA: Thank you, Middie.

(*Martha and Middie go upstairs. Bro helps Humphrey off with his coat, and takes it*)

BRO: Thank you, Humphrey.

HUMPHREY: I think you'll find it's all right. The lining's just coming away a bit behind the pocket there, but it's nothing to speak of.

BRO: (*Hanging up coat*) Oh, no. I'll get Middie to have a look at that.

HUMPHREY: In here, is it?

BRO: Yes—straight through, Humphrey. (*Humphrey goes into the living room, followed by Bro*)

Living Room. (*Humphrey walks around the compost heap with no more ado than if it were any other piece of furniture, and makes for the armchair*)

BRO: Sit down, Humphrey. Make yourself . . . (*He waves vaguely towards the chair*)

HUMPHREY: (*Sitting*) Thank you, Bro. It's a long lane that can't give itself a night off now and again, as the greengrocer's look-out man said to the Bishop of All Souls. (*He looks around the room*) There's something different since we were here last. You've had the place done up.

BRO: (*Sitting*) Just a coat of whitewash on the ceiling, Humphrey.

HUMPHREY: Oh.

BRO: It was the only place we could find room for it, to tell the truth.

(*Martha enters*)

MARTHA: We've just been . . . (*Her eye lights on the compost heap, which stops her momentarily in her tracks. She hastily recovers herself and goes on as though she has not noticed a thing*) We've just been looking at the view from the bedroom window, Humphrey. Did you know they could see to Crystal Palace?

HUMPHREY: I didn't know, but I'm not altogether surprised.

BRO: Sit down, Martha. (*She finds herself sitting on the settee right next to where the compost heap is. She darts it a glance of wary distaste out of the corner of her eye as she sits*)

MARTHA: I'd no idea you could see that from here.

BRO: Oh, yes. We've always been able to see to Crystal Palace from the bedroom window. Even before it was burnt down.

MARTHA: Well, I never.

MIDDIE: (*Off*) Bro!

BRO: Yes? (*No reply*) That's Middie. I'd better just . . .

MARTHA: She's in the kitchen, Bro.

BRO: (*Going out*) What is it?

(*Martha and Humphrey sit silent for a second*)

MARTHA: Did *you* know that?

HUMPHREY: I wasn't surprised.

Kitchen. (Bro and Middie with mixer)

MIDDIE: Isn't there a light that's supposed to go on?

BRO: Yes.

MIDDIE: It's not going on.

BRO: You haven't got it switched on over there. (*Middie switches it on. Sweet hum*) That's better. Now we can try it out. Where are the nuts?

MIDDIE: In here.

(*Bro quickly gets one and drops it in the mincer. Middie gets a shallow dish and holds it under the mincer, ready to catch what comes out. They wait expectantly*)

Living Room

MARTHA: What on earth are they up to out there?

HUMPHREY: I couldn't tell you, Martha.

MARTHA: Sitting here with this thing right under your nose.

HUMPHREY: I can't smell it myself, Martha.

MARTHA: No—you're not sitting here, are you!

HUMPHREY: It's just a . . .

MARTHA: What?

HUMPHREY: Well . . . it's more under the heading of what they call an object d'art.

MARTHA: Object *what?*

Kitchen. (Bro and Middie. The mincer had vouchsafed its offering. They are looking at it with stunned disenchantment. A few shreds of mangled nut and shell lie forlornly in the middle of the dish. They look at each other, and then down at the dish again)

MIDDIE: We can't offer them *that.*

BRO: No.

MIDDIE: It doesn't even *look* like a nut.

BRO: No.

MIDDIE: Just a minute. You stay here. (*She puts the plate down, and goes to the door*)

Living Room

MARTHA: (*To Humphrey*) All I can say is, I hope it's something worth waiting for. Asking you here and then sticking you down next to a heap of manure.

(*Middie enters*)

MIDDIE: You must think we're awfully rude, leaving you in here on your own like this.

MARTHA: (*Politeness itself*) Good heavens, Middie. (*Middie goes to the bureau and looks in the drawers*)

MIDDIE: We've got a new electric nutcracking machine, and it's chosen this moment to start acting up.

MARTHA: Oh, dear. Can we . . . ?

MIDDIE: No, it's all right, Martha. I'm just looking for something we can use instead.

MARTHA: As a matter of fact, we've just been admiring your . . . (*She waves towards the compost heap*)

MIDDIE: Oh. Do you like it? It's a compost heap.

MARTHA: Yes, I thought it might be something like that.

MIDDIE: To tell you the truth, it's only just come. We haven't had time yet to decide where we're eventually going to have it. (*Middie, having found what she was looking for, prepares to go*)

MARTHA: They're said to do very well out in the open air.

MIDDIE: They are and they aren't, Martha, funnily enough. It depends what kind they are. This is an indoor variety.

MARTHA: Oh. I never knew they made them.

MIDDIE: Apparently they used to be all the rage at one time. Now they're coming back.

MARTHA: Oh.

MIDDIE: (*Going*) I believe they *can* be quite valuable.

(*Middie goes out. Martha looks at the compost heap.*

Humphrey gets out of his chair to have a closer look at it)

MARTHA: I don't know about all the rage. *I've* never seen one before. (*Humphrey puts his glasses on, and gives the thing a sage and knowledgeable once-over*)

HUMPHREY: Could be a collector's piece, Martha.

MARTHA: A piece of old Victorian junk, more likely.

HUMPHREY: I think you'll find this is a good bit before Victorian, Martha. Unless I'm very much mistaken.

MARTHA: It's a monstrosity, whatever it is.

HUMPHREY: A thing like that could well be a thing of beauty, Martha, if it were properly authenticated by an expert.

MARTHA: Expert!

Kitchen. (*Middie with sugar tongs in her hand*)

BRO: You can't ask people to crack nuts with a pair of sugar tongs, Middie!

MIDDIE: Well, they've got to crack them with *some*thing!

BRO: Yes. With this. (*Bro indicates the mixer. The mincer attachment is still on it, but the mixer itself has been opened up, with the head raised*)

MIDDIE: It's ridiculous.

BRO: It isn't ridiculous at all, Middie. Look. I've just done it. (*We see nuts on the table, properly shelled*) All you do is use it manually, instead of the way it was meant to be used. (*He demonstrates. He puts a nut between the hinged parts of the mixer, and uses the whole thing as a nutcracker. The nut is cracked*)

MIDDIE: All right. Well, you bring that in on the cart, and I'll go through with the nuts. (*She starts hastily arranging the nuts properly in the dish*)

Living Room. (*Humphrey puts his glasses away and goes back to his chair*)

MARTHA: In its heyday when Bonnie Prince *Who* was on the throne?

HUMPHREY: Or one of them, anyway.

MARTHA: It's the first I've heard that Bonnie Prince Charlie was ever *on* the throne.

HUMPHREY: (*Sitting*) If the truth were known about Bonnie Prince Charlie, Martha, I wouldn't put it at all beyond the bounds of possibility that he's been on the throne more times than you've had hot dinners.

MARTHA: Nuts! (*Middie has entered, bearing the bowl of nuts. Martha has seen her, Humphrey has not*)

HUMPHREY: That's as may be, Martha.

MIDDIE: You must have thought we were never coming. (*Bro enters with the cart, on which is the mixer, in the open position*)

MARTHA: This *is* a treat.

MIDDIE: (*Handing bowl to Martha*) Which one are you going to have?

MARTHA: Oh, dear. They all look . . . I think I'll have this one, Middie.

MIDDIE: I think that's an acorn, Martha, isn't it?

MARTHA: Is it?

MIDDIE: I don't know how that can have got in there.

MARTHA: Well, it's all right, Middie. I'll . . .

MIDDIE: Good heavens, no. You don't want an acorn, Martha. Bro, take Martha's acorn.

BRO: (*Taking it*) That must have slipped in.

MARTHA: (*Taking another nut*) Can I . . . ?

MIDDIE: Those are rather nice, actually. (*Going with bowl to Humphrey and speaking to Bro*) Hand Martha the . . . (*Bro is already doing so*)

MARTHA: Oh, thank you, Bro. How do I . . . ?

BRO: Let me do it, Martha.

HUMPHREY: A very delectable assortment, as the retired airline pilot said to the earl's granddaughter. (*He takes one*)

MIDDIE: I know you both like nuts. (*To Bro*) When you've . . . (*She indicates Humphrey's nut*)

BRO: (*Having finished with Martha*) Yes, I'm just . . . (*He takes the mixer across to Humphrey, who cracks his nut with it and hands it back*)

HUMPHREY: Thank you, Bro.

MARTHA: (*To Bro*) We were saying to Middie, Bro, how much we liked your . . . (*She indicates the compost heap*)

BRO: (*Returning to cart with mixer*) Oh, yes? (*He cracks two nuts, one for himself, and one for Middie*)

HUMPHREY: Fetch a tidy price.

BRO: Do you think it would?

HUMPHREY: Oh, yes. Sotheby's. Just the kind of thing they'd . . .

BRO: (*Offering Middie her nut*) Middie.

MIDDIE: Oh. Thank you, Bro. (*Bro and Middie stand looking down, smugly proprietorial, at their compost heap*)

HUMPHREY: Especially if it's Regency. Or anything like that.

BRO: As a matter of fact, we were wondering ourselves what . . .

HUMPHREY: Hard to say, with anything like that, what it is.

BRO: Yes.

MARTHA: Humphrey seems to think it might be Queen Anne. (*Bro and Middie are looking down at the compost heap. We see their faces change. We see the compost heap. We see their faces*)

BRO: You mean her relics?

MARTHA: (*Oblivious*) No, I think he just meant . . . (*To Humphrey*) Didn't you? The period. Or whatever they . . .

BRO: (*Relieved*) Oh. Yes. Yes. (*They move away from the compost heap, in a way that rather suggests that they are never going to see it in quite the same light again, and sit down*)

MIDDIE: (*Brightly*) Well . . . it's very nice to see you both again. Bring the nuts over here, Bro, then we can dip in as we feel like it.

MARTHA: It's quite a long time, isn't it?

MIDDIE: It must be six weeks.

MARTHA: It must be at least that. How long ago is it since you had that experience in Lewisham High Street, Humphrey?

HUMPHREY: What experience?

MARTHA: When you were chased up that back alley by a firing squad.

HUMPHREY: Oh . . .

MIDDIE: A firing squad?

MARTHA: Yes. Oh, yes. Tell them about it, Humphrey.

HUMPHREY: Oh, it's nothing much. Just one of those things.

BRO: You mean you . . . ?

MARTHA: Yes. It's not the first time either. When was the other time you had to face a firing squad?

HUMPHREY: I wasn't facing a firing squad, Martha. I was standing with my back to it.

MIDDIE: But they've no business . . .

MARTHA: That's what I said, Middie, at the time.

MIDDIE: They could be had up.

HUMPHREY: I think, as a matter of fact, they were on the run from some military establishment or other and getting a bit desperate for food.

MIDDIE: Even so.

BRO: What were you doing at the time?

HUMPHREY: I was looking in a shop window. Next thing I knew, I'd turned 'round . . . (*Doorbell*)

MIDDIE: (*Getting up*) Oh, dear. Who can this be? Just as we've got settled down.

BRO: It'll be Laurence, Middie.

MIDDIE: Oh, yes. I expect that's who it is. (*She goes out*)

BRO: Laurence Grimsby. He comes in to watch television.

MARTHA: Yes, I believe we met him once.

MIDDIE: (*Off*) Laurence. Come in.

BRO: I thought so. He's usually here about now.

Hall

(*Middie closes door. Laurence is in hall. He is done up like some kind of Christmas tree. Over his ordinary clothes are bits of tinsel, paper chains, sprigs of this and that, bobbles, and he is carrying a sort of scroll tied with ribbon*)

MIDDIE: What . . . ?

LAURENCE: (*Exuding modesty*) Oh . . .

MIDDIE: Don't tell me . . .

LAURENCE: Yes. I've just . . .

MIDDIE: Well! (*Going into living room*) Bro! (*To Laurence*) Come in and . . . (*Middie goes in followed by Laurence*)

Living room

MIDDIE: Look what Laurence has . . . (*Laurence appears in doorway*)

BRO: Laurence! You've been decorated! (*Painful embarrassment from Laurence, as he nods to Martha and Humphrey*)

LAURENCE: How do you do?

BRO: This calls for a glass of tonic water.

LAURENCE: Oh, don't . . .

MIDDIE: Good heavens, Laurence. It's not every day we have someone come who's just been decorated. (*Bro has gone to cupboard*)

HUMPHREY: Just come from the Palace, have you?

LAURENCE: Yes, I've . . .

MIDDIE: Sit down, Laurence.

LAURENCE: (*Doing so*) Oh. Thank you.

MIDDIE: You can tell us all about it. (*Bro, with one bottle of tonic water, emerges from the cupboard*)

BRO: Glasses. (*He goes for them across the room*)

MIDDIE: They're in the . . .

BRO: Yes. (*He gets five tiny liqueur glasses*)

MARTHA: (*To Laurence*) Are we allowed to ask what . . . ?

LAURENCE: Oh—it's nothing. Just the usual . . . (*With scroll*) It's got it all in here, actually. For what it's worth. (*He hands the scroll to Humphrey*)

HUMPHREY: Oh, yes. (*He undoes the scroll, looks perfunctorily down it, and hands it to Martha*) They give you that, do they? (*Bro pours a quarter of an inch of tonic water into each glass*)

LAURENCE: Oh, yes. That's all . . .

MARTHA: Seal at the bottom and everything.

HUMPHREY: Oh, yes. They do you proud.

MARTHA: Have you seen this, Middie? (*Bro hands 'round the drinks*)

MIDDIE: No, I haven't, Martha.

MARTHA: (*Receiving drink*) Thank you, Bro.

MIDDIE: (*With scroll*) Oh, yes. This is very . . .

BRO: Humphrey.

HUMPHREY: Thank you, Bro.

BRO: I've put yours on there, Middie. (*He indicates the table with the compost heap on it*)

MIDDIE: Oh, this is mine, is it?

BRO: Laurence.

LAURENCE: Thank you, Bro. (*Bro gets ready to propose a toast*)

BRO: Well . . . (*They all, including Laurence, sit to attention with liqueur glasses at the ready*) . . . here's to Robert Louis Stevenson.

ALL: Robert Louis Stevenson.

(*In perfect unison, they all drink, toss the glasses over their shoulders, and carry on precisely as if nothing had happened*)

BRO: (*Sitting*) Did someone say there was a citation?

MIDDIE: Yes. It's . . . (*She hands it to Bro*)

BRO: Oh. My goodness. "Outstanding gallantry in the field." I say.

LAURENCE: It's all a lot of fuss, really, but you know what it is.

MIDDIE: You should have told us, Laurence. (*To Bro*)

Shouldn't he? (*To Laurence*) We didn't even know you'd been *in* a field.

HUMPHREY: What sort of a field was it, Laurence? As a matter of interest.

LAURENCE: Oh—nothing. It was . . . just a meadow, really.

MIDDIE: A *meadow?* That wasn't how *I* read it. It was more like a . . . (*To Bro*) what was it?

BRO: ". . . field a hundred and seventy-nine acres, bounded on three sides by a low hedge, and . . . and so forth."

HUMPHREY: I thought it couldn't be a meadow.

MIDDIE: You're being too modest, Laurence.

HUMPHREY: You don't get that kind of decoration by being gallant in a meadow.

MARTHA: Whereabouts? Or mustn't we ask?

LAURENCE: In the field? Oh . . . roughly . . . as a matter of fact, there's a . . . or should be . . . (*He indicates scroll*)

BRO: (*With scroll*) That's right. (*Showing Middie*) There's a diagram.

LAURENCE: X is where . . .

MIDDIE: Bottom lefthand corner.

BRO: Oh, yes.

MIDDIE: Near the gate. (*A slight sense that this revelation has tarnished the glory somewhat*)

MARTHA: Good vantage point.

LAURENCE: Well, there didn't seem much point in going all the way to the middle.

MIDDIE: Good heavens, no. I'm sure you can be just as gallant near the gate as you can farther in.

MARTHA: You don't have to worry so much about what you might tread in, either, on the way. (*She looks hostilely at the compost heap. Middie looks blackly at Martha*)

LAURENCE: (*Oblivious of the reference*) Well, that was partly it, really. Nobody wants that brought into the house, do they? Still less Buckingham Palace. So I thought rather than risk getting myself fertilized and smelling like a farmyard . . . (*He is out on a limb now, and is desperately trying to keep going*) It meant quite a lot of practice, of course. Start with something small, like an allotment, orchard, and then on to something bigger until eventually . . . (*He gives up*)

MIDDIE: I expect you'll be wanting to watch television.

LAURENCE: (*Glancing at watch*) Yes, I would, Middie, thank you very much. (*He gets up, so does Middie*)

MIDDIE: Otherwise you'll miss it. (*Laurence goes to the curtain which divides off the dining room*)

LAURENCE: Through here, is it?

MIDDIE: (*Going through*) Yes. I'll just move the chair for you. (*Laurence follows Middie. The curtains are drawn across from the other side*)

BRO: He's a member of the Television Watchdog League.

MARTHA: Ah, yes. I wondered if he might be.

BRO: Comes in every night on what they call Watchdog Patrol. On the lookout for smut.

MARTHA: It's not the smut, so much, it's the four-letter words I can't go for.

BRO: Oh, yes, they take four-letter words in their stride as well. In fact, all being well, they're talking of going on to five-letter words next year. Six-letter words the year after that.

MARTHA: Right old clean-up, then. (*Middie comes through curtains from dining room*)

MIDDIE: Are you absolutely sure, Laurence? I can always get Bro to bring one through for you.

LAURENCE: (*Off*) No, really, Middie. This is fine, thank you.

MIDDIE: It is switched on. (*Middie closes curtains and sits down*) I said you'd take him in a cushion, Bro, if he gets uncomfortable. (*Informatively, to Martha and Humphrey*) He's watching out for smut.

MARTHA: Yes, we . . .

BRO: Whereabouts . . . ?

MIDDIE: He's on the china cupboard.

BRO: Oh. He seems to make a beeline for that. He was on it last time.

MIDDIE: (*To Martha and Humphrey*) He likes to watch

the screen from different angles, in case they try to slip anything through out of the side.

MARTHA: Oh, yes. Well, they're up to anything, aren't they?

BRO: I think Laurence is pretty well on the alert, though, isn't he? For anything like that.

MIDDIE: Once it comes on. He's like a hawk.

Dining room. (*Laurence is crouched on a low cupboard in a corner diagonally opposite to where the television stands. He is watching the screen like a hawk with a pair of binoculars in his hand. The screen begins to flicker*)

Living Room. (*Bro, Middie, Martha, and Humphrey as before*)

MIDDIE: And then they report back, don't they, Bro, to Mrs. Whatever-her-name-is. At the end of each stint.

BRO: With a list.

MIDDIE: Yes.

MARTHA: Just as well there are people willing to do it.

HUMPHREY: Anyway, as I was saying, I'd no sooner turned 'round . . .

MIDDIE: Help yourself to a nut, Humphrey.

HUMPHREY: No, thank you, Middie. I'd no sooner turned 'round . . .

MIDDIE: You can surely manage another one.

HUMPHREY: No, no. Enough's enough, Middie, thank you very much.

BRO: Are you sure?

HUMPHREY: Yes, thank you, Bro.

MARTHA: He's driving.

HUMPHREY: Yes, as I was saying, I turned 'round, and next thing I knew . . . (*A crash from the dining room. Middie gets up and goes through the curtains*)

BRO: (*Calling*) What is it, Middie?

MIDDIE: He's only dropped his binoculars.

BRO: Oh. (*Middie comes back through the curtains*)

MIDDIE: (*To Laurence*) As long as they're not broken.

BRO: Is he all right?

MIDDIE: Yes.

BRO: (*To Martha*) He likes to be prepared for anything.

MIDDIE: I don't think Laurence is likely to let anything get past him, is he, in the way of smut. He's on to it like a flash.

BRO: He doesn't fall asleep on the job.

MIDDIE: (*To Martha*) And once he's spotted anything, he's straight back with his report.

MARTHA: He'll be lucky to get any smut now, won't he? There's only the Epilogue.

BRO: You'd be surprised, Martha. That's just where they like to try and slip it in. People off their guard. It's their big chance.

Dining Room. (*Laurence as before. On television a Parson talking*)

PARSON: . . . and so I went up to him and spoke to him. "Flake off!" he said to me. "Flake off, you stupid four-eyed twit and get beggared!" Flake off, you stupid four-eyed twit, and get beggared. How often have we had these words spoken to us in anger, at a moment of stress, perhaps, when things have not been going as well as they should that day, and the speaker's nerves are perhaps on edge through no fault of his own?

Living Room (*As before*)

MARTHA: We must be moving, Humphrey.

HUMPHREY: Yes.

BRO: Already? You hardly seem to have got here.

HUMPHREY: If we're going to get to Eastbourne.

MIDDIE: Can't I get you another nut or anything?

MARTHA: Really, Middie, thank you. I'm full to bursting as it is.

MIDDIE: Well, if you must . . .
(They go to the door)

Dining Room. (Parson talking as before)

PARSON: And what do we say in return? Do we say, "Flake you too, mate! Go and get beggared yourself!" Or do we, when the temptation comes, as come it must, to reply in some such vein as this, take firm hold of ourselves and remember the words of a famous hymn-writer who said . . .

Hall. (Humphrey and Martha are going out. Bro and Middie are speeding them on their way)

MARTHA: It's been a lovely evening, Middie.

MIDDIE: We mustn't leave it so long next time.

MARTHA: Goodbye, Bro.

BRO: Goodbye, Martha. Goodbye, Humphrey.

HUMPHREY: Goodbye, Bro.

MIDDIE: Have a nice journey. *(She closes the door, and immediately turns to look critically at Humphrey's coat, which is still hanging up)*

BRO: The lining behind the pocket's coming away.

MIDDIE: We can soon sew that up.

BRO: Otherwise it seems in fairly good shape.

MIDDIE: *(Turning away)* Have it cleaned . . . *(They go back into the living room)*

Car. (Humphrey is driving. Martha is beside him. They are looking straight ahead. Humphrey's face more or less expressionless, Martha's face set. She has clearly just finished saying something caustic and is likely any minute to say something caustic again. She does)

MARTHA: Six walnuts and a thimbleful of tonic water! And that's what they call a gay evening!

Living Room. (Bro and Middie are clearing up the debris. Bro stops, with a glass in his hand, to look at the mixer)

MIDDIE: I suppose they'll be halfway there by now.

BRO: Where?

MIDDIE: Eastbourne.

Car. (*As before*)

MARTHA: Not to mention a heap of old horse manure under your nose the minute you step inside!

Living Room. (*As before. Bro with mixer*)

BRO: I think where we were making our mistake, Middie, with this, was that we should have used it without the cutters or whatever they're called. (*He starts dismantling the mincer attachment*)

MIDDIE: Don't start doing it now, Bro.

BRO: It won't take a moment, Middie. Just let the nut work its way through in one piece and rely on the pressure inside to crack it as it goes.

(*Middie has paused at the compost heap, and is looking at it*)

Car. (*As before*)

MARTHA: At least she could have put something over it. A doily or something. Make it look presentable.

HUMPHREY: I think you'll find a doily would spoil the effect, Martha. They're meant to be left as nature intended.

(*Silence for a second*)

Living Room. (*Bro with mixer. Middie ostensibly watching, but with her eye on the compost heap*)

MIDDIE: I was wondering if we had a cake frill large enough.

BRO: It doesn't need a cake frill, Middie. It merely looks as though you're trying to gild the lily.

MIDDIE: Yes. I'll see what there is when I clear out the cupboard. How are you getting on with that?

BRO: I'm just screwing it up. Then we can have a final nut before we go to bed.

Car. (As before)

MARTHA: And as for whatever-his-name-was with the mistletoe all over him . . .

Living Room. (As before)

MIDDIE: I wonder if Laurence is all right in there. Do you think I ought to go in?

BRO: It'll be finished in a moment, Middie. If it isn't finished already.

MIDDIE: They'll be at Eastbourne now, I suppose.

BRO: Yes. They probably will.

Beach. (Humphrey and Martha are in deckchairs side by side, looking out to sea)

MARTHA: Take up a position in the middle of a field in full view of anybody who happens to be passing and then starts displaying his gallantry to all and sundry! He was lucky not to get six months.

Living Room. (Mixer now ready. The outlet of the mincer faces the dining room curtains. Middie ready with nut to drop in)

MIDDIE: What's supposed to happen, then?

BRO: It comes out here.

MIDDIE: Oh. Tell me when you're ready. (*Laurence emerges from behind the dining room curtains*) Oh, hello, Laurence. You're just in time for a nut. (*To Bro*) Where do I . . . ? (*She drops the nut in. A loud, demented whirr, followed by a report like a howitzer going off. We see Laurence. He is stretched out on the floor, out cold*)

MIDDIE: Oh dear.

Beach. (*Humphrey and Martha as before*)

MARTHA: And who, if it comes to that, is Robert Louis Stevenson when he's at home?

HUMPHREY: That's between him and his maker, Martha.

Living Room. (*Laurence is lying on settee covered with blanket, and coming partially 'round. Bro and Middie are hovering*)

MIDDIE: You were hit on the head by a nut, Laurence. (*She tries to get through to him*) N-U-T. Nut. (*No go*) He'll be all right when he's better. (*They stand back and look solicitously down at him*) You wouldn't think a nut could do all that damage.

BRO: One of the ironies of fate, Middie. Watching out like a hawk all evening for four-letter words, and he gets laid out flat by a three-letter one.

MIDDIE: Yes. Oh, well . . . We'll see what he's like in the morning. (*They make towards the door, and go out*)

Hall. (*They come out, put out the living room light and go contentedly upstairs*)

BRO: Barring accidents, not an entirely unsuccessful evening.

MIDDIE: I don't know why we don't do it more often, Bro.

BRO: Who can we ask next time?

MIDDIE: (*Calling down*) Goodnight, Laurence. (*As they disappear*) Yes. We must think. Who can we ask?

Fade

Alice Childress

WINE IN THE WILDERNESS

Alice Childress

Alice Childress was born in Charleston, South Carolina, and raised in Harlem, New York City, where she began her career with the American Negro Theatre. During the twelve years that she was associated with the history-making group, Miss Childress functioned as drama coach, director, writer and actress. She appeared in an important role in their production of *Anna Lucasta,* which initially was presented in Harlem and later transferred to Broadway (1944) where it ran for 957 performances.

Her first play, *Florence,* was written for and produced by the American Negro Theatre in 1951. This was followed by *Gold Thru the Trees* and *Just a Little Simple* (an adaptation of Langston Hughes' *Simple Speaks His Mind*), both presented in 1955 at the Club Baron Theatre in Harlem. Subsequently, Miss Childress moved downtown to the Greenwich Mews Theatre with her drama, *Trouble In Mind,* and it received the "Obie" Award for the best original Off-Broadway play of the 1955–56 season. The same play was produced twice by the B.B.C. in London.

Miss Childress received a Harvard appointment as scholar-writer to The Radcliffe Institute for 1966–68, and the University of Michigan presented her play, *Wedding Band,* as their professional theatre production of 1966, with Ruby Dee, Abbey Lincoln and Jack Harkins.

Wine in the Wilderness initially was seen in 1969 on television in Boston, Massachusetts. It was the first play in a series, *On Being Black,* produced under a Ford Foundation grant, and it starred Abbey Lincoln in the role of Tommy.

Miss Childress also is the author of *Martin Luther King at Montgomery, Alabama,* which toured schools and colleges from 1969 through 1971; *The African Garden;* and two published novels, *A Short Walk* and *The Habit,* the latter dealing with the problem of dope addiction and intended for young readers. She also has contributed articles to several major periodicals and is the editor of *Black Scenes,* a collection of fifteen scenes culled from the works of black playwrights.

As an actress, Alice Childress has appeared in many plays both on and off Broadway, on television, and in films.

Characters:

BILL JAMESON
OLDTIMER
SONNY-MAN
CYNTHIA
TOMMY

Place:

Harlem, New York City, New York, U. S. A.

Time:

The summer of 1964. Night of a riot.

Scene:

A one room apartment in a Harlem tenement. It used to be a three-room apartment, but the tenant has broken out walls and is half finished with a redecorating job. The place is now only partly reminiscent of its past tawdry days, plaster broken away and lathing exposed right next to a new brick-faced portion of wall. The kitchen is now a part of the room. There is a three-quarter bed covered with an African throw, a screen is placed at the foot of the bed to insure privacy when needed. The room is obviously black dominated, pieces of sculpture, wall hangings, paintings. An artist's easel is standing with a drapery thrown across it so the empty canvas beneath it is hidden. Two other canvases the same size are next to it. They too are covered and conceal paintings. The place is in a beautiful, rather artistic state of disorder. The room also reflects an interest in other darker peoples of the world: a Chinese incense-burner Buddha, an American Indian feathered war helmet, a Mexican serape, a Japanese fan, a West Indian travel poster. There is a kitchen table, chairs, floor cushions, a couple of box-crates, books, bookcases, plenty of artist's materials. There is a small raised platform for model posing. On the platform is a backless chair.

The tail end of a riot is going on out in the street. Noise and screaming can be heard in the distance: running feet, voices shouting over loudspeakers.

OFFSTAGE VOICES: Offa the street! Into your homes! Clear the street! (*The whine of a bullet is heard*) Cover that roof! It's from the roof! (*Bill is seated on the floor with his back to the wall, drawing on a large sketch pad with charcoal pencil. He is very absorbed in his task but flinches as he hears the bullet sound, ducks and shields his head with upraised hand, then resumes sketching. The telephone rings; he reaches for phone with caution, pulls it toward him by the cord in order to avoid going near window or standing up*)

BILL: Hello? Yeah, my phone is on. How the hell I'm gonna be talkin' to you if it's not on? (*Sound of glass breaking in the distance*) I could lose my damn life answerin' the phone. Sonny-man, what the hell you callin' me up for! I thought you and Cynthia might be downstairs dead. I banged on the floor and hollered down the air shaft, no answer. No stuff! Thought y'all was dead. I'm sittin' here drawin' a picture in your memory. In a bar! Y'all sittin' in a bar? See there, you done blew the picture that's in your memory . . . No kiddin', they wouldn't let you in the block? Man, they can't keep you outta your own house. Found? You found who? Model? What model? Yeah, yeah, thanks, but I like to find my own models. No! Don't bring nobody up here in the middle of a riot . . . Hey, Sonny-man! Hey! (*Sound of yelling and rushing footsteps in the hall*)

WOMAN'S VOICE: (*Offstage*) Damnit, Bernice! The riot is over! What you hidin' in the hall for? I'm in the house, your father's in the house, and you out here hidin' in the hall!

GIRL'S VOICE: (*Offstage*) The house might burn down!

BILL: Sonny-man, I can't hear you!

WOMAN'S VOICE: (*Offstage*) If it do burn down, what the hell you gon' do, run off and leave us to burn up by ourself? The riot is over. The police say it's over! Get back in the house! (*Sound of running feet and a knock on the door*)

BILL: They say it's over. Man, they oughta let you on your own block, in your own house . . . Yeah, we still standin', this seventy-year-old house got guts. Thank you, yeah, thanks but I like to pick my own models. You drunk? Can't you hear when I say not to . . . Okay, all right, bring her. (*Frantic knocking at the door*) I gotta go. Yeah, yeah, bring her. I gotta go . . . (*Hangs up phone and opens the door for Oldtimer. The old man is carrying a haul of loot: two or three bottles of liquor, a ham, a salami and a suit with price tags attached*) What's this! Oh, no, no, no, Oldtimer, not here. . . . (*Faint sound of a police whistle*) The police after you? What you bring that stuff in here for?

OLDTIMER: (*Runs past Bill as he looks for a place to hide the loot*) No, no, they not really after me but . . . I was in the basement so I could stash this stuff, but a fella told me they pokin' 'round down there . . . in the backyard pokin' 'round. The police doin' a lotta pokin' 'round.

BILL: If the cops are searchin' why you wanna dump your troubles on me?

OLDTIMER: I don't wanta go to jail. I'm too old to go to jail. What we gonna do?

BILL: We can throw it the hell outta the window! Didn't you think of just throwin' it away and not worry 'bout jail?

OLDTIMER: I can't do it. It's like . . . I'm Oldtimer, but my hands and arms is somebody else that I don' know a-tall. (*Bill pulls stuff out of Oldtimer's arms and places loot on the kitchen table. Oldtimer's arms fall to his sides*) Thank you, son.

BILL: Stealin' ain't worth a bullet through your brain, is it? You wanna get shot down and drown in your own blood—for what? A suit, a bottle of whiskey? Gonna throw your life away for a damn ham?

OLDTIMER: But I ain' really stole nothin', Bill, 'cause I ain' no thief. Them others, they smash the windows, they run in the stores and grab and all. Me, I pick up what they left scatter in the street. Things they drop, things they trample underfoot. What's in the street ain' like stealin'. This is leavin's. What I'm gon' do if the police come?

BILL: (*Starts to gather the things in the tablecloth that is on the table*) I'll throw it out the air shaft window.

OLDTIMER: (*Places himself squarely in front of the air shaft window*) I be damn. Uh-uh, can't let you do it, Billy-Boy. (*Grabs the liquor and holds on*)

BILL: (*Wraps the suit, the ham and the salami in the tablecloth and ties the ends together in a knot*) Just for now, then you can go down and get it later.

OLDTIMER: (*Getting belligerent*) I say I ain' gon' let you do it.

BILL: Sonny-man calls this "The people's revolution." A revolution should not be looting and stealing. Revolutions are for liberation. (*Oldtimer won't budge from before the window*) Okay, man, you win, it's all yours. (*Walks away from Oldtimer and prepares his easel for sketching*)

OLDTIMER: Don't be mad with me, Billy-Boy, I couldn' help myself.

BILL: (*After a moment*) No hard feelin's.

OLDTIMER: (*As he uncorks bottle*) I don't blame you for bein' fed up with us . . . fella like you *oughta* be fed up with your people sometime. Hey, Billy, let's you and me have a little taste together.

BILL: Yeah, why not.

OLDTIMER: (*At table, pouring drinks*) You mustn't be too hard on me. You see, you talented, you got somethin' on the ball, you gonna make it on past these white folk . . . but not me, Billy-Boy. It's too late in the day for that. Time, time, time . . . time done put me down. Father Time is a bad white cat. Whatcha been paintin' and drawin' lately? You can paint me again if you wanta. No charge. Paint me 'cause that might be the only way I get to stay in the world after I'm dead and gone. Somebody'll look up at your paintin' and say, "Who's that?" And you say, "That's Oldtimer." (*Bill joins Oldtimer at table and takes one of the drinks*) Well, here's lookin' at you and goin' down me. (*Gulps drink down*)

BILL: (*Raising his glass*) Your health, Oldtimer.

OLDTIMER: My day we didn't have all this grants and scholarship like now. Whatcha been doin'?

BILL: I'm working on the third part of a triptych.

OLDTIMER: A what tick?

BILL: A triptych.

OLDTIMER: Hot-damn, that call for another drink. Here's to the trip-tich. Down the hatch. What is one-a those?

BILL: It's three paintings that make one work. Three paintings that make one subject.

OLDTIMER: Goes together like a new outfit . . . hat, shoes and suit.

BILL: Right. The title of my triptych is "Wine In The Wilderness." Three canvases on black womanhood.

OLDTIMER: (*Eyes light up*) Are they naked pitchers?

BILL: (*Crosses to paintings*) No, all fully clothed.

OLDTIMER: (*Wishing it was a naked picture*) Man, ain' nothin' dirty 'bout naked pitchers. That's art. What you call artistic.

BILL: Right, right, right, but these are with clothes. That can be artistic, too. (*Uncovers one of the canvases and reveals painting of a charming little girl in Sunday dress and hair ribbon*) I call her "Black girlhood."

OLDTIMER: Awwwww, that's innocence! Don't know what it's all about. Ain't that the little child that live right down the street? Yeah. That call for another drink.

BILL: Slow down, Oldtimer, wait till you see this. (*Covers the painting of the little girl, then uncovers another canvas and reveals a beautiful woman, deep mahogany complexion, she is cold but utter perfection, draped in startling colors of African material, very "Vogue" looking. She wears a golden headdress sparkling with brilliants and sequins applied over the paint*) There she is . . . "Wine in The Wilderness." Mother Africa, regal, black womanhood in her noblest form.

OLDTIMER: Hot-damn. I'd die for her, no stuff . . . oh, man. "Wine in The Wilderness."

BILL: Once, a long time ago, a poet named Omar told us what a paradise life could be if a man had a loaf of bread, a jug of wine and a woman singing to him in the wilderness. She is the woman, she is the bread, she is the wine, she is the singing. This Abyssinian maiden is paradise . . . perfect black womanhood.

OLDTIMER: (*Pours for Bill and himself*) To our Abyssinian maiden.

BILL: She's the Sudan, the Congo River, the Egyptian Pyramids. Her thighs are African mahogany. She speaks and her words pour forth sparkling clear as the waters . . . Victoria Falls.

OLDTIMER: Ow! Victoria Falls! She got a pretty name.

BILL: (*Covers her up again*) Victoria Falls is a waterfall not her name. Now, here's the one that calls for a drink. (*Snatches cover from the empty canvas*)

OLDTIMER: (*Stunned by the empty canvas*) Your . . . your pitcher is gone.

BILL: Not gone . . . She's not painted yet. This will be the third part of the triptych. This is the unfinished third of "Wine in The Wilderness." She's gonna be the kinda chick that is grass roots. No, not grass roots. I mean she's underneath the grass roots. The lost woman, what the society has made out of our women. She's as far from my African queen as a woman can get and still be female, she's as close to the bottom as you can get without crackin' up. She's ignorant, unfeminine, coarse, rude . . . vulgar. A poor, dumb chick that's had her behind kicked until it's numb. And the sad part is . . . she ain't together, you know . . . there's no hope for her.

OLDTIMER: Oh, man, you talkin' 'bout my first wife.

BILL: A chick that ain' fit for nothin' but to . . . to . . . just pass her by.

OLDTIMER: Yeah, later for her. When you see her, cross over to the other side of the street.

BILL: If you had to sum her up in one word, it would be nothin'!

OLDTIMER: (*Roars with laughter*) That call for a double!

BILL: (*Beginning slightly to feel the drinks. He covers the canvas again*) Yeah, that's a double! The kinda woman that grates on your damn nerves. And Sonny-man just called to say he found her runnin' 'round in the middle-a this riot. Sonny-man say she's the real thing from underneath them grass roots. A back-country chick right outta the wilds of Mississippi, but she ain' never been near there. Born in Harlem, raised right here in Harlem, but back country. Got the picture?

OLDTIMER: (*Full of laughter*) When . . . when . . . when she get here let's us stomp her to death.

BILL: Not till after I paint her. Gonna put her right here on this canvas. (*Pats the canvas, walks in a strut around the table*) When she gets put down on canvas, the triptych will be finished.

OLDTIMER: (*Joins him in the strut*) Trip-tick will be finish . . . trip-tick will be finish . . .

BILL: Then "Wine in The Wilderness" will go up against the wall to improve the view of some post office. Or some library, or maybe a bank, and I'll win a prize. And the queen, my black queen, will look down from the wall so the messed up chicks in the neighborhood can see what a woman oughta be, and the innocent child on one side of her and the messed up chick on the other side of her . . . *my statement.*

OLDTIMER: (*Turning the strut into a dance*) Wine in the wilderness . . . up against the wall . . . wine in the wilderness . . . up against the wall . . .

WOMAN FROM UPSTAIRS APT.: (*Offstage*) What's the matter! The house on fire?

BILL: (*Calls upstairs through the air shaft window*) No, baby! We down here paintin' pictures! (*Sound of police siren in distance*)

WOMAN FROM UPSTAIRS APT.: (*Offstage*) So much-a damn

noise! Cut out the noise! (*To her husband, hysterically*) Percy! Percy! You hear a police siren! Percy! That a fire engine?

BILL: Another messed up chick. (*Gets a rope and ties it to Oldtimer's bundle*) Got an idea. We'll tie the rope to the bundle, then . . . (*Lowers bundle out of window*) lower the bundle outta the window and tie it to this nail here behind the curtain. Now! Nobody can find it except you and me. Cops come, there's no loot. (*Ties rope to nail under curtain*)

OLDTIMER: Yeah, yeah, loot long gone 'til I want it. (*Makes sure window knot is secure*) It'll be swingin' in the breeze free and easy. (*There is knocking on the door*)

SONNY-MAN: Open up! Open up! Sonny-man and company.

BILL: (*Putting finishing touches on securing knot to nail*) Wait, wait, hold on. . . .

SONNY-MAN: And-a here we come!

(*He pushes the door open. Enters room with his wife Cynthia and Tommy. Sonny-man is in high spirits. He is in his late twenties, his wife Cynthia is a bit younger. She wears her hair in a natural style, her clothing is tweedy and in good, quiet taste. Sonny-man is wearing slacks and a dashiki over a shirt. Tommy is dressed in a mismatched skirt and sweater, wearing a wig that is not comical, but is wiggy looking. She has the habit of smoothing it every once in a while, patting to make sure it's in place. She wears sneakers and bobbysocks, carries a brown paper sack*)

CYNTHIA: You didn't think it was locked, did you?

BILL: (*Looking over Tommy*) Door not locked?

TOMMY: You oughta run him outta town, pushin' open people's door.

BILL: Come right on in.

SONNY-MAN: (*Standing behind Tommy and pointing down at her to draw Bill's attention*) Yes, sireeeeee.

CYNTHIA: Bill, meet a friend-a ours. This is Miss Tommy

Fields. Tommy, meet a friend-a ours . . . this is Bill Jameson. Bill, Tommy.

BILL: Tommy, if I may call you that . . .

TOMMY: (*Likes him very much*) Help yourself, Bill. It's a pleasure. Bill Jameson, well, all right.

BILL: The pleasure is all mine. Another friend-a ours, Oldtimer.

TOMMY: (*With respect and warmth*) How are you, Mr. Timer?

BILL: (*Laughs along with others, Oldtimer included*) What you call him, baby?

TOMMY: Mr. Timer. Ain't that what you say? (*They all laugh expansively*)

BILL: No, sugar pie, that's not his name. We just say "Oldtimer," that's what everybody call him.

OLDTIMER: Yeah, they all call me that. Everybody say that . . . *Oldtimer.*

TOMMY: That's cute, but what's your name?

BILL: His name *is* . . . er . . . er . . . What *is* your name?

SONNY-MAN: Dog-bite, what's your name, man? (*There is a significant moment of self-consciousness as Cynthia, Sonny-man and Bill realize they don't know Oldtimer's name*)

OLDTIMER: Well, it's . . . Edmond L. Matthews.

TOMMY: Edmond *L.* Matthews. What's the L for?

OLDTIMER: Lorenzo. Edmond Lorenzo Matthews.

BILL & SONNY-MAN: Edmond Lorenzo Matthews.

TOMMY: Pleased to meetcha, Mr. Matthews.

OLDTIMER: Nobody call me that in a long, long time.

TOMMY: I'll call you Oldtimer like the rest, but I like to know who I'm meetin'. (*Oldtimer gives her a chair*) There you go. He's a gentleman, too. Bet you can tell my feet hurt. I got one corn, and that one is enough. Oh, it'll ask you for somethin'. (*General laughter. Bill indicates to Sonny-man that Tommy seems right. Cynthia and Oldtimer take seats near Tommy*)

BILL: You rest yourself, baby, er . . . er . . . Tommy. You did say Tommy?

TOMMY: I cut it to Tommy. Tommy-Marie, I use both of 'em sometime.

BILL: How about some refreshment?

SONNY-MAN: Yeah, how 'bout that. (*He starts to pour drinks*)

TOMMY: Don't y'all carry me too fast, now.

BILL: (*Indicating liquor bottles*) I got what you see and also some wine . . . couple-a cans-a beer.

TOMMY: I'll take the wine.

BILL: Yeah, I knew it.

TOMMY: Don't wanta start nothin' I can't keep up. (*Old-timer slaps his thigh with pleasure*)

BILL: That's all right, baby, you just a wine-o.

TOMMY: You the one that's got the wine, not me.

BILL: I use this for cookin'.

TOMMY: You like to get loaded while you cook? (*Old-timer is having a ball*)

BILL: (*As he pours wine for Tommy*) Oh, baby, you too much.

OLDTIMER: (*Admiring Tommy*) Oh, Lord, I wish, I wish, I wish I was young again.

TOMMY: (*Flirtatiously*) Lively as you are, I don't know what we'd do with you if you got any younger.

OLDTIMER: Oh, hush now!

SONNY-MAN: (*Whispering to Bill and pouring drinks*) Didn't I tell you! Know what I'm talkin' about? You dig? All the elements, man.

TOMMY: (*Worried about what the whispering means*) Let's get somethin' straight. I didn't come bustin' in on the party, I was asked. If you married and any wives or girl friends 'round here . . . I'm innocent. Don't wanta get shot at, or jumped on. 'Cause I wasn't doin' a thing but mindin' my business! (*Saying the last in loud tones to be heard in other rooms*)

OLDTIMER: Jus' us here, that's all.

BILL: I'm single, baby. Nobody wants a poor artist.

CYNTHIA: Oh, honey, we wouldn't walk you into a jealous wife or girl friend.

TOMMY: You paint all-a these pitchers? (*Bill and Sonnyman hand out drinks*)

BILL: Just about. Your health, baby, to you.

TOMMY: (*Lifts her wine glass*) All right, and I got one for you. Like my grampaw used-ta say, "Here's to the men's collars and the women's skirts . . . may they never meet." (*General laughter*)

OLDTIMER: But they ain't got far to go before they do.

TOMMY: (*Suddenly remembers her troubles*) Niggers, niggers . . . niggers! I'm sick-a niggers, ain't you? A nigger will mess up everytime. Lemme tell you what the niggers done . . .

BILL: Tommy, baby, we don't use that word around here. We can talk about each other a little better than that.

CYNTHIA: Oh, she doesn't mean it.

TOMMY: What must I say?

BILL: Try Afro-Americans.

TOMMY: Well . . . the Afro-Americans burnt down my house.

OLDTIMER: Oh, no they didn't!

TOMMY: Oh, yes they did. It's almost burn down. Then the firemen nailed up my door . . . the door to my room, nailed up shut tight with all I got in the world.

OLDTIMER: Shame, what a shame.

TOMMY: A *damn* shame. My clothes . . . Everything gone. This riot blew my life. All I got is gone like it never was.

OLDTIMER: I know it.

TOMMY: My transistor radio . . . that's gone.

CYNTHIA: Ah, gee.

TOMMY: The transistor and a brand new pair-a shoes I never had on one time. (*Raises her right hand*) If I never move, that's the truth . . . new shoes gone.

OLDTIMER: Child, when hard luck fall it just keep fallin'.

TOMMY: And in my top dresser drawer I got a my-on-ase jar with forty-one dollars in it. The fireman would not let me in to get it. And it was a Afro-American fireman, don'tcha know.

OLDTIMER: And you ain't got no place to stay. (*Bill is studying Tommy for portrait possibilities*)

TOMMY: (*Rises and walks around the room*) That's a lie. I always got some place to go. I don't wanta boast, but I ain't never been no place that I can't go back the second time. Woman I use to work for say, "Tommy, any time, any time you want a sleep-in place you come right here to me." And that's Park Avenue, my own private bath and T.V. set. But I don't want that. So I make it on out here to the dress factory. I got friends . . . not a lot of 'em, but a few *good* ones. I call my friend—girl and her mother they say, "Tommy, you come here, bring yourself over here." So Tommy got a roof with no sweat. (*Looks at torn walls*) Looks like the Afro-Americans got to you, too. Breakin' up, breakin' down, that's all they know.

BILL: No, Tommy, I'm redecorating the place.

TOMMY: You mean you did this to yourself?

CYNTHIA: It's gonna be wild . . . brick-face walls, wall to wall carpet.

SONNY-MAN: She was breakin' up everybody in the bar . . . had us all laughin', crackin' us up. In the middle of a riot, she's gassin' everybody!

TOMMY: No need to cry, it's sad enough. They hollerin' whitey, whitey . . . but who they burn out? Me.

BILL: The brothers and sisters are tired, weary of the endless get-no-where struggle.

TOMMY: I'm standin' there in the bar, tellin' it like it is. Next thing I know they talkin' 'bout bringin' me to meet you. But you know what I say? Can't nobody pick nobody for nobody else. It don't work. And I'm standin' there in a mismatch skirt and top and these sneaker-shoes. I just went to put my dresses in the cleaner . . . Oh, Lord, wonder if they burn down the cleaner! Well, no matter, when I got back it was all over.

They went in the grocery store, rip out the shelves, pull out all the groceries . . . the hams . . . the . . . the . . . the can goods . . . everything . . . and then set fire. Now who you think live over the grocery? Me, that's who. I don't even go to the store lookin' this way, but this would be the time, when folks got a fella they want me to meet.

BILL: (*Suddenly self-conscious*) Tommy, they thought . . . they thought I'd like to paint you. That's why they asked you over.

TOMMY: (*Pleased by the thought but she can't understand it*) Paint me? For what? If he was gonna paint somebody, seems to me it'd be one of the pretty girls they show in the beer ads. They even got colored on television now . . . brushin' their teeth and smokin' cigarettes. Some of the prettiest girls in the world. He could get them, . . . couldn't you?

BILL: Sonny-man and Cynthia were right. I want to paint you.

TOMMY: (*Suspiciously*) Naked, with no clothes on?

BILL: No, baby, dressed just as you are now.

OLDTIMER: Wearin' clothes is also art.

TOMMY: In the cleaner I got a white dress with a orlon sweater to match it. Maybe I can get it out tomorrow and pose in that. (*Cynthia, Oldtimer and Sonny-man are eager for her to agree*)

BILL: No, I will paint you today, Tommy, just as you are, holding your brown paper bag.

TOMMY: Mmmmmm, me holdin' the damn bag. I don' know 'bout that.

BILL: Look at it this way, tonight has been a tragedy.

TOMMY: Sure in hell has.

BILL: And so I must paint you tonight . . . Tommy in her moment of tragedy.

TOMMY: I'm tired.

BILL: Damn, baby, all you have to do is sit there and rest.

TOMMY: I'm hungry.

SONNY-MAN: While you're posin' Cynthia can run down to our house and fix you some eggs.

CYNTHIA: (*Gives her husband a weary look*) Oh, Sonny, that's such a lovely idea.

SONNY-MAN: Thank you darlin', I'm in there, on the beam.

TOMMY: (*Ill-at-ease about posing*) I don't want no eggs. I'm goin' to find me some Chinee food.

BILL: I'll go. If you promise to stay here and let me paint you, I'll get you anything you want.

TOMMY: (*Brightening*) Anything I want. Now, how he sound? All right, you comin' on mighty strong there. "Anything you want." When last you heard somebody say that? I'm warnin' you, now, I'm free, single and disengage, so you better watch yourself.

BILL: (*Keeping her away from ideas of romance*) Now this is the way the program will go down. First I'll feed you, then I'll paint you.

TOMMY: Okay, I'm game, I'm a good sport. First off, I want me some Chinee food.

CYNTHIA: Order up, Tommy, the treat's on him.

TOMMY: How come it is you never been married? All these girls runnin' 'round Harlem lookin' for husbands. (*To Cynthia*) I don't blame 'em, 'cause I'm lookin' for somebody myself.

BILL: I've been married. Married and divorced. She divorced me, Tommy, so maybe I'm not much of a catch.

TOMMY: Look at it this-a-way. Some folks got bad taste. That woman had bad taste. (*All laugh except Bill who pours another drink*) Watch it, Bill. you gonna rust the linin' of your stomach. Ain't this a shame? The riot done wipe me out, and I'm sittin' here havin' me a ball. Sittin' here ballin'! (*As Bill refills her glass*) Hold it, that's enough. Likker ain' my problem.

OLDTIMER: I'm havin' me a good time.

TOMMY: Know what I say 'bout divorce? (*Slaps her hands together in a final gesture*) Anybody don' wantcha later, let 'em go. That's bad taste for you.

BILL: Tommy, I don't wanta ever get married again. It's me and my work. I'm not gettin' serious about anybody.

TOMMY: He's spellin' at me, now. Nigger . . . I mean Afro-American . . . I ain' ask you nothin'. You hinkty, I'm hinkty too. I'm independent as a hog on ice and a hog on ice is dead, cold, well-preserved and don't need a mother-grabbin' thing. (*All laugh heartily except Bill and Cynthia*) I know models get paid. I ain' no square, but this is a special night and so this one'll be on the house. Show you my heart's in the right place.

BILL: I'll be glad to pay you, baby.

TOMMY: You don't really like me, do you? That's all right. Sometime it happen that way. You can't pick for *nobody*. Friends get to matchin' up friends and they mess up everytime. Cynthia and Sonny-man done messed up.

BILL: I like you just fine and I'm glad and grateful that you came.

TOMMY: Good enough. (*Extends her hand. They slap hands together*) You 'n me friends?

BILL: Friends, baby, friends. (*Putting rock record on*)

TOMMY: (*Trying out the model stand*) Okay, Dad! Let's see 'bout this *anything I want* jive. Want me a bucket-a Egg Foo Young, and you get you a shrimp fry-rice, we split that and each have some-a both. Make him give you the soy sauce, the hot mustard and the duck sauce, too.

BILL: Anything else, baby?

TOMMY: Since you ask, yes. If your money hold out, get me a double order egg roll. And a half order of the sweet and sour spare ribs.

BILL: (*To Oldtimer and Sonny-man*) Come on, come on. I need some strong men to help me bring back your order, baby.

TOMMY: (*Going into her dance, simply standing and going through some boo-ga-loo motions*) Better go get it 'fore I think up some more to go 'long with it. (*The men laugh and vanish out of the door. Steps heard descending stairs*) Turn that off. (*Cynthia turns off record player*) How could I forget your name, good as you been to me this day? Thank you, Cynthia, thank you. I *like* him. Oh, I *like* him. But I don't wanta push him too fast. Oh, I got to play these cards right.

CYNTHIA: (*A bit uncomfortable*) Oh, honey . . . Tommy, you don't want a poor artist.

TOMMY: Tommy's not lookin' for a meal ticket. I been doin' for myself all my life. It takes two to make it in this high-price world. A black man see a hard way to go. The both of you gotta pull together. That way you accomplish.

CYNTHIA: I'm a social worker, and I see so many broken homes. Some of these men! Tommy, don't be in a rush about the marriage thing.

TOMMY: Keep it to yourself, but I was thirty my last birthday and haven't ever been married. I coulda been. Oh, yes, indeed, coulda been. But I don't want any and everybody. What I want with a no-good piece-a nothin'? I'll never forget what the Reverend Martin Luther King said. "I have a dream." I liked him sayin' it 'cause truer words have never been spoke. (*Straightening the room*) I have a dream, too. Mine is to find a man who'll treat me just half-way decent. Just to meet me half-way is all I ask, to smile, be kind to me. Somebody in my corner. Not to wake up by myself in the mornin' and face this world all alone.

CYNTHIA: About Bill, it's best not ever to count on anything, anything at all, Tommy.

TOMMY: (*This remark bothers her for a split second but she shakes it off*) Of course, Cynthia, that's one of the foremost rules of life. Don't count on *nothin'!*

CYNTHIA: Right, don't be too quick to put your trust in these men.

TOMMY: You put your trust in one and got yourself a husband.

CYNTHIA: Well, yes, but what I mean is . . . Oh, you know. A man is a man and Bill is also an artist and his work comes before all else and there are other factors . . .

TOMMY: (*Sits facing Cynthia*) What's wrong with me?

CYNTHIA: I don't know what you mean.

TOMMY: Yes, you do. You tryin' to tell me I'm aimin' too high by lookin' at Bill.

CYNTHIA: Oh, no, my dear.

TOMMY: Out there in the street, in the bar, you and your husband were so sure that he'd *like* me and want to paint my picture.

CYNTHIA: But he does want to paint you. He's very eager to . . .

TOMMY: But why? Somethin' don't fit right.

CYNTHIA: (*Feeling sorry for Tommy*) If you don't want to do it, just leave and that'll be that.

TOMMY: Walk out while he's buyin' me what I ask for, spendin' his money on me? That'd be too dirty. (*Looks at books. Takes one from shelf*) Books, books, books everywhere. "Afro-American History." I like that. What's wrong with me, Cynthia? Tell me, I won't get mad with you, I swear. If there's somethin' wrong that I can change, I'm ready to do it. Eighth grade, that's all I had of school. You a social worker, I know that mean college. I come from poor people. (*Examining the book in her hand*) Talkin' 'bout poverty this and poverty that and studyin' it. When you *in* it you don' be studyin' 'bout it. Cynthia, I remember my mother tyin' up her stockin's with strips-a rag 'cause she didn't have no garters. When I get home from school she'd say, "Nothin' much here to eat." Nothin' much might be grits, or bread and coffee. I got sick-a all that, got me a job. Later for school.

CYNTHIA: The matriarchal society.

TOMMY: What's that?

CYNTHIA: A matriarchal society is one in which the women rule. The women have the power. The women head the house.

TOMMY: We didn't have nothin' to rule over, not a pot nor a window. And my papa picked hisself up and run off with some finger-poppin' woman and we never hear another word 'til ten, twelve years later when a undertaker call up and ask if mama wanta come claim his body. And don'cha know, mama went on over and claim it. A woman need a man to claim, even if it's a dead one. What's wrong with me? Be honest.

CYNTHIA: You're a fine person . . .

TOMMY: Go on, I can take it.

CYNTHIA: You're too brash. You're too used to looking out for yourself. It makes us lose our femininity. It makes us hard. It makes us seem very hard. We do for ourselves too much.

TOMMY: If I don't, who's gonna do for me?

CYNTHIA: You have to let the black man have his manhood again. You have to give it back, Tommy.

TOMMY: I didn't take it from him, how I'm gonna give it back? What else is the matter with me? You had school, I didn't. I respect that.

CYNTHIA: Yes, I've had it, the degree and the whole bit. For a time I thought I was about to move into another world, the so-called "integrated" world, a place where knowledge and know-how could set you free and open all the doors, but that's a lie. I turned away from that idea. The first thing I did was give up dating white fellas.

TOMMY: I never had none to give up. I'm not soundin' on you. White folks, nothin' happens when I look at 'em. I don't hate 'em, don't love 'em . . . just nothin' shakes a-tall. The dullest people in the world. The way they talk. "Oh, hooty, hooty, hoo." Break it down for me to A, B, C's. That Bill . . . I like him, with his black, uppity, high-handed ways. What do you do to get a man you want? A social worker oughta tell you things like that.

CYNTHIA: Don't chase him. At least don't let it look that way. Let him pursue you.

TOMMY: What if he won't? Men don't chase me much, not the kind I like.

CYNTHIA: (*Rattles off instructions glibly*) Let him do the talking. Learn to listen. Stay in the background a little. Ask his opinion. "What do *you* think, Bill?"

TOMMY: Mmmmm, "Oh, hooty, hooty, hoo."

CYNTHIA: But why count on him? There are lots of other nice guys.

TOMMY: You don't think he'd go for me, do you?

CYNTHIA: (*Trying to be diplomatic*) Perhaps you're not really his type.

TOMMY: Maybe not, but he's mine. I'm so lonesome. I'm *lonesome*. I want somebody to love. Somebody to say, "That's all right," when the world treats me mean.

CYNTHIA: Tommy, I think you're too good for Bill.

TOMMY: I don't wanta hear that. The last man that told me I was too good for him was tryin' to get away. He's good enough for me. (*Straightening room*)

CYNTHIA: Leave the room alone. What we need is a little more sex appeal and a little less washing, cooking and ironing. (*Tommy puts down the room straightening*) One more thing. Do you have to wear that wig?

TOMMY: (*A little sensitive*) I like how *your* hair looks. But some of the naturals I don't like. Can see all the lint caught up in the hair like it hasn't been combed since know not when. You a Muslim?

CYNTHIA: No.

TOMMY: I'm just sick-a hair, hair, hair. Do it this way, don't do it, leave it natural, straighten it, process, no process. I get sick-a hair and talkin' 'bout it and foolin' with it. That's why I wear the wig.

CYNTHIA: I'm sure your own must be just as nice or nicer than that.

TOMMY: It oughta be. I only paid nineteen ninety-five for this.

CYNTHIA: You ought to go back to usin' your own.

TOMMY: (*Tensely*) I'll be givin' that some thought.

CYNTHIA: You're pretty nice people just as you are. Soften up, Tommy. You might surprise yourself.

TOMMY: I'm listenin'.

CYNTHIA: Expect more. Learn to let men open doors for you.

TOMMY: What if I'm standin' there and they don't open it?

CYNTHIA: (*Trying to level with her*) You're a fine person. He wants to paint you, that's all. He's doing a kind of mural thing and we thought he would enjoy painting you. I'd hate to see you expecting more out of the situation than what's there.

TOMMY: Forget it, sweetie-pie, don' nothin' happen that's not suppose to. (*Sound of laughter in the hall. Bill, Oldtimer and Sonny-man enter*)

BILL: No Chinese restaurant left, baby! It's wiped out. Gone with the revolution.

SONNY-MAN: (*To Cynthia*) Baby, let's move, split the scene, get on with it. Time for home.

BILL: The revolution is here. Whatta you do with her? You paint her!

SONNY-MAN: You write her. You write the revolution. I'm gonna write the revolution into a novel nine hundred pages long.

BILL: Dance it! Sing it! "Down in the cornfield hear dat mournful sound . . . (*Sonny-man and Oldtimer harmonize*) Dear old Massa am-a sleepin', a-sleepin' in the cold, cold ground." Now for "Wine in The Wilderness!" Triptych will be finished.

CYNTHIA: (*In Bill's face*) "Wine In The Wilderness," huh? Exploitation!

SONNY-MAN: Upstairs, all out, come on, Oldtimer. Folks can't create in a crowd. Cynthia, move it, baby.

OLDTIMER: (*Starting toward the window*) My things! I got a package.

SONNY-MAN: (*Heads him off*) Up and out. You don't have to go home, but you have to get outta here. Happy paintin', y'all. (*One backward look and they are all gone*)

BILL: Whatta night, whatta night, whatta night, baby. It

will be painted, written, sung and discussed for generations.

TOMMY: (*Notices nothing that looks like Chinese food. He is carrying a small bag and a container*) Where's the Foo Young?

BILL: They blew the restaurant, baby. All I could get was a couple-a franks and a orange drink from the stand.

TOMMY: (*Tersely*) You brought me a frank-footer? That's what you think-a me, a frank-footer?

BILL: Nothin' to do with what I think. Place is closed.

TOMMY: (*Quietly surly*) This is the damn City-a New York. Any hour on the clock they sellin' the chicken in the basket, barbecue ribs, pizza pie, hot pastrami samitches; and you brought me a frank-footer?

BILL: Baby, don't break bad over somethin' to eat. The smart set, the jet set, the beautiful people, kings and queens eat frankfurters.

TOMMY: If a queen sent you out to buy her a bucket-a Foo Young, you wouldn't come back with no lonely-ass frank-footer.

BILL: Kill me 'bout it, baby! Go 'head and shoot me six times. That's the trouble with our women. Y'all always got your mind on food.

TOMMY: Is that our trouble? (*Laughs*) Maybe you right. Only two things to do. Either eat the frank-footer or walk on outta here. You got any mustard?

BILL: (*Gets mustard from the refrigerator*) Let's face it, our folks are not together. The brothers and sisters have busted up Harlem . . . no plan, no nothin'. There's your black revolution, heads whipped, hospital full and we still in the same old bag.

TOMMY: (*Seated at the kitchen table*) Maybe what everybody need is somebody like you, who know how things oughta go, to get on out there and start some action.

BILL: You still mad about the frankfurter?

TOMMY: No. I keep seein' pitchers of what was in my room and how it all must be spoiled now. (*Sips the orange *drink*) A orange never been near this. Well, it's cold. (*Looking at an incense burner*) What's that?

BILL: An incense burner. Was given to me by the Chinese guy, Richard Lee. I'm sorry they blew his restaurant.

TOMMY: Does it help you to catch the number?

BILL: No, baby, I just burn incense sometime.

TOMMY: For what?

BILL: Just 'cause I feel like it. Baby, ain't you used to nothin'?

TOMMY: Ain't used to burnin' incent for nothin'.

BILL: (*Laughs*) Burnin' what?

TOMMY: That stuff.

BILL: What did you call it?

TOMMY: Incent.

BILL: It's not incent, baby. It's incense.

TOMMY: Like the sense you got in your head. In-sense. Thank you. You're a very correctable person, ain't you?

BILL: Let's put you on canvas.

TOMMY: (*Stubbornly*) I have to eat first.

BILL: That's another thing 'bout black women. They wanta eat 'fore they do anything else. Tommy . . . Tommy . . . I bet your name is Thomasina. You look like a Thomasina.

TOMMY: You could sit there and guess 'til your eyes pop out and you never would guess my first name. You might could guess the middle name but not the first one.

BILL: Tell it to me.

TOMMY: My name is Tomorrow.

BILL: How's that?

TOMMY: Tomorrow. Like yesterday and *tomorrow,* and the middle name is just plain Marie. That's what my father name me, Tomorrow Marie. My mother say he thought it had a pretty sound.

BILL: Crazy! I never met a girl named Tomorrow.

TOMMY: They got to callin' me Tommy for short, so I stick with that. Tomorrow Marie. Sound like a promise that can never happen.

BILL: (*Straightens chair on stand. He is very eager to start painting*) That's what Shakespeare said, "Tomorrow and tomorrow and tomorrow." Tomorrow, you will be on this canvas.

TOMMY: (*Still uneasy about being painted*) What's the hurry? Rome wasn't built in a day . . . that's another saying.

BILL: If I finish in time, I'll enter you in an exhibition.

TOMMY: (*Loses interest in the food. Examines the room. Looks at portrait on the wall*) He looks like somebody I know or maybe saw before.

BILL: That's Frederick Douglass. A man who used to be a slave. He escaped and spent his life trying to make us all free. He was a great man.

TOMMY: Thank you, Mr. Douglass. Who's the light colored man? (*Indicates a frame next to the Douglass*)

BILL: He's white. That's John Brown. They killed him for tryin' to shoot the country outta the slavery bag. He dug us, you know. Old John said, "Hell no, slavery must go."

TOMMY: I heard all about him. Some folks say he was crazy.

BILL: If he had been shootin' at *us* they wouldn't have called him a nut.

TOMMY: School wasn't a great part-a my life.

BILL: If it was you wouldn't-a found out too much 'bout black history cause the books full-a nothin' but whitey . . . all except the white ones who dug us. They not there either. Tell me, who was Elijah Lovejoy?

TOMMY: Elijah Lovejoy. Mmmmmmm. I don't know. Have to do with the Bible?

BILL: No, that's another white fella. Elijah had a printin' press and the main thing he printed was "Slavery got to go." Well, the men moved in on him, smashed his press time after time, but he kept puttin' it back together and doin' his thing. So, one final day, they came in a mob and burned him to death.

TOMMY: (*Blows her nose with sympathy as she fights tears*) That's dirty.

BILL: (*As Tommy glances at titles in book case*) Who was Monroe Trotter?

TOMMY: Was he white?

BILL: No, soul brother. Spent his years tryin' to make it all right. Who was Harriet Tubman?

TOMMY: I heard-a her. But don't put me through no test, Billy. (*Moving around studying pictures and books*) This *room* is full-a things I don' know nothin' about. How'll I get to know?

BILL: Read, go to the library, book stores, ask somebody.

TOMMY: Okay, I'm askin'. Teach me things.

BILL: Aw, baby, why torment yourself? Trouble with our women, they all wanta be great brains. Leave somethin' for a man to do.

TOMMY: (*Eager to impress him*) What you think-a Martin Luther King?

BILL: A great guy. But it's too late in the day for the singin' and prayin' now.

TOMMY: What about Malcolm X.?

BILL: Great cat, but there again . . . Where's the program?

TOMMY: What about Adam Powell? I voted for him. That's one thing 'bout me. I vote. Maybe if everybody vote for the right people . . .

BILL: The ballot box. It would take me all my life to straighten you on that hype.

TOMMY: I got the time.

BILL: You gonna wind up with a king-size headache. The matriarchy gotta go. Y'all throw them suppers together, keep your husband happy, raise the kids.

TOMMY: I don't have a husband. 'Course, that could be fixed. (*Leaving the unspoken proposal hanging in the air*)

BILL: You know the greatest thing you could do for your people? Sit up there and let me put you down on canvas.

TOMMY: Bein' married and havin' a family might be good for your people as a race, but I was thinkin' 'bout myself a little.

BILL: Forget yourself sometime, sugar. On that canvas you'll be givin' and givin' and givin'. That's where you can do your thing best. What you stallin' for?

TOMMY: (*Returns to table and sits in chair*) I . . . I don't want to pose in this outfit.

BILL: (*Patience is wearing thin*) Why, baby, why?

TOMMY: I don't feel proud-a myself in this.

BILL: Art, baby, we talkin' art. Whatcha want . . . ribbons? Lace? False eyelashes?

TOMMY: No, just my white dress with the orlon sweater . . . or anything but this what I'm wearin'. You oughta see me in that dress with my pink linen shoes. Oh, hell, the shoes are gone. I forgot 'bout the fire.

BILL: Oh, stop fightin' me! Another thing . . . our women don't know a damn thing 'bout bein' feminine. *Give in* sometime. It won't kill you. You tellin' me how to paint? Maybe you oughta hang out your shingle and give art lessons! You too damn opinionated. You gonna pose or you not gonna pose? Say somethin'!

TOMMY: You makin' me nervous! Hollerin' at me. My mama never holler at me. Hollerin'.

BILL: I'll soon be too tired to pick up the brush, baby.

TOMMY: (*Eye catches picture of white woman on the wall*) That's a white woman! Bet you never hollered at her and I bet she's your girl friend, too, and when she posed for her pitcher I bet y'all was laughin'. . . and you didn't buy her no frank-footer!

BILL: (*Feels a bit smug about his male prowess*) Awww, come on, cut that out, baby. That's a little blonde, blue-eyed chick who used to pose for me. That ain't where it's at. This is a new day, the deal is goin' down different. This is the black moment, doll. Black, black, black is bee-yoo-tee-full. Got it? *Black is beautiful.*

TOMMY: Then how come it is that I don't *feel* beautiful when you *talk* to me?

BILL: That's your hang-up, not mine. You supposed to stretch forth your wings like Ethiopia, shake off them chains that been holdin' you down. Langston Hughes said let 'em see how beautiful you are. But you determined not to ever be beautiful. Okay, that's what makes you Tommy.

TOMMY: Do you *have* a girl friend? And who is she?

BILL: (*Now enjoying himself to the utmost*) Naw, naw, naw, doll. I *know* people, but none-a this "tie-you-up-and-I-own-you" jive. I ain't mistreatin' nobody and there's enough-a me to go around. That's another thing with our women. They wanta *latch* on. Learn to play it by ear, roll with the punches, cut down on some-a this "got-you-to-the-grave" kinda relationship. Was today all right? Good, be glad, take what's at hand because tomorrow never comes. It's always today. (*She begins to cry*) Awwww, I didn't mean it that way! I forgot your name. (*He brushes her tears away*) You act like I belong to you. You're jealous of a picture?

TOMMY: That's how women are, always studyin' each other and wonderin' how they look up 'gainst the next person.

BILL: (*A bit smug*) That's human nature. Whatcha call healthy competition.

TOMMY: You think she's pretty?

BILL: She was, perhaps still is. Long, silky hair. She could sit on her hair.

TOMMY: (*With bitter arrogance*) Doesn't *everybody?*

BILL: You got a head like a rock and gonna have the last word if it kills you. Baby, I bet you could knock out Mohamud Ali in the first round, then rare back and scream like Tarzan, "Now, I am the greatest!" (*He is very close to her and is amazed to feel a great sense of physical attraction*) What we arguin' 'bout? (*Looks her over as she looks away. He suddenly wants to put the conversation on a more intimate level. His eye is on the bed*) Maybe tomorrow would be a better time for paintin'. Wanna freshen up, take a bath, baby? Water's nice n' hot.

TOMMY: (*Knows the sound and turns to check on the look. Notices him watching the bed. Starts weeping*) No, I don't! Nigger!

BILL: Was that nice? What the hell, let's paint the picture. Or are you gonna hold that back, too?

TOMMY: I'm posin'. Shall I take off the wig?

BILL: No, it's a part of your image, ain't it? You must

have a reason for wearin' it. (*Tommy snatches up her orange drink and sits in the model's chair*)

TOMMY: (*With defiance*) Yes, I wear it 'cause you and those like you go for long, silky hair, and this is the only way I can have some without burnin' my mother-grabbin' brains out. Got it? (*She accidentally knocks over container of orange drink into her lap*) Hell, I can't wear this. I'm soaked through. I'm not gonna catch no double pneumonia sittin' up here wringin' wet while you paint and holler at me.

BILL: Bitch!

TOMMY: You must be talkin' 'bout your mama!

BILL: Shut up! Aw, shut-up! (*Phone rings. He finds an African throw-cloth and hands it to her*) Put this on. Relax, don't go way mad, and all the rest-a that jazz. Change, will you? I apologize. I'm sorry. (*He picks up phone*) Hello, survivor of a riot speaking. Who's calling? (*Tommy retires behind the screen with the throw-cloth. During the conversation she undresses and wraps the throw around her. We see Tommy and Bill, but they can't see each other*) Sure, told you not to worry. I'll be ready for the exhibit. If you don't dig it, don't show it. Not time for you to see it yet. Yeah, yeah, next week. You just make sure your exhibition room is big enough to hold the crowds that's gonna congregate to see this fine chick I got here. (*This perks Tommy's ears up*) You oughta see her. The finest black woman in the world . . . No, the finest *any* woman in the world. This gorgeous satin chick is . . . is . . . black velvet moonlight . . . an ebony queen of the universe. (*Tommy can hardly believe her ears*) One look at her and you go back to Spice Islands. She's Mother Africa. You flip, double flip. She has come through everything that has been put on her . . . (*He unveils the gorgeous woman he has painted: "Wine In The Wilderness." Tommy believes he is talking about her*) Regal . . . grand . . . magnificent, fantastic. You would vote her the woman you'd most like to meet on a desert island, or around the corner from anywhere. She's here with me now, and I don't know if I want to show her to you or anybody else. I'm beginnin' to have this deep attachment . . . She sparkles, man. Harriet Tubman, Queen of the Nile . . . sweetheart, wife, mother, sister, friend. The night . . . a black diamond . . . A dark, beautiful dream . . . A cloud with a silvery lining . . . Her wrath is a storm over the Bahamas. "Wine In The Wilderness." The memory of Africa, the *now* of things, but best of all and most important she's tomorrow. She's my tomorrow. (*Tommy is dressed in the African wrap. She is suddenly awakened to the feeling of being loved and admired. She removes the wig and fluffs her hair. Her hair under the wig must not be an accurate, well-cut Afro but should be rather attractive natural hair. She studies herself in a mirror. We see her taller, more relaxed and sure of herself*) Aw, man, later. You don't believe in nothin'! (*He covers "Wine In The Wilderness." Is now in a glowing mood*) Baby, whenever you ready. (*She emerges from behind the screen, dressed in the wrap, sans wig. He is astounded*) Baby, what . . . ? Where . . . where's the wig?

TOMMY: I don't think I want to wear it, Bill.

BILL: That is very becoming, the drape thing.

TOMMY: Thank you.

BILL: I don't know what to say.

TOMMY: It's time to paint. (*Steps up on the model stand and sits in the chair. She is now a queen, relaxed and smiling her appreciation for his past speech to the art dealer. Her feet are bare*)

BILL: (*Mystified by the change in her. Tries to do a charcoal sketch*) It is quite late.

TOMMY: Makes me no difference if it's all right with you.

BILL: (*Wants to create the other image*) Could you put the wig back on?

TOMMY: You don't really like wigs, do you?

BILL: Well, no.

TOMMY: Then let's have things the way you like.

BILL: (*Has no answer for this. He makes a haphazard line or two as he tries to remember the other image*) Tell me something about yourself . . . anything.

TOMMY: (*Now on sure ground*) I was born in Baltimore, Maryland and raised here in Harlem. My favorite flower is Four O'clocks, that's a bush flower. My wearin' flower, corsage flower, is pink roses. My mama raised me mostly by herself, God rest the dead. Mama belonged to The Eastern Star. Her father was a Mason. If a man in the family is a Mason any woman related to him can be an Eastern Star. My grandfather was a member of The Prince Hall Lodge. I had a uncle who was an Elk, a member of The Improved Benevolent Protective Order of Elks of the World: The Henry Lincoln Johnson Lodge. You know, the white Elks are called The Benevolent Protective Order of Elks but the black Elks are called The *Improved* Benevolent Protective Order of Elks of *the World*. That's because the black Elks got the copyright first but the white Elks took us to court about it to keep us from usin' the name. Over fifteen hundred black folk went to jail for wearin' the Elk emblem on their coat lapel. Years ago . . . that's what you call history.

BILL: I didn't know about that.

TOMMY: Oh, it's understandable. Only way I heard 'bout John Brown was because the black Elks bought his farmhouse where he trained his men to attack the government.

BILL: The black Elks bought the John Brown Farm? What did they do with it?

TOMMY: They built a outdoor theatre and put a perpetual light in his memory. And they buildin' cottages there, one named for each state in the union and . . .

BILL: How do you know about it?

TOMMY: Well, our Elks helped my cousin go through school with a scholarship. She won a speaking contest and wrote a composition titled "Onward and Upward, O, My Race." That's how she won the scholarship. Coreen knows all that Elk history.

BILL: (*Seeing her with new eyes*) Tell me some more about you, Tomorrow Marie. I bet you go to church.

TOMMY: Not much as I used to. Early in life I pledged myself in the A.M.E. Zion Church.

BILL: (*Studying her face, seeing her for the first time*) A.M.E.?

TOMMY: A.M.E. That's African Methodist Episcopal. We split off from the white Methodist Episcopal and started our own in the year 1796. We built our first buildin' in the year 1800. How about that?

BILL: That right?

TOMMY: Oh, I'm just showin' off. I taught Sunday School for two years and you had to know the history of A.M.E. Zion . . . or else you couldn't teach. My great, great grandparents was slaves.

BILL: Guess everybody's was.

TOMMY: Mine was slaves in a place called Sweetwater Springs, Virginia. We tried to look it up one time but somebody at church told us that Sweetwater Springs had become a part of Norfolk, so we didn't carry it any further. As it would be a expense to have a lawyer trace your people.

BILL: (*Throws charcoal pencil across room*) No good! It won't work! I can't work anymore.

TOMMY: Take a rest. Tell me about you.

BILL: (*Sits on bed*) Everybody in my family worked for the post office. They bought a home in Jamaica, Long Island. Everybody on that block bought an aluminum screen door with a duck on it . . . or was it a swan? I guess that makes my favorite flower crab grass and hedges. I have a lot of bad dreams. (*Tommy massages his temples and the back of his neck*) A dream like suffocating, dying of suffocation. The worst kinda dream. People are standing in a weird looking art gallery, they're looking and laughing at everything I've ever done. My work begins to fade off the canvas, right before my eyes. Everything I've ever done is laughed away.

TOMMY: Don't be so hard on yourself. If I was smart as you I'd wake up singin' every mornin'. (*There is the sound of thunder. He kisses her*) When it thunders that's the angels in heaven playin' with their hoops, rollin' their hoops and bicycle wheels in the rain. My mama told me that.

BILL: I'm glad you're here. Black *is* beautiful, you're beautiful, A.M.E. Zion, Elks, pink roses, bush flower . . . blooming out of the slavery of Sweetwater Springs, Virginia.

TOMMY: I'm gonna take a bath and let the riot and the hell of living go down the drain with the bath water.

BILL: Tommy, Tommy, Tomorrow Marie, let's save each other, let's be kind and good to each other while it rains and the angels roll those hoops and bicycle wheels. (*They embrace. The sound of rain*)

(*Music in as lights come down. As lights fade down to darkness, music comes in louder. There is a flash of lightning. We see Tommy and Bill in each other's arms. It is very dark. Music up louder, then softer and down to very soft. Music is mixed with the sound of rain beating against the window. Music slowly fades as gray light of dawn shows at window. Lights go up gradually. The bed is rumpled and empty. Bill is in the bathroom. Tommy is at the stove turning off the coffee pot. She sets table with cups and saucers, spoons. Tommy's hair is natural, she wears another throw [African design] draped around her. She sings and hums a snatch of a joyous spiritual*)

TOMMY: "Great day, Great day, the world's on fire, Great day . . ." (*Calling out to Bill who is in bath*) Honey, I found the coffee, and it's ready. Nothin' here to go with it but a cucumber and a Uneeda biscuit.

BILL: (*Joyous yell from offstage*) Tomorrow and tomorrow and tomorrow! Good mornin', Tomorrow!

TOMMY: (*More to herself than to Bill*) "Tomorrow and tomorrow." That's Shakespeare. (*Calls to Bill*) You say that was Shakespeare?

BILL: (*Off*) Right, baby, right!

TOMMY: I bet Shakespeare was black! You know how we love poetry. That's what give him away. I bet he was passin'. (*Laughs*)

BILL: (*Off*) Just you wait, one hundred years from now all the honkys gonna claim our poets just like they stole our blues. They gonna try to steal Paul Laurence Dunbar and LeRoi and Margaret Walker.

TOMMY: (*To herself*) God moves in a mysterious way,

even in the middle of a riot. (*A knock on the door*) "Great day, great day the world's on fire . . . (*Opens the door. Oldtimer enters. He is soaking wet. He does not recognize her right away*)

OLDTIMER: 'Scuse me, I must be in the wrong place.

TOMMY: (*Patting her hair*) This is me. Come on in, Edmond Lorenzo Matthews. I took off my hairpiece. This is me.

OLDTIMER: (*Very distracted and worried*) Well, howdy-do and good mornin'. (*He has had a hard night of drinking and sleeplessness*) Where Billy-boy? It pourin' down some rain out there. (*Makes his way to the window*)

TOMMY: What's the matter?

OLDTIMER: (*Raises the window and starts pulling in the cord. The cord is weightless and he realizes there is nothing on the end of it*) No, no, it can't be. Where is it? It's gone! (*Looks out the window*)

TOMMY: You gonna catch your death. You wringin' wet.

OLDTIMER: Y'all take my things in? It was a bag-a loot. A suit and some odds and ends. It was my loot. Y'all took it in?

TOMMY: No. (*Realizes his desperation. She calls to Bill through the closed bathroom door*) Did you take any loot that was outside the window?

BILL: (*Off*) No.

TOMMY: He said "no."

OLDTIMER: (*Yells out window*) Thieves . . . dirty thieves . . . lotta good it'll do you!

TOMMY: (*Leads him to a chair, dries his head with a towel*) Get outta the wet things. You smell just like a whiskey still. Why don't you take care of yourself. (*Dries off his hands*)

OLDTIMER: Drinkin' with the boys. Likker was everywhere all night long.

TOMMY: You got to be better than this.

OLDTIMER: Everything I ever put my hand and mind to do, it turn out wrong. Nothin' but mistakes. When you don' know, you don' know. I don' know nothin'. I'm ignorant.

TOMMY: Hush that talk. You know lotsa things, everybody does. (*Helps him remove wet coat*)

OLDTIMER: Thanks. How's the trip-tick?

TOMMY: The what?

OLDTIMER: *Trip-tick*. That's a paintin'.

TOMMY: See there, you know more about art than I do. What's a trip-tick? Have some coffee and explain me a trip-tick.

OLDTIMER: (*Proud of his knowledge*) Well, I tell you . . . a trip-tick is a paintin' that's in three parts but they all belong together to be looked at all at once. Now this is the first one . . . a little innocent girl . . . (*Unveils picture*)

TOMMY: She's sweet.

OLDTIMER: And this is "Wine In The Wilderness." The Queen of the Universe . . . the finest chick in the world.

TOMMY: (*Thoughtful, as he unveils the second picture*) That's not me.

OLDTIMER: No, you gonna be this here last one. The worst gal in town. A messed-up chick that . . . that . . . (*He unveils the third canvas and is face to face with the almost blank canvas, then realizes what he has said. He turns to see the stricken look on Tommy's face*)

TOMMY: The messed-up chick, *that's* why they brought me here, ain't it? That's why he wanted to paint me! Say it!

OLDTIMER: No, I'm lyin', I didn't mean it. It's the society that messed her up. Awwwwww, Tommy, don't look that-a-way. It's art . . . it's only art. He couldn't mean you. It's art . . . (*The door opens. Cynthia and Sonny-man enter*)

SONNY-MAN: Anybody want a ride down . . . down . . . down . . . downtown? What's wrong? Excuse me . . . (*Starts back out*)

TOMMY: (*Blocking the exit to Cynthia and Sonny-man*) No, come on in. Stay with it "Brother", "Sister." Tell 'em what a trip-tick is, Oldtimer.

CYNTHIA: (*Very ashamed*) Oh, no.

TOMMY: You don't have to tell 'em. They already know. The messed-up chick! How come you didn't pose for that, my sister? The messed-up chick lost her home last night, burnt out with no place to go. You and Sonny-man gave me comfort, you cheered me up and took me in . . . *took me in!*

CYNTHIA: Tommy, we didn't know you, we didn't mean . . .

TOMMY: It's all right! I was lost but now I'm found! Yeah, the blind can see! (*She dashes behind the screen and puts on her clothing, sweater, skirt, etc.*)

OLDTIMER: (*Goes to bathroom door*) Billy, come out!

SONNY-MAN: Billy, step out here, please! (*Bill enters shirtless, wearing dungarees*) Oldtimer let it out 'bout the triptych.

BILL: The rest of you move on.

TOMMY: (*Looking out from behind screen*) No, don't go a step. You brought me here, see me out!

BILL: Tommy, let me explain it to you.

TOMMY: (*Coming out from behind screen*) I gotta check out my apartment and my clothes and money. Cynthia . . . I can't wait for anybody to open the door or look out for me and all that kinda crap you talk. A bunch-a liars!

BILL: Oldtimer, why you . . .

TOMMY: Leave him the hell alone. He ain't said nothin' that ain' so!

SONNY-MAN: Explain to the sister that some mistakes have been made.

BILL: Mistakes have been made, baby. The mistakes were yesterday, this is today.

TOMMY: Yeah, and I'm Tomorrow, remember? Trouble is I was "Tommin'" to you, to all of you. "Oh, maybe they gon' like me." I was your fool, thinkin' writers and painters know more'n me, that maybe a little bit of you would rub off on me.

CYNTHIA: We are wrong. I knew it yesterday. Tommy, I told you not to expect anything out of this . . . this arrangement.

BILL: This is a relationship, not an arrangement.

SONNY-MAN: Cynthia, I tell you all the time, keep outta other people's business. What the hell you got to do with who's gonna get what outta what? You and Oldtimer, yakkin' and yakkin'. (*To Oldtimer*) Man, your mouth gonna kill you.

BILL: It's me and Tommy. Clear the room.

TOMMY: Better not. I'll kill him! The "black people" this

and the "Afro-American" that . . . You ain' got no use for none-a us. Oldtimer, you their fool, too. 'Til I got here they didn't even know your damn name. There's something inside-a me that says I ain' suppose to let *nobody* play me cheap. Don't care how much they know! (*She sweeps some of the books to the floor*)

BILL: Don't you have any forgiveness in you? Would I be beggin' you if I didn't care? Can't you be generous enough . . .

TOMMY: Nigger, I been too damn generous with you, already! All-a these people know I wasn't down here all night posin' for no pitcher, nigger!

BILL: Cut that out, Tommy, and you not going anywhere!

TOMMY: You wanna bet? Nigger!

BILL: Okay, you called it, baby, I did act like a low, degraded person . . .

TOMMY: (*Combing out her wig with her fingers while holding it*) Didn't call you no low, degraded person. Nigger! (*To Cynthia who is handing her a comb*) "Do you have to wear a wig?" Yes! To soften the blow when y'all go up side-a my head with a baseball bat! (*Going back to taunting Bill and ignoring Cynthia's comb*) Nigger!

BILL: That's enough-a that. You right and you're wrong too.

TOMMY: Ain't a-one-a us you like that's alive and walkin' by you on the street. You don't like flesh and blood niggers.

BILL: Call me that, baby, but don't call yourself. That what you think of yourself?

TOMMY: If a black somebody is in a history book, or printed on a pitcher, or drawed on a paintin' . . . or if they're a statue, dead and outta the way and can't talk back, then you dig 'em and full-a so much-a damn admiration and talk 'bout *our* history. But when you run into us livin' and breathin' ones, with the life's blood still pumpin' through us, then you comin' on 'bout how we ain' never together. You hate us, that's what! *You hate black me!*

BILL: (*Confused and saddened by the half truth which applies to himself*) I never hated you, I never will, no matter what you or any of the rest of you do to *make* me hate you. I won't! Hell, woman, why do you say that! Why would I hate you?

TOMMY: Maybe I look too much like the mother that give birth to you. Like the ma and pa that worked in the post office to buy you a house and a screen door with a damn duck on it. And you so ungrateful you didn't even like it.

BILL: No, I didn't, baby. I don't like screen doors with ducks on 'em.

TOMMY: You didn't like who was livin' behind them screen doors. Phoney nigger!

BILL: That's all! Damnit! Don't go there no more!

TOMMY: Hit me, so I can tear this place down and scream bloody murder!

BILL: (*Somewhere between laughter and tears*) Looka here, baby, I'm willin' to say I'm wrong, even in fronta the room fulla people . . .

TOMMY: (*Through clenched teeth*) Nigger!

SONNY-MAN: The sister is upset.

TOMMY: And you stop callin' me *the* sister! If you feelin' so brotherly why don't you say *my* sister? Ain't no we-ness in your talk. *The* Afro-American, *the* black man, there's no we-ness in you. Who you think *you* are?

SONNY-MAN: I was talkin' in general er . . . *my* sister, 'bout the masses.

TOMMY: There he go again. *The* masses. Tryin' to make out like we pitiful and you got it made. You the masses your damn self and don't even know it! (*Another angry look at Bill*) Nigger!

BILL: (*Pulls dictionary from shelf*) Let's get this ignorant "nigger" talk squared away. You can stand some education.

TOMMY: You *treat* me like a nigger, that's what. I'd rather be called one than treated that way.

BILL: (*Questions Tommy*) What is a nigger? (*Talks as he is trying to find word*) A nigger is a low, degraded person, *any* low degraded person. I learned that from my teacher in the fifth grade.

TOMMY: Fifth grade is a liar! Don't pull that dictionary crap on me.

BILL: (*Pointing to the book*) Webster's New World Dictionary of The American Language, College Edition.

TOMMY: I don't need to find out what no college white folks say nigger is.

BILL: I'm tellin' you it's a low, degraded person. Listen. (*Reads from the book*) Nigger, n-i-g-g-e-r . . . A Negro. A member of any dark-skinned people . . . Damn. (*Amazed by dictionary description*)

SONNY-MAN: Brother Malcolm *said* that's what they meant. Nigger is a Negro. Negro is a nigger.

BILL: (*Slowly finishing his reading*) A vulgar, offensive term of hostility and contempt. Well, so much for the fifth grade teacher.

SONNY-MAN: No, they do not call low, degraded white folks niggers. Come to think of it, did you ever hear whitey call Hitler a nigger? Now if some whitey digs us, the others might call him a nigger-*lover,* but they don't call him no nigger.

OLDTIMER: No, they don't.

TOMMY: (*Near tears*) When they say "nigger," just dry-long-so, they mean educated you and uneducated me. They hate you and call you "nigger." I called you "nigger" but I love you. (*There is dead silence in the room for a split second*)

SONNY-MAN: (*Trying to establish peace*) There you go. There you go.

CYNTHIA: (*Cautioning Sonny-man*) Now is not the time to talk, darlin'.

BILL: You love me? Tommy, that's the greatest compliment you could . . .

TOMMY: (*Sorry she said it*) You must be runnin' a fever, nigger, I ain' said nothin' 'bout lovin' you.

BILL: (*In a great mood*) You did, yes, you did.

TOMMY: Well, you didn't say it to *me.*

BILL: Oh, Tommy . . .

TOMMY: (*Cuts him off abruptly*) And don't you dare say it now. I'm tellin' you, it ain't to be said now. (*Checks through her paper bag to see if she has everything. Starts to put on the wig, changes her mind, holds it to end of scene. Turns to the others in the room*) Oldtimer . . . my brothers and my sister.

OLDTIMER: I wish I was a thousand miles away, I'm so sorry. (*He sits at the foot of the model stand*)

TOMMY: I don't stay mad. It's here today and gone tomorrow. I'm sorry your feelin's got hurt, but when I'm hurt I turn and hurt back. Somewhere, in the middle of last night, I thought the old me was gone, lost forever and gladly. But today was flippin' time, so back I flipped. Now it's "turn the other cheek" time. If I can go through life other-cheekin' the white folk, guess y'all can be other-cheeked, too. But I'm goin' back to the nitty-gritty crowd, where the talk is we-ness and us-ness. I hate to do it but I have to thank you 'cause I'm walkin' out with much more than I brought in. (*Goes over and looks at the queen in the "Wine in The Wilderness" painting*) Tomorrow Marie had such a lovely yesterday. (*Bill takes her hand, she gently removes it from his grasp*) Bill, I don't have to wait for anybody's by-your-leave to be a "Wine In The Wilderness" woman. I can be it if I wanta . . . and I *am*. I am. I am. I'm not the one you made up and painted, the very pretty lady who can't talk back, but I'm "Wine in The Wilderness," alive and kickin', me . . . Tomorrow Marie, cussin' and fightin' and lookin' out for my damn self 'cause ain' nobody else 'round to do it, don'tcha know. And, Cynthia, if my hair is straight, or if it's natural, or if I wear a wig, or take it off, that's all right. Because wigs, shoes, hats, bags, and even this . . . (*She picks up the African throw she wore a few moments before, fingers it*) They're just what you call access . . . (*Fishing for the word*) . . . like what you wear with your Easter outfit . . .

CYNTHIA: Accessories.

TOMMY: Thank you, my sister. Accessories. Somethin' you add on or take off. The real thing is takin' place on the inside. That's where the action is. That's "Wine in The Wilderness," . . . a woman that's a real one and a good one. And y'all just better believe I'm it. (*She proceeds to the door*)

BILL: Tommy. (*She turns. He takes the beautiful queen, "Wine in The Wilderness," from the easel*) She's not it at all, Tommy. This chick on the canvas . . . nothin' but accessories, a dream I drummed up outta the junk room of my mind. (*Places the queen to one side*) *You* are and . . . (*Points to Oldtimer*) . . . Edmund Lorenzo Matthews . . . the real beautiful people . . . Cynthia . . .

CYNTHIA: (*Bewildered and unbelieving*) Who? Me?

BILL: Yeah, honey, you and Sonny-man don't know how beautiful you are. (*Indicates the other side of model stand*) Sit there.

SONNY-MAN: (*Places cushions on the floor at the foot of the model stand*) Just sit here and be my beautiful self. (*To Cynthia*) Turn on, baby, we gonna get our picture took. (*Cynthia smiles*)

BILL: Now there's Oldtimer, the guy who was here before there were scholarships and grants and stuff like that, the guy they kept outta the schools, the man the factories wouldn't hire, the union wouldn't let him join . . .

SONNY-MAN: Yeah, yeah, rap to me. Where you goin' with it, man? Rap on.

BILL: I'm makin' a triptych.

SONNY-MAN: Make it, man.

BILL: (*Indicating Cynthia and Sonny-man*) On the other side, Young Man and Woman, workin' together to do our thing.

TOMMY: (*Quietly*) I'm goin' now.

BILL: But you belong up there in the center. "Wine in The Wilderness," that's who you are. (*Moves the canvas of the little girl and places the sketch pad on the easel*) The nightmare, about all that I've done disappearing before my eyes. It was a good nightmare. I was painting in the dark, all head and no heart. I couldn't see until you came, baby. (*To Cynthia, Sonny-man and Oldtimer*) Look at Tomorrow. She came through the biggest riot of all, somethin' called slavery, and she's even comin' through the "now" scene . . . folks laughin' at her, even her own folks laughin' at her. And look *how* . . . with her head high like she's poppin' her fingers at the world. (*Takes up charcoal pencil and tears old page off sketch pad so he can make a fresh drawing*) Aw, let me put it down, Tommy. "Wine in The Wilderness," you gotta let me put it down so all the little boys and girls can look up and see you on the wall. And you know what they're gonna say? "Hey, don't she look like somebody we know?" (*Tommy slowly returns and takes her seat on the stand. Tommy is holding the wig in her lap. Her hands are very graceful looking against the texture of the wig*) And they'll be right, you're somebody they know. (*He is sketching hastily. There is a sound of thunder and the patter of rain*) Yeah, roll them hoops and bicycle wheels! (*Music in low. Music up higher as Bill continues to sketch*)

Curtain

Ramon Delgado

ONCE BELOW A LIGHTHOUSE

Ramon Delgado

Presently chairman of the speech-drama department at Kentucky Wesleyan College, Owensboro, Kentucky, Ramon Delgado was born in 1937 in Tampa, Florida. He received his education at Stetson University, the Dallas Theatre Center, and the Yale School of Drama, from which he received an M.F.A. in 1967.

Although his academic duties absorb most or all of his working hours during the school year, Mr. Delgado's summers—frequently spent in Florida—are devoted exclusively to writing. "I can't do both teaching and writing," he admits. "I write in the summer. The rest of the year, I get ideas, write myself notes. I have a whole file full of ideas." Much of his writing is set in his home state, including *Once Below A Lighthouse,* which is published for the first time anywhere in this collection.

The author initially won recognition for his work in 1959 when his short play, *Waiting for the Bus,* took first place in a contest sponsored by the Theta Alpha Phi honorary dramatic society and subsequently was included in two play anthologies. In 1966, he once again came off with top honors, this time for a full-length drama, *Nest Among the Stars,* in the Baylor University religious drama competition. The play had been produced earlier at Chipola Junior College in Florida, where the author taught from 1963 to 1965.

Mr. Delgado's most recent award came in May, 1971, for his short comedy, *The Knight-Mare's Nest,* chosen as the best play in the University of Missouri's playwriting contest.

His other plays include: *Omega's Ninth; Fear of Angels; Hedge of Serpents; Snowbird;* and *Brother of Dragons.*

Characters:

LARRY

TERRY

ANITA GARCIA

Scene:

A few miles south of Daytona Beach, Florida. A cross section of the top floor of an ancient frame house, featuring a combined dining-bedroom and a small balcony overlooking a point between ocean and inlet. A rusty glider is on the balcony. A door connects balcony to the larger room. Inside the room a door opens to a kitchen and another door serves as the entrance from hall and stairs. Old furniture, pictures, stacks of magazines, newspapers, bric-a-brac, old shoes, umbrellas, a couple of old circus posters give the room a cramped, cluttered appearance. Furniture includes a desk and chair, a refrigerator, a stereo, a sink, a bed with a nightstand and lamp, a chair at the foot of the bed, and a table and chairs in the dining area. A monkey sits in a covered cage by the bed.

The room is in darkness. The sky beyond the terrace is purple-gray. A tropical thunderstorm is in progress. Dogs bark. In a moment the upstage door is unlocked, opened, and the beams of two illuminated flashlights appear. Larry and Terry enter. Larry is a slight, intense, dapper young man in his early thirties. Terry is a solidly built, innocent-faced boy of eighteen with a deliberately careless appearance.

LARRY: This is it! (*He turns on the lights*) The last room on the top floor in the last shack below the lighthouse.

TERRY: Somebody ought to fix those stairs.

LARRY: The owner doesn't give a damn, and when the caretaker's home, he stays too drunk to drive a nail straight.

TERRY: Did you see the wicked look his wife gave us?

LARRY: Did you see the one God gave her?

TERRY: Foreigner, isn't she? Some kind of Latin?

LARRY: Claims to be Mexican and her husband pure Indian. This land was once all theirs, and now we are their guests. Here, let me give your shirt a soak.

TERRY: You really don't have to bother.

LARRY: If you don't soak it now, it may leave a stain.

TERRY: Sure you don't mind?

LARRY: You can't go through life with a shirtful of pelican shit.

TERRY: Damn bird! (*He takes off his shirt and gives it to Larry, who soaks it in the sink*)

LARRY: Non-polluting detergent. How's that for saving the world?

TERRY: A twelve-dollar shirt! A gift, too.

LARRY: (*Admiring Terry's build*) My, all those juicy muscles! You lift weights or something?

TERRY: I work out now and then, and surf as much as I can.

LARRY: You like that—surfing, I mean?

TERRY: Out there, all alone, you're king of the sea.

LARRY: "Balls," said the queen, "if I had two, I'd be king."

TERRY: What's that supposed to mean?

LARRY: Damned if I know.

TERRY: (*Slapping at an insect*) Gee, you've got something vicious in this place.

LARRY: Sandflies, mosquitoes, tsetse flies, you name it.

TERRY: Tsetse flies in Daytona Beach? You're putting me on.

LARRY: Yeah, I'm putting you on. (*Giving Terry one of his shirts*) Here, no use advertising the feast.

TERRY: Thanks. (*He puts on the shirt*)

LARRY: Bit small, but it'll still do the job.

TERRY: So they say.

LARRY: Embroidered by Ethel, but faded with age.

TERRY: Fancy stuff. Who's Ethel?

LARRY: You'll meet Ethel later. (*Terry slaps again*) Still nibbling?

TERRY: Maybe it's a flea from one of those poodles downstairs.

LARRY: Those dogs are so pampered they need all the fleas they can get to remember they're dogs. It's probably mosquitoes; the rain drove 'em in. There's an insect strip hanging up there somewhere—but it's three years old.

TERRY: Why don't you throw it away and get a new one?

LARRY: Might upset the owner. He doesn't like a hair to be touched. Never throws out a thing and sometimes goes through the trash on the road to find some knickknack of questionable value. You think this room is full of junk, you ought to see the attic. (*Taking an insect spray bomb from the desk*) Here, spray this around the doors and under the bed.

TERRY: Why the bed?

LARRY: If you were a mosquito, wouldn't you hide under the bed?

TERRY: What happened to your concern for ecology?

LARRY: Present survival always comes first.

TERRY: (*As he starts to spray*) Say, I thought you invited me up to help you celebrate something.

LARRY: That's right.

TERRY: What's the occasion?

LARRY: My anniversary.

TERRY: Anniversary? Of what?

LARRY: My marriage.

TERRY: Isn't it the usual thing to celebrate marriage anniversaries with your—spouse?

LARRY: If one is spouse, then two is spice.

TERRY: And three?

LARRY: Three?

TERRY: Well?

LARRY: Is your curiosity piqued?

TERRY: Is it what?

LARRY: Piqued.

TERRY: I suppose.

LARRY: Only your curiosity?

TERRY: What else?

LARRY: Your—apprehension, your caution.

TERRY: She must have had some patience to put up with you.

LARRY: Who?

TERRY: Your wife.

LARRY: Spouse.

TERRY: You did say this was your anniversary?

LARRY: No. I said I was going to celebrate my anniversary. I didn't say this was it. And I didn't say "wife." You said "spouse," and I agreed on "spice," the variety of life. (*Dogs bark below. Larry crosses to the hall door, locks it*)

TERRY: Why're you locking the door?

LARRY: The caretaker—or rather, the caretaker's wife, she's feeding the dogs.

TERRY: So, she's not gonna feed 'em up here.

LARRY: She's making progress. They're on the second floor, you know.

TERRY: Still that's no reason . . .

LARRY: Once she came busting through that door and caught me half-naked taking a leak in the sink—to save a trip to the second floor john.

TERRY: That's not likely to happen now, is it?

LARRY: Nowadays you never know, do you?

TERRY: Maybe I'd better go.

LARRY: Go? What for? Your shirt's still soaking, and we haven't even decorated the place yet.

TERRY: Decorated?

LARRY: How can we have an anniversary celebration—with or without a spouse—if we don't decorate the place?

TERRY: Are you some kind of eccentric millionaire or something, and this is the way you get your kicks?

LARRY: Why did you bring up the question of money again? I told you I didn't have any.

TERRY: That car you drive. Lincoln Continentals don't come without "bread."

LARRY: Just because I drive it, doesn't mean it's mine.

TERRY: No?

LARRY: I could have rented it for the occasion.

TERRY: Oh?

LARRY: I wanted a Pontiac Grand Prix. Think about it for a minute.

TERRY: Uh-huh. (*Edging his way to the door*) I think I'd better go, mister.

LARRY: Larry. My name is Larry. And yours? You never did say.

TERRY: I don't think we're down to a first name basis. And I don't think we're ever going to be.

LARRY: Look, kid, I'm perfectly harmless.

TERRY: Give me the key.

LARRY: To the car?

TERRY: To the lock.

LARRY: There's no key on this side. Only a night latch. (*Terry opens the night latch and tries the door*)

TERRY: It won't open.

LARRY: Gets stuck in rainy weather. Swells up right in the hole.

TERRY: I want out of here.

LARRY: I told you it's stuck. (*He opens the door*) There, you see, I told you it was only stuck in the hole. (*Pause*) Well, aren't you going?

TERRY: You were telling the truth, weren't you?

LARRY: About the door? Most assuredly. You go out now, you'll have to explain to the caretaker's wife. She gets lonely with her Indian husband off on the shrimp boat—three hundred miles at sea. But maybe there's something in it for you. Maybe she's hoarding treasure from the Seven Cities of Gold, and you can prime her till she runs dry.

TERRY: I've never seen such a disgusting pig in all my life!

LARRY: Then stay here with me. I may pique your apprehension, but at least I don't disgust you. At least you haven't said that I do.

TERRY: No, you don't disgust me. In fact if you'd come off the hocus-pocus, I might even find you very interesting.

LARRY: That's what I thought. But the hocus-pocus is part of my charm. Besides, I've got more reason to be fearful of you than you of me.

TERRY: You're a heck of a lot older.

LARRY: Let's not mention age. Each anniversary (*Touching his hair*) brings new sprinkles of silver.

TERRY: You're creepier.

LARRY: But you're bigger.

TERRY: Height's about the same.

LARRY: But you've got more muscles.

TERRY: So what?

LARRY: (*Picking up a newspaper; suggesting headlines*) "Eccentric Anniversary Celebrant Strangled: Vagrant Beach Boy Sought."

TERRY: Now look . . .

LARRY: I have been.

TERRY: I'm not like that at all.

LARRY: Why not? Not that there's anything worth strangling me for, if that was your idea.

TERRY: What do you do around here, anyway?

LARRY: I rent Lincoln Continentals instead of Grand Prixes, I have anniversaries, I live in the last room on the top floor of the last shack below the lighthouse, and I pick up vagrant beach boy hitch-hikers to bring them back to my room to do God-knows-what-awful-things to their bodies and souls.

TERRY: (*After a moment, he starts laughing*) You're a fraud, a plastic, freaky fraud. You should have been an actor, or maybe you are. Who put you up to all this? Wendell? Gary? One of my friends from the beach?

LARRY: I just happened to see you walking along the . . . Now, see here, I can't have you make light of all my careful preparations. (*Crossing to door*) Not you and the weather, too. Hasn't cleared up yet, and we *were* scheduled to watch the eclipse . . . (*He picks up the binoculars hanging on a nail by the door and looks through them at Terry*) . . . through these.

TERRY: Is that what you use to spy on the lovers?

LARRY: I don't need to watch them. The sounds they make are revealing enough. (*He steps onto the balcony*) Come on.

TERRY: In the rain?

LARRY: It's cut to a drizzle. You can stand under the eaves if you're afraid of the wet. (*Looking through the binoculars*) Look, three cars. Can't go backward and can't go forwards, whipping around like stranded whales.

TERRY: I don't see a damn thing.

LARRY: They've stopped the cars now. All out in the wet sand, taking off their clothes, dancing in the rain in the headlights of their cars.

TERRY: Where you see all that?

LARRY: In my binoculars. (*He offers the binoculars to Terry*)

TERRY: You must be crazy!

LARRY: You have to come over here by me.

TERRY: How come?

LARRY: The angle's bad from where you are. (*Terry cautiously moves next to Larry and takes the binoculars. Terry looks. Larry puts his arm over Terry's shoulder and points*) There! Right there, don't you see?

TERRY: What the heck are you doing?

LARRY: I'm simply trying to show you where to look.

TERRY: Well, get your arm off my shoulders, will you?

LARRY: Tense as a kite string!

TERRY: Hovering over my shoulder like a vulture doesn't exactly turn me on.

LARRY: Sorry. (*He moves away*) Clouds started moving. We may get to see the eclipse yet.

TERRY: Moon's still covered. You can hardly see the lighthouse from here. What happened to it anyway?

LARRY: I thought you knew your way around here.

TERRY: I've only been here a couple of weeks. I don't know everything yet.

LARRY: You act like you did.

TERRY: Will you answer the question? What happened to the damn lighthouse?

LARRY: It doesn't work any more.

TERRY: Well, I can see that, for Christ's sake!

LARRY: They've got a smaller one across the channel now. See. Over there. Since they narrowed the channel, the big ships can't come this way anymore.

TERRY: Little boats, little lights.

LARRY: That's about the size of it.

TERRY: Imagine giving up that magnificent, old lighthouse.

LARRY: Light today, dark tomorrow.

TERRY: Changing the face of things.

LARRY: There used to be pelicans come over every five minutes or so.

TERRY: They're often enough as it is.

LARRY: They'd come gliding over in lines of twelve or thirteen. I used to think of Jesus and the twelve apostles.

TERRY: Why'd pelicans make you think of Jesus?

LARRY: Isn't that the way he fed the five thousand—five loaves of bread and two pelicans?

TERRY: Fish. They were fish, damn it! Don't you know *anything?*

LARRY:

What a wonderful bird is the pelican,
His beak holds more than his belly can.
He holds in his beak enough food for a week,
But I don't see how in the hell he can.

TERRY: Sounds freaky to me. (*Offstage, dune buggies race their engines*) There's the dune buggies you thought you saw.

LARRY: I saw them before they arrived.

TERRY: If you say so.

LARRY: This used to be a quiet place where a man could come close to nature, to think about life and stuff. But now, at all hours of the night and day, dune buggies and tourists circle the place like a fleet of vultures. There's a small blue heron left in the lagoon, and even a raccoon and skunk pass by now and then. Rabbits, but the dove and quail have been killed off, and there hasn't been a deer since the Second World War.

TERRY: Tide's rising.

LARRY: Full moon makes it high, and the winds beat it almost to the first floor porch. You can hear it lapping at the floorboards—almost like a live thing. (*Pause*)

TERRY: Let's go inside.

(*They cross back into the room*)

LARRY: I pulled some things out of the attic for the celebration.

TERRY: Just help yourself?

LARRY: I've known the owner since I was knee-high to a grasshopper. Collects lotsa junk, but there's some nice stuff, too. (*Taking black lace tablecloth from top of refrigerator*) Handmade lace—Spanish.

TERRY: Like the woman downstairs?

LARRY: She's Mexican plastic. This is the *real* thing. (*He spreads the cloth*) Never touched by the hands of machines. Basic black. It goes with the decor. (*He takes a string of Japanese paper lanterns from behind the refrigerator*) Here, help me hang these up.

TERRY: Don't tell me—made in Japan.

LARRY: Right. Goes with the decor.

TERRY: Most anything would.

LARRY: Inside, old Christmas tree lights. Made in Hong Kong. Rainbow colored. Goes with the decor.

TERRY: (*Simultaneously*) . . . With the decor. It's a regular U.N.

LARRY: "The people come and go, talking of Michelangelo."

TERRY: How do you make a living anyway?

(*They continue to decorate during this sequence*)

LARRY: "How do I make a living?" Let's rephrase the question. "How do I survive?" That's better. Survival—the first concern of the caveman—the prominent concern of the present, the full cycle of the evolution of a species. Adaptability to specialization, then extinction from overspecialization. What have we specialized in—babymaking and war. They each feed on the other. You supply more babies, I'll supply more bombs. Sounds workable, doesn't it? In theory, at least. But mass production of each has made the environment all but uninhabitable. And only the small boats can come and go with cargos of Michelangelo.

TERRY: I only wanted a simple answer, not a whole book.

LARRY: Answers are never simple, and questions rarely answerable—except in riddles. What's bigger than a breadbasket and full of holes?

TERRY: Bigger than a breadbasket and full of holes?

LARRY: I could have said smaller than a breadbasket without any holes.

TERRY: Is there an answer?

LARRY: Is there a question?

TERRY: I've met a lot of nuts in my day, but I never . . .

LARRY: (*Overlapping*) I never met a nut I couldn't eat.

TERRY: Then you're not going to tell me?

LARRY: "What I Do to Survive," by Lawrence of Arabia. I have preached a little, mainly in country churches and on streetcorners; one pays about as well as the other. I have worked as a professional killer under the sponsorship of the Selective Service. I have been a journalist, covering such international events as purse snatchings and the opening of new gymnasiums, and I have worked as a lifeguard.

TERRY: A lifeguard?

LARRY: At the kiddies' pool of the Family YMCA. And I have read in my spare time half the *Wisdom of the Western World*, volumes one through ten.

TERRY: And the other half?

LARRY: Lord, I've got to save something for my old age. Besides, if the second half is as unprofitable as the first half, I'd rather wait 'til my old age to see how the whole mess turned out.

TERRY: And now?

LARRY: Now? This moment? This spring, this vernal equinox, when life's night equals her day, the seventh anniversary of my three-day marriage—or is it the three-year anniversary of my seven-day marriage? Time is such a confusing maze of hours and faces, and putting the two together in their sequential order is quite beyond me and barely worth the effort.

TERRY: Anyone ever tell you that you dribble?

LARRY: (*Fixing two drinks*) I didn't know it still showed. Yes, my late spouse, or was I the one who was late? In any case, she used to make the same compliment—I dribbled. Not necessarily in words, you understand. I dribbled my clothes all over the house, a scarf here, a sock there, my unfinished volumes of the *Wisdom of the Western World,* complete in twenty volumes, under the rugs and Hepplewhite chairs—veneer, veneer, ornate veneer. I dribbled serpentine pieces of newspaper clippings from sky hook to sky hook, and my night's hard pillow with the salty shaft of tears. Oh, did I ever dribble! I was a born dribbler, and a dribbler I shall die. (*Handing Terry a drink*) But not a drop of *that* brew did I spill. (*Terry holds the glass, hesitating*) What's the matter? You do drink, don't you?

TERRY: I tasted some beer once.

LARRY: Then I don't suppose you ever tackled the really hard stuff like sherry and port? Come on, kid, who's leg you trying to pull? And why? Aren't you the liberated generation, the dropped-out, turned-on, groupie-feelie generation, the kids who could write a book on *Everything You've Always Known About Sex and Weren't Afraid to Try?*

TERRY: I suppose there were some like that, but I've led a sheltered life. Really, I have. This is the first summer I didn't have a nosy parent poking over my shoulder.

LARRY: What happened to them?

TERRY: I left. I was eighteen and old enough to find out a few things for myself.

LARRY: They don't know where you are?

TERRY: They know all right, and they also know better than to try to force me back home.

LARRY: What were they like, your parents?

TERRY: What difference does it make to you?

LARRY: I think maybe we rebelled against the same middle-class nightmare.

TERRY: Mister, my sob story is just like any other sob story.

LARRY: Larry, call me Larry.

TERRY: Why should I call you Larry?

LARRY: Because that's my name, damn it. You have a name too, don't you?

TERRY: Sort of.

LARRY: And you like to be called by it, don't you?

TERRY: Not particularly.

LARRY: Then tell me what it is, so I won't use it by accident.

TERRY: Terry. My name is Terry.

LARRY: Larry and Terry. The feminine syllables rhyme.

TERRY: Don't get smart.

LARRY: Merely an observation. (*Holding up his glass*) To Terry and Larry. (*Terry puts his glass down without drinking*) What's the matter? You're not gonna get drunk on one lousy sip. One swallow doesn't make a summer, or anything else, they say.

TERRY: It isn't that. I think I'd better . . .

LARRY: The "convenience"?

TERRY: The john.

LARRY: The "convenience" isn't very convenient at all. In fact it's a hell of an inconvenience. On the second floor—between the caretaker's wife and the dogs.

TERRY: So many doors we passed. I stopped counting at eight.

LARRY: From the foot of the stairs, take the second door

to the right. Open it, cross into the room, to your left will be three doors.

TERRY: "His," "Hers," and "Theirs."

LARRY: Pay attention.

TERRY: I am, I am.

LARRY: Take the third door.

TERRY: What happens if I take the first or second?

LARRY: Look, if you want me to go and hold your hand . . .

TERRY: Just give me a flashlight. (*Larry gives him one of the flashlights*) But what's behind the other two doors?

LARRY: You can't make a mistake. The first is only a closet. Empty, except for some rusty old coat hangers, pieces of yellow paper still covering some of 'em—one of those clean-in-an-hour places, I think. Leave the second door alone. The third door is the "convenience," the john. Use it, flush it, leave it for the next customer. No dimes. No change machine. Sometimes the water works and sometimes it doesn't, but it's usually when you're ready to shave—your face covered with creamy, rich lather, waiting for daily castration, then water pressure rattles the pipes, you turn the handle, and "foom!" Nothing but air, the faucet hanging limp and obscene, shamed by it's functional failure.

TERRY: I only want to go to the john, not hear a lecture on plumbing.

LARRY: (*Singing*)

When Fanny met John in the john,
It was dreadful how they carried on.
She sat on his lap,
Gave his what's-it a flap,
And said, "I'll see you anon."

TERRY: Can I go now?

LARRY: (*Stepping aside*) And hurry back, or your ice'll melt, and it'll be two hours before this old refrigerator'll have set up some more.

TERRY: What're you hiding behind that second door?

LARRY: Just leave it be and get on with it.

TERRY: All right. If I wasn't so polite, I'd pee in the sink.

LARRY: Help yourself. That's where I'm soaking your bird-shitted shirt.

TERRY: Damn pelican! (*There is a rumble of boards in the ceiling*) What's that?

LARRY: Rats.

TERRY: They sound big as dogs.

LARRY: They are big as dogs. Last week one ran off with a trap I set. Don't know what he plans to do with it. Set up a museum of captured enemy weapons, I guess.

TERRY: Rats big as dogs and dogs big as rats.

LARRY: That's the way life is a few feet below the lighthouse. We're all reduced to a common denominator—survival. I put out some poison, but I can't smell that it's done much good so far. I hated to do it, but it was my food or theirs.

TERRY: (*Making a peace sign as he leaves*) If I capture the enemy, I'll send up a flare. Piss for peace. (*He exits*)

LARRY: (*Inspecting the soaking shirt*) What a wonderful bird is the pelican! (*He crosses to the cage, but does not uncover it*) Well, dear Ethel, what do you think of our beautiful prize? Surprised? No, you're never surprised. The same goddam expression of boredom no matter what gorgeous gob of flesh comes trembling. Peanut? Ethel wants a peanut? How about a piece of banana as well? You never get enough of it do you, sweetheart? Hell, you never get any at all! Careful! You don't care what's attached to the finger that feeds you! Greedy glutton! (*Terry returns*) God, my child, you look like you got the piss scared out of you. The caretaker's wife didn't try to goose you in the hall, did she? (*Pause*) Oh, you peeked behind the second door, didn't you? Now that was a naughty.

TERRY: I'll be all right. It's just that you made such a big deal of it all. It still doesn't quite make sense.

LARRY: You remember what Bluebeard did with his wives when they opened the forbidden door? But I shan't take off your maiden's head or whatever—not tonight.

TERRY: You're not one of those weird freaks, are you?

LARRY: Depends on what you mean by "weird freaks."

TERRY: The dripping—that's what got me—the dripping.

LARRY: Blop-blop! Blop-blop!

TERRY: That's exactly the way it went. Blop-blop! Blop-blop!

LARRY: Did you notice the color?

TERRY: I didn't stay long enough to think about color.

LARRY: Rusty-red! Rusty-red! Blop-blop! Blop-blop! Comes from a leak in the old tin roof, down through the floor of the attic above.

TERRY: But it looks like it's coming from . . . (*He puts his hand to his heart*)

LARRY: I know, I know. Blop-blop! Blop-blop!

TERRY: Stop it!

LARRY: Blop-blop!

TERRY: Stop it!

LARRY: It's only a statue.

TERRY: I could take the statue, but it was the dripping. . . . And there's a strange shaft of light.

LARRY: (*Lighting the candles on the table*) Then you saw it, too? When I first saw it that way I thought it was only the last stray beam of the sunset, but it was too late for the sun. And then I thought it came from a crack in the floor from the caretaker's kitchen below, but she wasn't at home and my hand couldn't find a way to shadow the beam. Maybe it's paint, luminous paint. Anyway, it glows.

TERRY: The statue . . .

LARRY: The Sacred Heart of Jesus is a painted plaster saint, and the paint's peeling off like a worn-out glove. Strange, standing there with the rusty water from the tin roof and the stray ray of light hitting on his heart and trickling down his sleeve to the dead rat on the floor. Blop-blop! Blop-blop! How his stretched fingers must ache from that gesture which says sort of "come-unto-me-hither." And all that came was a dying rat on the next to last floor of the last shack on the last road below the lighthouse. (*Pause*)

TERRY: I think I'll take that drink now.

LARRY: I thought you might. (*Giving Terry the glass*) To all the lonely plaster saints and all the dead rats at their feet! (*They drink*) As Jesus said on the cross, dear child, "God, this stuff is strong!" (*Rain, lightning, thunder. He crosses to the door*) I bet the ocean's over the floorboards by now. Someday it'll all be empty, too, not even a dab of plankton left. And the sea that nourished all life will die.

TERRY: This is no way to run a celebration.

LARRY: You're right. (*He heads for the phonograph and puts on some sitar music. He turns off the lights, leaving the room lit by candles and Japanese lanterns*) We've only to blow our minds, and the whole dirty world is flushed down the drain. (*He produces a couple of "joints"*) Ever tried these before?

TERRY: Sure. It's easy as air around this place. But it doesn't mix so well with booze.

LARRY:

Eeny, meeny, miney, mo,
Catch a vice cop by the toe,
If he hollers let him blow,
Eeny, meeny, miney, mo.
My mother told me to choose this very one.

(*Larry puts down his glass and lights up a joint. He inhales, passes it to Terry, exhales. They share it during the next few moments*)

TERRY: You sure it's safe here?

LARRY: You're a real paranoid, you know that.

TERRY: I just don't want to get caught.

LARRY: Relax. Nobody's going to be out here in this weather.

TERRY: I think I'd feel more at ease with you if you'd tell me the truth about your—spouse.

LARRY: (*Taking a diary from the desk*)

The truth lies in an ancient book,
But can't be read by priest or crook.
The book's closed up with a rusty lock
And can't be forced with bar or rock.

The key's been thrown away, you see,
And the secret is known by only me.
Who am I?

TERRY: I give up. Who are you?

LARRY: Not even a guess?

TERRY: A bookworm!

LARRY: You cheated.

TERRY: I did not. Is that the answer?

LARRY: Not quite the one I had in mind, but it'll do in a pinch.

TERRY: What else could it be?

LARRY: Another clue:
Though shiny as a dime
My first will never rhyme.
I never swam the ocean
Though the last might give that notion.

Paper and glue's my favorite dish,
I'm a word-devouring silverfish!

TERRY: (*With Larry*) Silverfish!

LARRY: You guessed it. You win a year's supply of library paste and a lifetime subscription to the *Silverfish Digest*.

TERRY: And the truth's in the book, huh?

LARRY: A seven-year diary. Little golden letters and a clasp concealing the truth inside. And now it's full. But after the seven fat years came the seven lean.

TERRY: What the heck are you talking about?

LARRY: Your Jewish heritage, my boy. It's all in the book.

TERRY: May I see it?

LARRY: The book is sealed and so are my lips. (*The rec-*

ord player stops and the lanterns go off) Damn! Must be the electricity.

TERRY: What difference does it make?

LARRY: (*At switch*) Yep. They're off for sure. No ice tonight.

TERRY: Come on, let's finish the celebration. You were just about to tell me the truth.

LARRY: The truth'll have to wait while I repair the music.

TERRY: You can't fix the power failure.

LARRY: No, but I can reach back in history and bring forth magic. (*Leaving with a flashlight*) Be back in a sec.

(*While Larry is gone, Terry goes to the desk, takes the diary, tries to open it, using a letter opener and a knife. Then he tries tearing the latch. The diary remains intact*)

TERRY: Damn lock!

(*Larry returns with a portable hand crank victrola and several records. Terry quickly sticks the diary in the back of his shirt*)

LARRY: I told you the owner never throws away a thing.

TERRY: Quite an antique.

LARRY: Not as old as you think. I used to play one when I was a little boy.

TERRY: Maybe you lied about your age after all.

LARRY: We'll have to use old records, too. This needle'd ruin those microgrooves. Ah, here we are. Caruso, the final lament from the first act of *Pagliacci*. I hope this thing still works. There's a balancing device inside that's supposed to look like a pawnbroker's sign, but one ball was missing, so I fixed it with a lead fishing sinker. (*The record starts to play—a bit too fast*)

TERRY: Sounds like Caruso might be missing the same thing.

LARRY: Well, I've got some more sinkers. (*He slows down the record to the proper speed*)

TERRY: You really enjoy that Greek?

LARRY: Italian! The main character is a clown in a traveling show. His wife is running around, and he's got to go on making people laugh—but inside he is dying of passion. (*They listen to the ending of the piece. Pause*) You going to make some smart-ass remark after that?

TERRY: No. Somehow, I understand how he feels, and I don't even need a translation.

LARRY: Good. You're sensitive enough to appreciate refreshments.

TERRY: You must have heard my stomach growling.

LARRY: (*Behind Terry, blindfolding his eyes*) Sit still.

TERRY: What the hell are you doing? (*Larry puts a party hat on Terry and one on himself*)

LARRY: What's a party without hats! Careful. They're fragile as butterfly wings.

TERRY: I bet we look cute!

LARRY: Like a couple of clowns. At-ah! Don't peek. I'll only be a minute. (*He moves the animal cage to one of the chairs at the table*)

TERRY: What are you up to?

LARRY: (*Going to kitchen*) Just fixing everything for the refreshments.

TERRY: What is that God-awful smell?

LARRY: Probably cat litter.

TERRY: Cat litter! You got a cat in this place?

LARRY: (*Returning with a cake containing twenty-one candles. He then removes Terry's blindfold*) *Voilà!* Anniversary cake.

TERRY: You got enough candles to burn down the place.

LARRY: Twenty-one candles. So whether it's seven times three or three times seven, we're covered.

TERRY: And who's the guest that smells like a cat?

LARRY: In case you hadn't noticed, the cover also goes with the decor.

TERRY: (*Simultaneously*) . . . With the decor.

LARRY: (*Removing the cover. The monkey also wears a party hat*) *Voilà!* This is Ethel!

TERRY: A monkey? Ethel is a monkey?

LARRY: We've been married for seven years—ever since the first Ethel left. Not legally, of course.

TERRY: I'm glad to hear that!

LARRY: And of course we're not adding to the population problem.

TERRY: I should hope not!

LARRY: And very little to pollution. Ethel rides a tricycle occasionally on her way to market—no hydrocarbons, no sulfides.

TERRY: How is it with a monkey?

LARRY: How's what?

TERRY: I mean, you do go to bed with her, don't you?

LARRY: See how modestly she covers her face? Ethel's a born Puritan. She doesn't even play with herself like her relatives in the zoo.

TERRY: It's those tricycle rides that do it. But what about the real Ethel, or was there *ever* a real Ethel?

LARRY: You question my veracity?

TERRY: You have made certain statements, certain questionable remarks that I want to find out if they're true. (*He pulls out the diary*)

LARRY: My diary! Give it back to me!

TERRY: At-ah! It's impolite to take by force.

LARRY: That belongs to me!

TERRY: Possession is nine-tenths ownership.

LARRY: It has my name inscribed on the cover.

TERRY: "Little golden letters and a clasp concealing the *lies* inside."

LARRY: The truth! *My* truth.

TERRY: The lies! *Your* lies. Or is this the *truth* and your stories to me the lies?

LARRY: You little bastard! Give me the book!

TERRY: Are you going to tell me the truth?

LARRY: How will you know when I'm telling the truth?

TERRY: Were you *ever* married to a girl named Ethel?

LARRY: Spouse!

TERRY: Whatever she was!

LARRY: What difference does it make to you?

TERRY: Tell me the truth!

LARRY: You've no right to know. (*He has backed Terry to the bed and is nearly on top of him*)

TERRY: Leave me alone, you dirty old man! You want me to have you arrested!

LARRY: (*Realizing how physical they have become*) I'm sorry. I didn't mean to . . . just give me my dairy.

(*Terry turns on his stomach, falling over on the bed with the diary concealed beneath his stomach. Larry struggles on top of him, reaching left and right for the diary*)

LARRY: Give it to me! Give it to me!

TERRY: (*Turning over and holding the diary above his head*) Listen to him beg for it! The dirty old man is begging for his lies back!

LARRY: Without them I have nothing! No one—nobody!

TERRY: You have Ethel and the dead rats and the short-playing Caruso and the statue of the Sacred Heart of Jesus! Blop-blop! Blop-blop! (*He continues the beat through the next few lines*)

LARRY: Give it to me, goddam it, give it to me!

TERRY: My virgin ears are offended. Blop-blop!

LARRY: (*Almost in tears, sinking to his knees on the floor at the edge of the bed*) I want it! I want my life back!

TERRY: Will you tell me the truth?

LARRY: Yes, yes! Anything, anything you want to know.

TERRY: All right! Let's start with Ethel. Was there ever really an Ethel, besides the monkey, I mean?

LARRY: What can it matter to you?

TERRY: I only want to help you . . . to help you put your life back together. So you won't have to live this way, perched on the edge of the ocean ready to be covered by the tide any minute.

LARRY: Empty! The sea will be empty!

TERRY: You can hear it lapping, can't you? Licking like

mad to devour you? You've been backed to the shore by bigger and bigger lies, and I only want to keep you from drowning.

LARRY: It might be peaceful, restful, in the depths of inky brine.

TERRY: I'm waiting, Larry. I'm waiting to see if you can face the truth about your life.

LARRY: Yes, yes! The truth. (*Clawing at Terry's shirt. Dogs start barking below*) It's there somewhere beneath the embroidery—the faded lines of stencil—the programmed pattern beneath the meaningless string of words. I'll tell you all about Ethel . . .

(*Anita Garcia, a slovenly, earthy Mexican-American, bursts into the room. She wears a faded housecoat, her hair in curlers, covered by a net*)

ANITA: Did you see the eclipse?

LARRY: Mrs. Garcia!

ANITA: It's happening now. Let me borrow your spyglass. (*Anita takes the binoculars from the hook and hurries out to the balcony*)

LARRY: (*Following her*) You can't just come busting up here any time of the day or night!

ANITA: The eclipse of the moon. It happens only once every ten years. How many chances does that give in a lifetime?

(*Terry crosses as far as the door*)

LARRY: It just so happens I'm entertaining guests!

ANITA: (*Coming in from the balcony*) You're having a party and didn't invite me? (*The lights go on and the sitar music resumes*)

LARRY: The power, thank God!

ANITA: I'll have a bourbon on the rocks, thank you.

LARRY: (*Turning off the sitar music*) You're not welcome to the party, Mrs. Garcia!

ANITA: Prejudice! Prejudice! Everywhere you go, prejudice to the poor *chicano*.

LARRY: What would your husband say if he knew?

ANITA: How's he going to know, for Christ's sake? He's

three hundred miles out in a shrimp boat and won't be back for a week.

LARRY: Mrs. Garcia, if you don't get out of my apartment, I'm going to have to report this to the owner. *And* your dogs. If he knew what your dogs are doing to this place. . .

ANITA: Prejudice! All my life, nothing but *prejudice.* (*Noticing Terry for the first time*) Who is this boy, one of your guests?

LARRY: Yes, he's one of my guests.

ANITA: Say, haven't I seen you somewhere before?

TERRY: I don't recall that we've met.

ANITA: No, but I've seen. Boy, have I seen!

TERRY: You don't know what you're talking about!

ANITA: Down by the rocks. Parking your butt on the rocks.

TERRY: You're interrupting our party, lady. Get lost!

ANITA: Hustling your butt to every dirty old man in the street!

LARRY: He's my *nephew.* Get out of here and leave us alone!

ANITA: If he's your nephew, then he's got uncles all over the place!

LARRY: You are not welcome here, Mrs. Garcia!

ANITA: He ain't your nephew, mister. He's the greediest little hustler on the beach. You better check your money downstairs, if you want to have any left when he leaves.

LARRY: I think you must be mistaken!

TERRY: You fat Mexican slut, get out of here!

ANITA: Listen what he call me, the little whore!

LARRY: I guess I'll just *have* to tell the owner about your dogs!

ANITA: You tell him about my dogs and I have an entertaining bug for his ear. You think he approve of these going's on? You crazy, mister, you crazy as moondust. (*She holds out a shot glass from the table*) But we make a little bargain, you see. You never saw no dogs in this house, and I never saw no little boy whore. (*Pause*) My bourbon on the rocks, if you please!

LARRY: (*Fumbling with the bourbon*) We seem to be out of rocks.

ANITA: I got plenty downstairs. My dogs is always wanting their water to be cool, so I keep plenty of ice cubes. My dogs live on the second floor, you know, where they got no refrigerator. And now that I know about your little boy guest, I'm sure they will continue to live on the second floor without the crazy old man ever knowing a thing! (*She nods and exits with her glass of bourbon*)

TERRY: Out, you old pelican, out!

LARRY: (*Toasting Anita*) What a wonderful bird is the pelican! (*He locks the door. Dogs bark below. Pause*) Well?

TERRY: "Balls," said the queen, "if I had two, I'd be king!"

LARRY: Amazing what a small dose of truth can flush out.

TERRY: You really didn't know, did you?

LARRY: Truth—the best emetic for the unpalatable paradoxes of life. No, I didn't know.

TERRY: You didn't even suspect?

LARRY: Innocent me, suspect? (*Pause*) So you hustle on the rocks.

TERRY: I never said I didn't.

LARRY: Serves me right.

TERRY: Thanks for the attempted defense, anyway.

LARRY: What was it you said you wanted to know about Ethel?

TERRY: Ethel? She's the monkey you married, isn't she? And this is the celebration of the seventh anniversary of your three-day marriage.

LARRY: Give me my book. (*Terry complies*) You hadn't opened it, after all, had you? Had you?

TERRY: You knew all along?

LARRY: (*Unlocking the diary with the key around his neck*) Of course I knew. I knew that, at least. (*He opens the book and shows it to Terry*)

TERRY: It's empty.

LARRY: There was nothing to put in it, until tonight.

TERRY: Empty page after empty page.

LARRY: But about the money . . . If that's what you want, I haven't got any. What little I have's in travelers checks anyway.

TERRY: What the hell's use is money?

LARRY: Then why do you do it?

TERRY: I dunno. It gives some lonely bastard something beautiful to remember the world by, I suppose.

LARRY: But you don't refuse money.

TERRY: Why insult 'em. Sometimes it's all they've got. If they don't have any understanding of the real essence of it all at least I don't insult 'em.

LARRY: Then you take the money?

TERRY: Of course I take the money, goddam it! When a person has nothing else, you got to take the money, because that's all they understand. But if they're smart, they know it isn't the money. I'm no money-grabbing hustler. I do it for the . . . for the . . .

LARRY: Moments of pleasure?

TERRY: Half the time I don't get any pleasure at all.

LARRY: But you just said . . .

TERRY: Look, mister, either you want it or you don't. Now, I've listened to your stories and your records . . .

LARRY: Short-playing records of the past.

TERRY: . . . And shared your golden weed. Make up your damn mind. Either piss or get off the pot.

LARRY: (*Extinguishing all the lights except the lanterns and candles*) We've still got an anniversary to celebrate.

TERRY: Then there really was an Ethel?

LARRY: In the long run which is *more* true, the new little tales we make up every day, or the big lies we spread over a lifetime?

TERRY: And the dying rat asked, "What is truth?"

LARRY: And the plaster savior of lies replied, "Truth is what's left when the paint's all peeled off."

TERRY: But I still don't know . . .

LARRY: Layer after layer. We can never know when the last layer's off.

TERRY: (*Holding out his hand*) Then believe in the warmth of my hand and the tap of my pulse.

LARRY: But when the hand turns cold and the pulse grows faint?

TERRY: All I can offer is the new, little tale for today.

LARRY: And the big lie for a lifetime?

TERRY: *That* you'll have to find for yourself.

LARRY: It's so awfully dark.

TERRY: The clouds must have covered the moon again.

LARRY: Maybe when you put the little sprinkles of lies together, the heat of their conflict generates its own perverse light, a throbbing pulse of life. But if you can't see it, is it really there?

TERRY: It's got to be there. The clouds are only temporary.

LARRY: The earth's shadow and now the clouds again. Moonlight hardly has a chance.

TERRY: (*Reaching for Larry's hand*) If you hold that nub of candle any longer, you'll scorch your fingers.

LARRY: My hands are like ice.

TERRY: (*Holding the candle with Larry*) Let me melt the ice.

LARRY: I don't know if you can, if *anybody* can.

TERRY: You mean you never . . . ?

LARRY: Does five years old count? I did it twice when I was five years old.

TERRY: What can you do at five years old?

LARRY: More than I've done in the last twenty-five.

TERRY: By experience, I may have lived longer than you.

LARRY: That's quite possible.

TERRY: Age is no longer an obstacle.

LARRY: And your painted "innocence" no longer a reason to hesitate.

TERRY: So what are we waiting for?

LARRY: (*Turning off the Japanese lanterns*) *My* innocence stays trembling on the threshold, hesitating to open the forbidden door.

TERRY: (*Striking the pose of the statue*) Blop-blop! Blop-blop!

LARRY: (*Covering Ethel's cage*) Happy anniversary, Ethel. We'll celebrate the memory of what never happened on the ripe, bought lips of love. (*Larry turns on the Caruso record*) Enjoy your nuts and banana, Ethel.

TERRY: Terry. My name is Terry.

LARRY: And my name is Larry.

TERRY: The feminine syllables rhyme. (*Larry turns up the volume of Caruso*)

LARRY: Sing, dead Caruso! Burst your lungs with fire!

(*Terry blows out the last candle*)

Curtain

Edward Bond

BLACK MASS

Edward Bond

"One never quite knows whether it is an advantage or not for a playwright to arrive with a bang, in a storm of controversy, critical denunciations and enthusiastic counterblasts, letters to papers from luminaries of the theatrical profession and even—that one-time accolade of the advanced dramatist, now merely an historical footnote—complete banning by the Lord Chamberlain." So wrote John Russell Taylor in *Plays and Players* in a comprehensive essay on Edward Bond, who since has gone on to become one of the foremost writers of his generation. What Mr. Taylor refers to, of course, is the historic controversy sparked by the Royal Court's 1965 production of Bond's play, *Saved,* which incensed London's then-reigning censor, the Lord Chamberlain. The raging contretemps actually spurred Mr. Bond's career onward and upward by bringing him to international attention. Prior to the *Saved* episode, he had written some fifteen scripts, most of which he abandoned, and only one had been produced: *The Pope's Wedding,* at the Royal Court (1962) where he had been a member of its writers' workshop.

In 1968, the controversial author had another run-in with the Lord Chamberlain over *Early Morning,* which was banned altogether from the public stage. The play was presented, though, as a private dress rehearsal for critics and friends at the Royal Court on a Sunday afternoon in April, 1968, and, ironically, won the George Devine Award of the English Stage Society. With official censorship of the English stage ended, the play was revived in 1969 at the same theatre in repertory with *Saved* and *Narrow Road to the Deep North.* The latter work was commissioned for the Peoples and Cities Conference in Coventry and was first staged there at the Belgrade Theatre in June, 1968. It was given its American premiere in January, 1972, by The Repertory Theatre of Lincoln Center, New York.

Lear, Mr. Bond's most recent work for the theatre, opened at the Royal Court, London, on September 29, 1971. With Harry Andrews giving a virtuoso performance in the title role, the author has taken Shakespeare's play as a starting point and has written a modern tragedy. According to R. B. Marriott in *The*

Stage, "It is Lear in a wildly savage but modern world of power used insanely; of everyone resorting to force, cruelty and repression for the ends of a cause or for personal ends; of dehumanized people in command of a world which should be, and could be, richly human; of hell on earth, when the idea was for heaven to be on earth."

Black Mass, published in the United States for the first time in *The Best Short Plays 1972,* was written for the Sharpeville Massacre Tenth Anniversary Commemoration Evening, held by the Anti-Apartheid Movement at the Lyceum Theatre, London, on March 22, 1970. In the play, "Christ comes down from the cross and poisons the communion wine about to be taken by the South African Prime Minister. In retaliation for the minister's death, Christ is banished from the church and his place on the cross taken by young uniformed policemen in endless succession."

Edward Bond was born in Holloway, North London, in 1934. His father was a laborer, and he admits that if he couldn't make a living out of writing, he would be forced to be a laborer himself, since he has no educational qualifications of any sort, having left school at the age of fifteen. Nonetheless, the author states that he fell in love with language at a very early age. As for playwriting, Mr. Bond has said, "A play is an attempt to solve the problems which are posed to me by society and my life. In order for me to have a rational approach to life, in order for it to make sense and be workable and have some kind of future, I have to solve those problems for myself, and I do that by writing plays. Actually, it's a very good method of working out these problems."

In addition to writing for the theatre, Mr. Bond, who lives with his wife in the country near Cambridge, England, has worked on a number of film scripts including: Antonioni's *Blow-Up; Nicholas and Alexandra; Laughter In the Dark;* and *Walkabout.*

Characters:

PRIEST

PRIME MINISTER

INSPECTOR

Scene:

A church at Vereeniging. An altar and a large cross. The altar is plain and covered by a white cloth. The cross is made of simple wood. A life-size Christ is nailed to it. A Priest and a Prime Minister. The Prime Minister kneels for communion.

PRIEST: Ye that do truly and earnestly repent you of your sins and are in love and charity with your neighbors and intend to lead a new life, make your humble confession to Almighty God meekly kneeling upon your knees. (*Pause*) Meekly kneeling upon your knees . . .

PRIME MINISTER: (*After a pause*) You said something, padre?

PRIEST: You have a lot on your mind.

PRIME MINISTER: True.

PRIEST: Something in particular, Prime Minister? Perhaps I can help.

PRIME MINISTER: You are a help, padre. It's nothing in particular. I wish . . . I wish I got a little more understanding. Something more in the way of appreciation. Even a bit less abuse. But you know, padre, I tell myself—I only tell myself in secret, of course—that men of vision are bound to be misunderstood in their own time and being misunderstood is part of the privilege of being a man of vision. Well, let's get on. There's a cabinet meeting this afternoon. You were saying?

PRIEST: Meekly kneeling upon your knees.

PRIME MINISTER: Ah, yes. Almighty God, judge of all men, we acknowledge and bewail our manifold sins and wickednesses which we . . . and now there's that crowd of Kaffirs down the road . . . from time to time most grievously have committed by thought word and deed . . . just stuck there. We do earnestly repent and are heartily sorry for these our misdoings the remembrance of them is grievous unto us the burden of them intolerable have mercy upon us . . . You'd think they'd have the decency to go. They get pleasure out of causing trouble and giving me a bad name abroad—padre, yes, have mercy upon us —and what can I do? They tie my hands and stand in front of the gun and when I squeeze the trigger, it's my fault because they're aggressive enough to get hit. I must make a note of that for the cabinet meeting. (*He writes in a little notebook*) Did I say we acknowledge and bewail our manifold . . . Note how I'm on my knees. I wish they could see that abroad! I'm not ashamed to pray for guidance, how else could I be sure I was doing the right thing? But I mustn't stay here talking, padre, enjoyable though that is. We must put our hand to the plow, amen.

PRIEST: Lift up your hearts.

PRIME MINISTER: We lift them up.

(*An Inspector comes in. The Priest goes to the altar and prepares communion*)

INSPECTOR: The Kaffirs are still there, sir.

PRIME MINISTER: You showed them the planes?

INSPECTOR: Did do, sir.

PRIME MINISTER: And they still stayed?

INSPECTOR: So we brought in reinforcements. The lads didn't like it. They were playing rugger, tennis, cricket, and other mind-cleansing and body-building games, but they came when they heard the summons.

PRIME MINISTER: What about the Saracens?

INSPECTOR: As useless as the planes.

PRIME MINISTER: Oh.

INSPECTOR: They're British made, so you wouldn't expect them to work. You might as well send them out on the milk round. Never mind, we've got our own personal weapons, all made in the home country—they'll shift them. (*He goes to the altar, where the Priest is making ritual gestures*) Could I disturb you for a moment, padre? (*He takes rifles from under the altar*) Could you say a prayer for the boys while you're at it, padre?

PRIEST: I'm always praying for the boys.

INSPECTOR: Thank you, padre. We'll do you a good turn someday, man. (*The Inspector leaves. The Priest turns to the Prime Minister with the bread and wine*)

PRIME MINISTER: Time spent on your knees is never wasted.

PRIEST: I wish more people thought like you, Prime Minister.

PRIME MINISTER: So do I.

PRIEST: (*Offering the bread*) Take and eat this in remembrance that Christ died for thee and feed on him . . . (*Loud rifle fire, off. After twenty seconds he speaks again*) Do you hear a noise, Prime Minister?

PRIME MINISTER: No.

PRIEST: I think perhaps there *is* a sound. Perhaps we should go and see if we can . . .

PRIME MINISTER: I don't know what you hear, but I can't hear it. *My* mind is entirely concentrated on the appropriate holy thoughts.

PRIEST: Oh, so is mine! But I thought I . . . well, your hearing is better than mine.

PRIME MINISTER: Then let's get on. I can't keep the cabinet waiting. (*The rifle fire stops and the Inspector comes in*)

INSPECTOR: We had to use fire, sir.

PRIME MINISTER: Dear me.

INSPECTOR: They wouldn't go. And the lads were impatient. They'd been pulled away in the middle of their matches, you see, sir. Naturally they were keen to get back and win! There's no fun in shooting at people nowadays. Too many rules in the game. It doesn't really qualify as a sport any more, though mind you, the lads still try to play in the spirit of the old amateurs, even if they've turned professional. But it can't hold a candle to wildfowling. You've shot one man and you've shot them all. Still, they put up a show.

PRIME MINISTER: What was the final score?

INSPECTOR: Sixty-nine–zero. They certainly didn't let the opposition walk over them. The lads really put their backs into the training. There *were* a few they could have brought off if they'd been on the ball. They set them up, but they couldn't follow it through. Still, they showed real style and you can't ask fairer than that. They've gone off to the shower. Might be as well if you had a word with them, sir. After all, they won. They're good lads and I don't doubt for one moment they're their own hardest critics. I watched their faces and you could see how when one of them missed he knew he'd let the team down. The lady folk have prepared some beer and sandwiches and a few party dainties—perhaps you'd care to join us, padre?

PRIEST: Later on, I'd like that.

PRIME MINISTER: We'll just give them a pat on the head now, while they're hosing down. They like to see the board going 'round straight after the whistle. Show them you take an interest.

(*The Prime Minister, Inspector and Priest go. Christ comes down from the cross. He raises his hands to speak, but drops them. He puts something in the communion wine, and goes back onto the cross. The Prime Minister and Priest return*)

PRIEST: Most of them were shot in the back.

PRIME MINISTER: (*Kneeling*) It's the nature of the Kaffir to turn his back when confronted with the white man's weapons.

PRIEST: Shall we finish this?

PRIME MINISTER: It's a long day but it has its rewards.

PRIEST: (*Offers bread*) Take this and remember that Christ died for thee.

PRIME MINISTER: (*Swallows*) You know, the lads think it's all over now and they can go home and sleep quietly in their beds like little children, but I'll be burning the midnight oil. The paper work a thing like this involves. The paper work—it never stops! I only wish you could dispose of paper as easily as you dispose of people. Paper's more difficult to handle.

PRIEST: (*Offers wine*) Drink this in remembrance that Christ's blood was shed for thee and be thankful.

PRIME MINISTER: I don't begrudge them their sleep when they've earned it. But there are times when I could gladly lay down the burdens of the helm. (*Dies*)

(*The Inspector comes in*)

INSPECTOR: Did I hear a body falling? Too late! I shall examine the scene of the crime for clues and pounce on the accused with professional speed. Note how, as he faced his maker, he showed the whites of his eyes.

PRIEST: I wish it could have happened somewhere else. It looks bad here.

INSPECTOR: That's the mark of the black hand—no respect for the proprieties. This is a typical Kaffir foul—behind the umpire's back. I'm on to something here! A row of little spots. The accused was crying, unless I'm mistaken and he was peeing himself.

PRIEST: In church?

INSPECTOR: Just a little joke, padre. No intention of mocking the cloth. (*He follows the trail of spots to the cross*) And here we have just what I was looking for: a little puddle. (*To Christ*) Just a moment, sir. (*Takes out a notebook*) Would you mind telling me your name, permanent address and occupation and explain what you're doing trespassing on these premises?

PRIEST: I think there's a mistake, Inspector.

INSPECTOR: You know this fellow, sir?

PRIEST: Yes.

INSPECTOR: (*Starts to put his notebook away*) In that case I take it you're not prepared to vouch for this gentleman's bona fides.

PRIEST: Well . . . not entirely.

INSPECTOR: I see. Dearie me then. In that case I must ask the gentleman to accompany me to the station.

PRIEST: No. I . . . let me pray for guidance.

INSPECTOR: In the circumstances, I think prayer comes under the Conspiracy Act.

PRIEST: That makes it difficult. I'll have to guess the answer. (*To Christ*) I'm afraid I must ask you to leave.

INSPECTOR: I'm sorry, padre. It's gone further than that.

PRIEST: This is the best way. The whole incident could be blown up out of proportion.

INSPECTOR: You mean the gentleman has friends abroad?

PRIEST: Frankly, I'm not sure, but it's not worth the risk.

INSPECTOR: In that case I'll leave the matter in your hands, as there's no one here to represent Interpol.

PRIEST: (*To Christ*) You've heard, I've been able to spare you some of the public disgrace. But now I must ask you to collect your things and go immediately. I can't risk your contaminating the young people we have here. I'm very disappointed in you. Oh, I'm not thinking of myself and all the wasted effort I've thrown away, but you've let yourself down. It's too late to say it now, but you weren't without promise, and you've thrown all that away. You'll regret it in a few years and you'll look back on this and see we were right. I hope by then you'll have learned something. You'll never make anything of yourself if you go on the way you've started. I shall say no more. (*Christ comes down from the cross and starts to leave. He stops when the Priest talks again*) God knows what your family will think of this. You've got a good family. They gave you a start in life many others would envy, and you've let them down, too. I shan't go on. Please leave quietly. It's too late for explanations and apologies. It's past amends. There is some conduct that's too underhand to be put right. I've finished now. (*Christ leans against the cross in boredom*) Why didn't you say if something was troubling you? You know you could always turn to me. I'm not a hard man, I'm fairly reasonable and open—I think I can say that. There's nothing more to be said. The whole thing is best left in silence. In fact I'm too upset to speak (*Christ hangs one arm over the horizontal bar of the cross*) I'd give you another chance if I thought it would help. But there's no point. I have to remember the others in my charge. It's not fair on others to allow someone like you to continue to be in a respectable institution like this. Go, and I hope you find somewhere where you can fit in. Have I made myself clear? (*Christ goes*) It leaves a space. I shan't get used to a space up there. It seems wrong. The congregation expects something.

INSPECTOR: I'll help you out, padre. (*He gestures off-stage. A young Policeman comes on. He is dressed in a fascist-style uniform with an armband*) Here we are, Kedgie. Here's a nice easy job for you. Stand up there on that wooden appliance. Up you get, lad.

PRIEST: Won't he find it tiring?

INSPECTOR: No. He's used to controlling traffic. He'll be all right if he puts his mind to it. You can do anything if you put your mind to it. Comfortable, Kedgie? Keep staring straight ahead, lad. Just think how they taught you to keep watch on the frontier. (*To Priest*) That makes the place look tidier.

PRIEST: True, it's an improvement.

INSPECTOR: Didn't like the look of the other one. You can pick them out when you've had a few years in my job.

PRIEST: I sometimes had doubts myself. But he had such good references, so what can you . . .

INSPECTOR: You're looking fine, Kedgie. You'll be relieved in two hours, lad. Do you know what to do? We'll just have a little rehearsal. We don't want any slip-ups. Church parade is a parade like any other parade. The same smartness and superior turnout and every movement at the double. (*Shouts order*) Relief Christ, to your post, *march!* (*A replica of Kedgie marches in*) Relief Christ, *halt!* (*The Relief Christ halts in front of the cross*) Old Christ—descend—*cross!* Smartly, smartly, there! Stop waving your arms about, you're not blessing the multitude now! Watch your step, eyes front, head up, don't look down or you'll fall through the water! By god, I'll make martyrs of the pair of you! (*Kedgie has come down from the cross*) Relief Christ—wait for it, wait for it. Don't anticipate the word of command! Mount *cross!* I don't want to see you move, I want to see you there! Get up that cross there! Halt! Put your arms out. Put your arms out, lad! Don't stand there with your arms dangling! You look as though you're going to start playing with yourself! Wank in your own time, not the army's! (*Turns to Padre*) There we are, padre, now we're beginning to get somewhere. We're playing on our home ground.

PRIEST: I feel much safer. There's someone up there watching over me and I can trust and rely on him. (*Indicates bread and wine*) It's a pity to waste all this. Would you like to take communion?

INSPECTOR: Oh, I . . .

PRIEST: I've changed the wine.

INSPECTOR: In that case . . . It's a very civil thought of yours, padre, and I'd be glad to oblige. Call on me any time. (*The Inspector kneels and the Priest offers him communion*)

Curtain

René de Obaldia

THE UNKNOWN GENERAL

(*Translated by Donald Watson*)

René de Obaldia

Poet, novelist and dramatist, René de Obaldia was born in Hong Kong in 1918. His mother was French, his father Panamanian. He was educated in France and was a prisoner of war for four years. Since that time, he has produced several volumes of verse and prose, short stories and novels, of which *The Centenarian* (translated by Alexander Trocchi) is perhaps the best known. His first play, *Jenusia,* was produced by Jean Vilar in 1960 at the Théâtre National Populaire with considerable success. Drama critics immediately linked his name with writers such as Audiberti, Ionesco, Beckett, and Giraudoux. This play was performed in New York in 1969, after a previous production in London. His short plays, *Seven Impromptus for Leisure,* have been translated into twenty languages and performed all over the world. Other short plays followed, including *The Unknown General,* published for the first time in the United States in this collection. The comedy, which wittily satirizes the absurd pretensions of a little man with inflated military and political fantasies, was performed in Paris by the Comédie Française in 1971.

His full-length plays include *The Satyr of La Villette; Wind in the Branches of the Sassafras;* and his most recent, . . . *And Then Came the Bang.*

René de Obaldia has received numerous prizes for his work in various fields. It is characterized by great verbal dexterity and sensitivity. He is a humorous writer, but his humor is dark around the edges. He undeniably has affiliations with the Absurdist movement, but he contributes his own brand of *joi de vivre* to his work.

The play was translated from the French by Donald Watson, who was born in London in 1920. He spent the war years in Algeria, Italy and Austria, where he acquired a taste for languages. After the war he graduated from University College, London, and from 1950 spent five years in France doing research on modern French drama. A chance meeting with Eugène Ionesco in 1952 led to the translation of most of the latter's work for the theatre. For the past fifteen years he has been lecturing in the French department at Bristol University, specializing in French drama.

Two volumes of his translations of René de Obaldia's plays have been published in England and he also has translated plays by Marivaux and Musset as well as Robert Pinget's novel, *The Inquisitory,* and Ionesco's critical work, *Notes and Counternotes.*

He has directed students in a number of classic and modern French plays, and it was at Bristol that he launched the first English-language production of René de Obaldia's *Impromptus* in the early 1960's.

Characters:

MARGUERITE

ACHILLES, GENERAL BEAULIEU DE CHAMFORT-MOURON

CAPTAIN KRASPECK

Scene One:

"Nine rooms in a row," as the General says. Yes, but vertical. *The last one, where the action takes place, is the kitchen: a sort of anti-atomic shelter which is as clean and tidy as a hospital ward. There is no reason why the General should not make his entrance through the ceiling.*

Marguerite is sitting on a stool, peeling potatoes.

MARGUERITE: (*After a long moment of silence*) Is it better to talk? Or keep quiet? Or just mutter? (*With her knife in her hand, suddenly declaiming*) "Then, as they muttered together, the Lord moved up his Right Wing. A cloud of avenging angels swooped down from heaven. Their faces were brighter than their swords . . . A woman, who was holding her newborn child up to the empyrean, found, as she drew him closer to embrace him, that he was old and wizened. 'The time is not far off' she ventured . . . The whole city was destroyed . . ." (*To the audience*) My father was a clergyman. He reinvented the Bible out of large glasses of spirits. (*A pause*) Keep quiet? How can you keep quiet? Speak out? How can you speak out? How can you mutter? Yesterday, men would just come out with what they had to say, they bubbled over. Today, now, they're worn thin as old pebbles. Now they have nothing to say. They're trying to find a way to communicate nothing: all this proliferation of Civil Service reports on nothingness! (*Taking up her potato-peeling again*) Peeling potatoes is still perhaps the greatest adventure of our time . . . (*A pause*) "Civilization in pictures"! Cinema, television; we don't live any more, we watch ourselves live. It's utterly absorbing. Not a minute to ourselves, not a minute for other people. Where have the minutes gone? Time has turned into dough, time is blind, congealed. That's why I like peeling potatoes. The hand quiets the mind. I take my time . . . (*Another silence*) To listen to me anyone would think I was an abandoned, cast-off, bitter woman. A woman who's reflected on the condition of her sex and who still hasn't joined the Salvation Army. An extremely unhappy woman . . . (*With some violence*) Well, I'm not! See? Get that straight. I've all I need to make me happy: I'm married, my husband loves me, and he's a general. Not just any general, a brain! Specially entrusted with the aerial defense of the territory. When we realize how crumbly the earth is these days and know it's surrounded by air, we can estimate the crushing responsibility that weighs on my spouse's shoulders! If he turns out to be odd, apoplectic, mixed up, sporadic, Chinese, we can forgive him. No children: the general's no. (*Imitating him*) "I have no wish for the enemy to pulverize my sons. I have no wish to be the father of my orphans!" And yet I should have liked to know what sort of features and character would have stemmed from our embraces. No children. After us a vast desert. (*Noise of an explosion that shakes the whole house*) Here he is! (*Picking up a potato again, she peels it with great humility*)

(*Achilles bursts into the kitchen. He is in mufti, but has field glasses slung around his shoulders. Under his arm, a briefcase, which he throws on the table*)

ACHILLES: (*A tough and tense expression on his face*) Still in the kitchen!

MARGUERITE: Relax, Achilles! Relax.

ACHILLES: And this mania for peeling potatoes . . .

MARGUERITE: (*An attempted light touch*) From the earth, dear General! It's good to come down to earth now and again, back to our bodies, too . . .

ACHILLES: Words, more words. I married an intellectual.

MARGUERITE: Achilles! When I walk 'round the local district, I'm the only woman the grocers point at and say, "She hasn't written any novels yet. She hasn't even appeared on television."

ACHILLES: That would be the last straw! On top of all my other problems!

MARGUERITE: *More* problems?

ACHILLES: The same ones, always the same. But bigger ones.

MARGUERITE: They're growing older, like you, Achilles. That's natural.

ACHILLES: My position is untenable. (*Shouting*) Un-tenable! I'm entrusted with the defense of the territory. Well, the territory is indefensible.

MARGUERITE: Everyone knows that, my dear! Don't wake the dead!

ACHILLES: That's just it, everyone knows it. That's the worst of it. (*He takes a tube from his pocket, opens it and swallows a pill*)

MARGUERITE: You're not going to have another nervous breakdown?

ACHILLES: What do you expect, Marguerite? I'm an honest man, incurably honest. Helvetic blood runs through my veins. This comedy makes me sick. All these scratch solutions. All those dummies leaning over me in a jangle of medals and decorations. All those plans and counter-plans, those plandi-dandies flung in each other's faces, which won't do any good. They're born obsolete. Electronics move faster than thought. This very morning, at the close of the General Staff meeting, I gave in my resignation again. (*A worried look from Marguerite*) Once again, it was refused.

MARGUERITE: (*With a sigh of relief*) Ah!

ACHILLES: (*More and more downcast*) I'm irreplaceable!

MARGUERITE: There, you see, Achilles!

ACHILLES: Irreplaceable! (*With a sneering laugh*) If they put a she-monkey in my place, the whole world wouldn't notice a thing!

MARGUERITE: Achilles!

ACHILLES: Once the enemy presses that button, we disintegrate on the spot! An honorable spot, without distinction of sex or color. All of us, you hear? You and your potatoes!

MARGUERITE: Don't shout, Achilles. There are only two of us!

ACHILLES: No time even to rectify the position, to bat an eyelid . . . pulverized! Just a few pinpoints in the noosphere . . . (*He swallows another pill*) And I'm talking about the enemy. But if a friend has the same idea, if he wants to play games and launch a preventative attack, it's exactly the same old merry-go-round! Up we go! Everyone up to heaven! With just one difference, of course. That it's worse with friends. (*A silence*)

MARGUERITE: Achilles, do you believe in the resurrection of the flesh in eternal life?

ACHILLES: Those ridiculous questions of yours again! It's not because your father was a clergyman . . .

MARGUERITE: (*Dreamily*) I often think about the trumpets of the Last Judgment. I hear them. From the four points of the compass, bones stream out of their tombs, and gallop off and gather together, exalting in the face of the Lord.

ACHILLES: There won't be any more bones, Marguerite. Get that well fixed in your skull, no more bones! Nothing but intangible ashes the color of bricks, the ghosts of ashes. The death of death. An inconceivable void.

MARGUERITE: Well then, Achilles, what about the resurrection of the flesh?

ACHILLES: You really think you're so beautiful?

MARGUERITE: Achilles!

ACHILLES: An abstraction, that's all. The quintessence of abstraction. A bone, that's concrete, terribly concrete. The sovereignty of bones and forms is over! Now we live only in the abstract. Pinpricks, reflections, pictures, pictures, pictures. As if heaven itself had turned into a great television screen. No more flesh, no more blood!

MARGUERITE: (*Very gently*) I'm here, Achilles. My reactions are simple: I love you.

ACHILLES: Painting is abstract, music is abstract, literature, architecture, procreation, my command and the Ten Commandments. The object rules as Lord and master. (*With a sneering laugh*) The object! "Be objective, General." Who do they take me for? For a saucepan? We must admit the evidence. Man is obviously out of place on this planet. (*He swallows another pill*)

MARGUERITE: That's three pills you've swallowed already, since you came home! Be reasonable, Achilles!

ACHILLES: Don't worry, Marguerite, they don't explode. I bought them myself, and I take care to go to a different chemist each time. They won't get me that way.

MARGUERITE: Your life's in danger, Achilles?

ACHILLES: So what? Every life is in danger.

MARGUERITE: But you, Achilles, you . . . Oh! It makes me shiver. It was only by a miracle you escaped the last attempt.

ACHILLES: Not a miracle, a trick. The assassin's arm wasn't his own. A different one had been grafted on while he slept. He fired at me, but too high. It was Colonel Trochu who bit the dust.

MARGUERITE: What a life! Achilles, why don't you hire a double? Someone as like you as two peas in a pod. Two generals, who'd inspect the bases for you, who'd deliver your speeches, while you stayed peacefully with me in the kitchen, chattering and spinning away like an ordinary mortal.

ACHILLES: Don't tempt me, woman. (*A silence. He goes to the kitchen window and, seizing his field glasses, looks at the view*) The sea is pregnant today.

MARGUERITE: (*Terrified*) The sea?

ACHILLES: (*Inspecting the horizon*) One aircraft carrier, two cruisers, five destroyers, one battleship: "The Mauriac" . . . , one motor torpedo boat . . . Ah! Ah! A black seagull, all black!

MARGUERITE: (*In a thin voice*) But . . . but . . . the sea is more than three hundred miles away . . .

ACHILLES: Secret field glasses, with infra-red and ultraviolet. They cut out the landscape to show you nothing but the kappa point, the observation fallout point. If I wear them well in evidence, it's so no one gets the idea they're secret.

MARGUERITE: All these inventions, there's no time to keep up-to-date! (*Achille now training his field glasses on Marguerite*)

Achilles, don't look at me like that! Please! (*She covers herself with her hands as if she were naked*) Achilles, what are you doing?

ACHILLES: Your skeleton's just like you. As clean, as neat, as peremptory . . . (*Dropping his field glasses*) You're a fine woman, Marguerite.

MARGUERITE: Darling, instead of . . . (*Timidly*) You . . . you wouldn't like to help me peel potatoes?

ACHILLES: Potatoes! Potatoes! You, a general's wife! How can the Generaless Beaulieu de Chamfort-Mouron born Plouadec, take pleasure in this kitchen, in ancillary occupations!

MARGUERITE: Achilles, we won't start that again! You know very well that . . .

ACHILLES: I know, I know. I'm forbidden to employ any domestic servant, because of espionage.

MARGUERITE: Not even your nanny!

ACHILLES: But you could play your part in a different way and not look so much like the cook I haven't got. Why don't you ever get dolled up and show yourself off?

MARGUERITE: Get dolled up?

ACHILLES: Your undress uniform, with your breasts taking the air?

MARGUERETE: (*Submissively*) If that's what you want, Achilles. We've been joined by the sacrament of marriage, so it won't be concupiscence. (*A pause*) Do you want me to be quite naked, except for my jewels, like the other evening?

ACHILLES: No, stay here, Marguerite. I'm tired, terribly tired.

MARGUERITE: (*Moved, pressing her husband's head against her breasts*) Poor General. My poor little General's head . . .

ACHILLES: Undermined.

MARGUERITE: Poor little undermined General!

ACHILLES: This morning, they not only refused my resignation, but they gave me another increase!

MARGUERITE: (*Happily*) You'll go right through the ceiling soon!

ACHILLES: My monthly pay is now equal to a hundred-and-ninety-nine times the annual salary of a skilled craftsman! A turner and shaper, for example.

MARGUERITE: What sort of calculation's that! You can't compare a turner, even if he *is* a shaper . . . ?

ACHILLES: And, what's more, I'm quite incapable of preventing the poor bugger flying into dust through the atmosphere one fine Sunday morning like a flea that's been charged with dynamite!

MARGUERITE: That's life, Achilles!

ACHILLES: No, no, it's dishonest.

MARGUERITE: Once it used to be the plague, cholera, tsetse fly . . . what else? Monte Carlo! The number of people who committed suicide in the gardens of the Casino! Don't complain because the bride's too beautiful! (*A pause*) I agree, at the moment, while you're still in the service, we can hardly take advantage of the money. But think about your retirement, about our old bones . . .

ACHILLES: Our old bones! So you haven't understood a thing! The sovereignty of the bone is *fertig! Fertig!* Soon we'll be used as fertilizers for shooting stars, giving our last gasps to the asteroids and joining the gaseous group of the supernovae. Uranium is beckoning us! From the celestial depths, I can already hear a silent chuckle. Like octopuses, the galaxies hold out for us their slimy loathsomely milky arms. Relentless suction is about to follow!

MARGUERITE: You really do look on the black side. Do you know what I think, Achilles? You spend too much time with the military.

ACHILLES: I'm sorry, Marguerite, I admit I'm not a very lively husband.

MARGUERITE: You don't have to think about being lively, but being a general.

ACHILLES: That's right. And then I come back here, and see you relegated to the kitchen. Who would suspect we had nine rooms at our disposal, in a row?

MARGUERITE: With twelve armored doors!

ACHILLES: That's it! Armored.

MARGUERITE: You've no idea, Achilles, all those doors, each weighing three tons. I haven't got the strength to close them, and that makes for drafts. Here, in the kitchen, I feel all right. I think about you while I get on with the chores. I reread the Bible.

ACHILLES: You're a saintly woman, Marguerite.

MARGUERITE: Oh, no! Don't say that! If you only knew all the ideas that cross my mind . . .

ACHILLES: Oh, yes? For example?

MARGUERITE: (*Embassassed*) Nothing . . .

ACHILLES: What do you mean, nothing? What sort of ideas cross your mind that you hide from me? (*He takes hold of his field glasses*)

MARGUERITE: You're not going back to your field glasses!

ACHILLES: (*Inexorably*) I'm listening.

MARGUERITE: (*Confused*) Boloney . . . moonshine . . .

ACHILLES: Moonshine? What else?

MARGUERITE: I often have the same dream: you are an ironmonger, I am your wife, an ironmongress. We live in a little village. The schoolteacher, the parson, the lawyer, the woman taken in adultery, it's all so peaceful. When we shut up shop, all excited by the blue bags, the steel wool, the oil of turpentine, we go up to our bedroom and pull the curtains and . . .

ACHILLES: And then?

MARGUERITE: (*Whose voice is getting fainter*) . . . And nine months later, there is born a little ironmonger Beaulieu de Chamfort-Mouron . . . (*A silence*)

ACHILLES: A sense of occasion doesn't seem to be your strong point!

MARGUERITE: You're the one who persuaded me into . . .

ACHILLES: (*Seizes his field glasses and returns to the window*) Aha! The battleship has hoisted sail! What's that, a whale or a shrimp? (*He remains there contemplating the view, without uttering a syllable*)

MARGUERITE: Have I hurt you, Achilles? Please, say something!

ACHILLES: What is there to eat this evening?

MARGUERITE: Black pudding.

ACHILLES: Bravo! But don't cook it too long. I only like my black pudding blue.

MARGUERITE: (*After a moment*) Oh, I know what you're thinking, you know!

ACHILLES: (*In a controlled voice*) Marguerite, once and for all, you can cross out our children unless you want them to bear a terrible cross. I'm in a very good position to speak to you like this.

MARGUERITE: (*Exploding*) But, Achilles, miracles can happen! If you think of all the plagues that have scourged mankind since the flood, isn't it miraculous that we're here now, the two of us, in the twentieth century, and in the dry, as if nothing had ever gone wrong?

ACHILLES: Listen to me carefully, woman. Suppose a generation does survive the atom "by a miracle," that will be still more terrifying!

MARGUERITE: What do you mean?

ACHILLES: (*Getting carried away*) I have no wish for my offspring to have webbed feet, a plastic head with one rigid eye, three navels, a grubby nose, no testicles, an anal appendix, grass hair, and one ear shaped like an egg, and then start clamoring for bread made with plutonium, in a language he articulates like an eel!

MARGUERITE: Achilles! You're . . . you're . . . you're delirious!

ACHILLES: Yes, I . . . I am delirious. Forget what you've just heard. Forget it with all your might, Marguerite. That meeting of chiefs of staff upset my nervous system. (*He swallows another pill*)

MARGUERITE: Achilles! Oh, Lord! You make my flesh creep!

ACHILLES: Lucky is the flesh that still can creep!

MARGUERITE: Achilles! You . . . I . . . you . . . you. . . .

ACHILLES: Great weariness. Don't pay any attention. Even the mind becomes a distorting mirror.

MARGUERITE: Distorting? That's it! Deforming! Oh, Lord! What can I do for you?

ACHILLES: One thing would bring me relief . . .

MARGUERITE: Yes, yes . . .

ACHILLES: A footbath.

MARGUERITE: Why of course. Certainly. Why didn't you ask me before? The basin's just here, under the sink. Straightaway. At once, General! (*She gets busy*)

ACHILLES: You are a model wife, Marguerite. A model. As one speaks of a model prisoner, a model rocket, a model cow, a model co-operative store . . .

MARGUERITE: Relax, Achilles, please! Take the stool, it's better for you.

ACHILLES: Model stool. (*He obeys. He sits down on the stool, and turns up the bottom of his trousers. Marguerite brings the basin into which he plunges his feet*)

MARGUERITE: Too hot?

ACHILLES: Perfect. Just right. (*He lets out a huge sigh of satisfaction*)

MARGUERITE: And what if I added a little potassium? Or chlorine? It's toughening.

ACHILLES: No, no, thank you. After all, I'm not a footslogger! (*He moves his feet around in the basin*) Gentle waves and frothy scum, fluidity, fish nibbling at the clouds . . . Let's forget the heavy water, let's forget.

MARGUERITE: Don't think about anything any more. (*The General lifts up first one foot, then the other*) Your heel doesn't hurt you?

ACHILLES: Still a few twinges. It's a habit.

MARGUERITE: It's hereditary, all right.

ACHILLES: Yes, a question of genes, differential genes. Who's not got some little ailment? (*A pause*)

MARGUERITE: You wouldn't like me to settle down beside you and read you the Bible? (*A strange sound rings out, causing them both to jump*) Lord! Who's ringing at our door? This is not the moment!

ACHILLES: I'd forgotten. Captain Kraspeck.

MARGUERITE: Captain Kraspeck?

ACHILLES: An agent from the Seventh Bureau. Our future Head of Counterespionage. Of Czech origin, as the name suggests.

MARGUERITE: You could have done without that!

ACHILLES: Of the greatest importance.

MARGUERITE: Anyway, you can't see him in here . . . and with me looking like this. (*She hurriedly puts her hair straight*)

ACHILLES: Don't worry, Marguerite, the Captain's been around! (*Another ring*)

MARGUERITE: But, but . . .

ACHILLES: Go and open it. No, wait. What a fool I am! (*From his inside pocket he takes a minute box, to which is attached a lead with a small implement at the end. He fixes the implement in his ear*)

MARGUERITE: Now what on earth's *this* contraption?

ACHILLES: (*Bringing the box in front of his mouth as if it were a microphone*) Captain Kraspeck . . . ? Greetings, Captain. Press the ninth button along, starting from the top, and ignore the electric shock . . . That's right. You can go down the three steps and turn immediately to your left describing an angle of forty-six degrees. Mind your head! After that, no more problems. You go through nine rooms in a row. You only have to push open the armored doors. I'm right at the other end. Beg pardon? . . . Thanks. Not too bad. I'll expect you. *Bien, bien!"* (*He puts the box back in his pocket*)

MARGUERITE: I ask you!

ACHILLES: At headquarters, Captain Kraspeck is suspected of being a double agent. Personally, I'm convinced the captain's a treble.

MARGUERITE: Lord!

ACHILLES: Amazingly daring. This is the one who delivered us the Kong Plan.

MARGUERITE: The Kong Plan?

ACHILLES: Which can be translated as, "Gather ye rosebuds while ye may." The famous extermination plan. I'm going to have a hard nut to crack. (*He swallows a pill while the sound of an explosion is heard*)

MARGUERITE: Fancy slamming doors like that!

ACHILLES: The story of the Kong Plan deserves a whole volume.

MARGUERITE: Are you going to stay with your feet in the water?

ACHILLES: Thought out by us, stolen by the Naybabs, pinched again by the Naybis, then when it had fallen into the hands of the Naybots—our allies at the time—Captain Kraspeck managed to get it back for us, but distinctly improved. The enemy worked hard on it. (*A fresh explosion*)

MARGUERITE: He doesn't do things by halves! Our poor drawing-room chandelier!

ACHILLES: (*Dreamily*) Every now and again, the great powers ought to swap their chiefs of staff, their presidents, their prostitutes, their aluminum, their pineapples, their rivers . . .

MARGUERITE: One thing I can't understand, Achilles. You admit yourself the territory is indefensible . . .

ACHILLES: Ssh! Not so loud, Marguerite, not so loud!

MARGUERITE: (*In a low voice*) But it's no secret to anyone. So why this gigantic network of spies, all those lives which . . .

ACHILLES: Solidarity of caste. Everyone plays the game. On one side or the other a few fanatics would, in fact, suffice to reduce this globe to black crepe.

MARGUERITE: And so?

ACHILLES: (*Forced back to his defensive position*) And so, yes, yes, the army is quite useless. Anachronistic. But that's something the army doesn't admit. Will never admit . . . They'd rather blow up Uranus, Jupiter, Neptune, Venus . . . (*A strident sound. Achilles tightens the knot of his tie*) Come in. (*A long silence. Shouting*) Come in!

(*The door opens. Marguerite is bowled over. Captain Kraspeck turns up, in fact, in the form of a ravishing pinup, underage and decisive*)

CAPTAIN: (*Who was probably not expecting to see her superior officer taking a footbath*) Oh! Am I disturbing you, General?

ACHILLES: (*Excited, exaggerating the joviality*) Not at all! By no means! Come in! I like this sort of improvisation. You must just forgive me for not getting up . . . (*Making his introductions from a distance*) My wife . . . Captain Kraspeck.

CAPTAIN: *Comment allez-vous?*

MARGUERITE: (*Short of breath*) *Mademoiselle, Monsieur.* Captain.

ACHILLES: *Eh bien!* Now we've got that over . . . Make yourself comfortable, Captain: take your coat off. Your skirt. Take off anything you like.

MARGUERITE: (*Trying to pull herself together*) In here, it's not cold.

ACHILLES: Even if the month of December has succeeded the month of November. It's winter, what!

CAPTAIN: (*In a sophisticated baby-girl voice, like a starlet*) Yes, the seasons, nowadays, are just like men! All upset. (*Removing her raincoat, she displays a delectable figure*)

ACHILLES: And upsetting!

MARGUERITE: (*Dryly*) Pass me your leather coat. I'll hang it up.

CAPTAIN: (*Handing the raincoat over to her*) Please don't trouble yourself. (*She primps her hair*) It seems in Alaska the fields are full of violets.

ACHILLES: Oh, really! Well, well!

CAPTAIN: Whereas in Honolulu, a cemetery of snow.

ACHILLES: You're very well informed, Captain.

CAPTAIN: I listened to the last news bulletin, General.

ACHILLES: It's true the radio is a mine of information. We

don't pay enough attention to it. It was over the radio that the Woaks discovered they were at war. President Boro was getting a tan on the beach, with his transistor. When I say "getting a tan," it's only a manner of speaking, President Boro being as black as my hat. But sit down. Marguerite, pull up a chair!

MARGUERITE: (*Hurriedly*) Of course! What was I thinking of! Sit down, *Mademoi* . . . Ca . . . Captain.

CAPTAIN: (*Sitting down*) Oh! I can quite well remain standing! (*She crosses her legs, and takes up a voluptuous pose, more and more the starlet. An embarrassed silence*)

ACHILLES: The steam from the water doesn't trouble you, Captain?

CAPTAIN: So long as it's only the steam . . .

ACHILLES: Yes, obviously.

CAPTAIN: When I was a girl, I used to take hot baths as a precaution against rheumatism, at Roscoff.

ACHILLES: At Roscoff! Well, well!

MARGUERITE: *You* know, Achilles. Roscoff, in Brittany? I used to have an aunt . . .

ACHILLES: (*Dryly*) I know only too well that Roscoff is not in Russia. Thank you, Marguerite.

CAPTAIN: But still! Geography moves so fast these days . . . (*A fresh silence*)

ACHILLES: You've come empty-handed, Captain. But skilful with them, I'm sure.

CAPTAIN: You flatter me, General! (*A pause*)

MARGUERITE: If I'm in the way . . .

ACHILLES: Why, not at all, not at all, Marguerite!

CAPTAIN: On the contrary.

ACHILLES: I'll tell you when you ought to go. What if you brought us in a fruit juice? A nice fruit juice out of the top drawer? (*Marguerite stands up*)

CAPTAIN: Not for me, thank you.

ACHILLES: It *was* for you, Captain. (*Marguerite sits down again*)

CAPTAIN: (*Pointing to the field glasses lying on the table*) Very fine field glasses!

ACHILLES: Very old ones. They used to belong to my great-grandcousin, Commander Viermals von Tripp.

CAPTAIN: Did they!

ACHILLES: They've seen a few battlefields, and heroes of every hue: brand new grenadiers, amorous hussars, Kurds, Croats and Bulgarians, cornflowers, poppies and cyclamens . . .

CAPTAIN: How good to look through them and see everything you describe!

MARGUERITE: (*Swiftly snatching them up*) My husband always leaves them lying about. I spend my time tidying up after him.

CAPTAIN: I think all men are like that, even the greatest.

ACHILLES: Oh! The greatest. We mustn't cherish our illusions. One fine evening you turn 'round and realize the path you've followed has vanished behind you. The eternally virgin forest . . . No footprints left. Our footsteps have melted away.

MARGUERITE: No matter, if we find them again in heaven. If they've been counted by the Lord.

ACHILLES: My wife is a clergyman's daughter.

CAPTAIN: Oh, yes? I was nearly a clergyman's daughter myself.

MARGUERITE: Really?

ACHILLES: And you changed your mind?

CAPTAIN: At the last moment my mother swung 'round in favor of a South American peacock. He abandoned her as soon as he discovered his activities had made her pregnant. I came into the world deprived of a father.

ACHILLES: Your life is a novel, Captain Kraspeck.

CAPTAIN: A novel. Let's say *several* novels, General.

ACHILLES: Indeed! (*A silence*)

MARGUERITE: That water must be cold now, with all our chattering. Would you like me to warm it up?

ACHILLES: For heaven's sake, Marguerite, eyes front! Stay

where you are! Stand at ease! You see, Captain, I mistake myself for Balzac, but *he* used to soak *his* feet in basins of coffee. He used to stay up night after night . . .

CAPTAIN: I'm sorry to have intruded upon your private life.

ACHILLES: It was I who asked you to come. Standing between two drafts, conversation is difficult. Here. Tell me, Captain . . . ?

CAPTAIN: General?

ACHILLES: I have informed my wife about your brilliant exploits. A claim, that goes without saying . . .

CAPTAIN: Delighted to have met the general's lady at last.

MARGUERITE: You could be my own daughter.

ACHILLES: So there's no reason why I shouldn't . . . (*Sharply*) It appears you went in for striptease in Ankara?

CAPTAIN: Correct, General.

ACHILLES: And despoiling the enemy of the Kong Plan wouldn't be unconnected with this . . . this exercise?

CAPTAIN: Correct, General.

ACHILLES: Piquant.

MARGUERITE: Steady nerves, I imagine?

ACHILLES: Steady nerves, steady nerves.

CAPTAIN: You see, General, friend or enemy, what simplifies my task is that all men are subject to a one-track mind.

ACHILLES: Yyyyesss . . .

CAPTAIN: Primeval.

ACHILLES: By the way, how's that charming and intelligent friend of yours?

CAPTAIN: Which one, General?

ACHILLES: The bio-chemist who made such sensational discoveries about the isotope? Oh! I don't seem to remember his name . . .

CAPTAIN: (*In an icy voice*) He is nameless now, General.

ACHILLES: What!

CAPTAIN: He has lost his identity and some of his physical attributes as well.

ACHILLES: (*Suddenly jumping to his feet in the basin and shouting*) But that's monstrous! Monstrous!

CAPTAIN: Take care, General, or your trousers will be taking a footbath.

ACHILLES: (*Scarlet*) Anyway, what proof have I that you're telling the truth, Captain Kraspeck, born Rostopchine?

MARGUERITE: Achilles!

CAPTAIN: (*Standing suddenly to attention and affecting the mechanical tones of the radio messages put out by the BBC to the Resistance*) "Athalie's hat is brimming over. I repeat: Athalie's hat is brimming over."

ACHILLES: (*In the same tone*) "This virgin, vivacious and fair day and age." (*With irony*) This fair day and age!

CAPTAIN: "The catfish has bitten its tail. Three times."

ACHILLES: "Like a hail of grape-shot from the charnel vineyard."

CAPTAIN: "Watch out for the caliber of Caliban."

ACHILLES: "Pegasus' wings are trailing in the inkwell."

CAPTAIN: "Our years are fleeting as a snail."

ACHILLES: "The Archbishop has retired into his mother's womb. Nine times."

CAPTAIN: "Monsieur and Madame Barbituric and their children."

ACHILLES: "The sunbeams in my fist are blinding Jupiter."

CAPTAIN: "Come into the garden Maud."

ACHILLES: *"Pierre qui roule n'amasse pas mousse!"*

CAPTAIN: *"Si senor."*

MARGUERITE: Why . . . why . . . You speak with other tongues! You're inspired by the Holy Spirit!

ACHILLES: "Gaston's hoop rolls on down to hell. I repeat: Gaston's hoop rolls on down to hell."

CAPTAIN: Hell, General, means the shameful part of God.

ACHILLES: Scrofulous.

CAPTAIN: Shameful.

ACHILLES: "With my heel I crush the bull's-eye."

CAPTAIN: "Eat the lynx."

ACHILLES: "Lynx-eye."

CAPTAIN: "Bolt it, it stinks."

MARGUERITE: Now then, now then! (*A pause; the General sweats copiously*)

ACHILLES: Now listen to me, Captain Kraspeck . . .

CAPTAIN: I'm listening.

ACHILLES: (*Who must surely be playing his last card*) "Wanted. A practising pederast, Catholic on the side."

CAPTAIN: (*Very airily*) "Is there anything to beat a boojum with?"

ACHILLES: (*Who is visibly breaking up*) Beg pardon?

CAPTAIN: "I repeat: Is there anything to beat a boojum with?"

ACHILLES: (*Completely knocked off his feet*) A . . . a . . . a boojum . . .

(Blackout)

Scene Two

Marguerite, sitting on a stool, is peeling potatoes, as at the start of the play, but this time in front of the closed curtain.

MARGUERITE: It was from that very moment my husband, General Beaulieu de Chamfort-Mouron, went mad. (*Recalling the scene*) The basin overturned, thousands of fish on the tiles racing off to the sea . . . Of course, he'd already had several nervous breakdowns. In no time he was sobbing to the daisies, kissing the earth and refusing to eat meat. Superficially, nothing has changed. A state secret. The General is irreplaceable. He still does his rounds in an atom-bomber, inspecting bases, making speeches, decorating the mothers of overlarge families . . . But *I,* I know. And so does Captain Kraspeck, who witnessed that frightful scene and who was, moreover, compelled at revolver-point to perform a striptease in front of us. A beautiful girl, I don't deny it. It's terrible how many eyes these potatoes have. (*She digs into the potato*) And now, Captain Kraspeck and he are inseparable, bound by a ghastly secret. And the hostile powers shake in their bases. And I . . . I, his wife for the duration, where shall I found my patience, energy and faith if not on the Bible, sustained by the durability of Holy Writ? (*Opening the book at random and reading*) "And it shall come to pass in that day, saith the Lord God, that I will cause the sun to go down at noon, and I will darken the earth in the clear day: And I will turn your feasts into mourning and all your songs into lamentation, and I will bring up sackcloth upon all loins, and baldness upon every head; and I will make it as the morning of an only *son,* and the end thereof as a bitter day . . . In that day shall the fair virgins and young men faint for thirst." (*She closes the Bible*) Amos, chapter eight, verses nine to thirteen. We've been lucky to hit upon a minor prophet. As far back as we can go, man is destined to extermination. My father, the clergyman, became so conscious of it, he drank in order to forget, to forget what he could remember. Amos, Isaiah, Joshua, Jeremy, Habakuk, Malachi, Job, John of Patmos, he clinked glasses with all the prophets, the minor and the major. In the end, when he'd turned quite puce, stinking of alcohol ten miles off, none of us dared strike a match in his presence, lest he flared up like a torch. He died by drowning . . . One false step. Several of those who saw his body drifting down the river were struck by his hat, which, suddenly welded to his head, endowed him with a dark halo. A saintly man. (*She goes on peeling potatoes*) My marriage with the General was for him a cause for pride. A lovely wedding. Ringing bells that were swathed in silk . . . At that stage the General was still only a cadet. But everything about him proclaimed the general: the very obstinate set of his brow, the close-cropped hair, the splayed-out ears, deeply pitted eyes that skulked in ambush, and that staring gaze that put pay to all argument, that bared you like a bayonet. Incomparably right-minded even when he was gauche. How could one guess this very righteousness would drive him insane? (*She attacks a potato*) These potatoes! I ought to have a different kind and only buy English ones, those Buddy Girls. Meanwhile, life must go on. "The Last Judgement is still taking a long time to prepare." Live. Hope. Plot and plan. Be the strong woman Israel speaks of. And when he comes back here, to his home, let him find his wife where he left her, making the same gestures, saying the same words, preparing the same footbath . . . Perhaps then I shall manage to cure him, to pacify him? Make him forget the atrocious battlefield he has become for himself, take him away from that creature—that creature who now clings to him like his shadow, like Scotch whisky, who . . . that creature . . .

(*Music for a tango. The curtain opens on a scene in a cabaret. Soft lights. Dance floor. In one corner, a table. A bottle of champagne in a bucket. Two glasses. A vase of flowers.*

Achilles, in full dress uniform, and Captain Kraspeck, in an evening dress, are dancing amorously, very close together. Sometimes their bodies separate: this is when the General executes a skilful side-step only to press his partner more tightly to him than ever, a moment later.

At the front of the stage, Marguerite carries on as before)

ACHILLES: (*While he is dancing*) Do you like the sea?

CAPTAIN: I prefer the mountains. (*A few steps*) And you?

ACHILLES: With me, it's lakes.

CAPTAIN: Lakes?

ACHILLES: Yes, I only feel really well by the side of a lake.

MARGUERITE: To be a lake, liquid metal . . . The mountains dip their head in it on the quiet. A few sails, like handkerchiefs. Oh, to be that tranquil mirror! (*End of the tango. Achilles and the Captain return to their table*)

ACHILLES: Champagne?

CAPTAIN: Yes, lots of champagne. (*He has no sooner filled her glass than she empties it, almost at once, and holds it out to him again*)

ACHILLES: I'm going to order a whole bucket of them!

CAPTAIN: Why not rather arrange for a pipe line, General, to run direct from the cellar to this glass?

ACHILLES: Is it the tango that makes you so thirsty?

CAPTAIN: No, General, it's life! (*She drinks. The General seizes the chance to swallow a pill, in great haste*)

MARGUERITE: What a life! If Achilles had been an ironmonger . . .

CAPTAIN: General Beaulieu de Chamfort-Mouron?

ACHILLES: (*Smiling*) Present, Captain Kraspeck!

CAPTAIN: It is true your name is Achilles?

ACHILLES: Yes, Achilles.

CAPTAIN: Really, you're so witty!

ACHILLES: (*Seizing her hand*) And you're so beautiful, Captain Kraspeck, if . . .

CAPTAIN: Sonia . . . Sonia Kraspeck.

ACHILLES: (*Dazzled*) Sonia! (*Same music. He gets up and bows. They dance*)

MARGUERITE: An ironmonger! A decent profession . . . with real Sundays. And me in a print dress, in a hat with flowers or fruit. And him poured into a tweed suit, always saying the right thing. Our five children, well combed and polished, holding each other by the hand in order of size. Order. There's greatness for you . . . Military band. How-do-you-dos. Blessings all 'round. (*The music breaks off. Just as the Captain and Achilles are about to sit down, it starts up again: they return at once to the dance floor.*)

CAPTAIN: Still the same tango!

ACHILLES: It's I who asked for it.

CAPTAIN: What strategy! Never rock-and-roll? Or the twist? A boogie? A surf?

ACHILLES: There are a lot of people here.

CAPTAIN: (*Pressing herself against him*) There's you!

ACHILLES: Sonia! Sonia! (*He kisses her passionately*)

CAPTAIN: (*Ecstatically*) Achilles! (*The music has stopped*)

MARGUERITE: Achilles! He'd have been a Gustave . . . or an Adolph. No, not Adolph!

ACHILLES: Sonia!

CAPTAIN: Achilles!

(*Their passion gets wilder. Achilles and the Captain slip over to their table. Achilles fills up the glasses*)

ACHILLES: It's wonderful, isn't it, what's happening to us?

CAPTAIN: So original!

ACHILLES: It *had to* happen.

CAPTAIN: Yes, a vague sort of necessity . . .

ACHILLES: Your hair, your eyes, your hands, your neck, your fine bones . . .

CAPTAIN: Your strike force, your power of persuasion and dissuasion . . . (*In a still more ambiguous tone*) V to the power of four squared . . .

ACHILLES: (*Almost blushing*) Sonia!

CAPTAIN: You who used to spit on conventional armaments!

ACHILLES: Don't let's talk about that now. At this moment this is a different man here in front of you. A man! And this man is gazing at you and discovering the whole of nature in a small compass.

CAPTAIN: (*Very coquettish*) Flatterer! (*She drinks. He swallows a pill*)

MARGUERITE: To stretch out idiotically in some meadow, with a buttercup between your teeth. To remain for several hours, just with a cow, a sheep or a lark. To watch and wait, with a trembling heart, for the first star to appear and to greet it with your tears. That's what's missing, that's what he'll never have, Achilles. He's a general.

CAPTAIN: (*Quietly drunk, stroking his face and in a blurred voice*) General Beaulieu de Chamfort-Mouron . . .

ACHILLES: Ssh! Ssh! (*He seizes the delicate hand stroking him and turns it towards him to examine the lines on it*)

MARGUERITE: But nature herself has become his enemy. Earth and sky conspire together, rock crumbles away, the desert is overpopulated: a dump for arms and robots aimed at total destruction. The desert is breeding another desert which only itself will know—and now we realize that the bowels of the sea are bloody. At night, the General flings himself on his bed fully dressed, dripping with sweat and decorations: the stars and the planets take it in turns to spy on him!

CAPTAIN: Are you looking at my heart line?

ACHILLES: (*Bowled over*) Sonia! Sonia! You have *three* life lines!

CAPTAIN: Are you complaining!

ACHILLES: It's too much. It's really too much!

CAPTAIN: I give you all three of them, Achilles.

ACHILLES: Sonia! (*He feverishly kisses her hand*) I can't believe this is real, I can't . . .

CAPTAIN: Reality always surpasses reality.

ACHILLES: This deserted room . . . we two . . . and thousands of men everywhere, except in here . . .

CAPTAIN: Your orders have been carried out to perfection.

ACHILLES: (*With a gentle gleam in his eyes*) Gather ye rosebuds while ye may . . .

CAPTAIN: (*Severely*) Oh, please, General, not another word about the Kong Plan.

ACHILLES: (*Taken aback*) But . . . but I wasn't thinking about the Kong Plan!

CAPTAIN: (*Feline*) Casanova!

ACHILLES: The absence of your body burns me up. Let's dance! This table that separates us . . . Come, Sonia, let's dance. (*He stands up*)

CAPTAIN: Without music?

ACHILLES: One moment . . . (*He takes out his revolver and fires a shot into the air. Immediately the tango gets going. He puts his weapon back in his holster, then puts his arms amorously 'round the Captain*)

CAPTAIN: (*Pressed against Achilles*) I love powerful men. (*A few steps*)

ACHILLES: It's extraordinary how concrete you are!

CAPTAIN: (*In one breath*) Even more than you know, darling.

ACHILLES: (*In a paroxysm of passion*) Sonia! I'm going crazy! I'm afraid I shall lose you . . . I . . . I'd like to die . . .

(*The music stops. The couple stop moving. Achilles and*

Sonia, one against the other, exchange a kiss. Time no longer exists. However, behind the General's back, the Captain makes a slight movement of the hand. A fantastic creature emerges from the shadows and slowly advances towards the General, who is lost in ecstasy. The creature raises its arms as it moves forward, with the manifest intention of strangling Achilles. Its hands are webbed. The creature is now only a few steps away from the General. The Captain immobilizes her prey, both panting, close together, but she keeps a formidably clear head. The creature . . . All at once, the General tears himself away from the arms of his temptress, executes an about turn and with a movement, swift as the hero of a cowboy film, shoots the creature down with one pistol shot. Immediately taking aim at the Captain).

ACHILLES: Don't move, Captain Kraspeck. Hands behind your back!

CAPTAIN: You really are magnificent.

ACHILLES: (*Assuming the mechanical tones of the code messages again*) "The praying mantis has forgotten her Latin."

CAPTAIN: "Leon is drinking his café crème at Verdun."

ACHILLES: "Watch out!" The paralytic is decamping three times."

CAPTAIN: (*Correcting him*) Once, General.

ACHILLES: Correct, once. What a pity, Captain Kraspeck, that you're working against us.

CAPTAIN: (*Sliding her hands lasciviously up her breasts*) Are you so very sure?

ACHILLES: Hands behind your back, Captain. I know what's hidden in your brassiere.

CAPTAIN: Without your field glasses . . . My compliments, General.

ACHILLES: (*Indicating the shapeless corpse*) I fear that exquisite creature of yours has given up the ghost.

CAPTAIN: His Holy Ghost! How you like to exaggerate, General!

ACHILLES: Hands up, Captain Kraspeck! (*Sarcastically*) There is nothing to beat a boojum with!

(*Blackout. Thunderous applause can be heard, and cheers from a delirious crowd. A more penetrating voice crying: "Encore! Encore!" When the light returns, the General is alone in the center of the dance floor; he returns his weapon to its holster and acknowledges the anonymous and abstract crowd, which goes on giving vent to its enthusiasm. As he waits for peace and quiet, he swallows a good number of pills*)

ACHILLES: (*Trying to get a word in and ride the noise of the ovation*) Thank you! Thank you! I . . . Thank you! You . . . I don't . . . The . . . And I, too . . . and I, too . . .

MARGUERITE: (*Shouting*) Silence!

(*A sudden silence. It is with great humility and like a man tottering with fatigue that Achilles takes a few steps forward to address the audience*)

ACHILLES: And I, too . . . I, too, should love to be like you, an everyday man, with everyday problems and everyday habits, sharing the everyday ideas of my daily paper. The golden mean. Well balanced. Healthy! . . . I wake myself up, wash myself down, deck myself out, and have my breakfast. I kiss my wife on the brow, my children on the mouth and set off for the place where I work. Good mornings. Respect. Wage increase. Back home in the evening I take off my shoes, mumble a few words and sink into the television. (*Assuming the sugary voice of a lady announcer*) "Good evening, dear tele-spectators, dear little children of the regiment. I hope you've grown up since yesterday." And here is the freshest of news: the Pope's corpse is floating in my soup, there's pole-vaulting in my spaghetti, I'm gobbling Miss Universe with my cream cheese. That's it, goodnight everyone! I slip into my pajamas, my striped pajamas, and go to sleep . . . (*Exhausted*) Yes, I sleep! I spend a wakeless night . . . Thank you! On Sunday, I put on my Sunday suit and go off in the car with all my family. Objective: to absorb the fresh air compressed between two towns. We return home tired but happy.

On Monday, I put on my Monday suit, and if I sometimes chance to put on Wednesday's suit on Thursday, that is what's called "playing a prank." By nature man is subject to pranks. And so my wife forgives me. She opens the door and holds out her wifely arms weeping, and I weep with her . . . Joy perhaps *is* sad? . . . There we are. That's all. An everyday man. But you've seen! You have seen! Melodrama, pure and simple. I am condemned to greatness, to melodrama! Greatness consigns you to the pit and the pit crawls with monsters. Captain Kraspeck is legion. I sleep when I'm upright and wake when I lie down, ceaselessly mounting guard over my guts. Perhaps I should have let myself be strangled? At last I should have gone over to the other side—the stronger side—without weapons or luggage, press-ganged straightaway into the army of the Lord. (*Getting worked up by this wonderful idea*) Angels, archangels, cherubims and seraphims, thrones, dominions, virtues, come and take me away! I am only a poor general, stark naked beneath his uniform, a last minute cadet. Carry me off on your flaming wings, set me down up there on a carpet of moss, surrounded by trees and immutable birds, and I will gaze upon the virgins, a pack of invincible girls gathered 'round a sparkling brook pinching each other and laughing while they wash out the great blue sheets of heaven. (*He falls on his knees and passionately calls upon heaven*) You thrones that rest upon thrones, icy cherubims . . . All you friends of heaven, little sister corpuscles, my brothers the protons, the neutrons and the ions, Lord Archibald Isotope, Lady Bacteria, Sir Atmospheric Pollution . . .

MARGUERITE: That's it, he's off again! You're not in for another breakdown!

ACHILLES: (*Standing up again, bewildered*) Forgive me . . . My nerves. What time is it?

MARGUERITE: Time to come home, Achilles.

ACHILLES: I must go home, or Marguerite will throw another fit. My poor wife is mad. She spends her time in the kitchen peeling potatoes. A mild form of madness, I admit, compared with the crazy world we live in, a mild form. But this additional cross on my back—and such a prosaic one! "Your wife, General, is she still peeeling potatoes?"—"Still peeling, Monsieur Minister of War." It started in the seventh year of our marriage, when it became clear Marguerite could not have children. We attempted the impossible, raised heaven and earth and genesis, tried all the remedies, Soviet and Yankee. Nothing. *Nada.* Sterile flanks. A night on the bare mountain. My secret services made available a list of other males to whom clandestinely she had recourse, all without benefit, alas, except to them. One fine morning they all met up again, in the expeditionary force. A small company of shock troops. Interred with full honors in a distant land. No children. A vast desert after us. After that, the tragic death of her father, the clergyman, who fell into the river one day of strong gales and alcohol. Serenely she took refuge in insanity, assisted by Holy Writ, and I must confess with a certain nobility, a certain self-effacement. The classic sketch of a sterile wife who turns into a recluse. She imagines we live in a fortress with anti-conceptional walls, impermeable to radio-activity with phosphorous passages and armored doors. She imagines . . . It's strange, sometimes—for the space of a second—I have the startling impression she imagines that I, too, I, Beaulieu de Chamfort-Mouron, am only the figment of her raving imagination. Perhaps we are an old woman's dream, a very old woman sitting on a stool among the stars, eternally busy peeling potatoes?

(Blackout)

Scene Three

The kitchen. Exactly as at the start of the first scene.

ACHILLES: (*Very tired*) Still in the kitchen!

MARGUERITE: Relax, Achilles.

ACHILLES: And this mania for peeling potatoes!

MARGUERITE: *Potatoes!* Do you really think these are potatoes?

ACHILLES: Yesssss . . . Until I've proof to the contrary. (*Shouting*) After all you're not peeling new-born babies!

MARGUERITE: No, no, don't shout! And even if I was? I'm in my own home, aren't I? (*The General contains himself. He contends himself with walking 'round in circles*) You've put your full dress uniform on . . .

ACHILLES: (*Inspecting himself*) Yes, so I have.

MARGUERITE: I'm not blaming you, Achilles. It gives it an airing. And what with the moth . . .

ACHILLES: The moth! (*He swallows a pill*)

MARGUERITE: How pale you are, Achilles. Your face all drawn and that shifty look . . .

ACHILLES: Tired. Extremely tired. (*Marguerite makes a dive for the sink and fetches the basin*) No, no footbath today! No footbath. You want to make a spectacle of me again!

MARGUERITE: (*Putting the basin back into place*) All right, all right. As a general rule . . .

ACHILLES: A General who lets himself slide into the general rule, he's like . . . Like what? (*Cast down*) Even my scintillating similes escape me!

MARGUERITE: They'll come back, Achilles. If you did a little walking, or riding, or even . . .

ACHILLES: (*Reciting by heart*) The short incisive simile, which abbreviates like a punch, illuminates in a flash, and penetrates without laceration, always gains a hearing and wins the admiration of a Cartesian civilization.

MARGUERITE: (*With a great outpouring of pity*) Achilles, you desolate me! What can I do to help you?

ACHILLES: (*Severely*) My field glasses.

MARGUERITE: What about your field glasses?

ACHILLES: Where have you hidden my field glasses now? In the potato pail like last time? (*He starts making for it*)

MARGUERITE: It's no good. You're wasting your time.

ACHILLES: Where are they?

MARGUERITE: (*Quietly*) You can torture me if you like, Achilles, I won't tell you!

ACHILLES: (*Controlling himself with difficulty*) Marguerite, you were brought up on religious principles . . .

MARGUERITE: Precisely! "Thou shalt not curse the deaf nor put a stumbling block before the blind . . ." Leviticus chapter nineteen, verse fourteen.

ACHILLES: Woman, do not push me too far. If you will not give me the object I covet, I am capable of the worst. And you must know how, with me, the worst can easily take on cosmic proportions!

MARGUERITE: Achilles, be reasonable! You know perfectly well your field glasses wear you out. Your eyes, when you look at me afterwards, just like saucers! All these stupid inventions that already existed at the time of Atlantis . . .

ACHILLES: (*More weary*) Perhaps you're right. Who was it said, "You can only command nature by obeying her dictates"?

MARGUERITE: You see: you've started talking in parables again.

ACHILLES: Oh! Marguerite, there are some moments when I'd like to be a happy pig.

MARGUERITE: (*Pressing her husband's head against her breast*) But you are a happy pig, too, Achilles.

ACHILLES: (*Extremely weary*) Yes.

(*A strange and strident sound is suddenly heard. Immediately, Achilles takes from his pocket the minute little box and rigidly comes to attention*)

MARGUERITE: What is it now?

(*From the little box comes the voice of Captain Kraspeck*)

VOICE: (*Very sensual, in the "air hostess" style*) General Beaulieu de Chamfort-Mouron?

ACHILLES: Present, Captain.

MARGUERITE: Captain Kraspeck!

VOICE: From this moment on, count yourself under arrest.

ACHILLES: At your orders, Captain.

MARGUERITE: What's this, Captain Kraspeck giving you orders now!

VOICE: Grounds for the indictment: Traitor. Deserter.

Subverter. Fermenter. Fornicator. Cyst. Masochist. Deviationist. Numismatist. Neuropath. Cocoon. Quadroon. Pot shot. Usurper. Corruptor. Ventilator. Peeping Tom. Imposter. Gravedigger.

MARGUERITE: Lord!

VOICE: Backslider. Backslider. (*Short pause*) This is the voice of the Upper Echelons of the Supreme Joint Staff. This is the voice of the Upper Echelons of the Supreme Joint Staff. (*The wailing of a newborn babe is heard*)

MARGUERITE: Lord! (*A terrible silence*)

VOICE: General Mouron.

ACHILLES: (*Correcting*) Beaulieu de Chamfort-Mouron.

VOICE: Don't try and gain time with your particles. You have two minutes in which to leave your lair.

ACHILLES: May I bring a few personal effects with me?

VOICE: Your toothbrush. Only your toothbrush.

MARGUERITE: (*Taking a toothbrush from her apron pocket*) Here, my pet.

ACHILLES: Thank you, Marguerite.

VOICE: You will pass through your nine rooms in a row without turning 'round. Right at the end, you will find someone to speak to.

ACHILLES: At your orders, Captain Kraspeck.

VOICE: End of message. This is the voice of the Upper Echelons of the Supreme Joint Staff. This is the voice of the Upper Echelons of the Supreme Joint Staff! (*The wailing of the newborn babe redoubles. Then silence. Achilles puts the box back in his pocket*)

ACHILLES: Well! There you are, Marguerite. We've gone full circle.

MARGUERITE: It had to be expected. I was expecting it.

ACHILLES: (*Brandishing his toothbrush*) Intelligence was the enemy.

MARGUERITE: Intelligence, Achilles.

ACHILLES: You don't know how relieved I feel.

MARGUERITE: I know. You're not the only one.

ACHILLES: At last I shall be thrown into prison. At last I shall be free.

MARGUERITE: Human beings are never free, Achilles. They're incidental.

ACHILLES: Incidental . . . May your father, the clergyman, watch over you from his drunkard's heaven, Marguerite. (*He kisses her chastely on the brow*)

MARGUERITE: May your ascendants forgive you for having no descendants, Achilles.

ACHILLES: (*Addressing the audience*) All of you, my friends and enemies, civilly ensconced in your seats while the earth tears at a breakneck speed towards the constellation of Hercules; all of you who witness the obscure spectacle of your life, with your hand on your neighbor's thigh . . .

MARGUERITE: For goodness sake, Achilles, this is not the moment for lyricism now!

ACHILLES: That's true, Marguerite. Off we go then! It's time. It's time.

(*He does a regimental about turn and disappears. Marguerite picks up the Bible and opens it at random*)

MARGUERITE: (*Reading*) "And I saw heaven opened, and behold a white horse; and he that sat upon him was called Faithful and True; His eyes were as a flame of fire, and out of his mouth goeth a sharp sword, that with it he should smite the nations . . . And I saw an angel standing in the sun: and he cried with a loud voice, saying to all the fowls that fly in the midst of heaven: 'Come and gather yourselves together unto the supper of the great God; that ye may eat the flesh of kings, and the flesh of captains . . . (*The sound of machine-gun fire. The cries of a man who has fallen. She represses a shiver, and then continues*) . . . and the flesh of mighty men, and the flesh of horses, and of them that sit on them, and the flesh of all men, both free and bond, both small and great . . .'" Revelation, chapter nineteen, from verses eleven to eighteen. (*She lays the Bible down*) . . . Yes, we've gone full circle. There's one thing, however, I can say:

any resemblance with actual living or suspected persons you have already met, or may meet as you go about, is really striking. And I could add this . . . But no, better keep quiet, I'm sure, quite sure of that now, better keep quiet. Keep quiet . . . (*And, as she picks up and peels a very old potato:*)

The Curtain Falls

Jerome Lawrence

LIVE SPELLED BACKWARDS

(A Moral Immorality Play)

Jerome Lawrence

Jerome Lawrence was born in Cleveland, Ohio, on July 14, 1915, and was educated at Ohio State University. He began his career as a writer for radio and also as a short story writer for the *Saturday Evening Post.*

In 1942, Mr. Lawrence met his collaborator, Robert E. Lee, in a New York restaurant that catered to radio talent and personnel, and ever since that eventful meeting they have been one of the most productive and successful writing teams in the country. During their reign in radio, they turned out almost two thousand scripts for major network shows, won two Peabody Awards, and were co-founders of the Armed Forces Radio Service during World War II.

In 1948, the team journeyed from radio to the Broadway stage with their first musical venture, *Look, Ma, I'm Dancin'!* Produced and directed by George Abbott (with music and lyrics by Hugh Martin and choreography by Jerome Robbins), the show ran for 188 performances. Seven years later, they returned to the Broadway stage with a powerful drama, *Inherit the Wind,* based on the famous Scopes trial of 1925, with Paul Muni as the prototype of Clarence Darrow. The play was performed 806 times in New York, subsequently was translated into more than twenty foreign languages and presented in many world capitals, and was made into a film with Spencer Tracy and Fredric March.

The team's versatility again took successful hold with their adaptation of Patrick Dennis' novel, *Auntie Mame.* Rosalind Russell created the title role and the presentation delighted New York audiences for 639 performances. Miss Russell later recreated the flamboyant character in a screen version of the comedy and yet there was still mileage ahead for the property. In 1966, the authors (with the valuable assistance of Jerry Herman as lyricist and composer) turned out a musical version, *Mame,* and it sang and danced its way through 1,508 Broadway performances.

Another of the collaborators' work for the stage, *The Night Thoreau Spent in Jail,* though yet to be seen in New York, already has had over 140 different productions in resident, community and university theatres throughout the United States, presented under the auspices of the American Playwrights Theatre, an organization founded in 1963 to encourage dramatists to write for audiences beyond Broadway. The play is scheduled to receive its European premier at the 1972 Dublin Theatre Festival.

Other plays by the Messrs. Lawrence and Lee include: *Shangri-La* (a musical based on James Hilton's *Lost Horizon*); *The Gang's All Here; Only in America; A Call on Kuprin; The Crocodile Smile; Sparks Fly Upward;* the musical, *Dear World;* and *The Incomparable Max.*

In addition to being the recipient of many awards and prizes in the theatre, Mr. Lawrence received an honorary Doctor of Humane Letters degree from his alma mater, Ohio State University, in 1963; Doctor of Literature from Fairleigh Dickenson in 1968; and Doctor of Fine Arts from Villanova in 1969.

Live Spelled Backwards represents one of Jerome Lawrence's few recent works written without his collaborator, and it is published in an anthology for the first time in *The Best Short Plays 1972.*

Characters:

FRANK, *the bartender*

THE WOMAN WHO KNOWS ALMOST EVERYTHING (BADLY)

THE RICHEST GIRL IN THE WORLD

THE MOST FAMOUS PLAYWRIGHT OF OUR TIME

THE BEST HUSTLER IN MOROCCO

THE MOST EVIL MAN IN WASHINGTON COURT HOUSE, OHIO

Scene:

The American Bar, not far from the seashore of a sleepy town in Morocco. Any evening.

The bar itself is a short crescent downstage left, with its back side angled toward the audience. Behind the bar there is an assortment of liquor bottles and mixes and a brightly-polished Moroccan silver tray which contains a strange assortment: they might be hors d'oeuvres and then again they might not be.

There is a record player within arm's reach of the bartender. At the far end is a lamp, plastered with liquor labels. In front of the bar are several stools.

The room contains two small tables and a motley assortment of chairs. There is one arched doorway to the street.

Frank, the bartender, comes on, begins to set up shop for the evening. He polishes a glass, holding it up to the light to see if it shines. Frank is an expatriate American, forty-seven, uneducated but bright with an insolent kind of wisdom. He puts down the glass and slowly lifts the silver tray, studying it critically. The reflection of it plays on his face. Suddenly, he notices the audience.

FRANK: Oh. *Bonsoir!* (*Putting down the tray, he leans on the bar toward the audience*) The International Playground is open for the evening. All the naughty kiddies of the neighborhood are invited. Nothing rented here, nothing loaned. We sell for bucks or francs, pesetas or escudos, dirhems or kopecks all the delightful bottled wickedness known to man! (*He gestures around the commonplace, colorless and somewhat tawdry bar. His tone is slightly mocking and amused, mostly at himself*) "The Drunken Road to Heaven"—that is the slogan of the world-famous American Bar of Northwest Morocco. (*He turns to see a woman entering*) Ahh! We have a guest, The Woman Who Knows Almost Everything—Badly! (*He gestures with mock graciousness toward a bar-stool. The Woman Who Knows Almost Everything, Badly, is a Briton, bright-eyed, fussy. She carries a folded copy of the Paris Herald Tribune, a small pocket notebook, and an armful of assorted books*) Good evening. You are the lucky first, so you get an extra olive in your *Seven-Up!*

WOMAN WHO KNOWS: (*Making a wry face, distastefully*) Seven-Up! (*Sitting on a bar stool*) Brandy. Double. The usual. (*She doesn't notice that Frank is not moving to fill her order. With great relish, she consults her pocket notebook, then gushes a piece of information, dying to convey her latest discovery*) Frank, do you know what a palindrome is? (*She waits for his reply, eagerly*)

FRANK: (*With the patience of a regular straight man*) No, ma'am. I do not know. What is a palindrome?

WOMAN WHO KNOWS: I'm surprised at you, Frank. A man of your age and supposed worldly knowledge. From "palindromos," Greek, meaning running back. A delightful bit of phraseology which reads the same forwards or backwards.

FRANK: So, now I know. Is it going to make me a living?

WOMAN WHO KNOWS: Why, do you realize the first words ever spoken on earth were a palindrome? After the whole rib business. You know what they were? (*She leans in*) "Madam, I'm Adam!"

FRANK: According to who? They have a tape recorder going in the Garden of Eden?

WOMAN WHO KNOWS: No sensitivity to the refinements of life. Not a whit. Here's my favorite. "Ma is a Nun, as I am!"

FRANK: I knew that about you, kid, but not about your mother.

WOMAN WHO KNOWS: (*Disregarding the comment*) If

Errol Flynn and Peter Lorre had had a baby, what would they call it?

FRANK: A monstrosity, that's what *I'd* call it.

WOMAN WHO KNOWS: (*Irritably*) No, no, it's a palindrome. Errol Lorre! Backwards, also Errol Lorre. How about that?

FRANK: Just don't bring that kid in here, that's all I've got to say.

WOMAN WHO KNOWS: Wait a minute. Wait a minute. There's a classic one. Napoleon said it. "Able was I ere I saw Elba!"

FRANK: I suppose that works backwards and forwards in French, too, huh?

WOMAN WHO KNOWS: (*Slightly exasperated*) All right, all right! I'll give you an accurate bi-lingual, no—*tri*-lingual story about Napoleon which is the God's truth. (*Frank has turned his back and is pouring Seven-Up into a brandy snifter*) You know how pumpernickle got its name? You listening?

FRANK: Sweetheart, I've got ears in my ass.

WOMAN WHO KNOWS: (*Sailing right on with her story*) Well, anyway, Napoleon was riding triumphantly through Germany on his favorite horse, whose name was Nicolle. And the Bavarian peasants rushed out with their favorite delicacy, which was black bread, then called *Schwarzbrot,* and offered it like a wonderful gift in their outstretched hands. Napoleon took a piece, chewed on it, spat it out and said, *"Bon pour Nicolle!"* "Good for my horse." Well, the peasants got a real boot out of this. So they started calling their bread *Bon pour Nicolle.* But the Germans couldn't pronounce the French—so *Bon pour Nicolle* became Pum-per-nickle. (*Dead-faced, Frank stares at her, plunking down the brandy glass in front of her*) Am I a bore?

FRANK: Yes.

WOMAN WHO KNOWS: But am I a *good* bore?

FRANK: If they gave a Nobel Prize for bores, you'd win.

WOMAN WHO KNOWS: (*Sips at her drink, sputters*) What the hell is this?

FRANK: *What else? Seven-Up!*

WOMAN WHO KNOWS: (*Shoving the glass away*) In a brandy glass? It tastes like citrate of magnesia!

FRANK: Drink it. It'll clear your brains. We don't want any foggy minds here tonight. We've got important business.

WOMAN WHO KNOWS: What kind of business?

FRANK: Stick around, you'll see.

WOMAN WHO KNOWS: How old are you, Frank?

FRANK: What difference does it make?

WOMAN WHO KNOWS: I want to know.

FRANK: What are you, some kind of walking census bureau? What'll finding out how old I am add to your great useless store of knowledge?

WOMAN WHO KNOWS: I just want to know.

FRANK: Forty-seven. The lousiest age there is. You're nowhere when you're forty-seven. You're past everything and ahead of everything. Once I'm fifty, the thing I'm gonna forget most is being forty-seven. (*Woman Who Knows is jotting it down in her notebook*) What are you writing?

WOMAN WHO KNOWS: That you're forty-seven. Helps me to remember. It's a memory tickler.

FRANK: What good does it do to write down that I'm forty-seven? In five or six months your damn notebook won't be accurate.

WOMAN WHO KNOWS: You know, you could set bartending back a hundred years. You're supposed to be "mine host," genial, convivial, comforting to your guests. (*Still writing*) What's your last name, Frank? Frank what?

FRANK: What would you like my last name to be? Take your pick. Make it something glamorous. Hungarian, Transylvanian. Frank Esterhazy. Frank Dracula. Frank Frankenstein. Frank Diabolo. Or would you like something solidly American? Frank Eisenhower. Frank Kennedy. Frank Truman. Frank Rockefeller. Something more Empire for you, old Walking Encyclopedia? Frank Churchill? Frank MacMillan? Frank Windsor? The Duke of Fornification? Lord Love-Em-Young?

WOMAN WHO KNOWS: All right, all right. Just Frank. Frank's a good enough name all by itself.

FRANK: Frank's a lousy name. I'm not frank with anybody. I just pretend to be. And that's the most unfrank kind of frankness there is. I suppose Frank comes from Francis—and somebody said "That's a girl's name" and felt like a panty-waist and stuck a hard K on it to make it sound butch. But I don't like it. You suppose anybody ever called St. Francis of Assisi "Frank"? (*A handsome, well-coiffured girl of thirty enters. She is a little drunk but carries herself carefully. She wears dark glasses. This is the Richest Girl In The World*) Ah, come in, come in! Tell your Brink's truck to wait. (*The Woman Who Knows gets up from her stool, bows. Ignoring her, the Richest Girl goes to a bar stool*)

RICHEST GIRL: The usual.

FRANK: No, ma'am.

RICHEST GIRL: What do you mean, "No, ma'am"?

FRANK: No double vodkas for poor little rich girls tonight.

RICHEST GIRL: What are you pushing?

FRANK: (*Uncapping a bottle and pouring*) Pepsi Cola.

RICHEST GIRL: What're you trying to do—make Joan Crawford rich?

WOMAN WHO KNOWS: (*Leaning toward her confidentially*) Just between you and me, I think he has some kind of crazy idea that . . .

RICHEST GIRL: (*Sharply*) Please don't talk to me. You'll start asking questions. And the first question you'll ask is, "What do you do for a living?" And I'll have to say, "I inherit money." And you'll look at me as it were a worse crime than selling my body or pushing kif. So just don't talk to me. Clear?

WOMAN WHO KNOWS: Aloneness is the disease of the world. Don't spread it!

RICHEST GIRL: What do I have to do, pay money for quiet? How much does silence cost a kilo?

FRANK: Baby doll, if you want silence, stay home. We peddle liveliness here.

RICHEST GIRL: (*To Frank*) Don't *you* talk to me either.

FRANK: Suit yourself.

WOMAN WHO KNOWS: (*To Frank*) *I'll* talk to you.

FRANK: Big deal.

WOMAN WHO KNOWS: I am enamored of riddles. The Riddle of the Sphinx. The Riddle of the Universe. The Riddle of Homer. You know the riddle that killed Homer? He died from trying to figure it out. You want to hear it?

FRANK: I couldn't stop you if I wanted to.

WOMAN WHO KNOWS: "What I caught, I threw away; what I could not catch, I kept." You know what the answer is?

FRANK: (*Flatly*) No.

WOMAN WHO KNOWS: Fleas! Cooties! Lice!

FRANK: Crabs. They had 'em in the days of Golden Greece, too. You live and learn.

WOMAN WHO KNOWS: (*Wound up*) The most fascinating riddle of our time originated not far from here—Casablanca, to be exact—during the war. It was the favorite riddle of the G.I.'s. Get this. There are fourteen cities in the world, each in a different country, only one to a country, each with over half a million population, and they all begin with the letter M.

RICHEST GIRL: Moscow.

FRANK: I thought you weren't talking.

RICHEST GIRL: I'm not talking. I'm guessing.

FRANK: You think there's something Freudian . . . is that how you say it . . . ?

WOMAN WHO KNOWS: Freudian, that's right.

FRANK: . . . in the Richest Girl in the World giving Moscow as her first guess?

RICHEST GIRL: Mexico City.

WOMAN WHO KNOWS: Very good. That's two. Twelve more to go.

FRANK: Each has over half a million, right?

WOMAN WHO KNOWS: And only one to a country.

FRANK: Madagascar.

WOMAN WHO KNOWS: That's not a city, it's an island.

FRANK: (*Nettled*) If you're gonna run a quiz show here, pay money.

RICHEST GIRL: Madrid.

WOMAN WHO KNOWS: Good, very good indeed!

RICHEST GIRL: (*Pleased, thawing, turning*) What do they call you?

WOMAN WHO KNOWS: My French friends call me *Je Sais Tout Mal*—I Know Everything Badly. (*Turning to Frank*) See? See? Knowledge, even useless knowledge, is a better icebreaker than brandy!

FRANK: How about Marihuana, Massachusetts? Everybody gets high and burns a few witches. (*He flings the word "witches" right at the Woman Who Knows, who ignores him*)

RICHEST GIRL: Munich! (*Woman Who Knows applauds. Richest Girl laughs, delighted*)

WOMAN WHO KNOWS: Wonderful, absolutely wonderful. Only ten to go.

FRANK: (*Doggedly*) Minneapolis.

WOMAN WHO KNOWS: Sorry, no. With St. Paul it's over half-a-million; by itself it's not. 482,872. 1960 census.

FRANK: Is there one in the U.S.?

WOMAN WHO KNOWS: There's one.

FRANK: Memphis.

WOMAN WHO KNOWS: No, 497,524.

FRANK: Miami. Of course.

WOMAN WHO KNOWS: No, sir. 291,688. Throw in Miami Beach and you get another sixty-three thousand, give or take a few.

RICHEST GIRL: Milwaukee.

WOMAN WHO KNOWS: Fantastic. 741,324.

RICHEST GIRL: How do you know all this wonderful information?

FRANK: Badly—that's how she knows it.

WOMAN WHO KNOWS: I go to libraries. They fascinate me. Every library has the same smell, have you ever noticed that? The same taste in the air. Did you know your lungs have taste buds? No matter what library you go to, in any part of the world, you take a drawer from the card catalogue and it makes the same click against the hush. My favorite sound. And I ask myself, riffling through the cards, "What'll I find out about today?" Sometimes I deliberately go to the most silly subject, and invariably I find something intriguing. Cost accounting. Pigeon breeding.

FRANK: Montreal.

WOMAN WHO KNOWS: (*Disappointed that Frank guessed one, reluctant to give him credit*) Right.

FRANK: (*Proudly*) I got one!

WOMAN WHO KNOWS: Once I was sitting in the main reading room of the British Museum waiting for some books, I forget on what usbject. Anyhow, I was in the M section—"M"! You see? They alphabetize the room. And this old gent came up to me and whispered, "Young woman, you're going to have a very red bottom. You're sitting in the exact chair where Karl Marx wrote *Das Kapital!*" "Well," I told him, "better red than dead!" (*The Richest Girl laughs. The Most Famous Playwright Of Our Time enters. He is in his mid-thirties, pensive, piercing, bitter with barbs of amusement. He goes to a table*)

FRANK: I'm glad you came in. The intellectual tone of the room has suddenly gone up. (*Leaning in to the Woman Who Knows*) I should like to point out that The Most Famous Playwright of Our Time knows *absolutely nothing*—brilliantly.

PLAYWRIGHT: Stop! You'll turn my head.

RICHEST GIRL: Milan. We're got half of them. (*The Woman Who Knows pats her shoulder, gets down from her bar stool and crosses to the Playwright*)

WOMAN WHO KNOWS: I've been waiting to see you. The mail clerk at American Express says you should come in. There's a lot of stuff for you.

PLAYWRIGHT: I never pick up my mail. Mail is always bad news.

WOMAN WHO KNOWS: (*Handing him the newspaper*) I brought this paper for you. Paris edition of the *Herald Tribune.*

PLAYWRIGHT: (*Shoving it away*) You won't find any better news in the *Herald Trib* than you will in my mail.

WOMAN WHO KNOWS: There's something in it about the

blonde kid with all the teeth. The kid who used to hang around here a year or so ago, remember him? The one who wanted to be a playwright.

PLAYWRIGHT: Is it an obituary? If it is, I'll read it. Not otherwise.

WOMAN WHO KNOWS: What've you got against him?

PLAYWRIGHT: He's a thief.

WOMAN WHO KNOWS: What'd he steal?

PLAYWRIGHT: I'd rather not say.

WOMAN WHO KNOWS: (*Opening the paper as she goes back to the bar*) Well, it says here the kid won the Pulitzer Prize. (*Quickly, the Playwright gets up*)

PLAYWRIGHT: Let me see that. (*He takes the newspaper, reads it quickly*) I'll be damned. I always thought it was a pretty good play.

WOMAN WHO KNOWS: Did you read it?

PLAYWRIGHT: Read it? Hell, I wrote it! (*He gestures to Frank for a drink. Frank pours a glass full of Pepsi Cola. Absently the Playwright takes the drink back to his table, still studying the newspaper*)

WOMAN WHO KNOWS: You mean you helped him edit it, collaborated with him?

PLAYWRIGHT: No, no, it's my play. Every syllable. He stole the manuscript from me and suddenly disappeared. The next thing I heard, he'd turned up in New York. Then I found out the play was produced. As his.

RICHEST GIRL: (*Getting interested*) Didn't you do anything about it?

PLAYWRIGHT: (*Calmly*) No. Somebody brought me the reviews. "Exciting new *young* playwright!" That was a kick.

RICHEST GIRL: I have very good lawyers in New York. Expensive ones. I keep 'em on a retainer. But all they do for a living is endorse checks. Use 'em. I give 'em to you. Sue! Bring this faker to court. Lock him up.

PLAYWRIGHT: Why? I'm enjoying this too much. And the best part is yet to come!

RICHEST GIRL: But he's stolen your play.

PLAYWRIGHT: It's only a play. One year's work. You know what *I've* stolen? His life! His whole life! He'll be the greatest subject I've ever written about. Particularly when you watch him squirm—trying to write his *next* play! (*He takes a drink of the Pepsi Cola*) What the hell is this?

FRANK: *Pepsi Cola*. Hits the spot.

PLAYWRIGHT: Not mine!

WOMAN WHO KNOWS: You mean you knew about it all the time and you didn't do a thing?

PLAYWRIGHT: I'll tell you the truth. I was kind of curious to see what would happen to one of my plays without my name on it. You see, I've always had a theory: if Joe Schmo had brought *Long Day's Journey Into Night* to a Broadway producer, do you think anybody'd have touched it? Hell, no. But it gets on the stage, then on the screen, and it *explodes*. But without Eugene O'Neill's name on it, would anybody have let it be seen? No, I kept telling myself. Not a chance. Not a prayer. See? I guess I was wrong.

RICHEST GIRL: Are you writing another play?

PLAYWRIGHT: Always. Daily. Like a bowel movement.

RICHEST GIRL: I'll give you a subject: this bar, this goddam bar.

FRANK: If you write it, I want royalties. And I've got a title for you: *The Wrong Side of the Straits*.

PLAYWRIGHT: No. Never write a play that takes place in a bar. Nobody ever really believes it. Or they think you're trying to be symbolic, trying to say that the bar is hell or heaven—or *Outward Bound,* for Christ's sake, half-way-between the two. Worse than that, nobody believes the characters. Does a man speak a special kind of truth when under the influence of alcohol? No, ma'am, he does not. And swimming around publicly in the fishbowl that a bar is, isn't his personality a little distorted? Wavy mirrors in a fun-house? In a bar, is a man covering up the real person he is, or is he being too goddam much himself, an overblown caricature? Worse than anything, if you write a play about a bar, people will think you're Saroyan.

FRANK: This is not a bar. I prefer to think of it as halfway between a salon and a saloon.

PLAYWRIGHT: (*Staring at the Pepsi Cola*) Some saloon.

FRANK: The booze will be later. On the house. We're having a special entertainment first.

PLAYWRIGHT: What kind of entertainment?

FRANK: You'll see. As soon as just one more of my regular customers arrives, we'll start.

RICHEST GIRL: You putting in a floor show? Arab dancing boys?

FRANK: Patience!

WOMAN WHO KNOWS: (*To Richest Girl*) You haven't finished with the M's. Seven more to go. The seven most difficult.

RICHEST GIRL: I'm stuck. Marrakech? No, too small.

WQMAN WHO KNOWS: 190,000. Two hundred thousand if you count the people who've never been counted.

RICHEST GIRL: Is there one in Africa? All the cities seem to begin with C: Cairo, Casablanca, Capetown.

WOMAN WHO KNOWS: I'll give you that much of a hint, forget Africa.

FRANK: Africa is the easiest place in the world to forget—if you happen to be anywhere *except* Africa; then the trick is difficult!

PLAYWRIGHT: What are you trying to guess?

WOMAN WHO KNOWS: Cities, big cities that begin with the letter M.

PLAYWRIGHT: Every big city is an M. Metropolis. Megalopolis. *Manhattan!*

WOMAN WHO KNOWS: Manhattan doesn't count. It's really New York.

PLAYWRIGHT: *Nothing* is really New York. But why do you want to go messing around with Ms? It's a murderous letter. The big M—money! But also M for masochism, for mother, for man—and every madness of man; for masturbation and menstruation and menopause; for Mary and Moses; for Micky Finns; for the most, the maximum, the megatons; for magic, for mystery, for *miracles*. But most important—for me, for me, for *me!* The capital M in everybody's life. (*The Best Hustler In Morocco comes into the bar. He is eighteen, fiercely handsome, olive-tanned, with high Berber cheekbones. He moves like a dancer, smiles a great deal in a tremendous effort to please*)

BEST HUSTLER: (*Greeting everybody, speaking in song-lyrics*) "Summertime and the living is easy," yes? (*All laugh, except Frank*)

FRANK: Hustle your bottom someplace else tonight, Abdullah.

PLAYWRIGHT: Leave the kid be, Frank. Give him a drink.

FRANK: What d'ya want me to do, contribute to the delinquency of a minor?

PLAYWRIGHT: Give him a drink. Here, kid, take mine. (*Smiling happily, the Best Hustler takes the glass, lifts it in a toast*)

BEST HUSTLER: (*Speaking, not singing it*) "Fish are jumping!"

(*They howl. This time even Frank joins in. The Most Evil Man in Washington Court House, Ohio appears. He looks around the room. The Best Hustler is enjoying the laughter, laughing himself along with the others*)

MOST EVIL MAN: What's so funny about a kid learning English from records? They do it at Berlitz!

PLAYWRIGHT: Not *his* way.

MOST EVIL MAN: But it's cruel to laugh at him.

FRANK: Ah! We have the Defender of the Faith! You all know the Most Evil Man in Washington Court House, Ohio?

WOMAN WHO KNOWS: (*Taking out her notebook*) What make you the Most Evil Man in Washington Court House, Ohio? And where the hell is Washington Court House?

RICHEST GIRL: Who cares? Who needs it? It doesn't begin with an M.

BEST HUSTLER: (*Lifting his glass to the Most Evil Man, speaking, not singing*) "Night and Day, you are the one!" (*They laugh again*)

PLAYWRIGHT: Maybe Abdullah has the answer. All truths are in song titles. *I Love You Truly. All the World Is Waiting for the Sunrise. Yes, We Have No Bananas!* What nihilist ever said anything as profoundly nihilistic as that? *Yes, We Have No Bananas!* The *positive* negative! The absolutely positive negative!

FRANK: (*Waving the Most Evil Man into the room*) Come on in. Join our little world of madness and make-believe. But leave your shingle outside. You're just one of the crowd here, one of the fellas, one of the regulars. Around here, if you want to be evil, you've got to stand in line, wait your turn! (*The Most Evil Man moves toward a table to sit by himself apart from the others. He is in his early forties, looks like a typical small-town high school principal, a man completely without distinction. But he is intense, and there is something lost and pitiful in his attempts to find himself*)

MOST EVIL MAN: Anise. A short one.

FRANK: Later.

BEST HUSTLER: (*Speaking, not singing*) "Yes, We Have No Bananas!"

WOMAN WHO KNOWS: I'm curious.

FRANK: You bet your boots you are!

WOMAN WHO KNOWS: Just how do you know he's the hometown's most evil man?

FRANK: Oh, somebody came through a year or so ago and recognized him.

WOMAN WHO KNOWS: But why? What did he do?

FRANK: We don't know. (*To the Most Evil Man*) You want to tell us? What's your scene, your bag? What turns you on? Or off? Or over? What are you running away from? Or to?

MOST EVIL MAN: Forget it.

WOMAN WHO KNOWS: A living riddle!

FRANK: We're not asking for your name. No I.D.'s, no driver's licenses needed in this establishment. We live in the anonymous dark. Fine. People change their names as often as they change their underwear. Sometimes more often. Take Abdullah here. His name is probably Jussef or Ahmed. What's your name, kid?

BEST HUSTLER: (*Stretching out his hand, speaking the lyric*) "Appetizing young love for sale!"

FRANK: See? He's not interested in the label. He just wants to sell the merchandise.

WOMAN WHO KNOWS: (*Studying the Most Evil Man*) I can tell from looking at him. He's a remittance man. This town is full of them.

RICHEST GIRL: What's a remittance man?

WOMAN WHO KNOWS: Oh, it's an old Empire expression. A man who raped the mayor's daughter back home or relieved himself in the public square—and all his respectable relatives send him monthly checks—remittances—to keep him out of the country.

FRANK: Is that you? (*No answer. He points around the room*) *He's* the Most Famous Playwright because you can read it in *Who's Who*. *She's* the Richest Girl because Dun tells Bradstreet. *She* Knows Almost Everything Badly because she won't let us forget it. And Abdullah here is the Best Hustler in Morocco because he holds the local record of taking off and putting on his clothes more often than anybody living or dead.

PLAYWRIGHT: No. Abdullah's the best because he's got a gimmick. It's not down with the pants and into the sack. He puts on a floor show first. His customers get a laugh, and that takes the sting out of paying for love.

FRANK: (*To the Most Evil Man*) But you're the mystery guest.

MOST EVIL MAN: We'll keep it that way. Let me have an anise—or aren't you interested in my money?

FRANK: Among other things. (*Slowly, deliciously, Frank lifts the hors d'oeuvre tray*) We're having *hors d'oeuvres* first. Something special and wonderful for each of you.

PLAYWRIGHT: What're you peddling—a free lunch?

FRANK: (*Holding the tray aloft*) I am peddling *freedom*. Escape. I am inviting you all to fly without the help of Pan-Am.

RICHEST GIRL: Kif? Keep it. Doesn't work anymore. The kids in the Casbah offer you "the best grasses" for twenty dirhem, and nothing happens. We've had it, we've flown the route, we know the flight pattern.

FRANK: No! Nothing ordinary. Everything new. Look, my buddy-buddies, I am offering you *wings*. Psychedelic Flight 100 leaving for *everywhere* (*Holding up each hors d'oeuvre*) Peyote! Not mescaline, the real thing. Nourishment for the soul: the divine fleshy top of the magic cactus, where the gods live, or maybe the devil! (*Holding up the mushroom*) The most sacred mushroom of Egypt. Psilocybin, the Harvard boys call it when they take it synthetically on sugar cubes. But this is the real mushroom, smuggled in from where it grew, out of the breasts and brains of the Pharaohs. (*They all watch, fascinated, as he goes around the room, tempting them with the strange assortment on the tray. The tray reflects into their faces*) A cigarette. No ordinary drag of marihuana or kif or hashish here. A concoction out of Tibet. Momea, mixed in a cup made from a human skull. One puff means liberation. You are cordially invited to light up and crawl right out of the heavy suit of winter underwear called your skin! (*Holds up three blue pills, the size of saccharine tablets*) Best of all, the triumph of pure chemistry. LSD-25!

WOMAN WHO KNOWS: Hallucinogens.

FRANK: That's it. That's the name. Sister, when it comes to a fact, you are Daphne K. Reliability. *Hallucinogens!*

BEST HUSTLER: (*Again speaking, not singing*) "A trip to the moon on gossamer wings."

FRANK: Even a better description. Who'll have one? Who's first on the launching pad? (*There is a moment's pause. They all look at each other, waiting*)

BEST HUSTLER: (*Reaching for one*) Me.

FRANK: (*Pulling away*) Everybody's invited, except you, Abdullah. You're flying enough as it is. (*Offering the tray to the Most Evil Man*) You, Mr. Mystery Man?

MOST EVIL MAN: No. No, thank you. To hell with your

brave new world. Let me live peacefully in my cowardly old world. I don't want to be mixed chemically.

FRANK: They must all be pretty angelic in that burg with the long name—if you're the most evil.

MOST EVIL MAN: I just don't happen to think we should control ourselves with a lot of pills and chemicals. It's unnatural, against nature, that's what it is. And it might become a habit.

PLAYWRIGHT: Breathing is a habit, loving or even not-loving is a habit. Feeling sorry for yourself is a habit—a lousy one. When you're dead, all your habits are gone, good ones, bad ones.

WOMAN WHO KNOWS: (*Screwing up her face*) LSD-25, lysergic acid—isn't exactly a chemical. It's a semi-synthetic drug, which they get from ergot—E-R-G-O-T, a fungus which grows on rye. Discovered, quite by accident, in 1943 by a Dr. Hoffman in the Sandoz Pharmaceutical Laboratory in Switzerland.

FRANK: From rye! *Bon pour Nicolle!*

PLAYWRIGHT: From a fungus on rye. How about that? Isn't that something? All these centuries, everybody's been yelling, "I want something new, something fresh, something young." Fresh bread, yes sir, directly from the oven, *hot* cross buns. No stale loaves for me, no sir. Even day-old-bread—*one day old,* mind you—gets shoved onto a cut-price shelf! When all the time, all the penicillin and all the LSD was on the *stale* bread. Is the next discovery that there's something beautiful and healthy and dream-producing about old *people?*

RICHEST GIRL: (*Tempted by the tray*) How much?

FRANK: (*Eagerly*) Nothing. Not a dirhem. Not a penny. On me. On the house.

PLAYWRIGHT: What's your percentage? What do you get out of it?

FRANK: Nothing. A celebration for my old customers. An inducement to come in—like trading stamps.

RICHEST GIRL: What happens?

FRANK: Who knows? Who can tell? Miracles maybe. Reality is for the peasants.

PLAYWRIGHT: Aldous Huxley told me about his experiences with mescaline. He said he didn't dare look at anything he might consider beautiful—because it would be too terrible to behold. He didn't feel he could endure the beauty of it. So, under mescaline, he forced himself to look at the most commonplace, the most ugly, the most unattractive thing he could imagine, a sewer pipe. But he saw in the shadows, alongside that rusty old pipe, colors unimagined by the eyes of man. Purples beyond purples. Shades indescribable. Golds that made anything described before as golden seem cheap.

RICHEST GIRL: (*Suddenly*) Give me some.

FRANK: Which one?

RICHEST GIRL: The strongest. The absolute strongest. Nothing works for me anymore. And I want to float high, somewhere up there where there isn't even money.

FRANK: LSD-25 for the Richest Girl in the World. (*He pours the three tiny blue pills into her hand. She stares at them for a moment, then opens her mouth, throws back her head and pops them into her mouth, washing them down quickly with the Pepsi-Cola*)

PLAYWRIGHT: I'll try the cigarette.

FRANK: Delighted. (*Handing the Playwright the homemade cigarette*) Momea out of Tibet for the Most Famous Playwright of Our Time. (*The Playwright twists it into a cigarette holder*) In France, they are called *Defense de Fumer* Cigarettes. In Italy, the brand name is *Vietato Fumare!* (*He offers the tray to the Most Evil Man*)

MOST EVIL MAN: No! What for?

FRANK: Get away from reality.

MOST EVIL MAN: What's wrong with reality?

PLAYWRIGHT: I never made a dime out of it. Give me a light. (*The Best Hustler springs to his side with a match*)

BEST HUSTLER: (*As the match comes to life*) "I hear your name and I'm aflame."

PLAYWRIGHT: Thank you. Maybe I'll take myelf out of town and rewrite me. (*He takes a drag but lets it out just like cigarette smoke. The Best Hustler kneels at his side and indicates with pantomine how to inhale, breathing in very deeply and holding it, holding it, holding it in the lungs. The Playwright takes a very deep drag and tries it. The Best Hustler nods, pleased at being able to instruct*) Thanks. When they start selling this stuff in supermarkets, you'll have to do the TV commercials.

RICHEST GIRL: (*Disappointed*) Nothing happens. Nothing's happening.

PLAYWRIGHT: Take your time. *Let* it happen. Let go and let it happen. Plotinus called it the journey from the alone to the Alone. Small "a" to capital "A"!

FRANK: I'll turn down the lights. (*He switches off everything but the lamp, so there is a hazy glow of unreality*) Maybe a little music (*He puts on a dreamy tune, half-real, so the mood becomes increasingly vague, like an impressionist painting*)

WOMAN WHO KNOWS: What do I get?

FRANK: The Egyptian mushroom? The peyote? Help yourself.

WOMAN WHO KNOWS: (*Taking what looks like a small piece of melon rind*) The peyote. Do you know they use this as a sacrament in the Native American Church of the United States? "The Flesh of the Gods," the Indians call it: the Kiowas and the Comanches, the Omahas, and the Apaches. (*She chews a bit of it*) It's bitter and it's tough.

PLAYWRIGHT: Isn't everything? In a few minutes, it won't be.

MOST EVIL MAN: (*Striding toward the bar*) You're crazy, all of you. (*He picks up the lamp*) What is this? A lamp? Maybe. To you. To somebody else, it might be a weapon. Or to a savage who never saw an electric bulb, it might be a god and he'd bend down and worship it. (*He puts down the lamp*) Reality is difficult enough to define without getting outside our frame of reference. It's like a painting in a gallery, slipping out and visiting another painting in another frame.

PLAYWRIGHT: (*Dreamily*) Maybe it happens. How would

you like to be locked up every night, with guards patroling your corridors? (*He takes a deep drag of the cigarette and blows out a cloud of smoke*) I am suspicious of encyclopedias. I disbelieve the dictionaries. And the mystics are closer to the truth than the IBM machines. (*To the Richest Girl*) How do you feel? (*There is an imperceptible glow around the arched doorway and along the edge of the bar—subtly, a touch of gold*)

RICHEST GIRL: Better. Lighter. Tingly.

PLAYWRIGHT: Good. Good.

RICHEST GIRL: (*Distantly*) I've been so tired of laughing without smiling. So tired.

PLAYWRIGHT: Did you know that when he was a little boy, William Blake was beaten, badly beaten, by his own mother because he saw the Prophet Ezekiel in a summer field.

MOST EVIL MAN: *Said* he saw.

PLAYWRIGHT: *Saw!* I believe William Blake more than I believe you. Or his mother.

WOMAN WHO KNOWS: William Blake, born 1757, died 1827.

PLAYWRIGHT: (*Blowing smoke*)

"I will give you the end of a golden string,
Only wind it into a ball.
It will lead you in at Heaven's Gate,
Built in Jerusalem's wall."

RICHEST GIRL: "The end of a golden string." That's beautiful.

PLAYWRIGHT: I've always wanted to write a play about a dentist, a wonderful man, a sensitive man, full of delicate nerve endings. And he hates being a dentist. He's sick of looking into mouths, sick of having the foul breath of cavities blown up into his face, sick of pain, sick of prophylaxis, and "Rinse, please!" So he takes nitrous oxide himself, sitting in his own dentist's chair, the head-piece adjusted to fit, even putting a bib on himself almost by reflex. Then deliciously, he inhales the nitrous oxide and whammo he's on a desert, twenty centuries ago . . . (*The Best Hustler begins to dance, slowly, sensuously*) . . . and there's

Ingrid Bergman, who makes a ferocious kind of desert love to him, kissing his feet, rubbing her head over his body. The name of the play is *Open Wide!*

WOMAN WHO KNOWS: Your dentist has great taste. Ingrid Bergman. That's high class. Most dentists would have met Brigette Bardot or Diana Dors. I always say even in dreams you should pick bed-partners who can do something besides grunt. After it's over, even in dreams, you've gotta have somebody to talk to.

PLAYWRIGHT: (*In a rozy daze*) Open wide. Open *wider!*

RICHEST GIRL: (*Rising slowly*) Now. *Now. Now!* (*The energy level in the room goes up, as if a car pulling up a hill suddenly went into second gear. The Richest Girl takes off her dark glasses for the first time, climbs onto a chair then onto the table, and makes an announcement with stentorian clarity*) Ladies and gentlemen, I have an announcement to make. *Marseilles! Mukden in China! Madras in India! Melbourne! Manchester! Manila! and Montevideo in Uruguay! Mon-te-vi-de-o*—did you ever hear such a beautiful word? I see a mountain, rising above the Rio de la Plata. (*Looks around, sees the dancing Best Hustler*) I want to dance!

BEST HUSTLER: "You and the night and the music!" (*She holds out her hand, graciously stepping down. She dances with the Best Hustler, slowly, deliciously*)

PLAYWRIGHT: (*Suddenly*) Shhhh! Listen! I can hear it! (*He climbs up, kneeling on one of the bar stools, one open hand raised. The dancing stops. He gestures for the music to be cut off. Frank lifts off the record player arm. The Playwright moves his open hand, as if clapping it against air. There is a low, hushed hum, as if inside his head, like a distant sitar vibrating a lost note*) The great trick question of Zen is, "What is the sound of one hand clapping?" And I always thought it was a kook question, deliberately designed *not* to be answered. Also I am pre-conditioned, like one of Pavlov's salivating dogs, to wait for, expect, want, *desire* applause—the sound of two hands clapping, multiplied by the capacity of the Morosco or the Music Box. And the sound of *one* hand clapping is rejection, disapproval, darkness, hell, an entire audience turning off its love for me. (*He climbs up onto the bar, reaching toward the ceiling*) But I hear it now. And it's beautiful. The most beautiful silence. Fur-lined quiet. (*Caressing the silence with his raised hand, as if stroking velvet*) Hush, hush, hush, hush, hush. You want to come up for air into it. You've been swimming around in the world, then you come up into it. (*On tiptoe, reaching even higher*) Ohhhhh, you can touch the silence, velvet, goat's hair silence. (*The Most Evil Man has been watching, holding his breath with excitement. Now he moves deliberately to the bar*)

MOST EVIL MAN: Give me some of it!

FRANK: Sure. (*Holding up the mushroom*) This?

MOST EVIL MAN: Yes!

FRANK: The sacred Mushroom of the Pharaohs for the Most Evil Man in Washington Court House, Ohio. (*The Most Evil Man takes the mushroom, hesitates, then glances up at the Playwright. Quickly, he eats the mushroom*)

WOMAN WHO KNOWS: (*Her eyes closed*) I've never seen so much with my eyes closed!

(*The Richest Girl moves toward the bar, in an ecstatic trance. She begins to kiss the Playwright around the feet, hugging his legs, his ankles*)

RICHEST GIRL: I kiss your shoes, your socks, your feet, your ankles—because you are truly creative. And I am barren. You bring forth babies, and I bring forth nothing.

MOST EVIL MAN: (*Pale*) I'm sick. I'm nauseated.

FRANK: (*Pointing*) The can's that way. (*The Most Evil Man hurries off. The Playwright is still staring up at his hand, moving it against empty air. There is a flicker of lights from front, a ghost-train passing in the night. Do we see it?*)

RICHEST GIRL: (*Looking front, her eyes moving back and forth*) My God, this is the most amazing experience. I, me, I, this person, me—I am on one train and another me, a me I've never seen before, is on a track alongside and I am watching it, looking into a pullman car riding at the same speed, and all the shades are up.

WOMAN WHO KNOWS: (*Opens her eyes and slowly stares*

up at the ceiling) I'm tongue-tied. I cannot say the words that can possibly, possibly describe the beauty of this ugly room.

RICHEST GIRL: That poor girl, that poor girl—she's all alone on that train. All by herself, because she won't let anybody else on. She's so scared that nobody will love her for anything but her bank account, so she hides, in that brightly lit train, with all the shades up. I'm so sorry for her. Why doesn't she stop the train and let somebody else on? (*There is a shimmer of jewels from the ceiling*)

WOMAN WHO KNOWS: The ceiling is a waving field of fire and jewels. The walls are breathing! (*The Best Hustler crouches alongside her, trying to see what is on the ceiling also, but sees nothing, and is confused. He raises his hand as if to say "I don't see." The Woman Who Knows grabs it and holds it aloft*) Your dirty hand, your filthy fingernails, are like the hand of a saint painted by Titian!

PLAYWRIGHT: Oh, God, God, why have you hidden from us so long? Have you been keeping these silly chemicals just out of reach all these centuries to taunt us? Have all the fascinating legends you've allowed to be manufactured for our delight and confusion hinted—just *hinted*—at these magic formulae? Was the apple in the Garden of Eden a piece of peyote? Was the potion that put Sleeping Beauty to sleep really a squirt of primitive LSD? Did the little men in the Catskills slip a dram of mescaline into Rip Van Winkle's brew? Are all the fairy tales true and all the history books false?

RICHEST GIRL: (*As if calling to the girl on the train*) Care! Care! Care about something! About somebody! Myself is too much with me, getting and spending. (*The Playwright comes down from atop the bar and points toward the farther bar stool*)

PLAYWRIGHT: I saw him first right there—on the first bar stool—and he smiled at me and handed me his drink. And I began to think he was Death, Death was following me. Because it didn't make any sense. Why would anybody with teeth like that and eyes like that and cornsilk hair like that want to be a writer when he could be loved for his body and his face? But he said he desired me. And I told him, "You *must* be Death then, for only Death could find me beautiful." (*Laughs without humor*) But Death didn't want my body. All Death wanted was the Pulitzer Prize. (*The Playwright lifts up the bar stool and hugs it, holding it close to him*)

FRANK: (*As the Most Evil Man comes back into the room, a little dazed*) You better?

MOST EVIL MAN: I think so. (*Pulling up a bar stool*) I have a weird feeling, very strange. As if I'd been here before.

FRANK: You have. You're one of my best customers.

MOST EVIL MAN: No. I mean as if *now* had happened before, this minute, my talking to you. (*Suddenly, intensely*) Can I tell you a story? Will you listen to a story?

FRANK: Sure.

MOST EVIL MAN: (*Impelled, helpless, plunging—as if from a high building*) It's about . . . this man . . . this man I know. He was a principal of a high school in a town in a . . . well, in a midwestern state. He was a good administrator . . . he thought he was, because he tried to look at things the way the kids would. You know, understand their mentality, their motives and their feelings. Like . . . well, like once he grabbed away some Benzedrine inhalers the kids were using. They used to rip them open and swallow the insides, like aspirins washed down with cokes, hyping themselves up like souped-up flivvers. He was a principal, and I want to point out that it was not unprincipled of him to try it himself. He had to find out what went on inside the minds of the kids. So he locked the door of his office and swallowed the stuff, using a paper cup from the water cooler. But it was awful. It only made him dizzy, like a cheap drunk. It made his mind fuzzy, it narrowed his awareness, like putting on horseblinders. He tried to straighten himself up with coffee, but some people saw him, the janitor and the cleaning woman. It was hushed up, but the rumor was all over town that he was a secret drunk, and people began to look at him strangely. (*He leans in farther, speeding up his story*) Then one day he . . . this man took over a civics class as a substitute and he told the students that he thought McKinley deserved to be shot. Well, that got all over, that the high school principal could say that about a president, and it shocked everybody in that town, which is very republican and very American Legion. There, being unpatriotic is synonymous with being queer—as if waving the flag was partly waving your you-know-what in the breeze, both of 'em on a flagpole. (*Closes his eyes*) Then his wife left him. And that's always the man's fault. It means he's no good in bed. And there'd never been any kids, so this man was less than a man and not really able to lead and train other men's children. (*Shaking his head*) Nobody ever said this out loud. It was all rumor and speculation and suspicion. Until one day something definite happened. This young girl came into his office—a student, I guess she was only about sixteen. But standing there, the sunlight catching her blonde hair, she looked like the most beautiful creature that ever lived. And this man had a wild impulse. He had to . . . *hug her,* just once, nothing else. Because he wanted to honor the girl's beauty with his affection. Does that make him a child-molester? (*Nobody answers. The Playwright puts down the bar stool. The Most Evil Man wheels around to the Woman Who Knows*) You. You've been to all the libraries of the world, and to all the art galleries. If . . . if this man admires, even worships a great statue, a great painting, if he gives his love to, say Venus de Milo, does that necessarily mean he wants to possess it, steal it from the Louvre? (*No answer. The Woman Who Knows is staring, dazed at the ceiling*)

FRANK: I think he'd get in trouble if he tried to hug it.

MOST EVIL MAN: (*Wheeling around to Frank again*) There's an end to this story you won't believe. They got him out of town, *bought* him out of town: his brother, who was a deacon in the church, and his sister-in-law who was head of the Ladies' Aid, and his cousin who was one of the heads of the Chamber of Commerce. (*Recklessly*) And so this man decided to go to the most wicked place he could find on the map of the world and *try* all the things he'd been accused of, everything. And he hated them. They revolted him, they made him sick! (*Very quietly*) He has tried every evil and he is sick of them. Doesn't that make him purer than the people who never dare? The people who cling to their longing for sin and hang onto it and live with it all of their lives—aren't *they* the dirty ones?

RICHEST GIRL: Can we have some music, Frank?

FRANK: Sure. (*He puts on a record, a slow dance tune. The Richest Girl goes over and taps the Most Evil Man on the shoulder. He turns around, surprised*)

RICHEST GIRL: Will "this man" dance with me?

MOST EVIL MAN: Why, yes. That would be very nice. (*They begin to dance, both in a strange glow*)

RICHEST GIRL: I like Washington Court House, Ohio. You want two reasons? It doesn't begin with an M, and it doesn't have over half a million population.

MOST EVIL MAN: I'm sure of that. (*The Playwright takes the butt of the "cigarette" out of his holder and puts it into an ashtray on the bar. The Best Hustler watches it carefully. The Playwright takes an ordinary cigarette and inserts it into his holder. Frank leans across the Woman Who Knows to light it. Now the effects turn psychedelic, over all the walls: moving, curved finger-painting by some idiot-genius*)

WOMAN WHO KNOWS: (*Hiding her eyes from the match-light*) You're blinding me! I've never seen such a bright light! (*Through her hands, still covering her eyes*) Until now, I have known nothing. Absolutely nothing. Book knowledge, fact knowledge, card-catalogue knowledge is just a fake substitute—like reading on a jar, "Artificial Coloring." It's synthetic, false, temporary, meaningless, worthless. You stuff your head with it to avoid facing the hard, pure light of God! (*Looking up, beatifically*) I am Joan at the stake, I am Teresa of Avila, I am Saint Monica with black hands and face . . . !

FRANK: What the hell is Joan of Arc doing, talking in English—and with a British accent? (*He hits the record player head, so that it smears across the record to a stop. All the effects suddenly cut!*) You're fakes, all of you. Phoneys. Frauds. I always knew it! (*They all freeze, staring at the shouting bartender*) My hors d'oeuvre tray was the big joke of the year. And the joke's on all of you. (*He switches on more lights, further shattering the mood*) You think that was LSD? Three saccharine tablets dipped in ink! (*Laughing*) Peyote my ass! That was melon rind soaked in goat urine. (*Turning abruptly to the Playwright*) Your fancy cigarette from Tibet was a bunch of old Chesterfield butts mixed with camel dung. You've switched to Camels all right, Buster—*real camels!* (*Holding aloft an opened tin can of mushrooms*) And did you know that the greatest truth serum in the world is Heinz's mushrooms? Yes sir, 57 varieties of heaven! (*There is a great silence. It seems as if the blood has drained from all of their faces, as if a moment of cherished youth has slipped away from all of them. The Richest Girl hides again, putting her dark glasses back on*)

RICHEST GIRL: (*Bewildered, low*) Why? Why would you do a thing like that?

FRANK: Why? Because you're the richest, you're the most famous, you're the most evil, you're the most hustling. Me? Up until tonight I've been the most *nothing*. Not even the most frank. But now I'm the best maker of false camel dung cigarettes ever, that's what I am! The bunco artist of the wrong side of the Straits. Oh, God, God, go create yourself, so I can get down on my knees and thank you.

WOMAN WHO KNOWS: I don't believe you.

PLAYWRIGHT: (*Quietly*) *I* believe him. (*He looks at the others, who have sagged almost hopelessly*) Why not? Did St. John of the Cross use mescaline, for Christ's sake? Did Joan of Arc have a shot in the arm before she saw her visions and heard her voices?

RICHEST GIRL: Where is it? Where do we find it again?

PLAYWRIGHT: In the head, in the heart, in the glands, in the gonads!

RICHEST GIRL: (*To the Most Evil Man*) Will you take me home?

MOST EVIL MAN: I would be delighted. (*They start out*)

FRANK: (*Desperately*) Drinks. For everybody. On the house. Real booze.

WOMAN WHO KNOWS: (*Gathering up her things*) Get yourself some new customers.

FRANK: (*Trying to stop them*) It was a joke.

WOMAN WHO KNOWS: I didn't laugh. Goodnight. (*The Most Evil Man and the Richest Girl have gone. The Woman Who Knows follows, not looking back*)

PLAYWRIGHT: Goodbye, Frank. Goodbye, Abdullah. Keep your powder dry. And your lipstick.

FRANK: (*Physically trying to stop him*) Where you going?

PLAYWRIGHT: (*Pushing him aside*) Back to New York. I've just decided. I'm going to tell the whole story to Walter Kerr.

FRANK: Walter Kerr? Who's he?

PLAYWRIGHT: (*Who else?*) A dentist. (*He leaves. The Best Hustler stares after him, then quickly takes the Playwright's discarded cigarette butt in the ashtray on the bar and nervously lights it, holding it carefully between his thumb and forefinger*)

FRANK: Kid. Didn't you listen? It's a fake. It's camel dung. (*But the Best Hustler continues to draw on it, leaping up on the bar. He stares at the ceiling, waiting for the miracle, searching for the flames and the flowers, but he sees nothing and is almost in tears. He lifts his hand in the air, trying to hear the sound of one hand clapping. Again he is frustrated, hearing nothing. He hits the air, harder and harder, in a frenzy. Now he seems to touch something up there and he strokes it*)

BEST HUSTLER: Hush, hush, hush . . . !

FRANK: Camel dung, kid. Camel dung. (*Slowly, as if hypnotized, Frank picks up the can of Heinz's mushrooms. He looks lost, bewildered, mystified by the Best Hustler's apparent ecstasy. Then slowly, Frank begins to eat a mushroom. Then he looks up. As if in a trance, his hand goes up to try to touch the silence*)

Curtain

Terence Kelly

STELLA

Terence Kelly

A prominent British novelist as well as dramatist, Terence Kelly was born in 1920, and educated at nine schools culminating in a scholarship to the City of London School.

During World War II, he was a fighter pilot flying Hurricanes in the United Kingdom, over the Continent, Africa and the Far East. Captured by the Japanese in March, 1942, he was a prisoner of war until August, 1945, and spent his internment partly in Java and largely in Japan in a camp very close to Hiroshima. After his release and subsequent discharge from military service, he engaged in a number of commercial jobs, all the while focusing his sights on an eventual literary career.

Mr. Kelly's published novels include: *Carnival in Trinidad; The Carib Sands; The Developers; The Genki Boys;* and *Properjohn.*

His produced plays are: *A Share in the Sun; Four Sided Triangle; Divorce in Chancery; The Genki Boys; The Masterminds;* and *Stella,* which appears here in print for the first time.

Married and the father of two children, Mr. Kelly lives in an old Thameside converted pub and is a Freeman of the City of London and a member of the Painter Stainers Company.

Characters:

ALAN GRAY

MARGARET GRAY

Scene:

Alan and Margaret Gray's sitting room, Brighton, England. A Sunday evening in spring. He is a successful businessman of about fifty; she is about forty. They have good taste and this is reflected in the furnishings. Essential items of furniture are a nest of small tables, a television set, a record player and equipment, a shelf or cupboard where records are stored, two armchairs and a cabinet where drinks are kept. There is an open fire and it is lit, protected by a fireguard, and a pile of logs is stacked beside it.

The room is empty, then after a moment or two, Alan and Margaret come in. He goes to fire and removes fireguard.

ALAN: It's doing well.

MARGARET: Isn't that a lovely fire! (*Kneels and throws a couple of logs on it*) That was a very good idea of yours. It's usually me who suggests a walk.

ALAN: Funny how little that pub's changed, isn't it; not one of those stuffed fish looks a day older. I wonder what he was like?

MARGARET: Who?

ALAN: Jesse Blackall. (*Margaret frowns*) The man who caught them. Didn't you notice the capitals among the weeds? Painted on all the cases. What do you think he was like?

MARGARET: Now how on earth would I know?

ALAN: You can tell a lot from names.

MARGARET: Nonsense.

ALAN: It isn't nonsense. (*Ponders*) Jesse Blackall. Dark,

obviously. Big moustache. Dressed in tweeds and heavy boots. But quiet, shrewd.

MARGARET: Beats his wife?

ALAN: Probably.

MARGARET: Has a mistress on the side?

ALAN: A country girl. Big bosomed, thick legged and apple cheeked.

MARGARET: Owns a big dog, tremendously well trained.

ALAN: And wears one of those hats which points in opposite directions.

MARGARET: Deerstalkers?

ALAN: I wonder why they do anyway? Do you think it's to confuse the deer?

MARGARET: Darling, you're a fool. I always said you were a fool. What would you like for supper?

ALAN: Oh, I don't mind. Anything. What's on the tube?

MARGARET: There's that play with Keith Michell you wanted to watch.

ALAN: You mean there's that play with Keith Michell you said might be worth watching.

MARGARET: No. You said you wanted to see it. Really.

ALAN: I said nothing of the sort. But I don't mind. When was the last time we went to that pub?

MARGARET: It was a long time ago.

ALAN: Must be ten years, I should think.

MARGARET: I know when it was! We were bringing Roddy back for the holidays after his first term at Abingdon. You pretended you'd run out of cigarettes and we went in for a quick one. We left Roddy in the car.

ALAN: That's right. And when we came out he'd got your latest novel out of the glove compartment, had found a dirty passage and was breathing heavily.

MARGARET: Go on with you.

ALAN: I used to go with my father to that pub when I was a child. He used to leave me in the sitting room . . .

MARGARET: . . . And one day you found an old medical

dictionary and by the time he took you home you'd got everything from acidosis through to zoanthropy. That's the third time today alone.

ALAN: The scourge of marriage is its endless repetition. You run out of new things to say. Which is why you can always tell if the woman with a man in a restaurant is his wife or someone else's. Even when they obviously don't accept a word that's being said, they still disbelieve with tremendous concentration.

MARGARET: It's rather sad, isn't it?

ALAN: It always looks hard work to me. How about a drink?

MARGARET: D'you know I don't think I will. I got some paté from Waitrose. Real paté. Farmhouse. Not in a tin.

ALAN: No wonder the lights in the village stores throughout England are being extinguished one by one. Waitrose!

MARGARET: You're just obstinate.

ALAN: No, I really would prefer you didn't use them.

MARGARET: Will's quite right. You're square and stuffy. Paté and toast? By the fire? And watch Keith Michell?

ALAN: When does he come on?

MARGARET: In about half an hour. (*Exits*)

(*Alan goes to the drinks cabinet, takes out a bottle of gin, then changes his mind and puts the bottle back. He exits and comes back a moment later with a half bottle of red wine, a corkscrew and two glasses. He sets these down near the fire, selects a record and puts it on the record player. As the music blares, Margaret returns with napkins in silver rings, table mats and knives*)

MARGARET: Why do you always have to have it so *loud?*

ALAN: Before I was married . . .

MARGARET: You used to have it so loud that the glass used to shiver in the window panes. (*Then, contritely*) Sorry. (*She turns the volume down*)

ALAN: You say sorry, then go and turn the bloody volume down!

MARGARET: Oh well, if you want to . . . (*Pause*) Darling, do you think we ought to give ourselves a change?

ALAN: A change? What do you mean a change?

MARGARET: I don't know . . . Why don't you go off and have a holiday on your own. Play some golf or something?

ALAN: I can play golf here . . . what an extraordinary idea.

MARGARET: No. It might be a good thing . . . for both of us.

ALAN: I'd be bored stiff and my ego would go right down to my boots.

MARGARET: You can't get rid of things just by pretending they aren't there.

ALAN: And you can't make them exist by pretending that they are. I don't understand you, Maggie. We have a marvelous day . . . a marvelous weekend . . . the first we've felt truly on our own for twenty years. We light a fire, go out for a walk and a beer and come back to Keith Michell and Waitrose paté and suddenly . . . bang! I'm supposed to be off to Zanzibar.

MARGARET: All right, let it go.

ALAN: My ego really would go down to my boots, you know.

MARGARET: (*Flatly*) Would it? (*Then, seeking reassurance*) Would it really?

ALAN: Really. I hated those weeks in the States without you. Or did you think . . . ?

MARGARET: No. I never thought that. Not for a moment. They're rather good those records, aren't they?

ALAN: (*Relieved*) All the better for not having to pay for them.

MARGARET: You're not really serious about that are you?

ALAN: I'm absolutely serious.

MARGARET: But you can't just keep them. It's dishonest.

ALAN: No more dishonest than *Readers Digest* sending them without so much as a by-your-leave and then relying on human indolence to see them through. Serve them right. Don't worry they can afford it.

MARGARET: Are you boiling the wine? (*This is a family cliché without sarcasm*)

ALAN: Yes.

MARGARET: I'll get the toaster. (*Exits*)

(*Alan gets two of the occasional tables and places them in front of the armchairs. He puts a mat on each, then collects wine glasses from hearth. He handles them gingerly as they are hot, places them beside mats, then moves wine away from the fire and begins to draw cork as Margaret returns with loaf on breadboard, knife and toaster*)

ALAN: It really is boiled this time. *And* I forgot to draw the cork.

MARGARET: How could you? It's supposed to breathe.

ALAN: Probably choked itself to death. (*Pulls cork*) There.

(*Margaret plugs in toaster. She cuts two slices of bread and puts them in*)

MARGARET: Butter! (*Crosses to door; turns*) Watch the toaster.

ALAN: Won't it pop up?

MARGARET: After twenty-two years?

ALAN: Well, *I* pop up after twenty-two years.

MARGARET: (*Lightly*) Don't be disgusting. (*Exits*)

(*Alan turns up volume of record player, then turns it down a little. He warms himself by the fire and looks about him. It is getting dark now. The room looks inviting, yet he conveys a shade of tension, as if this evening, for all its normality, is not quite real, that he and Margaret are overplaying it—which they are. Then, he shrugs, picks up wine bottle, fills the glasses and drinks a little from his own. Margaret comes in with butter*)

MARGARET: You've turned it up.

ALAN: Haven't touched it.

MARGARET: That's where Will gets his capacity for lying from. How's the toast?

ALAN: Damn! (*He crosses to toaster, snaps up the lever so that the slices of toast shoot out. He gives one piece to Margaret and puts the other on his own plate. Margaret, already seated, helps herself to paté and butter. Alan does the same.*)

MARGARET: Do you want the light on?

ALAN: No. (*For a moment or two, they sit quietly eating their supper, sipping their wine and listening to the music*)

MARGARET: I wonder when we'll *hear* from Will.

ALAN: Uhm?

MARGARET: I said I wonder when we'll hear from Will?

ALAN: (*Without much interest*) Oh, I don't know. By next weekend, I expect.

MARGARET: I hope he won't find Canada disappointing. It's terribly young to go off on your own. Especially for a boy. (*Pause*) It's funny, isn't it; after all this time suddenly not having children any more.

ALAN: I'm trying to listen to the music.

MARGARET. (*With slight sarcasm*) Sorry. (*There is another long pause. Alan is staring into the fire. Margaret looks at him keenly, obviously reaching a decision*) Would you like another piece of toast?

ALAN: (*Impatiently*) It's all right. I'll get it.

MARGARET: No, don't worry. (*Margaret cuts a slice of bread, puts it in toaster and stations herself there*)

ALAN: It's all right, Maggie. I'll watch it. For heavens' sake! (*Margaret sits. There is silence for a moment. Then, the record catches in a groove. Edgily*) God Almighty! (*He removes record, takes it to the window and examines it*) What a bloody racket! It's got a crack in it.

MARGARET: (*Ironically*) And after all that money you laid out.

ALAN: Well, I might have. (*Puts record into sleeve and begins to select another one*)

MARGARET: No, don't put on another record. Let's just sit here watching it get dark. (*Suddenly*) The toast!

ALAN: Oh, damn. (*Examines toast*) It's all right. Caught it in the nick of time. Want another piece?

MARGARET: No, thanks.

ALAN: (*Half grumbling*) I can't see why we can't have music while we're watching it get dark.

MARGARET: If that's what you really want.

ALAN: Well . . .

MARGARET: No.

ALAN: Why not? It's a good idea. A sort of celebration.

MARGARET: Don't be silly.

ALAN: What have I said that's silly?

MARGARET: Well, you can't . . . not just like that.

ALAN: I can. You can't. With you it has to be telegraphed in advance and when delivered, all wrapped up in tinsel.

MARGARET: That isn't fair.

ALAN: Isn't it?

MARGARET: No . . . it's not. (*Pause*) It's going to be funny, isn't it, Alan, having both Roddy and Will permanently away? It's going to take some getting used to.

ALAN: Oh, I don't know. They were away at boarding school.

MARGARET: That was different. (*Pause*) I'm glad we had them when we did. Just think of Jean and Douglas . . . he'll be sixty-two when Charles is Will's age.

ALAN: Well, I'm fifty.

MARGARET: Not until September.

ALAN: That's not long. Anything in the bottle?

MARGARET: No. Go and open another one if you want to.

ALAN: It doesn't matter.

MARGARET: Oh, for heavens' sake. If you want another glass of wine, have it! Why shouldn't you?

ALAN: I said it doesn't matter. Don't crowd me, Maggie.

MARGARET: (*A little grimly*) Sorry.

ALAN: All right. But . . . well, maybe you don't realize it but . . . oh, hell!

MARGARET: I told you. It might be a very good thing if we had a change.

ALAN: And I told you that it wouldn't.

MARGARET: What are we going to do then?

ALAN: Do?

MARGARET: Yes. Do. Let's face reality, Alan. With Roddy in the Navy and Will in Canada, we're really on our own. For twenty years we've been protected from each other. Worrying about bringing up two children. First it was about them smothering themselves in their cots; then how they'd fit in at school and what sort of school. After that it was grades and sports. And then what they were going to do. Oh, we had our good times and our bad and occasionally even a holiday on our own, but mostly we concentrated on *them,* more so probably than the majority of parents. And although we've never openly admitted it to each other we both know exactly why. Because we couldn't face the reality of *our* personal relationship. Well, now we've got to. *Now.* We can't concentrate on *them* any more. We're right out in the open and twenty years older than the last time.

ALAN: That's why you didn't want the music?

MARGARET: That's either a very shrewd question or a very stupid one.

ALAN: And what does that mean?

MARGARET: It hurt sitting here, watching it get dark, listening to that music. At least it hurt me. It didn't hurt you, did it?

ALAN: As a matter of fact, it did.

MARGARET: Yes. But in your case it was masochism. You were wallowing in pain. Do you think I don't understand you by now, Alan? Do you think I don't know the moment you've gone away from me? The moment I cease existing as a human being? And do you think that when those moments come and I'm left . . . in a dreadful sort of vacuum, dismissed, shrugged off . . . I don't realize *where* you've gone? *Why* you've gone? (*There is a long silence*) Well?

ALAN: This is a very dangerous conversation, isn't it? Of course, there are times when I go away from you. But what's so heinous about that? Aren't we all entitled to a little privacy, to have in our minds a box to which we can retreat? Does marriage imply such all embracing possessiveness as that? On his wedding night, my father said to my mother, standing with his back to her looking into the street outside their hotel bedroom, that she wasn't to worry if sometimes he went off on his own—

that he had a kingdom of imps of which he was the ruler and sometimes he had to be with them. She didn't understand that it was allegory, not then, but she did later. Well, I have my imps too, Maggie, but they don't harm you.

MARGARET: I don't mind your imps.

ALAN: Oh yes, you do. You're jealous of them.

MARGARET: No. I promise you. I like you having them. All men should have them, and all women. And they do.

ALAN: Well, then . . . oh, Maggie! This is stupid. Come and sit here. (*Pats side of chair*)

MARGARET: No. There's no purpose.

ALAN: Please.

MARGARET: Oh, very well. (*She comes over and sits on floor, her back against Alan's chair. She stares into the fire. Alan puts his hand on her shoulder, then after a moment slides it to her breast*) Don't do that!

ALAN: But why not?

MARGARET: Please. (*Abruptly she stands, becoming businesslike and a little bitter*) Shall I make some coffee?

ALAN: (*Stiffly*) If you like.

MARGARET: (*With a sudden change of mood*) Oh, don't be like that, Alan.

ALAN: I'm not being like anything. *You* are.

MARGARET: Yes. I know. But. Well, I know it sounds silly to you . . . (*Giving up*) Oh, damn! Why do you always try to make me explain what you understand already? (*Alan remains silent*) I'll go and make the coffee. What do you want? Perked or Turkish?

ALAN: I don't mind.

MARGARET: Well, they're both as easy . . . For goodness sake.

ALAN: Turkish.

(*Margaret exits, carrying one or two mats, etc. with her. Alan rises, selects another record and puts it on. After a few moments, Margaret returns with coffee. She pours a cup for Alan and hands it to him*)

ALAN: (*Absently*) Thank you.

MARGARET: (*Sits with her own coffee; then, after a long pause*) Look, if you like . . . Oh, damn! I can't shout against that. (*She gets up and turns off record player*)

ALAN: (*Angry, but calm*) Maggie!

MARGARET: I was going to say that if you like . . . when we've had our coffee we could go upstairs.

ALAN: Well, that's a sacrifice, isn't it.

MARGARET: Oh, don't be ridiculous!

ALAN: I'm not being ridiculous. My God, I don't know why we don't go and live in suburbia and be done with it. "When we've finished our coffee we could go upstairs."

MARGARET: Well, before we have our coffee then. I don't care.

ALAN: But you do care. That's the trouble. You care very much. Everything in its appointed place. Everything at its appointed time. Eat, drink, and *then* be merry. But only upstairs. What's the matter with downstairs? On the floor. In front of the fire with music playing in the background.

MARGARET: (*With a spurious show of making an attempt to lighten it*) It's more comfortable.

ALAN: (*Interrupting*) Who the devil *cares* where it's more comfortable? What's the matter with doing it here? On a hard floor. Or in a field on a summer's day? Or in a railway carriage? Or in a motor car? Why does it always have to be so organized and clinical? God's truth. You say something to me. Okay, I misunderstand you. Never mind, I look at you. And you're attractive to me. As attractive as any woman I've ever known. (*Unconvincing*) You know that. Whatever else you say you've never denied I feel like that about you. Have you?

MARGARET: (*Without interest*) No.

ALAN: No. And you know that suddenly . . . And what do you suggest? That we go upstairs after we've finished our coffee. That's not what I want! What I want is you, of your own accord, to go upstairs and use your bloody imagination and then . . .

MARGARET: What a pitiful defense.

ALAN: (*Astonished*) What's that supposed to mean?

MARGARET: I know how you are, Alan. And you know I've accepted you as you are. That I do things which make me feel uncomfortable because that's what you want—or say you want. Pointless and unnecessary things which . . .

ALAN: When! When have you?

MARGARET: The last time you asked me. Whenever that was.

ALAN: I'm asking you now.

MARGARET: No. All you're doing is trying to prevent me saying what I want to say. We won't make love tonight. You don't want to make love tonight. You haven't the least interest in making love tonight. But your conscience, or something or other, tells you that as this is, in its way, a special occasion you *ought* to want to make love tonight. Or that I probably expect you to make love tonight. So what do you do? Create a situation which makes it impossible for us to make love. I don't think you really ever want to make love to me again. You will, of course. You've got your reasons. But they aren't sexual ones.

ALAN: I've suddenly become a different person.

MARGARET: No. Older. Sex doesn't blot out the considerations suddenly like it used to. That's all.

ALAN: (*Quietly*) That's not true.

MARGARET: It is true. As you said, you're nearly fifty.

ALAN: What the hell has that got to do with it except in the eyes of narrow-minded ignoramuses and teen-aged children! Oh, I agree, in Roddy and Will's eyes I'm an old man already. The idea of my taking off my clothes and rolling with you on the carpet would probably astonish more than nauseate them.

MARGARET: And that's totally unconvincing, too. Why do you exaggerate sex all the time, Alan. Do you think I don't see through it?

ALAN: Take a walk down Dean Street sometime. What is remarkable is that I have to justify myself. God, in three years we'll be celebrating our silver wedding and we're still trying to get to terms on sex!

MARGARET: (*Unmoved*) You're still exaggerating.

ALAN: I suppose we'll have a party and they'll all come 'round. Your family, my family. What's left of it. People from the golf club. People whose names we'll even find difficulty in remembering. And they'll drink our health in our champagne and say what a splendid couple we are and how obviously happy we've been over the last twenty-five years . . .

MARGARET: And haven't we been?

ALAN: You were the one who started querying it, not me. You were the one who started us off on this ridiculous and quite unnecessary row. Yes. We have been happy—in the sense that there's nothing I could tell anyone, except maybe a psychiatrist, that would earn me anything but envy.

MARGARET: Whereas in fact you're to be pitied because your wife won't act the prostitute with you.

ALAN: If you like.

MARGARET: (*Pause*) Tell me, Alan. How many women do you think out of all those we know . . .

ALAN: What do *I* care? What do I care if *none* of them do? We're talking about you and me.

MARGARET: It's remarkable you still have to justify yourself. You're still doing it. But it's really phoney, isn't it, Alan? Even that business of your complaints is phoney. I'd have done anything you wanted me to—anything—if you'd really wanted it. You know that. And if I haven't, it's been because you never wanted to push me to the ultimate. Because if you had, then you'd have been left with nothing to complain about. So long as you could justify *that,* it wasn't your fault if our marriage was not . . . what is it you say? Completely fulfilled. So long as you could justify that, you could also justify a rather uneasy conscience.

ALAN: Which means?

MARGARET: Oh, no. I'm not accusing you of being unfaithful to me.

ALAN: Which I haven't been.

MARGARET: I believe you. And you must have had your

opportunities. Do you remember those annual reunions you used to have?

ALAN: What on earth has that to do with this?

MARGARET: Quite a lot. You used to come home with the milk. Pie-eyed. And those were the days when London crawled with open prostitution, weren't they? When if you wanted a woman all you had to do was slow your car down in the street. Women, who for a few pounds you wouldn't have noticed, would have willingly done all those exaggerated things you have continually accused me of being too squeamish to indulge you in. Don't you think it's rather strange that if your tastes are what you hint at, you didn't take a willing substitute? Or did you?

ALAN: No.

MARGARET: Why not? (*Alan does not answer*) That's a very difficult question to answer, isn't it? Except in the obvious way, which I wouldn't believe and you wouldn't expect me to. (*Pause*) You know I haven't been unfaithful either, don't you?

ALAN: Yes. Of course.

MARGARET: But then I had my prudishness to help me, didn't I?

ALAN: I don't understand you.

MARGARET: No. That's the truth, isn't it? You don't understand me. And you never have. And, Alan, I'm not all that difficult to understand. Not really. Do you know why you've never understood me? It's quite simple really. You've never tried to. And why not? Because you just weren't interested. Because you never loved me, Alan, did you?

ALAN: That's not fair.

MARGARET: Cleverer than saying not true. And much easier. But let's not bother if it's fair or not. You never loved me, Alan, did you? (*Alan does not answer*) No. For a little while I thought you did. But that was because I was so in love with you that when I looked at you I saw my own love reflected in your eyes. There's been only one woman in your life, hasn't there, Alan? And her name was Stella. (*Short pause*) No, I could hardly expect you to answer that.

ALAN: But why shouldn't I . . . ?

MARGARET: (*Interrupting*) I'll tell you. Before you get yourself into a muddle. Because the facade of our marriage, which means your *life* as well, couldn't stand you admitting it. At least that's the way you've been looking at it for twenty years. That's only one reason. I'll tell you another: because the facade of your mental relationship with Stella couldn't stand it either. You're in a very comfortable position, Alan. You're a reasonably happily married man with all the trimmings, children, a home and so on, with, on the side, an affair that's foolproof.

ALAN: Are you suggesting . . . ?

MARGARET: Don't be so pompous and no! I've already said I'm not suggesting you're having a physical affair with Stella. Only a mental one. And that you've been having that ever since you broke it off with her God-knows-how-many years ago.

ALAN: Oh, don't be so absurd.

MARGARET: Even you can manage that kind of remark. Have you ever really asked yourself why you didn't pick up one of those prostitutes?

ALAN: The idea disgusted me.

MARGARET: And I don't believe one word of that. Not one word. You didn't pick up a prostitute because you had your own prostitute waiting for you at home. Why pay twice for the selfsame article? (*Pause*) What do you think I've felt like, Alan, through all those hundreds of times you've made love to me when I knew that in every case if you were thinking of anyone except yourself it was Stella you were thinking of? Do you think that what I felt was so very different from what a prostitute feels when she's earning *her* keep? Do you think there haven't been scores of times when I couldn't have screamed out for the hatefulness of it?

ALAN: (*Genuinely shocked*) You couldn't have felt like that.

MARGARET: Oh, but I did. Many times.

ALAN: I never realized.

MARGARET: There are many things you never realized,

Alan. You never realized how deeply I was in love with you. How could you? To know how much a person loves you you have to love that person. And Stella was the person that *you* loved. And there was something else you didn't realize . . . you didn't realize how sorry I was for you. That I understood what a lonely man you were, a man who'd missed the chance of marrying the only woman who got through to his roots.

ALAN: If you thought this, felt this, why *did* you marry me?

MARGARET: I didn't think this when I married you, Alan. If I had, I wouldn't have married you. Oh, I don't know . . . perhaps that's not true. I was very young then and, as you've said often enough, women don't marry the man they see standing at the altar, but the man they're going to make that man at the altar be. But I didn't think it then. I just thought that Stella was a fool and was grateful that she was. Have you ever seen her since we got married?

ALAN: Never.

MARGARET: Not even for lunch? Not even bumped into her accidentally Christmas shopping?

ALAN: No.

MARGARET: That's surprising really, isn't it? With you going up to London every day . . .

ALAN: She probably doesn't live in London. Maybe she's gone abroad.

MARGARET: Supposing she hasn't. Supposing she still lives in London. Supposing when you're up in town tomorrow, and I'm safely tucked down here in Brighton, you bumped into her? You'd not just raise your hat to her, would you? I mean you'd buy her a drink, or lunch or something?

ALAN: I suppose so.

MARGARET: And then supposing *she* suggested you met again. What would you do, Alan?

ALAN: I don't know.

MARGARET: Then I suggest you find out. Stella isn't abroad. And she *does* live in London. She's got a house in Walton

Street. I saw her a little while ago, Alan. We had a long chat. Oh, it's all right, there's nothing sinister about my seeing her . . . and she didn't spill any beans.

ALAN: There aren't any beans to spill.

MARGARET: No. I believe you.

ALAN: How did you come to see her?

MARGARET: Oh, that's quite simple. We happened to use the same restaurant for lunch.

ALAN: When was this?

MARGARET: Does it matter?

ALAN: Not particularly . . . oh, all right! Yes, of course I'm interested. She did mean a lot to me. I've never pretended otherwise.

MARGARET: Aren't you going to ask me what she looked like?

ALAN: What's the point? Did you lunch together?

MARGARET: No. I wasn't by myself for lunch.

ALAN: What were you doing in town?

MARGARET: Well, considering I go up every week . . .

ALAN: I'm sorry. So you just chatted briefly by the table. Or she did.

MARGARET: On that occasion.

ALAN: You mean you've met her since?

MARGARET: We had tea together.

ALAN: I don't believe it. Stella?

MARGARET: Now don't be silly, Alan. Why shouldn't we have tea together? You don't think a woman who had a man as much in love with her as you were, and who even if she didn't love him enough to marry, still liked him well enough, could resist it do you? All I can say is, you don't know women very well. Not women like Stella. No wonder she didn't marry you.

ALAN: She suggested it? The tea?

MARGARET: Suggested? She *insisted.*

ALAN: How extraordinary!

MARGARET: Not at all. Her marriage didn't work out, you know.

ALAN: How should I know? What happened to her marriage?

MARGARET: She didn't say. She just said it foundered five years ago.

ALAN: Did she divorce him?

MARGARET: She didn't go into details. In fact she said hardly any more than what I've just told you. She was much more interested in talking about you. You know, Alan, if it had been you in that restaurant, instead of me, I very much doubt if she'd have agreed to leave it there.

ALAN: You don't know Stella. She's far too . . .

MARGARET: Cool? Sensible? (*Pauses*) Incidentally, I noticed you said "is."

ALAN: You're not going to try to make something out of that, are you?

MARGARET: I'm *certainly* going to make something out of it! Twenty years and when you think of her it's still in the present tense. *There's* the ghost that's been lying between us, isn't it, Alan? *Stella.* And she'll go on lying between us for the next twenty years, won't she? Unless we do something about it.

ALAN: (*Astonished*) You're suggesting I do see her.

MARGARET: Yes. I am.

ALAN: I suppose she's suddenly fat and blowsy?

MARGARET: I'd hardly call her that.

ALAN: What do we do? Ask her 'round for the weekend?

MARGARET: *We* don't do anything. You do. You take her away for a holiday. Somewhere abroad, I should think. Somewhere where you won't have to keep looking over your shoulder to make sure no one's watching you.

ALAN: You can't be serious!

MARGARET: I'm absolutely serious, Alan. For twenty years I've shared you with another woman. I'm not prepared to do so for another twenty. You either get *her* out of your system . . . or me.

ALAN: I don't believe a word of this.

MARGARET: You don't?

ALAN: No.

MARGARET: Why not?

ALAN: Because if you felt as strongly as you say you do, you didn't have to wait for an accidental meeting. You could have telephoned her.

MARGARET: That's another one of those remarks that's either rather clever or utterly stupid. And do you think until I knew how she felt about you I'd have risked being left a grass widow with two children to bring up?

ALAN: But now they've gone . . .

MARGARET: No, Alan, that's not what I mean. Not what I mean at all.

ALAN: I see. But supposing you were wrong?

MARGARET: I'm not wrong.

ALAN: But you could be. Are you really prepared to take that risk?

MARGARET: I think that is probably the most conceited remark I have ever heard in all my life.

ALAN: Then why try to persuade me into this . . . this adventure?

MARGARET: The fact that that's how you refer to it shows you don't need much persuading.

ALAN: Let's stop being clever, Maggie, shall we? And stop trying to score points. Out of the blue, you make the almost unbelievable suggestion that I telephone a woman I haven't seen for more than twenty years and invite her to go abroad with me. You go on to say, or intimate, that while she'll accept the offer you're not worried . . . (*Margaret reacts*) All right. I'll withdraw that bit . . . that while she'll accept the offer it won't turn into a permanent affair because after a week or two of my uninterrupted company she'll tire of me.

MARGARET: Now when did I say that?

ALAN: You intimated it.

MARGARET: I did absolutely nothing of the sort.

ALAN: But you said . . .

MARGARET: I know exactly what I said. You'd better work it out again when you're less hot and bothered.

ALAN: I am not hot and bothered!

MARGARET: You are *very* hot and bothered. And I wouldn't blame you. Our Stella is a most attractive woman. There can't be many men who wouldn't jump at the opportunity. (*Crosses to her handbag, takes out diary and looks through it*) The number is (*Reads*) 01 373 4241. (*Margaret looks directly at Alan as she speaks and afterwards, but he does not hold the look for long*)

ALAN: This is ridiculous. Totally ridiculous! (*Alan crosses to pour himself a drink*)

MARGARET: Aren't you even going to ask me what she looks like now?

ALAN: I'm not interested in what she looks like.

MARGARET: Rubbish. You're shaking like a leaf.

ALAN: Well, perhaps I am. Are you surprised? All right then. What *does* she look like?

MARGARET: Well, to start with, she's still got that look about the eyes. The one I haven't got. The one you used to joke about when we first got married. You used to say you'd give it to me before you were done. It was a poor joke, Alan. And in dreadful taste.

ALAN: Never mind that now. What else?

MARGARET: What else? Well, she's still got the rather husky voice that you used to say went so well with the look and which you always used to draw my attention to when you heard it in other women.

ALAN: Go on.

MARGARET: She's kept her figure. She smiles a lot. Dresses beautifully. Do I whet your appetite?

ALAN: Yes. Yes, Maggie, you do.

MARGARET: Then telephone her.

ALAN: (*More in control*) Let's just for a moment suppose I go through with this ridiculous game of yours. That I do telephone her. That I invite her to spend a couple of weeks with me in . . . well, somewhere, and she agrees. Where do you gain?

MARGARET: Gain?

ALAN: Well, there must be something behind all this.

MARGARET: You're not prepared to take it at face value?

ALAN: Of course I'm not. There must be something behind it. (*Waits for Margaret to reply which she does not*) Well, suppose it didn't work the way you planned it should?

MARGARET: And how was that?

ALAN: For God's sake, stop talking in this affected manner and call a spade a spade! The only alternatives that make any sense at all are that either she'll tire of me or I'll tire of her. Well, supposing you're wrong. Supposing we didn't tire of each other. Supposing, once started, we wanted to carry on. How would that help you?

MARGARET: It would help me tremendously.

ALAN: To do what?

MARGARET: To make my *own* mind up.

ALAN: I don't see how.

MARGARET: I ought to leave you just for that.

ALAN: For what?

MARGARET: For not asking what *my* alternatives are. For not even contemplating that I've got alternatives.

ALAN: Well, of course you've got alternatives. You can want me back or not want me back. You called me conceited. All right, but I'm not so conceited as not to realize that if I did go away with Stella, you might come to the conclusion you didn't want me back.

MARGARET: I might come to the conclusion I didn't want you back. And you make out that your conceit is limited. My dear Alan, it isn't limited. It's boundless. You're blind with it. Don't you realize I've had an offer too?

ALAN: What!

MARGARET: An offer. A proposition. An invitation.

ALAN: I don't believe it.

MARGARET: Well, that was pretty predictable even if everything else hasn't been. Poor Alan.

ALAN: (*Pause; then, with heavy irony*) I suppose this offer came the same day you met Stella?

MARGARET: A long time before that.

ALAN: You mean to try to tell me . . .

MARGARET: Yes, Alan, I do. The first time the invitation was offered was three years ago.

ALAN: Three years! You'd have me believe . . . No, I don't believe it! I won't believe it.

MARGARET: (*Quietly*) I think you better had, Alan. For the last three years I've been regularly unfaithful to you.

ALAN: No. I don't believe this, Maggie. What I do believe is that this is the selfsame game we've been playing for the last hour or so. You've got a bee in your bonnet about Stella. You're trying to persuade me I've got to choose between two alternatives.

MARGARET: That's right. Absolutely. But you're wrong in thinking what I've just said isn't true.

ALAN: Only a little while back you told me you hadn't been unfaithful to me. Now you say you have been.

MARGARET: What I said a little while back, was, "You know I haven't been unfaithful either, don't you?" And what do you reply. "Yes. Of course." As if the possibility that I could ever cuckold *you* was so totally ridiculous as not to be contemplated for a moment. Well, you'd better start contemplating it now, Alan. At our level of life it's very much easier for a woman to get away with adultery than for her husband, particularly if the man she's doing it with happens to be unmarried which this one is. One can always fit it in between shopping and having one's hair done. Particularly if one happens to prefer a London hairdresser.

ALAN: It's incredible!

MARGARET: No. Surprising, perhaps. But not incredible.

ALAN: For God's sake, do you have to be so flippant about it?

MARGARET: That wasn't too convincing either. I wonder how much time you need to work out what your correct reaction ought to be. In any case I'm making no joke of this, Alan. I'm far too hurt for that.

ALAN: Oh, I see. It's my fault. I'm the guilty party.

MARGARET: Yes.

ALAN: It's because of me you've been carrying on this sordid little middle-aged love affair!

MARGARET: Yes. It is. And why so bitter about *when* it's happened? Do you think there's something nauseating about love affairs between people of our age? (*Alan does not reply*) I'm surprised you didn't pick that up, Alan. Or perhaps you don't want to.

ALAN: Why shouldn't I want to?

MARGARET: Because you'd have to apply it to Stella and yourself. And you wouldn't want to do that, would you, not with your romantic nature. When women get to our age, they ought to insist on separate bedrooms and avoid the covert glances shot at odd bits of them that aren't quite as good as they used to be by husbands who'd do better looking to their own incipient paunches. Not that the paunches matter all that much. On the whole women rather like it when their men start putting on weight. Perhaps subconsciously it makes them feel secure. After all *we're* not so sensitive. *We* concentrate on practical things. Such as, for example, that a woman of forty has only a few years left during which she can reckon to appeal sexually to a man she isn't married to. Which is another reason why it's time we brought this to a head.

ALAN: But wouldn't it be a fraud in your case?

MARGARET: I don't understand.

ALAN: An extension of your prostitution?

MARGARET: That's a pretty hard remark to take.

ALAN: It was you that called yourself a prostitute.

MARGARET: A lot of married women are prostitutes all their life, but they don't necessarily want it thrown back in their face. In any case it doesn't apply.

ALAN: Why doesn't it apply? Sex has never meant anything to you.

MARGARET: It does now.

ALAN: Not with me.

MARGARET: It might.

ALAN: Why should it suddenly? After half a lifetime?

MARGARET: Because I've discovered what it is like when you're lying in the arms of a man who isn't using you as a substitute.

ALAN: Do you love him? This man?

MARGARET: Who? John? No.

ALAN: Then he can accuse you of what you've been accusing me.

MARGARET: No. Because I've always been honest with him.

ALAN: (*Bitterly*) And, of course, his ideas of what a sexual relationship should be aren't exaggerated like mine.

MARGARET: I never said your ideas were exaggerated. Only that you exaggerated what your ideas were. In any case how do you know his ideas aren't exaggerated?

ALAN: Because you'd soon send him packing if they were.

MARGARET: And how do you know that?

ALAN: Because I know you.

MARGARET: No. Knowledge of a woman isn't part of her dowry, Alan. It doesn't come with a wedding ring. Nor like a free gift after you've collected five thousand breakfast labels. Knowledge comes from study. When you take a woman for granted, as you've taken me for granted, all you see in her is what you expect to find. Sometimes you find too little, sometimes too much.

ALAN: And that's a cue. Isn't it? Like all the rest. Telephone Stella. Meet her. Take her away. Have a good look at her. Note her imperfections. Bear in mind she's got a few years left in which she can possibly appeal sexually and when they're over, where's the profit? Remember she's aware of those years as well. It's so transparent, Maggie.

MARGARET: You've got to do it, haven't you, Alan? What you've just said proves you must. It proves how important she still is to you. No man would go to those lengths to prove an idea of this kind absurd unless he didn't find it absurd at all. You don't crack nuts with sledgehammers.

ALAN: But that's what you're trying to do. I don't believe

any of this, Maggie. I don't believe that you've met Stella; I don't believe there is a John.

MARGARET: I was with John when I met Stella. (*Pause*)

ALAN: When was this?

MARGARET: Last week. On Thursday to be precise. (*Pause*) I introduced them. John and Stella.

ALAN: As your lover, I suppose?

MARGARET: Good heavens, no! As my lawyer. (*Apologetically*) It was the first thing that came into my head.

ALAN: Ingenious! And for the first time this evening you're making sense. You get caught out skulking in some restaurant . . .

MARGARET: It was in Leoni's. I'd hardly call that skulking, would you? And we weren't caught out. I said he was my lawyer.

ALAN: And did she believe you?

MARGARET: Well, as a matter of fact I don't believe she did. But what of it? If this is all a charade, as you were leading up to saying, why should she tell you? Anyway, what am I trying to cover up? I've just told you everything.

ALAN: Subtle. You have an affair on the side. You get yourself caught. You're aware that what's been nicely tucked away for three whole years may suddenly be blown wide open. So what do you do? Try to throw a smoke screen over the whole messy business by coming up with some weird idea as a test case for our marriage. It's monstrous!

MARGARET: What tremendous righteous indignation! Are you going to phone her?

ALAN: Of course I'm not going to phone her!

MARGARET: Oh, don't be absurd, Alan. Of course you're going to phone her. And see her. How could you resist it? How could any man resist it? Here's a beautiful woman you've been mooning about for twenty-five years, who you once asked to marry you, available, and quite possibly willing. Here's a wife who isn't just looking the other way but is positively encouraging you to re-open a book you secretly wish you'd never closed. Here are *you*—fifty. Conscious your powers are a little on the wane and that from now on you'd only feel ridiculous taking out a typist. And here's your wife admitting her own infidelity, removing your last restriction—conscience. Of course you'll phone her.

ALAN: It's remarkable how you manage to turn defeat into a kind of victory.

MARGARET: It's more remarkable how you keep managing to avoid the issue. It isn't a question of victory or defeat. It's a question of you and me. I happen to have an alternative, Alan, but it's not the one I want to choose. I married you because I loved you. That love's a bit battered, but it's still alive, just as you believe your love is still alive for Stella. I have had to live with Stella for twenty years. I'm not going to any more. Suddenly, with Roddy and Will off on their own, we're free agents with alternatives for probably the last time in our lives. And even more than that, at least from my point of view, looking for a purpose in living at all. Up to now I've had my children. Now, I haven't anything! And there's something else I haven't told you yet, something I held back. Something that makes a tremendous difference. Stella and her husband did get a divorce. She's a free agent, too. (*There is a pause; then Margaret crosses to the telephone and begins to thumb through her diary*)

ALAN: No!

MARGARET: (*Calmly*) Now don't be silly, Alan. You know you'll only telephone her tomorrow when I'm out. (*She dials, listens, then holds telephone out to Alan. He takes it and puts it to his ear and listens. He jams it back onto the hook*) Was that Stella?

ALAN: Yes, damn you! That was Stella.

MARGARET: I was right, wasn't I? She hasn't changed.

ALAN: How should I know?

MARGARET: I mean her voice.

ALAN: No. No, it hasn't changed.

MARGARET: Did it do things to you? Give you butterflies in your tummy?

ALAN: Oh, shut up!

MARGARET: It did. Poor Alan. After all these years. Why *didn't* you marry her?

ALAN: You already know; because she wouldn't have me.

MARGARET: So you took me as second best.

ALAN: That isn't true. Not true at all. I didn't have to marry you because I'd been turned down by Stella. I didn't have to marry anyone. I married you because I wanted to marry you.

MARGARET: But why? You were still in love with Stella. You're still in love with Stella now.

ALAN: It's not like that. It's not so simple.

MARGARET: What is it like? Tell me, Alan. (*Gently*) I have to know now, don't I?

ALAN: I couldn't have married Stella. Never. We'd got our relationship onto different tracks. We could never have got onto the same lines again.

MARGARET: And yet you asked her to marry you?

ALAN: Yes. Several times. But I could hear her refusal in my own voice as I asked her. Asking her to marry me was *part* of our relationship—an acceptance of the fact that it could never be more than limited. Can you understand what I'm saying?

MARGARET: Yes. I think so. Because she hadn't reached the point where she was thinking of the possibility of marrying anyone.

ALAN: Yes. (*Bitterly*) She still had too many things to do. Too many experiences to taste. She hadn't any need of me; no need of anyone. She was very hard in a way. Giving and taking simply didn't enter into her philosophy. She was astonishingly direct, uncomplicated. She lived for each day as it was. Oh, I don't mean wildly. In fact she was probably the most self-disciplined woman I ever met. But she never regretted anything she did. If it was wrong, well, it was over and done with and tomorrow was more important anyway.

MARGARET: And you tried to tie her down?

ALAN: But I didn't, did I? By asking her to marry me I was merely bringing myself face to face with facts earlier than I would otherwise have done.

MARGARET: Deliberately?

ALAN: I'm not sure. But there was a compulsion in it. Subconsciously I knew.

MARGARET: What *did* she think of you?

ALAN: (*Smiling*) Well, she didn't want to throw away my adulation.

MARGARET: Not many women would. But what did she think of you?

ALAN: She thought a lot of me.

MARGARET: You were just . . . too early?

ALAN: Yes.

MARGARET: You slept with her, of course.

ALAN: Yes.

MARGARET: She was very young.

ALAN: She was never young. You were.

MARGARET: Is that why you married me? Because I was young and Stella wasn't?

ALAN: That came into it.

MARGARET: But you weren't in love with me.

ALAN: I didn't say that.

MARGARET: You never said it . . . or denied it.

ALAN: There are times when things are better left unsaid, or seem better left unsaid. And there are things which, if not said at the time they should have been, never can be said. When we got married, I still had Stella in my system. You knew that. You knew the hold she had on me. That I'd created a picture of what life should be which had revolved about her even though I knew it never would. Love. Love is a word which, it seems to me, is thrown around too easily. It's not a word *I* used very often, not even to Stella. And I couldn't say it in honesty to you so long as I couldn't think of Stella dispassionately.

MARGARET: And you never could. You can't now.

ALAN: That isn't quite the point. What applied at the beginning . . . our beginning, didn't later. Our own relationship was changing all the time. As it had to. Marriage in itself was a new, a tremendous thing, sufficient in itself. In all sorts of ways. That wonderful freedom from the slavery of continual sexual want which up to then had been only spasmodically satisfied. That in itself was a kind of miracle. And we were busy finding our feet in a new way of life. I had my business. Then there was Will, then Roddy. There was always something happening which radically changed our attitudes to each other.

MARGARET: And meanwhile you found the way to deal with Stella?

ALAN: Yes, I put her into a compartment of my mind which I didn't think you knew existed. I thought she was out of our life altogether. Apparently I was wrong. But that's what I thought. And then I could have told you that I loved you.

MARGARET: No. You couldn't have said that. All you could have said was that so far as that aspect of your life was concerned you loved me.

ALAN: Would that have been enough? Or was it better left unsaid?

MARGARET: Should any woman expect more than that? Does any woman hope for so very little? That's an unanswerable question, Alan. But you didn't say it.

ALAN: No. The time had gone when it could be said. There was resistance to my saying it—from you.

MARGARET: Yes. I think there was.

ALAN: Your love for me had been blunted by your disappointment. I know. And you'd found your substitutes. You'd had to.

MARGARET: Yes.

ALAN: We struck a bargain really, didn't we? Except perhaps in sex itself.

MARGARET: I didn't realize you knew we had.

ALAN: Oh, it was only in a vague sort of way, I know. It's only this evening it's become so clear. I never let myself probe too deeply. Where would it get me?

MARGARET: And meanwhile you were considerate. Or thought you were. And all the time were quite wrong, Alan. You drove yourself into a corner. You convinced yourself your sexual appetite was so much the greater, then didn't insist that it was gratified. That solved your conscience and gave you something to justify your thoughts and actions. It was very neat, really.

ALAN: And now you're saying it wasn't necessarily so at all.

MARGARET: I know it wasn't.

ALAN: (*Ironically*) Then it's very sad we should have wasted so much of these twenty years. Tell me about this man.

MARGARET: No.

ALAN: I've told you about Stella.

MARGARET: You've told me nothing I didn't know already. Except perhaps that where you went wrong was meeting her too early. She must have thought a lot about that herself. Particularly in these last five years. And before then, when her marriage was heading for the rocks? Do you think when he was making love to her she let herself imagine you were him?

ALAN: No. Not Stella, any more than I did. You were always you, when I made love to you.

MARGARET: Was I? It's a time for truth, however much it hurts.

ALAN: That is the truth. I swear to God that is the truth. (*Pause*)

MARGARET: I was wondering.

ALAN: What?

MARGARET: If I were Stella. I loved you, Alan, but suppose I hadn't. Suppose after marrying you, I found myself regretting I hadn't married someone else, someone who'd loved me and I'd loved as well, even if I hadn't realized it at the time. And that man had shrugged his shoulders and done the only possible thing, gone off and married someone else. Made his own way of life, had children, cut himself utterly away from me. What would *I* feel? Wouldn't I do the same as you did? Create my own compartment?

ALAN: Would you?

MARGARET: Yes. I think I would. But would Stella, Alan?

ALAN: I suppose so.

MARGARET: No. Don't just suppose so. Ask yourself?

ALAN: No. No, she wouldn't.

MARGARET: What would *she* have done? You know, don't you? She'd have got in touch with you. The moment she discovered she loved you and not the man she'd married, she'd have got in touch with you somehow and told you so. It's true, isn't it?

ALAN: Yes.

MARGARET: You're quite right about her. She would never regret anything she did. She's too straightforward altogether, too clear thinking. Too uncomplicated. She never had conscience—good or bad. I knew that before. And I knew that the other day when I sat and talked to her. I was talking to a woman, a very dangerous and attractive woman, who would take my husband away from me with a snap of her fingers if she wanted to.

ALAN: And you want to gamble on it?

MARGARET: To gamble involves weighing up the pull of the alternatives against the risk involved. I believe the risk is limited. I think she'd go to bed with you. Go on holiday with you. Have you as her lover. But I don't think she'd want you as her husband, Alan. If she'd wanted you as her husband, she'd have had you as that right in the beginning. She'd have found the way to make you wait till she was ready for you.

ALAN: What was that number? (*Margaret hands him the diary. He looks through it; picks up the telephone*) You understand what you're forcing me to do?

MARGARET: *I*'m not forcing you. (*Alan puts down telephone*)

ALAN: I want to get this quite clear first.

MARGARET: I thought it was.

ALAN: You don't mind if I do go away with her. You want me to. You believe the result will be a disenchantment so complete that I shall have got her finally out of my system. If you're right, you'll send your fellow packing; if I'm not, you'll accept his offer.

MARGARET: That's not what I think at all.

ALAN: It isn't?

MARGARET: (*Blithely*) No. I've changed my mind. But you do what you like. (*She picks up her bag*)

ALAN: Where are you going?

MARGARET: To London.

ALAN: To see this . . . John?

MARGARET: Yes.

ALAN: Then you'd better not come back.

MARGARET: I hadn't intended to. Except that you asked me. I'll telephone you in a couple of hours or so. To see what you've decided. Oh yes, Alan, I'm quite serious. I've never been more serious in my life. As soon as I've gone, you'll telephone Stella. In a couple of hours or so I'll telephone you. To see what you've decided. Then I'll decide—assuming I have a choice.

ALAN: I don't need to telephone Stella. I already know what I'm going to do.

MARGARET: I don't believe that's necessarily true. And there's no point in being precipitate. I'll phone you in an hour or two. (*She starts for the door*)

ALAN: Maggie.

MARGARET: Yes, Alan?

ALAN: What made you change your mind?

MARGARET: I'm not prepared to answer that.

(*She exits. There is silence in which the sound of Margaret's departure can be heard. Alan crosses to window and watches her go. For a second or two, he is indecisive; then he picks up the telephone and dials. In the following conversation only Alan's voice is heard*)

ALAN: Stella?

(STELLA): (Yes.)

ALAN: Alan.

(STELLA): (Where are you?)

ALAN: At home. It's all right. Maggie's just left.

(STELLA): (Left?)

ALAN: Yes. She's gone to London. To the man she's been living with for the last three years.

(STELLA): (Maggie!)

ALAN: Yes. Maggie. Incredible, isn't it?

(STELLA): (Do you mean she's left you? For good?)

ALAN: I don't know what she's going to do. She's going to phone me from London and see what *I've* decided.

(STELLA): (You mean about her?)

ALAN: No. I mean about me. Or rather about us. She's made the remarkable suggestion that I telephone you and invite you to go abroad with me.

(STELLA): (You mean she's found out?)

ALAN: No. It's not that.

(STELLA): (It must be.)

ALAN: I tell you it isn't that, Stella. She believes I haven't seen you since before we got married.

(STELLA): (You're wrong, Alan.)

ALAN: I'm not wrong, Stella. I tell you she hasn't the least idea.

(STELLA): (This man she's gone off to. Do you know him?)

ALAN: No. But *you* do. She introduced you to him last Thursday.

(STELLA): (What on earth are you talking about?)

ALAN: Last Thursday. At Leoni's.

(STELLA): (I wasn't in Leoni's last Thursday. I wasn't even in London.)

ALAN: Good God! But you must have been! She described you.

(STELLA): (I wonder how long she's known? Oh, well, I suppose it doesn't matter. What matters is that she does know. What are you going to do, Alan?)

ALAN: (*Almost impatiently*) I don't know. My God, to think that for all I know . . . for all these years . . .

(STELLA): (Is that important?)

ALAN: Of course it's important!

(STELLA): (Which means you aren't going to do what she suggested.)

ALAN: Does it? Why shouldn't I do what she suggested? She's given me carte blanche.

(STELLA): (Well?)

ALAN: I don't know. Listen, Stella. For the last hour it's been as if you've been here in this room. We talked as much about you as about ourselves.

(STELLA): (I see.)

ALAN: No, it wasn't like that. It . . .

(STELLA): (It *was* like that, wasn't it?)

ALAN: Yes. I suppose it was.

(STELLA): (She's a very clever woman.)

ALAN: Clever? Would you call it clever?

(STELLA): (Very clever. Because you're not going to do what she suggests are you, Alan?)

ALAN: No. But if I had . . . you wouldn't have come away with me, would you?

(STELLA): (I don't know. I wouldn't now.)

ALAN: Why not *now?*

(STELLA): (Because it wouldn't work. Because she's destroyed what there was between us.)

ALAN: Destroyed? Yes, she has, hasn't she? She's brought it in the open and destroyed it. She said a lot of things. You can imagine. Said them through herself, put herself up as a sort of . . . of Aunt Sally. Only it was *you* she was really talking about. I wonder . . .

(STELLA): (What do you wonder?)

ALAN: If there really is a John? That's the name of the man she's supposed to be having this affair with. Do you think there is a John? . . . I'm sorry. You're rather left out of this, aren't you?

(STELLA): (I expect she intended that as well.)

ALAN: I expect she did. It wouldn't work now, would it?

(STELLA): (No, it wouldn't. There'd always be her ghost between us. That's what she meant it to be.)

ALAN: It's funny. That's what she said of you, about a ghost between us, I mean. For these last twenty years. And it was true and would be true. On my part, anyway, Maggie's ghost would be tugging at my elbow, making me look in directions I wouldn't have thought to look in and saying "I told you so." Oh, Stella . . . I'm so sorry.

(STELLA): (I'm sorry, too.)

ALAN: Are you? But it doesn't have to be the end . . .

(STELLA): (It does, Alan.)

ALAN: Yes. You'd hate me now, wouldn't you? Or worse, despise me. In your eyes, I'd be an ineffectual coward scuttling out of harbor to see you now and then. What will you do, Stella?

(STELLA): (I don't know, Alan. Go away for a while, I think.)

ALAN: Away? Abroad? Like we used to say we would if only we had the chance? And now we have the chance. And we're not taking it. And yet I love you, Stella. I always shall. At least that's not destroyed.

(STELLA): (How strange.)

ALAN: Strange?

(STELLA): (That it's only now that you can say it.)

ALAN: Yes, that's true. Suddenly it's an easy thing to say. We should leave it there.

(STELLA): (Yes, we should.)

ALAN: Even if it were true about this John? Even if she wouldn't come back to me?

(STELLA): (Even then.)

ALAN: Yes.

(STELLA): (Goodbye, Alan.)

ALAN: Goodbye, Stella. (*Alan slowly puts down the telephone. He stands for a moment, then crosses and pours a drink. He puts it on table, then goes to record player and puts on a record low. He sits in his chair. Then suddenly he chuckles ruefully, rises and gets the telephone and places it on the table beside his drink. He glances anxiously at his watch and sits again—to wait*)

Curtain

Julie Bovasso

SCHUBERT'S LAST SERENADE

Julie Bovasso

Julie Bovasso is one of the contemporary theatre's rarities—a multiple talent who functions equally and successfully as actress, director, producer and playwright. Born in Brooklyn, New York, and a graduate of the City College of New York, Miss Bovasso has left a permanent imprint in various areas of the modern theatre. As founder, in 1953, of the Tempo Playhouse, the first professional experimental theatre in New York, she successfully introduced the works of Jean Genet, Eugene Ionesco and Michel de Ghelderode to this country. Generally considered to be one of the pioneer companies in the development of the Off-Broadway movement, Tempo Playhouse also became one of the forerunners of the Theatre of the Absurd in the United States.

The Tempo Playhouse established Miss Bovasso as a leading figure in the Off-Broadway citadel and brought her the first "Obie" (for Off-Broadway excellence) ever awarded, for her performance in Genet's *The Maids,* 1955. A second "Obie" was presented to her for "best experimental theatre work." In 1969, she created a record by receiving a triple "Obie" award for writing, directing and acting in *Gloria and Esperanza,* produced at the La Mama Experimental Theatre Club which subsequently moved to the ANTA Theatre on Broadway.

In addition to the aforementioned, Miss Bovasso's produced plays include: *The Moondreamers,* Ellen Stewart Theatre, New York, 1969; *Monday On the Way to Mercury Island,* La Mama, 1971; and *Down by the River Where Waterlilies Are Disfigured Every Day,* Trinity Square Repertory Company, Providence, Rhode Island, 1971.

Schubert's Last Serenade, which appears in print for the first time in this anthology, originally was presented at the La Mama Experimental Theatre Club in June, 1971. The play was directed by Miss Bovasso.

A playwright with distinct Absurdist leanings, Julie Bovasso's work often has stirred fierce controversy as well as fervent admiration. As Marilyn Stasio, the drama critic for *Cue* magazine, has written, "It's a tough, angry humor, which seems to flow from a cynical sense of disgust with the mess humanity has made of itself in the name of civilization, and whenever it's focused squarely it can be extremely potent satirical stuff."

As an actress, Miss Bovasso has appeared extensively on and Off-Broadway, at regional theatres throughout the country, on television, and in films. Her most recent appearance was as one of the principals in the American premiere (1971) of Genet's *The Screens* at the Chelsea Theatre Center, Brooklyn, N.Y.

A recipient of a Rockefeller Foundation playwriting grant in 1969 and a Guggenheim Fellowship in 1971, Miss Bovasso also is a drama instructor at Sarah Lawrence College and a member of the faculty of the New School for Social Research.

Author's Note

The action of the play occurs exactly as described by the Maître D'. There are a few stage directions which are not spoken by him and which are indicated in the usual manner. The Maître D' stands outside the action of the play and should have no contact with the actors nor they with him.

Characters:

THE MAÎTRE D'

ALFRED

BEBE

THE WAITER

THE COOK

FRANZ SCHUBERT

The houselights fade to black. A single spotlight picks up the Maître D' standing at a lectern in a corner of the stage. He reads from a manuscript.

MAÎTRE D': An elegant French restaurant. In the darkness we hear Schubert's Serenade played on a violin. (*The music begins and the lights fade up very slowly on the scene*) Alfred, a young construction worker, dressed in overalls and hard-hat, is seated at a table with Bebe, a young Radcliffe sophomore with a badly bandaged head. They stare at each other with intense love. Behind a large potted palm, Franz Schubert can be seen through the leaves, playing his violin. The waiter stands at his station, napkin folded over his arm, waiting.

(*There is a long silence*)

BEBE: I think it means something.

ALFRED: (*Nods*) Yeah.

BEBE: I mean, two people . . .

ALFRED: (*Nods*) Yeah, right.

MAÎTRE D': The cook appears in the archway and shakes

his fist fiercely at the palm tree. Franz Schubert stops playing and appears from behind the palm. The waiter looks from the cook to Franz Schubert. Franz Schubert looks from the waiter to the cook. The cook looks from Franz Schubert to the waiter; he makes another fierce gesture with his fist and exits angrily. The waiter follows him off quickly. Franz Schubert disappears behind the palm tree.

(*Franz Schubert plays again*)

BEBE: I mean . . . it means something.

ALFRED: Yeah.

BEBE: Happenstance.

ALFRED: Yeah.

BEBE: Accident.

ALFRED: Yeah.

BEBE: Don't you think it means something?

ALFRED: Yeah.

MAÎTRE D': Bebe brings her hand slowly up from her lap and moves it along the table toward Alfred. Alfred then brings his hand slowly up from his lap and moves it along the table toward Bebe. As their hands meet and touch they knock over a large glass vase. The music stops abruptly. Alfred and Bebe rise in confusion and embarrassment. Franz Schubert appears from behind the palm tree and glares at them. The waiter appears with a dustpan and brush and cleans up the mess. He glares at Alfred and Bebe, and exits. Franz Schubert disappears behind the palm tree, and Alfred and Bebe resume their original positions and try to recapture their love spell. There is a long silence. Franz Schubert plays again. Alfred and Bebe recapture their love spell and sit staring at each other with intense passion.

BEBE: Twice in two weeks.

ALFRED: Twice, right.

BEBE: It can't be an accident.

ALFRED: No.

BEBE: It has to mean something.

ALFRED: Right.

BEBE: It has to mean *something*.

ALFRED: Yeah.

MAÎTRE D': The cook pokes his head through the archway again and shakes his fist at the palm tree. The music stops abruptly. Suddenly, Bebe turns to the cook and shakes her fist fiercely at him. He rushes off. Alfred wipes his brow nervously with the napkin.

ALFRED: Wow! Some goings on.

MAÎTRE D': Franz Schubert plays again. There is another long pause while Alfred and Bebe get back into their love spell.

BEBE: I mean, why us?

MAÎTRE D': Alfred nods. But he does not make eye contact.

BEBE: It's such a large city, millions of people . . . why us?

MAÎTRE D': Pause.

BEBE: And twice. *Twice* in two weeks.

ALFRED: Right, twice.

BEBE: It's no accident.

ALFRED: No.

BEBE: It was planned.

ALFRED: Right.

BEBE: By some higher power.

ALFRED: Right.

BEBE: It was planned by some higher power that we should meet.

MAÎTRE D': Bebe listens to the serenade, wistfully carried off by the romance of the moment. Alfred is uncomfortable and sits with his head down, glancing around with lowered eyes.

BEBE: I mean, you and me . . . from opposite ends of the stratum.

MAÎTRE D': Alfred looks up, startled.

BEBE: Opposite ends of the stick.

ALFRED: Oh.

BEBE: In a city with millions of people . . .

ALFRED: Yeah.

BEBE: We stumble, we fall. Twice.

ALFRED: Right. We stumble, we fall.

BEBE: Twice.

ALFRED: Right.

MAÎTRE D': The waiter appears with two glasses of red wine. He places them on the table and, with a hostile glance at Alfred, exits. Alfred shifts uncomfortably in his seat. Bebe picks up her glass in a toast. Alfred does likewise.

BEBE: You know, the first time we stumbled across each other, I fell.

ALFRED: Oh, yeah?

BEBE: Down there in front of the Customs Building. Did you fall for me the first time we stumbled across each other?

ALFRED: Yeah.

BEBE: I knew it.

ALFRED: I didn't mean to crack your skull.

BEBE: Oh, but it was meant to be. I mean, why *my* head? Why not some other head? Don't you see? Don't you understand?

ALFRED: Yeah. I think so.

BEBE: *Your* club found its way to *my* head. I mean . . . *mine!*

ALFRED: That's true. It was your head. Not some other head.

BEBE: Not just *any* head. Don't you think that's magical?

ALFRED: Yeah.

MAÎTRE D': Franz Schubert stops playing and appears from behind the palm tree. He stands looking at them with an expression of unbelievable disgust.

BEBE: And just before I blacked out and fell, I knew that I had fallen.

ALFRED: For me.

BEBE: Yes. Just before I fell, I knew that I was falling . . . for you. Oh, I mean I was falling for The Cause, but while I was falling for The Cause, I simultaneously fell for you. It was a double fall, you might say. The moment you raised your club,

I started to fall. I fell even before you struck. But if you hadn't struck, I wouldn't have fallen.

ALFRED: For me.

BEBE: No, for The Cause.

ALFRED: Would you have fallen for me if you hadn't fallen for The Cause? I mean, anyway?

MAÎTRE D': Bebe frowns suddenly and, with a nervous little gesture, brings her hand to her chin.

BEBE: (*Evasively*) Have you got a cigarette?

ALFRED: (*Insistently*) Would you?

BEBE: I really would like a cigarette.

ALFRED: Answer my question!

BEBE: What question? (*The Cook and the Waiter appear*)

ALFRED: If I hadn't cracked your skull with my club and given you cause to fall for your Cause, would you have fallen for me anyway?

BEBE: I don't understand the question.

MAÎTRE D': She starts to rise. Alfred grabs her roughly by the arm.

ALFRED: Would you have fallen for me if you hadn't fallen for The Cause?

BEBE: You're hurting my arm!

ALFRED: Is it me or The Cause, baby?

BEBE: You're making a scene.

ALFRED: Let's have it straight or I'll break your skull!

MAÎTRE D': Bebe emits a cry of ecstasy and falls into his arms in a swoon. The waiter, the cook and Franz Schubert look from one to the other. Alfred holds Bebe's limp body, not knowing quite what to do with it. Finally, he puts her back into her chair. The cook and the waiter exit with hostile glances at Alfred. Franz Schubert disappears behind the palm tree. Alfred sits stiffly in his chair. Bebe finally opens her eyes.

ALFRED: Well?

BEBE: I haven't been quite honest with you.

ALFRED: That's what I thought.

BEBE: If you hadn't struck me that first time and given me the opportunity to fall for The Cause, I might not have fallen for you at all.

MAÎTRE D': Alfred rises angrily. . .

ALFRED: That's what I thought!

MAÎTRE D': . . . Flings his napkin on the table, picks up his tool box and starts to leave.

BEBE: Alfred, wait! (*She rises and grabs his arm. Alfred stops, stands with his back to her*) Don't leave me like this. Give me a chance to explain. It's all very complex. Please don't destroy something precious. It was the second time that I was really hooked, and whether or not the first time had happened, the second time would have happened anyway.

MAÎTRE D': Franz Schubert has come out from behind the palm tree and stands listening with interest.

BEBE: Don't you see? Whether or not I knew consciously that first time whether I had fallen for you because you'd made me fall for The Cause or whether I'd have fallen for you anyway doesn't matter. It was the second time, on the Ganesvort Street pier.

MAÎTRE D': Franz Schubert is confused.

BEBE: That second time was the time I knew that this time it was for real. (*The Waiter has entered with the Cook*) When I saw you marching on that line in front of the pier, carrying that picket sign which read "Save the Pier," and I arrived carrying a sign which read exactly the same thing! Oh, Alfred! That was the moment. It was the moment I realized that *we were on the same side!*

MAÎTRE D': She pauses and waits for some reaction. None is forthcoming. Desperately, she turns to Franz Schubert, the cook and the waiter for help.

BEBE: Don't you see? I realized that we were on the same side! (*Turning back to Alfred*) You, who had cracked my skull viciously two weeks earlier and sent me reeling to the ground for my Cause!

MAÎTRE D': Alfred does not respond. She turns to Franz

Schubert, the cook and the waiter again and attempts feverishly to explain.

BEBE: (*To Franz Schubert*) Don't you see? All my mixed emotions suddenly came together. All the confusion of love and hate jelled.

MAÎTRE D': Franz Schubert looks at the waiter.

BEBE: (*To the Waiter*) Love jelled into hate . . .

MAÎTRE D': The waiter looks at the cook.

BEBE: (*To the Cook*) Hate jelled into love . . .

MAÎTRE D': The cook looks at Franz Schubert.

BEBE: And suddenly I understood everything!

MAÎTRE D': They all look at each other in total confusion.

BEBE: *I understood my feelings about that first time at the Customs House!*

MAÎTRE D': Bebe turns desperately to Alfred, who is still not listening.

BEBE: I understood why I had felt that gnawing guilt about loving you, Alfred!

MAÎTRE D': At the mention of his name, Alfred turns.

BEBE: And because of that guilt, I had denied the truth to myself. I understood why I wanted to fling myself into your arms the moment you raised your club. I understood why I wanted to wrap myself around you and kiss you madly on the eyes in front of the world while the clubs were swinging and the rocks were flying and the bricks were hurtling through the air!

MAÎTRE D': The cook and the waiter leave. Franz Schubert straightens his tie self-consciously and goes behind the palm tree.

ALFRED: Are you saying that you would have fallen for me anyway? Even if I hadn't clubbed you?

BEBE: Yes!

ALFRED: Okay.

MAÎTRE D': They return to the table and resume their love spell with even greater intensity. Franz Schubert plays again, slightly off key.

(*The music plays for awhile, before Bebe speaks*)

BEBE: You know, Alfred, life is funny.

ALFRED: Yeah.

BEBE: I might not have known it if the second time hadn't happened.

MAÎTRE D': Alfred is immediately suspicious.

ALFRED: (*Suspiciously*) Waddayamean?

BEBE: I mean the Ganesvort Street pier. When I saw that we were on the same side it substantiated all the irrational emotions which I experienced at the Customs House.

ALFRED: Oh, right.

BEBE: You were fighting to save the pier. I was fighting to save the pier . . .

ALFRED: It's the union. The union is behind it all. The union is behind everything.

BEBE: The union is behind its men.

ALFRED: The men are behind the union.

MAÎTRE D': Franz Schubert appears from behind the palm tree with a savage look on his face.

BEBE: The union is behind our love!

MAÎTRE D': Franz Schubert flings his violin violently across the room. Alfred and Bebe rise in confusion. Franz, in a state of utter agitation, is feverishly mopping his face with a handkerchief. He then crosses the room and picks up his violin. The waiter enters hurriedly and tries to calm Franz Schubert, patting his head and brushing off his coat. Then, with an angry glare at Alfred and Bebe, he takes Franz behind the palm tree. Alfred and Bebe return to their chairs and sit stiffly. The waiter approaches them.

WAITER: (*Coldly*) Would you like to order now, please? The cook is getting impatient.

ALFRED: Oh, yeah. Sure. We'll order now. Fine.

BEBE: No! We'll wait!

MAÎTRE D': The waiter glares at her with fury, turns abruptly and exits.

ALFRED: You shouldn't have done that. He's really mad. Maybe he needs the table.

BEBE: Posh. We're not here to accommodate him; he's here to accommodate us.

ALFRED: That's true. I never thought of it that way.

MAÎTRE D': Franz Schubert comes out from behind the palm tree. He has completely recovered his composure and his manner is very disdainful and haughty. He moves to a table upstage and sits, crossing his legs and looking smugly at Alfred and Bebe. They glance at him; he smirks back at them and turns away with a derisive grin. He then raises his hand and summons the waiter.

ALFRED: (*Leaning across the table and whispering*) He's mad, too. I don't think he's going to play anymore.

MAÎTRE D': The waiter enters with a glass of wine for Franz Schubert. Franz raises the glass in mock toast to Alfred and Bebe. The waiter laughs. Then Franz Schubert laughs with the waiter.

ALFRED: I'll rap 'em *both* in the head!

BEBE: Don't pay attention to them. They're trying to arouse us. If we ignore them they'll stop.

MAÎTRE D': Alfred glares angrily at Franz Schubert and the waiter, who smirk back at him. The waiter then leans over to Franz and whispers something in his ear. Franz nods. The waiter laughs. Then they both laugh and glance at Alfred and Bebe.

ALFRED: I'll break that violin over his fat head!

MAÎTRE D': Alfred rises.

BEBE: No, Alfred, no! Sit down. I hate violence.

ALFRED: (*Advancing on Franz Schubert and the Waiter*) Did you hear me? I'll break that violin over your fat head!

MAÎTRE D': Franz Schubert scurries behind the palm tree and the waiter rushes off into the kitchen. Alfred stands in the center of the room with his fists clenched and bellows loudly.

ALFRED: Let's have a little service around this dump!

BEBE: Alfred, please! You're making a scene. Sit down.

ALFRED: What is this shit around here? Who the hell runs this joint? What kind of help have you got in this freak house restaurant? (*Franz Schubert, the Waiter and the Cook appear*)

BEBE: Alfred, please. Come and sit down. We were talking about us, Alfred, remember? Us. Look at me, Alfred. Love. It's the only solution.

MAÎTRE D': Alfred rises suddenly and slams his fist on the table.

ALFRED: You! Bring us some menus!

MAÎTRE D': The waiter rushes off. Alfred turns to Franz Schubert.

ALFRED: You! Go play your violin!

MAÎTRE D': Franz Schubert disappears behind the palm tree and plays frantically, at a much faster tempo. Alfred turns to the cook.

ALFRED: You! Get back into your kitchen, quick!

MAÎTRE D': The cook hobbles off. Alfred sits. Bebe stares at him with admiration.

BEBE: You're marvelous.

ALFRED: (*Modestly*) It was nothing.

BEBE: No, it was something. It really was something. I mean . . .

ALFRED: It was nothing. Nothing.

BEBE: . . . To be aroused to such passion, such fury, such . . .

ALFRED: It was nothing.

BEBE: Just like that! Without any cause.

MAÎTRE D': Alfred is immediately on his guard.

ALFRED: Waddayamean?

BEBE: I mean, I envy you. I really do. I mean, I wish *I* could be aroused without any cause.

ALFRED: Waddayamean, without any cause? I had a cause. *They* caused it.

BEBE: Well, small cause to warrant such a big reaction.

ALFRED: Oh, yeah?

BEBE: You overreacted.

ALFRED: Oh, yeah?

BEBE: And I suspect it's because you don't have a larger cause to react to.

MAÎTRE D': She leans over and touches his hands gently.

BEBE: Poor Alfred. If only you could harness your fury to an ideal.

ALFRED: (*Pulling his hands away*) Getattaheah.

BEBE: What's the matter? You're suddenly angry with me.

ALFRED: Yeah, I'm angry. I'm angry as hell! First you say I'm marvelous and then you take it all back.

BEBE: I didn't take it all back. I simply adjusted my initial reaction.

ALFRED: You adjusted it all right.

MAÎTRE D': He rises angrily . . .

ALFRED: You threw a wet rag on the whole thing!

MAÎTRE D': . . . Flings his napkin on the table . . .

ALFRED: Shit!

MAÎTRE D': . . . And starts to leave.

ALFRED: I'm going home!

BEBE: No, Alfred, please! Don't leave like this. Why can't we discuss things without getting angry and walking out? You're so compulsive, so irrational. You don't leave any room for differences. If you don't like something you get up and walk out. That's running away, Alfred, running away from infinite possibilities.

ALFRED: Yeah? Well, I'm still going home.

BEBE: I want to understand you, Alfred. I want to know you. And I want you to understand me and know me. What good is love without understanding? How can we love each other if we don't know each other and understand each other? How can we understand each other if we don't know each other? And how can we know each other if we don't love each other?

ALFRED: Okay.

MAÎTRE D': Alfred returns to the table, somewhat sullenly. There is a long silence. Bebe observes him clinically.

BEBE: (*Patronizingly*) Why did you come back?

ALFRED: What?

BEBE: Why did you come back?

ALFRED: (*Angrily*) I came back because I came back.

BEBE: (*Persisting*) But *why?* Why did you come back? Do you *know* why? Have you thought about it?

ALFRED: No, I haven't thought about it. I haven't had time to think about it.

BEBE: There you go, getting angry again. Why are you angry? What did I say to make you angry? (*She begins to cry*) I can't open my mouth without you shouting at me. Every word I say, you shout at me . . . like a bully.

MAÎTRE D': The cook enters disguised as a lady flower-seller.

ALFRED: Do you want a flower? Don't cry. I'll buy you a flower. Hey, you! (*The Cook crosses to their table*) Which one do you want?

BEBE: That one. (*She takes the flower and Alfred gives the Cook a dollar. The Cook leaves. Bebe sits sniffing it for a moment*) It doesn't smell. It's fake.

MAÎTRE D': She flings the flower on the table. Alfred picks it up and sniffs it.

ALFRED: You're right. It's fake.

MAÎTRE D': He rises quickly and begins to bellow again.

ALFRED: Fake! She sold us a fake flower! Where did she go? Hey! Flower-seller! Come back here, you fake! We don't want your fake flowers, understand?

MAÎTRE D': Franz Schubert and the waiter appear.

BEBE: Alfred, sit down. It doesn't matter.

ALFRED: Waddayamean, it doesn't matter? (*To Franz Schubert and the Waiter*) Where's that flower-seller? She sold me a fake flower!

BEBE: Alfred, sit down, please. You're making a scene. It's nothing.

ALFRED: Waddayamean, it's nothing! It's a fake! When I buy something real I don't want it to be fake.

BEBE: It doesn't mean that much. It's only a flower.

ALFRED: It's not a flower, it's a fake! A flower is a flower and a fake is a fake and I can't stand anything that's fake. Fake is shit! I shit on fake!

BEBE: This is embarrassing. Alfred, I don't care about the flower. It doesn't mean that much to me. Please, sit down.

MAÎTRE D': Alfred finally calms down and sits. Franz Schubert disappears behind the palm tree; the waiter starts to leave but decides not to.

BEBE: You see what I mean? You get so violent and passionate over such small things.

ALFRED: It's not a small thing.

BEBE: It's only a flower.

ALFRED: It isn't a flower!

BEBE: It isn't the end of the world.

ALFRED: It's the idea behind it!

BEBE: There is no idea behind it. You feel cheated, that's all.

ALFRED: All! All! Damned right I feel cheated! And that's not all! I feel so fucking cheated over that goddamn fake paper flower . . .

MAÎTRE D': He picks up the flower and rips it to shreds . . . and flings it into the air.

ALFRED: I hate anything that's fake!

MAÎTRE D': Exhausted, he sits down, his head in his hands. Bebe strokes his back gently.

BEBE: I understand. Poor Alfred. You get so passionate over nothing.

ALFRED: That's why I clubbed you. Because you gimme that fake smile. Fake!

BEBE: (*Startled*) What?

ALFRED: Yeah, yeah, fake. Waddaya think, I'm blind? I seen the expression on your face when I raised my club down there at the Customs House. You were ready to kill. You were ready to tear me apart, and I thought, Wow! This chick is outa sight. This chick is gonna beat the living shit outa me! But no! Waddaya do? You cop-out, that's what. Pppftt! Just like that. Sudden. You go soft on me and you smile. You gimme that little Jesus-Christ-on-the-cross smile, and in a second I know that you want *me* to club *you*. You expect me to club you. So I club you! Otherwise you wouldn'ta gimme that fake smile. You woulda tore into me the way you really wanted to. You'da scratched my face and bit my flesh and kicked me in the balls, and I'd of thought, Wow! This is a real chick! But no. Waddaya do? You stop. You stop just long enough to . . . adjust your initial reaction and you fake-out! Fake! Fake! Fake! Somebody should've split your skull long ago, let you know where it's at!

BEBE: You really are a beast, aren't you? An animal. And you're a coward on top of it all. Oh, big strong man with a steel hat and a club, coming at a lot of defenseless women and students . . .

ALFRED: Fakes! Fakes! And I hate anything that's fake. You're no woman. You're a *fake*. Fake-out! Fake!

BEBE: Oh, how could I have deluded myself into thinking I loved you? You are the lowest, the most primitive, the most despicable . . .

ALFRED: Right! But I'm *real*. I'm not fake!

BEBE: You're everything I've always loathed. How can I have imagined that I loved you?! How is it possible? How can I have even conceived the idea? Oh, Daddy! Daddy! All these years I've despised you, Daddy, because you were a gentleman, a man of refinement, a man of sensibilities, a man of education. Quiet, understanding, always willing to sit down and discuss a problem. Oh, Daddy, Daddy. I've betrayed you, Daddy. Betrayed you with this *beast!*

MAÎTRE D': The waiter approaches the table.

WAITER: Excuse me, sir. I'll have to ask you to remove your hat.

ALFRED: Remove my hat?

WAITER: Yes. We don't permit gentlemen in the dining room with their hats on.

ALFRED: I'm sorry, but I'm not removing my hat.

WAITER: You'll have to leave unless you remove your hat.

ALFRED: I'm not removing my hat and I'm not leaving!

BEBE: (*Screaming*) Oh, God! Oh, God! You're making a scene. Take off the hat!

ALFRED: Shaddap!

BEBE: My father would take off *his* hat!

ALFRED: I'm not your father!

BEBE: Oh, God!

WAITER: Why won't you take off your hat?

ALFRED: Because it's my hat!

WAITER: (*To Bebe*) Why won't he take off his hat?

BEBE: Because it's a symbol. Not a hat. If he takes it off he'll have an identity crisis.

WAITER: I see. (*He exits*)

MAÎTRE D': Bebe rises and begins to collect her things.

ALFRED: What are you doing?

BEBE: I'm leaving, that's what I'm doing.

ALFRED: Leaving?

MAÎTRE D': Alfred rises and grabs her arm.

ALFRED: Waddayamean, leaving?

BEBE: It's over. Let go of my arm!

ALFRED: Waddayamean, over? Where do you think you're going?

BEBE: Home. It's all over. Finished. I don't love . . . love you. It was a mistake.

ALFRED: Waddayamean, a mistake?

BEBE: Let me go!

MAÎTRE D': Bebe pulls away and rushes toward the exit.

ALFRED: What's a mistake? Come back here!

MAÎTRE D': Alfred grabs her again. She struggles.

BEBE: Let me go. It was all an illusion. A mistake.

ALFRED: Well, which was it, an illusion or a mistake?

BEBE: Let me go, you brute!

MAÎTRE D': Alfred cracks her across the jaw. (*Alfred does not follow this direction. Repeating*) Alfred cracks her across the jaw. (*Alfred still does not follow the direction. He holds Bebe's arms*)

ALFRED: You can't go. I dig you.

MAÎTRE D': Bebe screams and rushes off. (*Bebe does not follow this direction. They both remain fixed, looking at each other. The Maître D' repeats the direction very firmly*) Alfred cracks her across the jaw. Bebe screams and rushes off.

BEBE: (*Softly*) You called me a fake.

ALFRED: So what? So you're a fake. I dig you.

MAÎTRE D': (*Shouting*) *Alfred cracks her across the jaw. Bebe screams and rushes off.*

BEBE: You said you hate fakes.

ALFRED: I do. But I still dig you.

MAÎTRE D': (*Commanding like a Nazi*) *Alfred cracks her across the jaw . . . !*

ALFRED: . . . And something is telling me that I oughta crack you across the jaw but I don't want to.

MAÎTRE D': *Bebe screams and rushes off!*

ALFRED: Because I dig you.

MAÎTRE D': *Bebe screams and rushes off!!*

BEBE: (*Softly*) I dig you, too.

MAÎTRE D': *Bebe screams and rushes off, do you hear what I am saying?* (*The Waiter returns, alarmed*)

BEBE: . . . And something is telling me that I should leave, but I don't want to. It's as though something has *always* been telling me to do one thing when I've wanted to do something else. It's been that way all my life . . . as though I've been following some invisible stage directions.

MAÎTRE D': (*Desperately*) *Alfred cracks her across the jaw!* (*Alfred kisses Bebe tenderly*) *Bebe screams and rushes off!*

WAITER: Franz Schubert appears from behind the palm tree, smiling. (*Franz Schubert appears, smiling*)

MAÎTRE D': (*Whirling on the Waiter*) You're fired!

FRANZ SCHUBERT: (*Raising his bow*) Franz Schubert raises his bow and begins to play, magnificently. (*He plays*)

MAÎTRE D': You're *all* fired!

COOK: (*Entering with tray*) The cook appears with a tray of coconut milk.

MAÎTRE D': What coconut milk? I will have no coconut milk!

WAITER: The Maître D' flings his script across the room, kicks over the lectern and charges off like an angry savage.

MAÎTRE D': (*As he does so*) You're all fired! Through! Finished! Do you hear? You're finished, Schubert! D'ya hear me?! Finished! And you! And you! And you! And you! (*He disappears*)

WAITER: (*Taking the tray from the Cook and serving*) The waiter hands a coconut to Alfred, to Bebe, and to the cook, and they all drink their coconut milk while Franz Schubert plays, magnificently. (*The music swells and the lights fade on all drinking coconut milk*)

Curtain

Paul Hunter

AN INTERVIEW WITH F. SCOTT FITZGERALD

Paul Hunter

When *An Interview With F. Scott Fitzgerald* opened at the Evergreen Stage, Hollywood, in March, 1971, it was warmly greeted as "an absorbing footnote to the growing library on F. Scott Fitzgerald's final years." An affecting dramatic account of an actual fortieth birthday interview with Fitzgerald, one of America's most celebrated authors who, as spokesman for the "Jazz Age," captured the essence of the carefree madness of the 1920's, the play appears in print for the first time anywhere in *The Best Short Plays 1972*.

"An Interview With F. Scott Fitzgerald," wrote the drama critic of *The Hollywood Reporter,* "is that special kind of theatre that chills down into the marrow with true excellence. . . . More than just an interview, this play posed serious questions concerning the validity of probing into a public person's private life." The reviewer for the *Los Angeles Free Press* was equally enthusiastic and declared, "This is a beautiful piece haunted by the ghost of F. Scott Fitzgerald, the ultimate masochist, dying in a bog of self-pity and yet strangely tragic."

Paul Hunter was born on November 30, 1933, in Los Angeles, California. After graduating from Principia College, Elsah, Illinois, in 1955, he served for two years with the U.S. Army in Korea. Following his discharge, he embarked on a career that embraced a diversity of jobs. In his own words, "Professionally, I've worked in many capacities in the communications industry: as an advertising copywriter, a graphics designer, a magazine editor, a free-lance journalist and a photographer. I also worked in television as writer for a syndicated travel series, *Cesar's World,* narrated by Cesar Romero. Travel is one of my passions: I've been in over thirty countries in the Middle East, Far East and Europe."

Although Mr. Hunter has put in time as a television writer, he admits, "I don't consider the television credits important. I've never made any real effort to find television work; I consider myself a writer for the theatre, not for television. Television is commerce and I'd rather labor in the advertising world, which I like, if I'm going to sell my writing only for money. . . . The reason I mention the variety of writing jobs I have had is because I think it's an interesting example of what someone who is serious about writing for the theatre has to do to keep going."

In addition to *An Interview With F. Scott Fitzgerald,* Paul Hunter's other produced theatre works include: *Dino and Dad-Babe,* presented at the University of California at Los Angeles, 1966; *When In Rome,* Pioneer Playhouse, Kentucky, 1966; and *The Turncoats,* Harvard University, 1968. The latter, dealing with American prisoners of war who chose to go to China at the end of the Korean War, previously was seen on educational television in 1967.

The author now has his own advertising company in Los Angeles and also is a frequent contributor to *The Christian Science Monitor,* mainly writing about the theatre and films. His most recent work for the stage is a full-length play about the Fitzgeralds entitled *Scott and Zelda.*

Characters:

F. SCOTT FITZGERALD

NURSE

REPORTER

Scene One

A small, modest bedroom in a well-established resort hotel in Asheville, North Carolina. There is the usual hotel furniture: a bed, an armchair with a small table next to it, a straight-backed chair in a corner, and in the center of the room a dresser with a mirror over it. Doors lead off to the hall, a closet, and an adjoining bathroom; a curtained window overlooks the quiet hotel gardens below.

The occupant of this room is the writer F. Scott Fitzgerald. Aside from the picture of his wife on the dresser, the only personal touches we see are the books piled neatly on the table. Fitzgerald has been ill; the medicine bottles and bandages that line the top of the dresser tell us this, and there is an oppressive sterility in the atmosphere. It comes in part from the disciplined orderliness of the room; the Nurse who attends Fitzgerald is constantly straightening things. Even more, it comes from, and reflects, a barrenness and sterility in Fitzgerald's present situation and attitude toward life.

It is September 24, 1936, Fitzgerald's fortieth birthday—early in the afternoon of a gray day. Fitzgerald and the Nurse are seated on the bed playing gin rummy. Fitzgerald wears pajamas, slippers and a robe which is pulled over a cast on his right shoulder. He looks all of his forty years, but with his blond hair and his sensitive features, there is still something boyishly handsome under his tired, faded exterior. Not only has he been suffering from a broken shoulder and a light case of arthritis, but too many years of not caring for himself and too many years of too much drinking have taken their toll on his health, his face, and his nervous system. His hands sometimes tremble;

his face occasionally twitches; and his mind doesn't react as immediately as it once did.

The Private Nurse who attends Fitzgerald is a rather ordinary woman of simple tastes in her middle fifties. She and Fitzgerald have grown fond of each other, and while she hasn't the background to discuss or understand his writing, she is a good listener, and this has helped greatly in her efforts to nurse his depleted ego. Fitzgerald knows how to charm her, and she is perhaps more indulgent with him than she feels she ought to be.

At the moment, Fitzgerald is bored with the card game. The Nurse is engrossed; she arranges the cards in her hand and begins to hum happily.

FITZGERALD: When you hum like that, it means you're about to go out.

NURSE: (*Laying her cards on the bed*) Some of us have a talent for writing, and some of us have a talent for cards.

FITZGERALD: (*Throwing down his cards*) Skunked again!

NURSE: (*Picking up his cards*) Don't you want to keep score any more?

FITZGERALD: I wish there was a radio in this room.

NURSE: You're not going to quit just because I'm winning?

FITZGERALD: I don't want to play any more gin rummy. How about a game of strip poker?

NURSE: You're just playing with me.

FITZGERALD: (*With innuendo*) No, I have no intention of playing with you.

NURSE: Mr. Fitzgerald! (*She smiles, slightly embarrassed. Fitzgerald rises and walks around the room restlessly. He goes to the window and looks out*)

FITZGERALD: Is it always gray in North Carolina?

NURSE: This time of year. (*Fitzgerald continues roaming around aimlessly. Then he goes to the dresser and starts to open one of the drawers*) Do you want me to have room service send us up some tea? (*The telephone rings*)

FITZGERALD: I'll get it. (*He crosses and answers it*) Hello . . . Yes, this is . . . Who? . . . I can't imagine that people are still interested in reading about me . . . I don't think so . . . I haven't been well; I broke my shoulder . . . My experiences with reporters haven't been particularly happy these past few years. So many of you seem to have your minds made up *before* you talk to me . . . I'm sure you wouldn't . . . (*He smiles*) Then I really should see you, shouldn't I? . . . Are you downstairs in the lobby? . . . You're at the station? You came all the way without even knowing if I'd see you? . . . I suppose for a few minutes . . . Yes. (*He puts the telephone down*)

NURSE: You're in no condition to see a newspaper reporter!

FITZGERALD: He's come down from New York to interview me on my fortieth birthday.

NURSE: You should have turned him down.

FITZGERALD: I know. But he's a young man, and this is his first important assignment. I couldn't deny him his chance to make good. I've always helped young writers. I helped Ernest Hemingway, you know, when he was starting out in Paris.

NURSE: I'll send him away.

FITZGERALD: No, I want to see him.

NURSE: You want to see him!

FITZGERALD: Just to know that *everyone* hasn't forgotten me.

NURSE: You're supposed to be resting.

FITZGERALD: (*Turning on the charm*) Come on. Please.

NURSE: You know I'll give in, don't you?

FITZGERALD: That's what I like about you; you spoil me. I'll have to put on a suit.

NURSE: Why don't you stay in your robe?

FITZGERALD: I don't want him to see me like this.

NURSE: He'll understand why you're wearing a robe.

FITZGERALD: Maybe that's a good idea. My clothes have

gotten so shabby. You be sure to emphasize that I've been sick.

NURSE: I'll make it good. (*She starts straightening the bed*)

FITZGERALD: (*Looking around the room*) Can't we do something to brighten up this room? I don't want it to look like I've died. Too many people think that *already*. We need some dancing girls and some crepe paper streamers. And a five-piece jazz band headed by Benny Goodman.

NURSE: (*Pleased with his high spirits*) You *are* excited, aren't you?

FITZGERALD: A good interview could mean a new start for me. People might start buying my books again. (*Pausing a moment, almost to himself*) I wonder what he'll ask me. His editor probably read about my crack-up and decided I'd be a good example of how famous people go to pieces under stress. That'd make all his readers who managed to survive the depression feel superior to me. (*Planning his approach*) I'll have to pretend it wasn't as bad as I said. I'll tell him I'm all over it now. (*He paces a moment longer, the Nurse watching him with concern. He goes to the dressser and opens a drawer*)

NURSE: Mr. Fitzgerald, don't . . .

FITZGERALD: (*Bringing out a bottle of gin, pouring himself a drink*) Don't worry; I won't drink while he's here. I'm too smart for that. (*He takes a sip of the drink, and it seems to relax him. He sighs appreciatively, then begins to pace again*)

NURSE: Are you *sure* you want to see him?

FITZGERALD: I know how to handle reporters. Zelda and I used to be interviewed all the time back in our heyday. (*Pausing, taking a sip of his drink*) I remember one afternoon doing handstands in the lobby of the Plaza because I hadn't been in the papers all week and I was afraid I was slipping. (*Looking at his wife's picture. Quietly, with regret*) We were so young then. I wonder if we'd have acted differently if we'd known how it was going to end? (*He studies the picture a moment, then hides it in a dresser drawer*) I don't want to talk about my wife in this interview. Some reporters are bastards! They don't care what their stories do to you.

NURSE: Let me send him away. I'll tell him . . .

FITZGERALD: I won't have to worry about this one. He's young, and they're always a bit awed by famous people.

NURSE: I don't see *why* you go through with it.

FITZGERALD: (*Pacing nervously*) I can't sit here day after day knowing I've been forgotten. I was the country's most important young novelist. I have to reaffirm myself. I have to keep hoping. I always hope, even when there is *no* hope. You Bible-quoting Baptists believe in hope, don't you?

NURSE: It's the best thing you can do.

FITZGERALD: Sometimes I've wondered why. When Hemingway wrote that about me in *The Snows of Kilimanjaro,* about what a wreck I was . . . I got him the best editor and the best publisher in America . . . (*Sadly, uncomprehendingly*) I always considered him my best friend. It's incredible the way some people repay your generosity. I thought about committing suicide when Ernest did that to me.

NURSE: You must never think about that. You have so much to live for.

FITZGERALD: (*Amused, without bitterness*) Ah! The nurse's all-purpose cliché. Well, I appreciate your saying it.

NURSE: I mean it.

FITZGERALD: What *do* I have to live for? My public's gone, my friends are gone, my wife is gone. My health, my money . . .

NURSE: You still have your daughter.

FITZGERALD: I haven't been a very good father.

NURSE: You have your writing.

FITZGERALD: I don't know. I wonder if my talent hasn't gone, too. I used to get four thousand dollars a short story. Now the best I can do is four hundred. I ought to be writing now; I have all this time. But there's nothing I want to say anymore. (*Brightly, trying to pull himself out of the dark mood*) How do I look?

NURSE: You look fine.

FITZGERALD: Not too much like the drunken has-been everyone thinks I am?

NURSE: (*Going to him, straightening his robe*) You're still a good-looking man, and I think you know it.

FITZGERALD: What would I do without your lies?

NURSE: (*Joking, trying to build him up*) That's not a lie. I could take quite a shine to you if you weren't so young.

FITZGERALD: Young!

NURSE: Forty's still young.

FITZGERALD: (*Amused at himself*) I was very depressed when I woke up this morning and realized I was forty. (*There is a knock at the door. He finishes off his drink, then washes his mouth and gargles with a mouthwash which he swallows*)

NURSE: You *sure* you want to see him?

FITZGERALD: Should I be standing or sitting down? I think I'll stand. It looks healthier. (*He takes a pose by the bed*) All right. Let him in.

(*The Nurse goes to the door and opens it*)

REPORTER: (*Off*) Mr. Fitzgerald?

FITZGERALD: (*Smiling, motioning him in*) Yes, come in, please.

(*The Reporter enters; an ambitious, self-assured man in his middle twenties. He is wearing a rather rumpled suit and carries a briefcase. His dark hair and olive complexion suggest his Eastern European heritage, and his alert eyes move continually as he mentally notes what he sees. He is not at all impressed by Fitzgerald; in fact, if anything, he is a bit scornful of him. His obliging, slightly naive manner is the pose he has chosen as best for this interview. He will drop it and become aggressive to get the answers to his questions. As he enters, he looks a bit dubiously at the way Fitzgerald is dressed, then crosses to him, his right hand extended. Fitzgerald offers his left, and they shake*)

REPORTER: You're very kind seeing me like this.

FITZGERALD: Glad to do it.

NURSE: Your interview will have to be short. Mr. Fitzgerald has been ill.

REPORTER: All right.

FITZGERALD: (*A bit too heartily*) I'm well on the way to recovery now. You can't keep a good man down, you know. Please, have a seat. (*He indicates the armchair*)

REPORTER: Thank you. (*He sits, taking a moment to look around the room. Fitzgerald sits on the bed as the Nurse takes the chair in the corner and starts to knit. As the two men talk, it is almost as if they were adversaries measuring each other: Fitzgerald worrying how sympathetic the Reporter will be, the Reporter studying Fitzgerald to see how closely he fits his preconceived idea of him*) You really did break your shoulder, didn't you!

FITZGERALD: Yes. Then to complicate things, one night I tripped going into the bathroom. It took me forty-five minutes to pull myself to the telephone and get help, and lying in the cold, perspiring, gave me a touch of arthritis. Very dramatic. I'm going to write a story about it someday.

REPORTER: (*Opening his briefcase, getting out a pad and pencil*) How did you break it?

FITZGERALD: Diving off the high board.

REPORTER: (*Surprised, almost amused*) Diving!

FITZGERALD: I was showing off for some girls. I was doing a beautiful swan dive, and my shoulder broke right in the middle of it. I'm sure there's a story in that, too. I should stop showing off for girls.

REPORTER: You always were a ladies' man, weren't you?

FITZGERALD: Yes! I'm still as impetuous as a college boy; I'm just not as young any more.

REPORTER: I haven't congratulated you on your birthday.

FITZGERALD: Don't.

REPORTER: (*Smiling*) Is it terrifying to turn forty?

FITZGERALD: Only a young man could ask that with a smile on his face! Yes, it is.

REPORTER: Why?

FITZGERALD: (*Not wanting to pursue it, rising and walking around*) You're not as young as I expected you to be. You sounded so desperately eager over the telephone.

REPORTER: I was afraid you wouldn't see me after I'd

come all this way. Not just because of the interview. I wanted to meet you. I'm a great admirer of yours. I've read all your books.

FITZGERALD: Have you, really?

REPORTER: I remember passing around a secret copy of *This Side of Paradise* when we were in the sixth grade. We considered ourselves terribly dissolute reading it.

FITZGERALD: (*Reminiscing, fondly*) It created quite a scandal when it was published. I was accused of corrupting morals, advocating free love. Suddenly I became the spokesman for the younger generation. I must admit at twenty-three it was all very exhilarating. Of course, that generation's grown up now. The stock market crash *made* us grow up.

REPORTER: Are you sorry you're no longer the spokesman for that generation?

FITZGERALD: I was never that wild, Jazz Age, golden boy people thought I was. I could see the disastrous end to the Jazz Age almost before it began. That's what my second novel, *The Beautiful and Damned,* was all about, and that was seven years *before* the crash.

REPORTER: You must be sorry you're not as popular as you once were.

FITZGERALD: (*Trying to make it unimportant*) Well . . . I've never tried to write *popular* books. I've always tried to write *good* books and hoped they'd be popular. The public is like a high school girl, always falling in love with someone new. You get used to it!

REPORTER: Still, it must bother you.

FITZGERALD: I've been disappointed some of my books haven't sold better. Any author's disappointed about that. *This Side of Paradise* was such a success, I suppose I imagined the others would be, too.

REPORTER: We called all over the country trying to find you. What are you doing in North Carolina, hiding out?

FITZGERALD: I wanted to get away for a while.

REPORTER: Why?

FITZGERALD: To . . . recharge my batteries. Writers have

to do that, you know. Do a little "recollecting in tranquillity," as Wordsworth called it.

REPORTER: It seems pretty quiet here for a man like you.

FITZGERALD: You get to a point in life where you *like* it quiet. I can be anonymous here.

REPORTER: (*Trying to put him on the defensive*) You want to be anonymous! This is a new Scott Fitzgerald, isn't it? (*Fitzgerald smiles weakly*) Isn't the real reason because your wife's in a sanitarium near here? (*Fitzgerald stiffens. The Nurse stops her knitting and looks up*) She *is* in a sanitarium near here, isn't she?

FITZGERALD: (*Nervously*) Yes.

REPORTER: How is she?

FITZGERALD: (*Evasively*) They seem to be helping her.

REPORTER: Will they be able to cure her?

FITZGERALD: (*Pause; then changing the subject*) You said this interview is your first real chance to show what you can do. What'll happen if it's good?

REPORTER: I might get some national recognition, a chance to do some really important interviews. (*Fitzgerald laughs. Realizing what he's said*) Not that you're *not* important.

FITZGERALD: I'm not important anymore.

REPORTER: I mean political interviews: senators, congressmen. I'd like to interview the President someday.

FITZGERALD: (*Sympathetically*) You're ambitious, aren't you?

REPORTER: I want to be a success.

FITZGERALD: *I* was ambitious when I was your age. I'd warn you success isn't all that wonderful, but I doubt if you'd believe me!

REPORTER: You started out with a lot more than I did. You went to Princeton. Your parents were rich.

FITZGERALD: My parents were never rich.

REPORTER: My parents were immigrants. I've had to work hard to get where I am. And I'm not going to stop till I get all the way.

FITZGERALD: (*Tightens at the determination in his voice;*

then, returning to the bed) What's your slant on this story?

REPORTER: Scott Fitzgerald at forty. How the prophet of the Jazz Age looks at the world today. Something like that.

FITZGERALD: How about Scott Fitzgerald at forty—still developing as a novelist?

REPORTER: Do you think you *are* still developing?

FITZGERALD: Of course!

REPORTER: Most people seem to think you're . . . (*Stopping, not knowing how to say it*)

FITZGERALD: What? Written out?

REPORTER: Those essays you wrote about your crack-up seemed to suggest . . .

FITZGERALD: (*Getting up, walking around again*) I've been through my share of hell recently; I won't deny that. But you always struggle out of your low periods and the struggle deepens your work.

REPORTER: What's the *truth* behind your crack-up?

FITZGERALD: That's not important. The only thing important about me is my work.

REPORTER: Did you really crack-up?

FITZGERALD: My whole generation cracked-up, didn't we?

REPORTER: I mean you, personally.

FITZGERALD: *Crack-up* is probably an exaggeration.

REPORTER: You seemed to be describing a mental breakdown in those articles.

FITZGERALD: Well, I'm not crazy—if that's what you mean. On the other hand, I'm not the gay, reckless, golden boy I once was. You can see that by looking at me.

REPORTER: Did you have a breakdown?

FITZGERALD: I suppose it depends on what you call a breakdown. I . . . It's all in the articles; you can read them again.

REPORTER: (*Picking up his briefcase, opening it*) You called yourself a "cracked plate."

FITZGERALD: It made a good symbol. There were a lot of "cracked plates" around after the crash.

REPORTER: (*Taking some magazine pages from the brief-case*) I have it right here. Let's see . . . (*Reading from the article*) "Now the standard cure for one who is sunk is to consider those in actual destitution or physical suffering—this is an all-weather beatitude for gloom in general and fairly salutary daytime advice for everyone. But at three o'clock in the morning . . . the cure doesn't work—and in a real dark night of the soul it is always three o'clock in the morning, day after day . . ." That's not it. (*He searches through the article*)

FITZGERALD: (*Quietly repeating*) ". . . In a real dark night of the soul it is always three o'clock in the morning, day after day." (*More to himself*) It gives me strength to know I can still write like that.

REPORTER: Here's what I want! ". . . One is not waiting for the fadeout of a single sorrow, but rather being an unwitting witness of an execution, the disintegration of one's own personality . . ." Doesn't that describe a breakdown? (*Fitzgerald shrugs*) Did you feel your personality was disintegrating?

FITZGERALD: I suppose I did at the time. But, of course, I dramatized it.

REPORTER: There were all kinds of theories going around after you wrote those articles. People predicted you'd commit suicide. Everyone seemed to think you were through as a writer.

FITZGERALD: (*Getting angry*) Then they didn't read very well! What I said was that at last I had become a writer *only*. When you establish a certain reputation, a lot of little people want nothing more than to topple you off your pedestal and call you a has-been. (*Proudly*) I've lived all my life by my writing, and I've lived very well. There aren't many writers who can say that.

REPORTER: You're not sorry you wrote those articles?

FITZGERALD: (*Defensively*) I'm not ashamed of them. They're written with a kind of burning honesty few writers can match.

REPORTER: And you had no hesitation about baring your soul like that?

FITZGERALD: (*Reflectively*) Maybe I shouldn't have written them. But I was trying to understand what had happened to me, why things had disintegrated, why I had cracked-up.

REPORTER: But why did you let them be published?

FITZGERALD: I needed the money. And I thought people might be interested.

REPORTER: Why?

FITZGERALD: I was the spokesman for that generation. I was . . . the symbol of the age. I thought people might understand what happened to the age if they understood what happened to its symbol.

REPORTER: What were the causes of your crack-up?

FITZGERALD: I thought you wanted my views on the world today? Nobody's interested in all this gloomy stuff about me.

REPORTER: Yes, they are. And this is your chance to stop those rumors. If you're still writing, why let everyone think you're a has-been? (*He lets this sink in a moment*) What were the causes of your crack-up?

FITZGERALD: I'm sure you can guess.

REPORTER: Too much success at too early an age? Too many wild parties, too many sprees?

FITZGERALD: Not enough respect for the talent I have.

REPORTER: How much was the fault of your wife?

FITZGERALD: (*Stiffening, nervously*) I don't want to talk about my wife.

REPORTER: It *was* her fault, wasn't it?

FITZGERALD: What difference does it make whose fault it was?

REPORTER: Isn't that what you're saying in *Tender Is the Night?* That it was her fault?

FITZGERALD: Does it seem stuffy in here to you?

REPORTER: Not to me.

NURSE: Shall I open a window?

FITZGERALD: No, no, forget it.

REPORTER: Do they allow you to visit your wife?

(*The Nurse watches the interplay, ready to break in if necessary*)

FITZGERALD: Please! I don't want to talk about her.

REPORTER: Why not?

FITZGERALD: My wife's in very delicate health. Going over our problems in the newspapers, trying to assess blame, might destroy her. It might destroy both of us.

REPORTER: But it *was* her fault, wasn't it?

NURSE: (*Firmly*) Mr. Fitzgerald doesn't want to talk about it.

FITZGERALD: (*Pacing nervously, his hand trembling slightly*) My wife is a very remarkable woman. She's published a novel. She's had a gallery showing of her paintings. She could have been a fine ballerina. If you want to write about her, write about that.

REPORTER: Mr. Fitzgerald, your wife's insanity is no secret. (*He waits for a reaction from Fitzgerald but gets none*) I understand your reluctance to talk about it. My wife went through a breakdown. I know how you feel. (*Underplaying it*) I came home one night and she was sitting in the corner, sobbing. Our little boy was trying to comfort her. It's terrifying for the children. (*Knowing how to win Fitzgerald*) She was just like Nicole in *Tender Is the Night.* Nicole *is* a portrait of your wife, isn't she?

NURSE: Why do you keep after him?

FITZGERALD: (*Stopping her*) It's all right. (*More willing to talk now, feeling a bond of shared experience*) How is your wife?

REPORTER: She's much better now. Of course, we don't know whether it will last. Your wife's had a couple of breakdowns, hasn't she?

FITZGERALD: (*Sitting on the bed again*) Yes. She'd seem cured, and then . . .

REPORTER: Is there any hope for her?

FITZGERALD: No. I hoped for such a long time, but . . . this is her third breakdown. It haunts me what's happened to her. I keep wondering how much of it is *my* fault.

REPORTER: How much of what's happened to you is *her* fault?

FITZGERALD: (*More to himself*) I should never have married her. She might have been happy with a kind, simple man in a southern garden. She didn't have the strength for the big stage. Sometimes she pretended, and she pretended beautifully, but she didn't have it. It hurts me to see her so helpless and pitiful now.

REPORTER: And you don't blame her for what she did to you?

FITZGERALD: How can I blame her when there's still hope for me, and there's none for her anymore?

REPORTER: Isn't it true she was jealous of your work?

FITZGERALD: Can't we talk about something else? Please.

REPORTER: Of course, I'm sorry. Whenever I think of what you've been through . . . of what we've *both* been through. (*Then, to see how he'll react*) Every time I think of the evening you and your wife were strolling by that railroad track and she threw herself in front of the train . . .

NURSE: (*Trying to protect Fitzgerald*) Why don't you go on to something else?

REPORTER: And you were in such poor health you could barely pull her away. (*Fitzgerald rises nervously, crosses to the dresser and gets out the gin bottle*) I felt great pity for you when I heard that story. It must have been horrible.

FITZGERALD: Would you care for a drink?

REPORTER: No, thanks.

FITZGERALD: Not while you're working? It's good gin. (*Turning to the Nurse*) It's my birthday. (*To the Reporter*) You've heard about my drinking, haven't you?

REPORTER: Yes.

FITZGERALD: (*Turns away from the Reporter, takes a drink and pauses to regain his composure*) Dr. Barleycorn can be a great relief. I used to think you could do anything if you had talent and worked hard enough. It took me a long time to realize that isn't true. (*He begins to pace again*) Some people think I'm an alcoholic, but I'm not. People don't know why other people drink. My father drank. It embarrassed me when I was a boy because I didn't understand it. He cracked-up, too, in a way.

REPORTER: He did? How?

FITZGERALD: When he was a boy, he rowed spies across the river during the Civil War. My family's been mixed up in quite a bit of American history. My great-grandfather's brother was Francis Scott Key. I was named for him. My great-aunt was Mrs. Suratt who was . . .

REPORTER: What about your father?

FITZGERALD: I'm wandering, aren't I? The Civil War was the high point of his life. He worked at a number of things, but he was never a success. One afternoon—I was ten or eleven—the phone rang. I don't know why, but I felt disaster had struck us. I began to pray. "Dear God," I prayed, "please don't let us go to the poorhouse, please don't let us go to the poorhouse." A little while later my father came home. He had lost his job. (*Smiling ironically*) You thought I had rich parents! (*Then, reflectively*) He went out that morning a comparatively young man, full of strength, full of confidence. He came home an old man, a completely broken man. He was a failure the rest of his days. I've thought a lot about my father these last few years.

REPORTER: Do you think you're doomed to failure like he was?

FITZGERALD: No, I don't give up. You can't be a successful writer if you give up. In one four month period when I was first starting out, I wrote nineteen short stories and collected a hundred and twenty rejection slips. But I didn't give up. The next year *This Side of Paradise* was published, and I could sell stories anywhere I wanted.

REPORTER: You will admit these last few years there's been a decline.

FITZGERALD: In my output, perhaps. Not in my quality.

REPORTER: What about *Tender Is the Night?*

FITZGERALD: The best thing I've ever written.

REPORTER: (*Incredulously*) Do you really think so?

FITZGERALD: Yes, and many of the critics thought so, too.

REPORTER: It didn't sell.

FITZGERALD: Just because it didn't sell doesn't mean it isn't good. You read it. What did you think?

REPORTER: I'm no critic.

FITZGERALD: But you read it.

REPORTER: It seemed old-fashioned to me.

FITZGERALD: (*Trying to hide the hurt*) Did it? (*After a pause, musing*) I worked four years on that book. I wanted it to be my masterpiece. I was terribly disappointed when it didn't sell.

REPORTER: Did it surprise you? We've just come out of a depression. We're on the brink of another war. Who wants to read about a bunch of rich, neurotic Americans living in Europe!

FITZGERALD: (*Quietly*) I guess nobody does.

REPORTER: People today want to get down to the basics; they want to solve the problems of the world. You can't expect them to buy your books if you don't give them what they want.

FITZGERALD: Do you always give your readers what they want?

REPORTER: I try to.

FITZGERALD: (*Musing, to himself*) That's the way you sell newspapers.

REPORTER: (*Not hearing him*) What?

FITZGERALD: What do they want to read about *me?*

REPORTER: The truth.

FITZGERALD: What *is* the truth about me? (*Laughs; ironically*) I wish *I* knew!

REPORTER: That's what I'm here to find out.

FITZGERALD: Do you think you can find it in half an hour?

REPORTER: Some of it.

FITZGERALD: (*Envying the simplicity of his outlook*) I wish I were as young again as you are.

REPORTER: Do you ever think you might be one of those authors who writes a best seller when he's young, then loses his appeal because he has nothing new to say? (*He stares at Fitzgerald, knowing this must be one of his greatest fears. Fitzgerald rises and walks away, turning his back to the Reporter*) They have a couple of failures, then are never heard from again. (*Fitzgerald's hands are trembling*) You ever worry about that?

FITZGERALD: (*Unable to take it any longer*) Would you excuse me a moment? (*He exits into the bathroom, taking his drink with him. The Reporter starts making notes as the Nurse goes to the bed and straightens it*)

NURSE: (*After studying the Reporter a moment*) You really go after him, don't you?

REPORTER: (*Without looking up*) I had no idea he was in such bad shape. Is he always like this?

NURSE: You're making him nervous. He so wants to make a good impression on you.

REPORTER: How'd he *really* break his shoulder?

NURSE: Diving, just like he told you.

REPORTER: (*Disbelieving*) Really? You have to be pretty far gone to break your shoulder diving.

NURSE: Don't you believe it?

REPORTER: (*To test her reaction*) He might have broken it in a fight while he was drunk . . .

NURSE: He didn't. (*There is a pause. Then, quietly*) Be kind to him. You can help him get on his feet again if you want to. Don't describe his nervousness . . .

REPORTER: I have to write it the way it is, not the way he'd like it to be.

NURSE: How do you know the way it is? Do you realize . . . ?

REPORTER: (*Interrupting her*) He knows what an interview's like. If he didn't want me to tell the truth, he shouldn't have asked me to come.

NURSE: *You* asked *him* to come. (*The Reporter ignores her*) It took a lot of courage to write those articles about his crack-up. Then all his friends told him what a fool he'd been. They didn't understand what he'd been through. He's gotten letters from Sing Sing and Joliet about those articles, comforting him, telling him not to give up.

REPORTER: (*Making a note of it*) Has he really? Letters from Sing Sing!

NURSE: One night when I came in to check on him, he was lying here in the dark staring at the ceiling. He seemed so alone. I said to him, "What's going to happen to you, Mr. Fitzgerald?" He said—in a way I'll never forget—he said, "God knows."

REPORTER: Has he ever tried to commit suicide?

NURSE: No.

REPORTER: Aren't you afraid he will?

NURSE: He told you he doesn't give up.

REPORTER: What's he have to live for? He wants to be important, and he'll never be important again.

NURSE: You should see him sitting in that chair trying to write. He only writes three or four hours a week now, but he still writes.

REPORTER: He's living in a world that doesn't exist anymore.

NURSE: You can afford to be kind. He was kind when you wanted help.

REPORTER: What do you know about his wife?

NURSE: Nothing.

REPORTER: The stories I've heard about her! Swimming in the fountain in front of the Plaza, dancing on tables in restaurants, riding down Fifth Avenue on the tops of taxis! It doesn't surprise me she's crazy. Does he ever talk about her?

NURSE: No.

REPORTER: The taxi driver told me he'd brought them over from the station one afternoon. He said she was wearing a faded flapper dress and a little girl's bonnet tied under her chin. She started ballet dancing right in front of the station.

Fitzgerald just acted like nothing was wrong, and all the way here he told her a story: she was a fairy princess and he was the prince who'd searched all over the world for her. (*Shaking his head*) God!

NURSE: Your wife's never *had* a breakdown, has she? (*The bathroom door opens, and Fitzgerald emerges. The Nurse watches him, ready to come to his rescue if needed*)

FITZGERALD: (*Trying to disguise his fatigue*) We should celebrate the author's birthday, kill the fatted calf or something. (*To the Reporter as he goes to the dresser*) You sure you won't have a drink?

REPORTER: No, thank you.

FITZGERALD: (*To the Nurse, as he pours himself another drink*) What about you, my dear? Sure I can't tempt you?

NURSE: (*Aware of what Fitzgerald is going through, trying to help him. To the Reporter*) Mr. Fitzgerald loves to tease me about being a non-drinker.

FITZGERALD: One of these days I'm going to spike her tea and start her off down the road to hell.

NURSE: I'll have to watch out then, won't I? A country girl is easy pickings for you celebrities.

FITZGERALD: (*Enjoying the game, relaxing*) Celebrity! She didn't even know who I was the first time she met me.

NURSE: But you told me, didn't you! And I went home and read all your books, and now you're my favorite writer. (*She pats him affectionately*)

FITZGERALD: (*To the Reporter*) She's buttering me up for a raise.

NURSE: I'm interrupting your interview. (*She goes back to her chair*)

FITZGERALD: Yes, let's go on with the interview. What else would you like to ask me?

REPORTER: What are your plans for the future, Mr. Fitzgerald?

FITZGERALD: To keep writing, of course. A writer can't stop writing.

REPORTER: Are you working on anything now?

FITZGERALD: Oh, all sorts of things.

REPORTER: What are they?

FITZGERALD: I don't really want to talk about them yet. You talk about things too early, it takes something from them.

REPORTER: Are you working on a novel?

FITZGERALD: I'm *always* working on a novel.

REPORTER: What's it about? (*Fitzgerald shrugs but doesn't answer*) When will it be finished?

FITZGERALD: I don't know. It always takes longer than I expect. I keep revising. And my ideas change.

REPORTER: What will you live on while you're writing this novel?

FITZGERALD: I'll write for magazines.

REPORTER: Will you be able to live on that? You're pretty heavily in debt, aren't you? (*A pause; Fitzgerald says nothing*) Your expenses must be terrific, with your wife's care. And your daughter's in a boarding school, isn't she?

FITZGERALD: Yes.

REPORTER: I suppose you can always put her in public school.

FITZGERALD: (*The Reporter has gone too far*) And my wife in a public insane asylum! I'll take care of them, thank you, one way or another! My daughter's only fourteen; a good education's the onc thing I can *still* give her.

REPORTER: What if you can't meet your expenses writing? Have you ever thought of going to work?

FITZGERALD: *Writing* is work.

REPORTER: I meant for a salary.

FITZGERALD: I have thought of writing for the movies. I've done that before. There's a great novel waiting to be written about Hollywood. I'm toying with some ideas.

REPORTER: Will you have time to work on a novel if you're writing for the movies?

FITZGERALD: I'd find the time. Unless, of course, I became so successful writing movies it wouldn't be possible. Then I could afford to take the time. Write a movie or two between novels.

REPORTER: What if you can't get a job in Hollywood?

FITZGERALD: (*Wearily, with a trace of derision*) Maybe I could get a job on a newspaper . . . doing interviews. I suppose I could always sweep out a bar somewhere.

NURSE: (*Seeing a danger signal, getting up*) I think it's time you ended the interview.

REPORTER: (*Quickly, before the Nurse can stop him*) Where do you think you'll be ten years from now?

FITZGERALD: I'll be dead ten years from now.

NURSE: (*Lightly*) What a thing to say!

FITZGERALD: It's the truth.

NURSE: You'll have written your novel about Hollywood and several others by that time.

FITZGERALD: The prospect of dying doesn't scare me. Lying in the warm earth somewhere, snuggled next to Zelda, sounds very peaceful to me.

REPORTER: What makes you think you'll be dead? Has your doctor . . . ?

NURSE: (*Stepping in*) You'll have to excuse Mr. Fitzgerald!

REPORTER: Just a few more questions . . .

NURSE: I'm sure you have more than enough material.

FITZGERALD: (*Fondly*) Isn't she a tyrant!

REPORTER: (*Realizing his time is up, putting away his notes*) You're right. I've taken too much of your time already.

FITZGERALD: I hope you've gotten everything you need.

REPORTER: (*Rising, picking up his briefcase*) I'm sure I have.

FITZGERALD: Tell your editor how hard you had to talk to get in here.

REPORTER: (*Shaking Fitzgerald's hand*) Thank you, Mr. Fitzgerald.

FITZGERALD: Maybe we'll meet again someday—when you're an important columnist.

REPORTER: Good-by. (*The Nurse shows him to the door*) Thank you, too. (*He exits. The Nurse closes the door as Fitzgerald sighs exhaustedly*)

FITZGERALD: I'm glad you told him to leave. I had to go in the bathroom and sit down for a few moments just to rest.

NURSE: (*Putting the gin bottle and glass away in the dresser drawer*) Why don't you take a nap now? You've had an exhausting afternoon.

FITZGERALD: How did I do?

NURSE: You were fine.

FITZGERALD: I was scared the entire time.

NURSE: Well, you certainly didn't show it.

(*Fitzgerald stands and takes off his robe and slippers as the Nurse removes the spread from the bed*)

FITZGERALD: He kept staring at me, studying the lines in my face, watching my hands when I couldn't keep them still.

NURSE: He knows you've been ill. He'll write a good interview, and people will remember you and start buying your books again.

FITZGERALD: You'd tell a dying man he was going to live, wouldn't you?

NURSE: What do you mean?

FITZGERALD: I wonder what he will say about me? I'm afraid I won't think about much of anything else until I see the interview. You'll arrange to get a copy of it for me, won't you?

NURSE: Yes. (*Fitzgerald gets into the bed. The Nurse pulls the covers over him, then crosses to the door*) You have a good nap.

FITZGERALD: Do you think he'll be kind to me?

NURSE: I'm sure he will.

FITZGERALD: God, I hope so! (*The Nurse watches him a moment, then goes out. Fitzgerald lies in the bed, staring at the ceiling as:*)

The Lights Dim Out

Scene Two

It is noon, several days later. Fitzgerald, in his pajamas, is stretched out on his bed, his head propped up on the pillows, staring absently in front of him, ignoring the book in his hand. After a moment, the Nurse enters, carrying a letter and a newspaper which is folded under her arm. She is more than ordinarily cheerful.

NURSE: Only one letter in the mail this morning.

FITZGERALD: Did the interview come?

NURSE: (*Handing him the letter*) And it looks like an advertisement.

FITZGERALD: (*Seeing the newspaper, ignoring the letter*) Is that it?

NURSE: Your lunch is almost ready and guess what you're having!

FITZGERALD: Have you read it? Is it good?

NURSE: Chicken fried steak and mashed potatoes!

FITZGERALD: (*Getting up, crossing toward her*) Let me see it. What'd he say?

NURSE: (*Hiding the newspaper behind her*) Why don't you wait until . . .

FITZGERALD: It's bad, isn't it? (*She nods*) Where'd they put it?

NURSE: On the front page.

FITZGERALD: (*Going back to his bed, tired now*) It would have to be bad then, wouldn't it? Good news doesn't get on the front page. Read it to me.

NURSE: What good will it do?

FITZGERALD: It can't be *that* bad . . . can it?

NURSE: Wait till you've had your lunch, then we'll laugh at it.

FITZGERALD: Read it to me now . . . please. (*He stares at the ceiling. The Nurse unfolds the newspaper and starts to read*)

NURSE: "The Other Side of Paradise. Scott Fitzgerald, Forty, Engulfed in Despair." (*She pauses, turning to him*) Mr. Fitzgerald . . .

FITZGERALD: (*Without looking at her*) Go on.

NURSE: "Asheville, N.C., Sept. 25—Long ago, when he

was young, cocksure, drunk with sudden success, F. Scott Fitzgerald told a newspaperman that no one should live beyond thirty.

"That was in 1921, shortly after his first novel, *This Side of Paradise,* had burst into the literary heavens like a flowering Roman candle.

"The poet-prophet of the post-war neurotics observed his fortieth birthday yesterday. He spent the day as he spends all his days—trying to come back from the other side of paradise, the hell of despondency in which he has writhed for the last couple of years.

"He had no company except his soft spoken, indulgent nurse and this reporter. He chatted bravely, as an actor, consumed with fear that his name will never be in lights again, discusses his next starring role . . ." (*She stops, not wanting to go on*)

FITZGERALD: Go on.

NURSE: "Physically he was suffering the aftermath of an accident. But whatever pain his fracture might still cause him, it did not account for his jittery jumping off and onto his bed, his restless pacing, his trembling hands, his twitching face with its pitiful expression of a cruelly beaten child.

"Nor could it be held responsible for his frequent trips to a highboy, in a drawer of which lay a bottle. Each time he poured a drink . . ." (*She can't go on*)

FITZGERALD: (*After a moment*) Does he mention Zelda?

NURSE: The story about throwing herself in front of the train. (*Fitzgerald says nothing*) Don't think about it, Mr. Fitzgerald. What that boy says about you isn't worth worrying over!

FITZGERALD: I open myself up to people like that! I want to help them, and I assume they'll want to help *me*. You'd think I'd learn, wouldn't you? I think I'll try and rest.

NURSE: Don't go to sleep now. Your lunch is almost ready.

FITZGERALD: I'm not hungry.

NURSE: You'll feel much better after a good meal, and . . .

FITZGERALD: Please . . . (*She stops trying to be cheerful*) Leave the paper, will you? Thanks for bringing it to me. (*She wants to comfort him but doesn't know how. She puts the newspaper on the dresser and starts out the door. He watches her leave*) Do you think . . .

NURSE: (*Hopefully*) What?

FITZGERALD: (*Looking away*) I guess I *am* a has-been.

(*The Nurse pauses, watching Fitzgerald anxiously, then exits. Fitzgerald has been shattered by the article, and he tries to reconcile himself to the picture others have of him. After a pause, he slowly rises from the bed, crosses to the dresser and picks up the newspaper. He reads it for a moment, then puts it down and buries his face in his hands. Then he takes down his hands and studies himself in the mirror. He turns away from the mirror, defeated by what he sees. He starts to open the dresser drawer where the gin bottle is kept when he sees the medicine bottles. He stares at them, then picks one up and looks at it thoughtfully. He slowly opens it, puts it to his mouth, pauses a moment, then drinks all of it. He stands waiting and then begins to cough and retch violently. He staggers into the bathroom, and we can hear him vomiting. After a moment, he returns and starts toward his bed. But it is too much for him, and he falls dizzily to the floor. He lies there, breathing heavily. After a moment, the Nurse enters carrying the lunch tray*)

NURSE: (*As she enters*) Here's something that will cheer you up! (*Seeing Fitzgerald on the floor, putting the tray down*) Mr. Fitzgerald, what happened? (*She rushes to him and sees the empty medicine bottle in his hand. She takes it from him*)

FITZGERALD: (*Trying to make a joke of it*) I never could stand the taste of medicine. (*The Nurse grabs a towel from the dresser and begins to clean up Fitzgerald*)

NURSE: Ssh! You're all right now.

FITZGERALD: (*Terrified by what he's done*) I guess I've hit bottom. I can't go any lower than this. Thank God it didn't work.

NURSE: Don't try to talk. Let's get you in bed. (*She puts her arm around him and with great effort manages to get him into the bed. She makes him comfortable*) You're not going to give up, Mr. Fitzgerald. You're going to write more books, and they'll be better than anything you've ever written. I just know you will.

(*She wipes his brow tenderly. He smiles at her weakly. She crosses to a chair and sits in it, just to be there if he needs her. The lights dim out slowly except for a spot on Fitzgerald's face, as he stares exhaustedly into space. After a moment, he closes his eyes and breathes heavily. The spot fades out*)

Curtain

Olwen Wymark

STAY WHERE YOU ARE

Olwen Wymark

With Olwen Wymark's introduction as a playwright—in 1966 at the Close Theatre, Glasgow, and subsequently at the Edinburgh Festival and abroad—most critics perceived a new writer for the theatre of considerable originality and power. A consensus of opinion that has continued unabatingly, it reached new heights with the 1969 premiere of *Stay Where You Are* at the Traverse Theatre, Edinburgh.

The play, published here for the first time in the United States, was proclaimed "a fascinating example of theatrical chamber music" in which Mrs. Wymark continues to pursue the theme that interests her most: the crystallization of the personality out of the slurry of existence, and its vulnerability to external manipulation. Several members of the Scottish press cited *Stay Where You Are* as "the best new play produced in Scotland in 1969," one that again vividly demonstrates that "Mrs. Wymark's way with words and ideas is indeed rather like a firecracker: but there are feelings behind them and powers of organization at work upon them that provide not only intellectual stimulants but a profound dramatic satisfaction." The critic for *The Scotsman* found "the wisdom and wit of the play constantly absorbing" and described the author as "a very articulate and imaginative dramatist, with a grasp of ideas as well as words."

B. A. Young, the influential reviewer for London's *The Financial Times* who journeyed to Edinburgh for the premiere, concurred: "Olwen Wymark not only has a remarkable, vivid and original imagination, she has an immaculate sense of what is effective on the stage. Many writers today seem to be writing for themselves alone: if we can't follow them, so much the worse for us. Mrs. Wymark's writing is always theatrical, full of humor, tension and poetry that are *shared* with the audience. She is a writer of unusual merit."

Olwen Wymark was born in Oakland, California, in 1929 and grew up in Palo Alto, where her father was a professor at Stanford University. Her mother is English and the daughter of the noted writer, W. W. Jacobs, who with Louis N. Parker wrote *The Monkey's Paw,* one of the theatre's most popular short plays.

Mrs. Wymark spent two and a half years at Pomona College, then went to England to complete her education at University College, London, where she met her husband, Patrick Wymark, a distinguished British actor who died in 1970.

After their marriage, the couple "lived in stimulating poverty in South London" while he was a drama student at the Old Vic School. In 1954, he was engaged by the Royal Shakespeare Company and the Wymarks moved to Stratford-on-Avon where they remained for five years. Upon their return to London, they took a house on the edge of Hampstead Heath where Mrs. Wymark now lives with her four children, three cats and a dog.

The author readily admits, "I started writing at about the age of seven and began the Great American Novel nine or ten times but never finished it. I also wrote a great many rather tiring short stories and quite a lot of intense and bad poetry. In 1956, I wrote three radio plays, all of which were produced on the B.B.C., and immediately had two more babies in order not to have to write any more. But when all the children were in school, I ran out of excuses and wrote my first short play, *Lunchtime Concert,* which had its premiere in 1966 at the Close Theatre." The following year that play and two others by Mrs. Wymark, *The Inhabitants* and *Coda,* were produced at the same theatre under the overall title of *Triple Image*. The production was revived during the summer for the Edinburgh Festival, then toured Poland, Yugoslavia and Belgium before coming to London. In 1969, Mrs. Wymark's *The Technicians* was presented at the Leicester Festival of Experimental Drama. Among her other works for the theatre are: *Jack the Giant-Killer; Neither Here Nor There;* and *The Committee,* produced in London in 1971.

In addition to an active writing career and running a large household, Olwen Wymark does a good deal of voluntary work in the field of mental health, mainly for the Richmond Fellowship, an independent charity which sets up therapeutic communities for people who have suffered mental or emotional breakdowns.

Characters:

ELLEN

NINA

TADDY

DAVID

The stage is dark. There is the sound of footsteps outside.

ELLEN: Are you all right? Be careful.

NINA: You be careful with that bag. (*We hear her fumbling with the key in the lock*) Swinging it about. There's breakables in that bag. Bloody key. (*Wails*) There! I've dropped it now. I've dropped my key.

ELLEN: Wait. I'll get it. Here it is. Shall I do it?

NINA: Do, dear. There's a good girl.

(*The door is opened and the light from the street shows us a basement flat, near-slum, cluttered, dank, smelly. They come in.*

Nina is a fat old woman in her seventies, derelict looking, spectacles, a knitted hat. Ellen, about thirty, is pretty and well-dressed. Nina leans heavily on a stick and Ellen helps her through the door)

ELLEN: Well, if you're all right now . . . Oh. Your bag. (*Puts it down*) I'll have to go.

(*Nina puts her head back and makes a noise between a howl and a groan*)

ELLEN: (*Startled*) What is it?

NINA: The pain's come back. Me leg. I've got a blood clot under me knee.

ELLEN: Here. Sit down.

NINA: (*Sits, with Ellen's help*) Oh . . . that's better. That's a bit better. Turn on that light. (*Ellen looks about*) Over there!

(*Ellen does. Nina rocks back and forth in the chair, holding her leg and groaning. Ellen stands watching her, aghast. Eventually, Nina stops rocking and is silent, eyes closed*)

ELLEN: (*After a pause*) Are you all right?

NINA: The pain's gone now. (*But she doesn't open her eyes*)

ELLEN: Well . . . I'm awfully sorry but I really have to be going.

NINA: (*Opening her eyes and turning her head slowly to look at Ellen*) Going? How am I to manage?

ELLEN: I have to go. I was waiting for someone when I saw you. He'll be there now.

NINA: Stuck here in this chair. I won't be able to move for a hour now. I know that. I get these attacks. I know them.

ELLEN: He'll think I'm not coming.

NINA: I've only been out of hospital three days.

ELLEN: But isn't there somebody here? To take care of you?

NINA: Who—him? I have to cry like a baby before he'll take me up to the toilet.

ELLEN: Your husband?

NINA: I wouldn't have *him* for a husband. He's not right.

ELLEN: Does he live here?

NINA: He lives here all right. Oh yes, he lives here.

ELLEN: Well, he'll be back soon, won't he?

NINA: Who knows? Stays out all night, sometimes. (*Piteous*) All on my own here. Can't move. No one to protect me and the pain so bad sometimes I cry out in prayer, I can tell you.

ELLEN: (*Now desperate*) I have to *go!*

NINA: Make us a cup of tea first, eh? Will you just make a cup of tea for a poor rubbishy old woman?

ELLEN: But he won't know where I am.

NINA: Your husband, is it?

ELLEN: (*Brief pause*) Yes.

NINA: Well, he'll wait. He'll wait for his pretty wife.

ELLEN: No, I must go. He'll be worried.

NINA: But you're not worried about *me,* are you? Oh no. Help an old woman across the road. That's right. That's a good deed. Didn't want to help me back here though, did you? You'd have left me there. Got me across the road and just left me. What's the good of that? I had to beg for it. There's your good Samaritan.

ELLEN: Well, why were you out? You shouldn't have been out at all.

NINA: Someone had to get some food, didn't they? He's brought *nothing* in. Perish from hunger—he wouldn't care. It's took me hours just to get down to that little shop across the road. People going past making out I was drunk. That's what they think if you're poor. "Oh, she's drunk," they say. "What a frightful old woman. Look at her," they say. Never think you're just out of hospital. Nearly died. I won't last long, I know that.

ELLEN: Oh, you will . . . I'm sure . . .

NINA: It'd be easier for you if I'd popped off before you ever seen me. And *he'd* be glad. He'd be ever so glad to come home and find I'd popped off. (*Pause*) And I don't know nobody else.

ELLEN: Nobody?

NINA: Nobody . . . I'd like a cup of tea.

ELLEN: (*After a pause*) Where's the kettle?

NINA: It's behind that curtain. All the comforts of home. Sink, gas ring—we'll need a bob or a sixpence. Got a tanner, my duck?

ELLEN: I think I've got a shilling. Yes.

NINA: Meter's under the sink.

(*Ellen goes behind the curtain. We hear her fill the kettle, put the shilling in the meter and light the gas.*

Meanwhile Nina has, with difficulty, taken off one shoe, pulled her skirt up and peeled off one stocking. She starts to unwind a dirty elastic bandage from her leg)

NINA: (*Calls*) I say. Ducky. (*Ellen comes out*) Give us a hand with this bandage, dear, will you, while the kettle's boiling. I'm too weak, that's all. Got to be done twice a day, see. (*Ellen crouches down and gingerly starts to unwind the bandage and roll it up*) Has to be tight to stop this clot moving up to my heart. That's it. That's got it. (*Ellen has wound up the bandage*) Now put it back on again. (*Ellen crouches down again*) No, not like that. You got to start it right up here. (*She pulls her skirt even further up*) Right round here. That's right. Move over a bit, dear. Then I can rest my foot on your knee there. That's the way. That's better. (*She puts one hand on Ellen's shoulder as she rewinds the bandage, her leg stretched out straight, the foot resting on Ellen's lap*) That's it. Right round. Round again. Nice and tight.

(*The door opens quietly so that they don't hear it. A man, Taddy stands in the doorway watching them. He is in his fifties with grey hair but a youthful face. He's wearing a tattered greatcoat and sucking a lollypop*)

TADDY: (*Takes the lollypop out of his mouth and makes a sweeping gesture*) Mother-and-Child.

(*Ellen cries out, startled*)

NINA: Mind *out!* (*Looks round*) Oh, it's you. (*To Ellen*) It's only Taddy. Finish it off then. There's a pin on the end. Not so fast. Ow-oh-oh-ow-not so fast!

(*Ellen finishes and, putting Nina's foot on the floor, she gets up*)

NINA: (*Querulous*) What about my stocking?

TADDY: (*Strides briskly over*) I'll do that. (*Holding the lollypop in his mouth, he puts on her stocking and her shoe. Then he takes the lollypop out of his mouth and holds it up to Nina*) Suck?

NINA: No, I want my tea. (*Throws lollypop across the room*)

ELLEN: (*Who has been edging over to the door*) The kettle's boiling—in there. (*To Nina*) You'll be all right now, won't you. Your—he'll get you some tea.

TADDY: Oh, no. She won't let me make the tea. Not when somebody else is here. Hates my tea.

ELLEN: But I'm just going.

TADDY: Well, you can make the tea before you go.

ELLEN: (*Helplessly*) Please . . .

TADDY: (*To Nina*) What's she doing here?

NINA: How do *I* know?

ELLEN: I . . . I just helped you up the road! (*To Taddy*) She didn't seem to be able to walk. I don't think she ought to be out so soon after being in hospital.

TADDY: *She* wasn't in hospital.

ELLEN: Oh?

NINA: I was.

TADDY: All right, you were.

ELLEN: Well . . . goodbye.

TADDY: Why don't you just make her some tea?

ELLEN: But you're here now. You can do it.

TADDY: (*Goes over to bed and lies on it*) I could. But I'm not going to.

ELLEN: Why? Why not?

TADDY: Because I don't want to. (*Brief pause*) You don't want to either.

ELLEN: But I don't live here. I don't even know her.

TADDY: You have to *know* people before you can make them a cup of tea?

ELLEN: That isn't fair.

TADDY: Did you want to help her home?

ELLEN: (*Miserable*) I don't know.

TADDY: Why did you do it then?

ELLEN: I don't *know*.

TADDY: You must have had some reason. Felt sorry for her?

ELLEN: Yes. Yes I did!

NINA: Sorry enough to see me across the road. Not sorry enough to get me home.

ELLEN: I did bring you home. I put the kettle on. I did your bandage.

NINA: Yes, but you didn't want to. I had to make you, didn't I?

(*Taddy sits up and pats the end of the bed*)

TADDY: Here.

ELLEN: What?

TADDY: Come and sit here.

ELLEN: No!

NINA: (*Closing her eyes*) Don't be naughty, dear. Do as you're told.

TADDY: (*Still patting the bed; gently but firmly*) Come here. (*Ellen comes over but doesn't sit. She stands looking down at him*) Now. Try and think. Why did you help her across the road?

ELLEN: Because I couldn't think of any way out of it.

TADDY: *Very* good. That's very good.

NINA: That kettle will be boiling its liver out!

TADDY: And why did you bring her home?

ELLEN: She wouldn't let go of my hand.

TADDY: And then you put the kettle on.

ELLEN: Yes.

TADDY: And then you did her bandage.

ELLEN: Yes.

TADDY: Why?

ELLEN: She *told* me to.

TADDY: And you always do as you're told. (*Pause; then raps it out*) Make the tea!

(*They look at each other. Ellen turns and runs to the door*)

ELLEN: I won't! I don't have to! (*She pulls at the door handle*)

NINA: (*Opening her eyes; surprised*) You going?

ELLEN: Yes! I didn't want to come here in the first place. You never thanked me; that doesn't matter. But I did help you even though I didn't much want to. You can't make me stay here!

(*Taddy rises and walks over to her and stands with his back to the door. She backs away from him nervously*)

TADDY: (*Points to the curtained kitchen, his eyes steadily on Ellen*) Get in there and make the tea, do you hear me?

(*As if by reflex, Ellen turns and starts for the kitchen. Taddy and Nina roar with laughter*)

ELLEN: (*Stops; scared*) Why are you laughing?

NINA: Talk about a monkey on a string!

TADDY: You *do* do what you're told. Well, well. Amazing.

NINA: (*Banging her stick on the floor with great violence*) Tea! I want my tea! I want my tea!

TADDY: Stop that!

(*Nina subsides into mumbling. Ellen looks from one to the other, starts to speak, then changes her mind and walks with artificial purposefulness to the door*)

TADDY: Now what?

ELLEN: (*Firmly*) I must go! I have to meet . . . my husband. Would you let me by, please.

TADDY: (*Blocking the door again*) Oh, come on. It's not your husband—now is it?

ELLEN: I . . . I . . . I don't know what you mean . . .

TADDY: There's no need to pretend. We've known all along. Haven't we, Nina?

NINA: Well, o' course we have.

ELLEN: Known what?

TADDY: You must have thought we were very naïve. She must have thought we were just a couple of old fuddy-duddies, eh, Nina?

NINA: Sticks-in-the-mud.

TADDY: (*To Ellen; the Victorian father, grave and pompous*) Now we don't want to give you advice. Heaven knows, you should be old enough now to make your own decisions. But there is one thing I'd like to say. Just one last word. I think we're agreed on this point, my dear? (*He looks down inquiringly at Nina. Her attention has wandered and she is picking her teeth. She quickly folds her hands in her lap and nods at him. To Ellen*) We'd just like you to reflect a little about family life. The protection of the young. The little lives which have been put into your care. The home. The nest . . . (*He points at Ellen, in sad accusation*) How many innocent people will suffer —answer me that!

NINA: He's right, dear. It wouldn't be fair. Poor little pretties—it wouldn't be right.

ELLEN: You're both mad! I mean . . . insane.

(*They look at her steadily*)

TADDY: How many children has he got—two is it?

ELLEN: (*Shocked*) How . . . ?

TADDY: And you've got three, haven't you?

ELLEN: Yes.

TADDY: Well, that's five for a start, isn't it—to suffer, I mean? Not to speak of the other wife and other husband of course. Seven.

NINA: Oh, don't forget the grannies, dear. Don't leave them out. They'll be heartbroken.

TADDY: A good deal of pain, I'm afraid.

NINA: And the granddads o' course. (*Getting quite involved and counting on her fingers*) Not to mention the uncles and aunties. And with the cousins there would be . . .

TADDY: (*Firmly*) That'll do! (*Then, lightly*) I'll go and make that tea now. (*He goes*)

(*Ellen has been standing frozen through this. After a pause, she goes quickly over to Nina. We hear Taddy whistling in the kitchen*)

ELLEN: Is he a detective?

NINA: *I* don't know.

ELLEN: You said . . . You said he came in at all sorts of hours. (*Pause*) Does he have a tape recorder?

NINA: Yes! He does! You could be right. He never tells me nothing.

ELLEN: No, it can't be. It's too silly.

NINA: Expect you're right. Silly. Yes. (*Pause*) Still—it's funny. Your saying that, I mean. For *example,* sometimes he'll go out with this other bloke—a photographer he is—and they always go ever so late at night and most times he don't get back here till morning.

ELLEN: A photographer!

NINA: That's right.

ELLEN: Oh God! I suppose he could be . . .

NINA: Well, he *could*. I mean it would hang together, wouldn't it?

ELLEN: I don't know . . . I don't know . . . Maybe it would make it worse to go now. I don't know. Do *you* think I should stay?

NINA: You must do as you think fit, my dear. I wouldn't like to advise.

ELLEN: But it's such an impossible coincidence. How can he know anything about me? He couldn't know I was coming here. I mean, I'm only here by accident . . . (*She breaks off and stares at Nina. Taddy's whistling in the kitchen stops abruptly*)

NINA: Yes, dear? Go on.

ELLEN: (*Puzzled; not believing this but knowing it*) You brought me here! You did it all on purpose.

NINA: (*Bit dangerous*) Oh, I see. *He* sent me out to fetch you, is that right? (*Ellen is silent*) Is that what happened? (*Still no answer. Then, in a strong cruel tone*) Eh?

ELLEN: Yes. Yes, I do think that happened! It all fits in.

NINA: (*More dangerous*) Fits in. Oh, yes. (*Very sweet voice*) And where does my leg fit in? You'd say there's nothing wrong with it, would you? (*Ellen nods*) All part of the act, eh? (*Ellen nods again*) It's all about you, isn't it? The story's *always* got to be about you. (*Brief pause; then, spits it out with pain and venom*) Selfish little bitch! (*She closes her eyes, puts her head back and speaks privately*) *I* was in hospital. I was the one lying in bed awake all night waiting for that clot to get up to my heart. Sweating and crying—all alone. Nurses—cheeky hardbitten little madams. Doctor doesn't even look at you. Just a useless heap of rubbish nobody cares about. (*Opens eyes and looks clearly at Ellen*) Nor do I care, mind. Just enough to stay alive.

(*Taddy has come through again, unseen by them, and has been listening*)

TADDY: You were *not* in hospital. (*Ellen starts and stares at him. Nina doesn't move. Pause*)

NINA: (*Throwing her stick violently across the room*) Oh, all *right!*

ELLEN: You *weren't!* (*To Taddy*) She *wasn't!* None of that was true. There's nothing the matter with her!

TADDY: Oh, I don't think I'd say *that.*

NINA: Oh, very funny and witty I'm sure!

ELLEN: (*Effort at calm*) Before I go, I would like some kind of explanation. I think—I think . . .

TADDY: Yes?

ELLEN: (*Rather quavering dignity*) I think you may both regret all this—regret it very much.

NINA: Well! Well then! Ah, it's a shame. (*To Taddy*) And where's my bloody tea?

TADDY: (*Irish*) Now aren't I the great ninny? (*Bustles out and comes in again with the tray*) Tea is served, gentlemen. (*Then, own voice:*) Keep a cup hot for me in the pot. I'm just going up to make a couple of phone calls. (*He goes out another door*)

NINA: (*Pouring*) Milk and sugar, dear?

ELLEN: I don't want any. Calling who? *Who's* he telephoning?

NINA: How would I know, dear? How would I ever know? Here. You take this tea. (*Proffers cup*) It's good and strong and it's good and sweet. You're looking very peaky. (*Ellen automatically takes the cup*) There's my duck. Go on now—sit down.

(*Ellen does*)

NINA: (*Takes a swig of her own tea*) Ah, that's good. (*Looks over at Ellen who is just holding her cup and staring at nothing*) Drink it up, old lady.

ELLEN: (*Puts cup on floor*) I don't want it!

NINA: Well, poor mite. (*Shouts toward the door Taddy left by*) Poor mite I say! (*Pause; confidentially*) Here. Don't believe all I say when *he's* here, eh?

ELLEN: What do you mean?

NINA: I got no home of my own, you know. Nowhere to go but here. No Visible Means of Support.

ELLEN: Do you mean he pays you?

NINA: Pays me! All you young people think about is money. You don't understand nothing, do you?

ELLEN: (*Desperate*) No! No, I don't! (*Puts her face in her hands and sobs*) I don't know what to *do!*

(*Nina watches her in silence; then, holding her cup in her lap, she sings softly*)

NINA:

"Warm hands warm
The men have gone to plough
If you want to warm your hands
Warm your hands now."

My gran use to sing me that. Nice, isn't it?

"Warm hands warm
The men have gone to plough
If you want to—"

(*She breaks off and speaks briskly*) Tell you what we'll do!

ELLEN: (*Wiping tears off her face with her fingers*) What?

NINA: Now where's that stick? (*Ellen looks around vaguely*) Never you mind. I'll get it.

(*She heaves herself off her chair and starts to crawl grotesquely in the direction of the stick, grunting and puffing. Ellen gets up and backs away staring at her, horrified*)

ELLEN: But you said you *hadn't* been in hospital.

NINA: (*Briefly*) *He* said. (*Ellen starts to go forward to help her but Nina waves her away*) Never mind. Never mind. I'm used to this. Go and listen at that door. See if he's coming back.

(*Ellen goes over to the door and puts her ear to it*)

ELLEN: I can't hear anything.

NINA: (*Getting herself up to a standing position with the stick*) Ups-a-daisy! He thinks he knows everything. . . . There's a lot he *doesn't* know. For one thing he is jealous! Now that is one thing I am not. My dad used to say to me, "Nina, there is not a jealous bone in your body." What's *your* name?

ELLEN: Ellen.

NINA: Hmm. Bit plain. Elaine would have been nicer. More style. What did *your* daddy call you?

ELLEN: El. He always called me El.

NINA: Don't think much of that. *I'll* call you Elaine.

ELLEN: Please . . .

NINA: Don't rush me, dearie. You think old Nina's just rambling on. But all the time I'm thinking. I'm planning.

ELLEN: Planning what? Are you going to help me?

NINA: Well, o' *course* I'm going to help you, silly little juggins.

ELLEN: Will you tell me what to do? Can I go? (*Starts to cry again*) I want to go and find . . .

NINA: Find who?

ELLEN: M-m-my husband.

NINA: Oh, now. There's no use starting that again, is there? I told you before. Jealous! Taddy! He's jealous!

ELLEN: (*Utterly puzzled*) But you don't mean he's jealous of *me?*

NINA: Oh, Elaine, Elaine. Oh, dearie, dearie, dearie. We shall never get on at this rate. Here. Sit down will you? I can't get on with my planning—you standing about like a scared rabbit. (*Ellen sits*) Now, you just listen to Nina. When he comes back—the minute he comes in—I want you to faint! Flat on the floor!

ELLEN: Why?

NINA: Because I say so.

ELLEN: I can't. I don't think I can.

NINA: 'Course you can. 'Course you can. Easy enough. Just keel over. Any fool can do that. I'd show you myself if it wasn't for this sodding stick. All right then. There you are, stretched out. That'll stop him. "It's the shock," I'll say. (*Dramatically*) "She may never recover from this," I'll say.

ELLEN: Then what will happen?

NINA: "Fetch a doctor, quick!" I'll say. Then—while he's out of the way—up you get and off you run safe home to beddy-byes.

ELLEN: But how *can* I go? He *knows* things about me. (*She suddenly rises*) He's a blackmailer!

NINA: Shhhhhh! *I* didn't say it. (*Low*) Now you listen to me, Elaine. He knows nothing. He never saw you before tonight. It was me picked you.

ELLEN: But why did you do it? *Why?*

NINA: (*The reproving Nanny*) Try and think of others, Elaine dear. I got to do what I'm told or it would be the old heave-ho for Nina. Tipped out in the street.

ELLEN: (*Painfully trying to work it out*) Do you mean you just go out . . . I mean he sends you . . . to choose someone . . . anybody . . . and then frighten them about some secret they might have?

NINA: Everybody's got secrets, duck, and I must say you weren't much cop at hiding yours. Candy from a baby with you. That's why I felt sorry for you.

ELLEN: You *say* you're sorry for me. I don't believe you.

NINA: Don't then. I can see as how you wouldn't.

ELLEN: (*Pause*) You really *will* help me?

NINA: (*Licks her finger, draws it across her throat and holds it up*) Promise!

ELLEN: I do believe you.

NINA: There's my good girl! Now the minute we hear him coming, over you go. Can you do that?

ELLEN: Yes, I can. I'll do it.

NINA: That's right. I knew you could. You stay here and I'll be by the door. You watch me for the signal. Right?

ELLEN: (*Nods*) Right.

(*Nina goes over to the door. Ellen watches her, trembling a little*)

NINA: Don't worry, then. It'll be all right. Don't you worry. (*Ear to door*) Nothing yet. Not a sound. (*Straightens*)

Do you know? I get a funny sort of dream sometimes. Well, it's not really a dream because I'm awake. Like just before I get up out of bed in the mornings or like before I drop off at night. I get this feeling they've taken off the top of my head. Doesn't hurt or anything. It's just gone and I feel all lovely and empty, and then I can feel this sort of *growing* right inside my head. It's growing up and up and I stay ever so still. Flowers. All growing out of the top of my head. Lilacs and honeysuckle and daffs and bluebells—all sorts. There's this lovely sweet smell and I can feel the flowers hanging down and brushing against my face, just rustling like against my ears and my eyes. (*She smiles to herself, then looks over at Ellen*) You think I'm daft.

ELLEN: (*Quickly*) No, I don't. I don't. (*There is the sound of footsteps*)

NINA: He's coming. Quick! Now!

(*Ellen looks wildly about and then awkwardly and in a panic throws herself face down on the floor*)

NINA: (*Loud*) Oh, my God! Oh, my God!

(*Holding her stick under her arm, Nina runs very lightly over to Ellen and kneels beside her. The door opens. Taddy comes in followed by a young man, David. They go over to Nina and Ellen*)

TADDY: What have you done to her?

NINA: Me! What did *I* do? She's just had a fit or something, that's all. You've scared her into convulsions, that's what you've done!

DAVID: Oh Jesus! Ellen!

(*He tries to get to her but Taddy neatly intervenes. Ellen pulls herself up to her hands and knees and looks unbelievingly at David*)

ELLEN: David! Oh, you're here! You're here. How did you find me?

DAVID: (*To Taddy*) I'll go and get some brandy.

TADDY: Right.

(*David goes quickly*)

ELLEN: (*After a blank silence*) He's gone.

TADDY: He'll be back. Nina. Go and wash up these tea things. And find a glass in there.

NINA: (*Cheerful*) Right-oh, Taddy. Right-oh, right-oh, right-oh. (*She puts her stick down, collects the cups and waltzes out with the tray*) Anything to oblige. Mind your backs, ladies and gentlemen, *please.* (*When she gets through the curtain she starts to sing*) "She was a sweet little dickeybird, tweet tweet tweet she went . . ."

TADDY: *All* right!

NINA: (*Sticks her head through the curtain*) Spoilsport! Isn't he a mean old spoilsport, Elaine?

TADDY: Nina!

NINA: (*Sulky*) Oh, all right! (*She disappears behind the curtain*)

ELLEN: She *is* crazy.

TADDY: Yes! Now what about this fit of yours?

ELLEN: It wasn't . . . I mean I didn't. She *told* me to.

TADDY: Ah. I should have known that. You know, sometimes it gets to be a bit too much for me. It really does.

ELLEN: What does?

TADDY: (*Rubbing his eyes with the heels of his palms*) I'm tired. (*Looks at Ellen*) I can't *always* know the right thing to do, can I?

ELLEN: I don't know.

TADDY: You say that a lot, don't you? (*Ellen doesn't answer*) You'll have to do *some* of this. I can't do it all.

ELLEN: Some of what?

TADDY: After all, you've got responsibility for it, too.

ELLEN: How? What do you mean?

TADDY: Well, for Nina, for example. You *came* here with her.

ELLEN: Yes, but I didn't want to.

TADDY: I'm talking about what you did, not what you felt. (*He begins walking about, speaking more or less to him-*

self) Well, now what? What's for the best I wonder? I wonder. . .

ELLEN: He'll come back and he'll take me away.

TADDY: Possibly, possibly. Let's wait and see about that, shall we? It's not, after all, the main issue.

ELLEN: It is for me! I want to go.

TADDY: We all *always* want to go. Does it occur to you that this might be hard for me, too? And for Nina, God knows. No, I can see that it wouldn't.

ELLEN: You said she was crazy. She is.

TADDY: Yes, yes.

ELLEN: And . . . and . . . and I think you are, too!

TADDY: A possibility not to be discounted. And you? What about you? (*Laughs kindly*) Throwing yourself on the floor? Pretending to have a fit?

ELLEN: I didn't *want* to do that.

TADDY: But you had to because she told you to. Another one of your little sayings.

(*David returns with the brandy. Ellen rushes over to him*)

DAVID: Are you all right?

ELLEN: Yes! Can we go now?

TADDY: (*Friendly, apologetic*) I'm afraid it was all Nina's idea—one of her famous charades. (*To Ellen*) And you went along with it. Very generous.

ELLEN: (*To David*) Can we go?

(*Nina comes through the curtain, a cloth shopping bag over her head*)

NINA: Come on, Tad, Marco! Marco!

(*Taddy gives an elaborate rueful shrug to the others and goes up to Nina*)

TADDY: Polo!

(*Nina lunges and he moves quickly out of the way. He motions the others to join in*)

NINA: Marco!

DAVID: (*Moving towards her and grinning back at Ellen*) Polo!

NINA: I'll get you! (*Lunges; misses*) Marco!

TADDY: (*Quickly*) Polo!

NINA: Marco!

DAVID: Polo! Come on, Ellen.

(*Nina has been going toward one and then the other; now comes straight for Ellen*)

NINA: Marco!

ELLEN: (*Fast; nervous*) Polo! (*She doesn't move; Taddy darts back and moves her out of Nina's path*)

NINA: Marco!

TADDY: Polo!

NINA: Marco!

DAVID: Polo!

(*Ellen runs over and stands by David. He puts an arm 'round her*)

NINA: Marco!

DAVID: (*To Ellen*) Go on.

ELLEN: (*Bit braver*) Polo!

(*Nina moves in fast. David shoves Ellen aside and Nina gets him. She pulls the bag off her head*)

NINA: Ha! Ha-ha! (*She dances him 'round and then gives him a rather long slobbery kiss. Looks over her shoulder at Ellen*) Don't mind, do you, dear? I did win.

TADDY: That's the only reason she plays this game. For the kissing. Great slut!

NINA: (*Delighted*) Who you calling a slut?

TADDY: (*Genially*) You. You're a great slut and a fat sow.

NINA: Oh, naughty. Personal remark. (*To others*) That's right, isn't it? Personal remark—bad manners. (*To Taddy*) Weasel!

TADDY: Walrus!

NINA: Cheat. Cheat. Walruses are men. Snake!

TADDY: Snakes are women.

DAVID: (*Suddenly*) Wait! Stop! I can hear something outside. Turn out the lights. (*Taddy immediately does*)

ELLEN: (*Whispers*) What is it? David, where are you? What is it?

DAVID: Shhhhh! Don't know yet. Wait.

(*Silence*)

NINA: (*Quavering*) It's not them again, Taddy? It's not them, is it?

TADDY: (*Tense, clipped*) Don't think so. Don't be frightened, Nina.

NINA: Hold my hand, Taddy. You know I can't stand being alone in the dark.

TADDY: Here. I'm here. Be quiet now. Shall I go and have a look?

DAVID: No. Stay where you are. *I'll* go.

ELLEN: David, don't go. Please don't go!

DAVID: It's all right. Just stand quite still. (*We hear him going over to the door*)

NINA: (*Muttering it rapidly*) Soul of Christ sanctify me. Body of Christ save me. Blood of Christ intoxicate me. Water from the side of Christ wash me. Passion of Christ strengthen me. Oh good Jesus hear me. Within Thy wounds hide me. Never let me be separated from Thee. From the malignant enemy defend me. At my death call me and bid me come to Thee that with Thy saints I may praise Thee forever and ever Amen.

TADDY: Amen.

(*Silence again*)

DAVID: (*Cheerful*) All clear! Let's have the lights.

TADDY: (*Turns on the lights*) Phew! What we all need now is a drink.

ELLEN: (*To David*) Who was it? What was it?

TADDY: Nobody this time, thank God. Where are those glasses, Nina?

NINA: There's only one, Taddy. (*She brings out a half pint mug*)

TADDY: Well, we'll just have to have a loving cup. (*He holds mug out to David who pours brandy into it. Then hands it to Ellen; very courtly*) Our guest first.

DAVID: Drink, Ellen. It'll do you good.

TADDY: That's it. (*He then hands it to David but Nina intervenes and grabs it*)

NINA: Ladies first. (*Drinks*)

TADDY: Nina, Nina. You're supposed to be the hostess.

NINA: (*To David, handing him the mug*) Sorry, ducky.

DAVID: Quite all right. Well. Here's to the good life. (*He drinks and hands it on to Taddy*)

TADDY: (*Raising mug*) The Good Life. Champagne and Cadillacs and a month in the country!

ELLEN: (*Goes up to David and whispers*) Please, can we go now?

DAVID: Hang on, love.

ELLEN: (*Whispering*) But why can't we?

NINA: Whisper, whisper! (*Wags her finger*) Bad manners again.

DAVID: She's a bit upset.

NINA: I'm not surprised, poor little Elaine. Frightened into a fit like that. I don't wonder. Oh, it's a man's world, my dear. Take it from me.

TADDY: She didn't *have* a fit.

NINA: There now, there I go again. Mixing things up. It's the shock. Have some more brandy, Elaine lovey.

TADDY: That's right. Come and sit down. (*He pours some more and leads her to a chair. To David*) She's trembling.

(*David goes and sits by Ellen on the floor. He puts his arm across her legs and hugs them*)

DAVID: It's all right. It's all right. (*Ellen drinks; Nina comes over and takes the mug*)

NINA: Better now? I know how you feel. It's hard on a woman. (*Moves about orating and drinking*) Night after night I'll sit here, sometimes without no light if I haven't got a tanner. Oh, and I *hate* the dark! I'll just sit waiting, waiting. Him out

(*Indicating Taddy*) God knows where—larking about. And I think to myself, "Nina," I think, "This could be the night." Knock on the door. In they'll come. Break the door down most likely—*I* wouldn't open it. Paralyzed with fear in my chair waiting for it to happen. Crash! (*Ellen jumps; Nina pats her and says softly:*) Crash. In they'd come. There they'd be. "Your turn, Missus! (*Dramatic, thrilling tones*) It's your turn now!"

TADDY: You always think it's *your* turn, Nina. Why should it be you? Bet you thought it was your turn tonight.

NINA: Might have been. Might have been. Why not, I'd like to know?

TADDY: It might have been mine. Or his. (*Pause*) Or hers.

(*Silence; they all look at Ellen*)

ELLEN: My turn for what? (*To David*) What do they mean?

NINA: (*Through laughter; to Taddy*) She thought you were a detective! (*David and Taddy laugh heartily*)

ELLEN: *She* said you were a blackmailer.

NINA: Oooooh I never! What a fib! I didn't, Taddy. (*To Ellen*) That was *your* story.

DAVID: (*To Ellen*) Really? Did you really think that?

ELLEN: I didn't know what to think. I didn't understand what was happening.

TADDY: (*To the others*) Be fair. It's not surprising. (*To Ellen*) Everything happening so fast. Not a bit surprising.

NINA: *I* couldn't tell her, could I, Taddy? I mean, I couldn't tell her all about you. It wouldn't have been right.

TADDY: (*Formal; grave*) No, that's true, Nina. It would not have been right and I thank you for your discretion.

NINA: (*Humble*) Thank you, Taddy. But *you* could tell her, couldn't you.

TADDY: (*Looks down pensively; then looks up*) Yes. Yes. I could tell her.

NINA: (*Pulls up a chair near Ellen and sits down*) Taddy'll tell you.

TADDY: (*Mannered and actorish, but not parody*) It's a sad little story and rather stupid. I was a doctor—quite a good doctor in fact. When I was forty, something happened to me. (*Deprecatory*) I won't say it was the Voice of God. (*Serious again*) But I did feel I'd been . . . well . . . called. I suppose you could say it was a sort of vocation—mission—something like that. I left my home.

NINA: Muswell Hill.

TADDY: (*Shoots her a brief glance; nods and smiles reminiscently*) Muswell Hill. (*Then very seriously, to Ellen*) I left my wife and children. I left my excellent practice—the whole life I'd known and loved. And I went down to the East End of London. To the worst, slummiest part of the docks. I wanted to live with the Meth's drinkers. I felt I could help them to . . . find their way back. (*Pauses*)

DAVID: (*Respectful*) What happened?

TADDY: (*Shrugs; ironic*) What happened was that my capacity for suffering, my zeal for combating the ugliness and waste turned out to be less than my sense of personal despair. The despair being, I suppose, why I went into the absurd thing in the first place.

DAVID: (*Sympathetic*) I suppose so.

TADDY: (*Jaunty*) Well, I cracked up all over the shop, became an alcoholic myself and ended up far worse than those people I'd gone out to "spend my compassion" on. They had none for me. They hated me. (*Turns away, moved*) I couldn't run. I didn't know where to run to. Or why. So I tried suicide. A pathetic attempt. (*Turns back*) Nina found me. She saved my life. (*Nina smiles and shakes her head*) We came here.

DAVID: (*After a pause*) And now *you* look after *her*.

TADDY: That's about it. I do what I can. One-to-one salvation. (*To Ellen*) How does that sound to you? (*She looks into Taddy's face. The other two look at her*)

ELLEN: I . . . I'm sorry.

(*Nina and David exchange a very faint smile*)

TADDY: Ah, don't be sorry for me. I'm safe here. Nina's safe.

NINA: You never know, Taddy, you never know. The knock on the door. . .

TADDY: No, you never *do* know. It's best not to forget. (*To David*) You understand that, I think.

DAVID: Yes, I think I do. (*Shakes his head*) It's uncanny. Do you know, my own father died when I was thirteen—a hopeless alcoholic.

NINA: Funny old world.

ELLEN: (*To David*) You never told me that.

DAVID: I've never told anyone, Ellen, until just now. And I could never forgive my father either. But now, somehow, I think I do forgive him.

NINA: That's right. God rest him. We're *all* sinners, dear. All miserable sinners.

DAVID: I'd worshipped him, you see. I was the only child and I thought he was the most wonderful man in the world.

NINA: And what was your mummy like, dear? It must have been terrible for her.

(*David, as Taddy did, looks at her briefly*)

DAVID: My mother? Oh, she was a beautiful, foolish woman. (*Laughs fondly*) I never took her very seriously, I'm afraid. All she seemed to care about was parties and pretty clothes. I hadn't any idea, you see, that she was just putting up a front on a hideous situation. She kept it from me. Then, when . . . when it happened . . . Oh, I don't want to bore you with all that.

TADDY: No no, please. I think you should tell us.

NINA: What did she do, poor thing?

DAVID: Well, there was no money of course. She just went out to work. She didn't know how to do anything, really. Jobs in shops, working in a laundry, dishwashing. . . . Oh, she'd always lose the job but she just went on—on to another and another. She so desperately wanted me to stay in school and have a career. But she just wasn't strong enough. (*Pause*) She couldn't take it.

ELLEN: (*Taking his hand*) Did she die?

(*Now Taddy and Nina exchange the same faint smile*)

DAVID: No. She didn't die. She's in an asylum not far from Eastbourne.

TADDY: Do you see her?

DAVID: Oh, yes. Once a week I go down there. She lives in a kind of dream, really. Sometimes I wonder why I go. You see, she doesn't know who I am.

NINA: Doesn't recognize you—her own son?

DAVID: No. (*Pause*) Sometimes she thinks I'm my father. (*Pause*) Those are the worst times.

(*There is a silence*)

NINA: Oh, what a tragedy. What a sad and tragical story. It reminds me. . . . Oh, it has taken me back; just all that about the pretty clothes. I had such lovely clothes once. (*To Ellen*) In Paris, if you could believe that.

TADDY: No, she couldn't.

NINA: Why not, pray? (*Ellen takes her hand from David; touches Nina's knee*)

ELLEN: Go on. Go on. Please tell me.

NINA: (*Sulky*) You heard what he said.

ELLEN: (*Urgently*) No. I didn't. I didn't. What were you doing in Paris? Tell me.

TADDY: Ran away from home at sixteen? Artist's model in the Latin Quarter? It's a hopeless, ridiculous story, Nina, and you know it.

NINA: I don't see why. What about him trying to shoot me on that channel steamer?

ELLEN: Who? Who did? Tell me.

NINA: The painter chappie, dear, what I lived with.

TADDY: Oh, give over, Nina! We can't take all that.

NINA: (*Triumphantly indignant*) See! Spoilsport again! We can take *your* story. Oh, of course. Oh, definitely. Doctor in Muswell Hill indeed!

TADDY: *You* said Muswell Hill.

NINA: Well, I was a bit cross. Naturally, I was thinking it was going to be the one about you being a master in that public school and caught in bed with one of the boys. All the scandal and the disgrace. (*To Ellen*) I was the school cook, see.

ELLEN: No. No. No. No. No.

TADDY: That's where that one falls to bits. *You* a cook? You can't even make a cup of tea.

NINA: I could.

TADDY: Yes, you could. But you won't and you don't. (*To David*) How *is* your mother?

ELLEN: Don't!

DAVID: Wonderful for her age, really. She and my father have a cottage in the country. He's retired now.

(*Ellen puts her hands over her eyes and doubles up, hiding her face in her lap. David gets up and moves away and they all three stand looking at her. There is a silence*)

NINA: Got a pain perhaps.

TADDY: Looks more frightened to me.

DAVID: I expect both.

NINA: *I* get a pain in *my* tum when I'm frightened. (*Brightly*) No need to be scared, Elaine dear. (*Ellen sits up and looks at them all*)

ELLEN: I'm not Elaine! I'm Ellen. Ellen! Ellen!

DAVID: Yes? (*A pause; she stares at him*)

ELLEN: That's all. (*She hugs herself tightly*)

TADDY: Well, it's quite a lot. (*Another pause as they regard her*)

NINA: She *is* frightened, you know. Look at her. Like a little wild creature in a trap.

DAVID: Well, actually that's one of her favorite parts. She's extremely good at that one.

NINA: Oh, is she an actress? Are you an actress, duck?

DAVID: More of a performer really. (*Ellen stares at him with real pain and then convulsively doubles up again*)

DAVID: (*Strong and sharp*) Don't do that! Sit up! (*Slowly, Ellen does but she can't look at him*)

NINA: Well, there's no need to shout, surely. Poor little poppet. You're not to shout at her. (*Claps her hands*) I tell you what—we'll have another little game. That'll cheer her up.

Hide-and-seek. (*To Ellen*) You can be "It" first. (*Then, louder to her*) Hide-and-seek, dear. Quick now! We're only going to count to twenty.

(*She claps her hands over her eyes. Taddy and David follow suit. Nina starts counting and they join her; all count louder and faster to twenty. Ellen just sits absolutely still, staring*)

NINA: Ready or not, here we come!

(*They uncover their eyes and start looking elaborately and silently 'round the room under things and behind things*)

DAVID: Nobody found her yet?

NINA: Not a sausage.

TADDY: She's very good at this—remarkable.

NINA: Well, where can she be?

ELLEN: (*Suddenly; wildly*) I'm here! (*They all turn 'round and look at her astonished and delighted*)

NINA: There she is!

TADDY: Well, you certainly had us fooled!

NINA: (*To David*) Your turn now, dear.

(*She and Taddy put their hands over their eyes. They have counted to five when Nina takes her hands down and looks at Ellen*)

NINA: Oh, naughty. Mustn't cheat. (*She goes over to her and puts her hands over her eyes for her*) No peeking now. Back to one, Taddy. We weren't ready. One! (*Again she and Taddy count faster and louder to twenty*)

TADDY: Ready or not here we come!

(*They take their hands down. David has moved and sits on his heels directly in front of Ellen. Her hands are still over her eyes. Taddy and Nina start looking 'round the room again*)

NINA: (*Turning and looking at Ellen*) Oh, now. Who's being naughty again? Play up, play up and play the game. Open your eyes.

TADDY: (*Goes over to Ellen and takes her hands down*) You've got to look, too.

NINA: We can't find him anywhere.

ELLEN: He's here! He's here!

NINA: There now. She's found him!

TADDY: Very quick. Very quick indeed. This girl's a champion, Nina.

(*Ellen looks into David's face and speaks with real entreaty*)

ELLEN: David?

(*He looks impassively back at her. She gets up quickly and backs away. David gets up and steps back to join the others*)

DAVID: Something wrong?

ELLEN: Don't speak to me! You're one of *them*.

DAVID: And who are *they?*

ELLEN: (*Pointing*) Them! Them! They're the ones who *made* me come here.

TADDY: (*Quiet, but a little dangerous*) Made? Made? How *made?*

NINA: Who started it then? Who began?

ELLEN: *You did!*

NINA: Oh, no, you came up to me. *You* began.

ELLEN: You kept me. You wouldn't let me go.

DAVID: (*Sharply*) Forced you?

ELLEN: I didn't say that!

TADDY: Locked all the doors, did we?

ELLEN: No, it wasn't . . .

DAVID: Are you saying you've been kept a prisoner here?

ELLEN: (*Desperately*) No! No! No!

(*There is a pause*)

NINA: Well, o' course she wasn't.

TADDY: (*Laughs gently*) A prisoner . . . dear, dear, dear.

DAVID: (*To Ellen: clinical and interested*) You *are* frightened.

ELLEN: Yes!

DAVID: What of?

ELLEN: You all told *lies*. All of you! You just go on telling lies.

NINA: Stories more, really.

ELLEN: And games. And turning off the lights. And something bad outside, only nothing really. Pretending not to see when you could. Another lie or a game or a joke. Nothing ordinary. Nothing *real*.

TADDY: If it's not ordinary it can't be real?

NINA: No surprises, eh?

ELLEN: It's not that. I don't mean that.

DAVID: What *do* you mean?

ELLEN: (*Haltingly, but emphatic too*) I mean, you have to understand things. You have to *know* what to expect. You have to know what's going to happen, what to do.

DAVID: (*With real feeling*) No! No! You don't!

ELLEN: *I* do.

DAVID: Why? You tell me why, Ellen.

ELLEN: Because . . . because if everybody breaks all the rules then . . . then it *all* falls apart.

TADDY: What rules?

ELLEN: (*To David*) *You* know. Everybody knows! The rules about what you ought to do.

NINA: And what you oughtn't?

ELLEN: Yes! Yes! *I* broke the rules . . . (*To David*) . . . and I'm being punished for it now! I *knew*, I knew all along I'd be punished for it!

(*There is a pause and then Taddy goes over to her. He speaks directly to her with a gentle intensity*)

TADDY: Listen. There was once an old woman who lived in a little house facing a mountain. Now in order to get to church, which she did every day, she had to cross over the mountain. She was old and she was tired. One day she was reading her Bible and she came across the bit that says faith can move mountains. And she thought to herself, "Well," she thought. So that night she closed her little chintz curtains and she sat up the whole night through, praying that the mountain would be moved. When morning came, she drew the curtains and there was the mountain. And she looked, and she said, "I *knew* He wouldn't."

(*Silence. Nina and David make a slight movement forward. Ellen looks from one to the other*)

ELLEN: (*Turns away*) I don't understand. I don't understand.

(*David steps swiftly forward, takes her by the shoulders and turns her 'round to look at him*)

DAVID: (*Angry and desperate*) No, of course you don't! How could you? Ellen, that story's about *you*. That's what *you* do. Can't you see? If you find you can't plan and decide ahead and make sure everybody, including you, plays the parts you've given them, you just stop being anyone at all. You can't control the situation so then you believe that the situation is controlling *you*. Then it all has to be a conspiracy, you the victim. Either way—*either way*, Ellen, nothing is allowed to *occur!*

ELLEN: (*Releasing herself from his grasp; defiantly*) And does everyone have to be *mad* before anything can *occur?*

DAVID: (*Turning away; wearily*) Maybe. Yes. Probably. Up to a point.

ELLEN: It isn't like that! It *can't* be like that.

DAVID: (*Facing her again*) It isn't *like* anything. It just *is*. Look, look! I'll *show* you what you would have wanted all this to be like. (*He goes over to Nina*) What were you doing when she came up to you? Go on. Show me.

NINA: I wasn't *doing* nothing. Just standing there leaning on my stick. (*Starts to act this as she goes on*) Oh yes, that's right, I did get a bit cross. All them bleeding cars. None of them would stop for me. Rush, rush, rush, back and forth. So I starts shaking my stick and shouting a bit. "Bastards! Stop will you! Let me across, one of you buggers!"

DAVID: Well, that would be wrong for a start. (*To Ellen*) That's wrong, isn't it? Poor old ladies don't swear. (*To Nina*)

Just be helpless and pitiful. I'm her coming up to help you. (*He takes a few steps away and then walks back looking solicitous*)

NINA: Oh, oh what shall I do? I'll never get home. Won't somebody help a poor old woman?

DAVID: Can *I* help?

NINA: Oh, would you, sir—miss, I mean. God bless you, miss. (*They act crossing the street*)

DAVID: Are you sure you're all right? Can you get home by yourself?

NINA: I'll manage. Don't you worry your pretty little head about me. It's only just up the hill.

DAVID: I'll see you home. No, it's no trouble. Here, take my arm.

(*They walk a few more steps. Then Taddy comes forward and mimes opening a door*)

TADDY: Oh, there you are, mother.

NINA: (*Indignant*) Mother!

TADDY: Shut up, Nina. I was getting quite worried about you, mother. You know you didn't ought to be out on your own.

NINA: This young lady seen me home.

TADDY: There's kind. Please do step in, miss. Now mother, you come and sit down. (*He and David sit her down*) She's not been out of hospital long, you know.

NINA: (*Shivering*) I'm cold, *son*. I'm cold. Put the fire on.

TADDY: I've got no money for the meter, mother. I'll get you a blanket.

DAVID: Please. I've got plenty of sixpences and shillings in my purse. Take them, do.

TADDY: Oh, you're too kind. She's too kind isn't she, mother?

NINA: Ah, you don't meet many Christian people these days.

TADDY: At least let us give you a cup of tea.

DAVID: No, no. I must go. (*And then with a kind of smiling savagery*) I've "done" you two, you see, and now I've got to go and "do" him.

(Now, slowly, Taddy and David turn to look at Ellen. She looks back. Then she gets up violently from her chair, knocking it over deliberately)

ELLEN: I hate this place!

(She starts to move 'round the room, methodically turning over chairs and tables, pulling pictures off the walls, etc. She is silent, concentrated and swift. The others just watch her attentively)

ELLEN: There! (*She looks 'round at the mess*) I did that!

TADDY: Yes.

NINA: Why?

DAVID: Were you angry?

ELLEN: (*With glad rage*) *Yes!*

DAVID: (*Nice, loving laugh*) Good. Good. Good.

ELLEN: (*To David; ferocious and loving*) *You* can go to hell!

(She picks up her bag and walks straight out the door. The others stand still for a moment)

NINA: She's left the door open. (*To David*) Aren't you going after her, dear?

DAVID: Yes!

NINA: That's right. That's right, isn't it, Taddy?

TADDY: Yes.

Curtain

Tom Topor

ANSWERS

Tom Topor

Born in Vienna in 1938, Tom Topor was brought to London the following year and remained there until he came to New York in 1949.

While attending Brooklyn College (where he took his B.A. in English), he wrote, directed and acted in plays, a natural outgrowth of years of acting as a child in school productions in England.

Mr. Topor's plays have been seen Off-Off-Broadway at The Playwrights Unit, The Extension, Caffe Cino and the La Mama Experimental Theatre Club. During a three-year stay in Paris, he had several productions at The Studio Theatre of Paris, organized his own "Theatre of Games," and wrote and performed in a number of dubbed films.

Answers is Mr. Topor's first published play and is based on personal observations and experiences acquired during his tenure as a newspaperman which began in 1960. Since then, he has worked for *The Daily News* (New York), *The New York Times* (Paris), and presently is on the staff of *The Post* in New York.

The journalist-author's first novel, *Tightrope Minor,* was published in August, 1971, and a second is due later this year. At the moment, he is at work on a third novel and two new plays.

Characters:

ED

FRANK

THE SUSPECT

Scene:

The interrogation room in the headquarters of Homicide South in Manhattan. No windows. Pale green, dirty walls; institutional furniture. On one wall, a Playmate of the Month; on another, a Police Department leaf calendar. There is an old, scarred desk with papers, file folders, a telephone and an electric coffee-maker on it. At the desk, a chair

In the center of the room there is a small table. On it, a box of file cards, a cassette recorder and a fan with no guardwire.

The Suspect is sitting at the table with his head on his arms.

Frank and Ed, detectives, are standing at either end of the table. Each has a pistol in a belt holster and a set of handcuffs. They are passing file cards to each other.

A long silence.

ED: Byron, Frank thinks you're lying. (*The Suspect doesn't move. Ed leans toward his ear*) Byron, Frank thinks you're lying.

FRANK: Ed, I never said Byron was lying. I said his story has a couple of soft spots.

SUSPECT: (*Lifts his head*) My name isn't Byron! (*He lets his head fall*)

ED: Byron, Frank thinks your story has a couple of soft spots. (*He lifts the Suspect's head*) Is that true, Byron? Does it?

SUSPECT: My name isn't Byron.

ED: Does your story have a couple of soft spots?

SUSPECT: I didn't do it!

FRANK: That's one of the soft spots.

ED: (*Lifts the Suspect's head*) Byron, tell us what you didn't do. Tell Frank. He wants to believe you.

SUSPECT: Nothing.

ED: Nothing. You mean you did nothing? Is that what you mean, Byron? (*He lifts the Suspect's head*) Nothing? (*Suspect nods*) Frank, Byron says he did nothing.

FRANK: Hmmmmmmmmmmmmm.

ED: Byron, did you hear that? (*He signals Frank*)

FRANK: Hmmmmmmmmmmmmm.

ED: I know that hmmmmmmmmmmm. It gives me hives.

FRANK: Hmmmmmmmmmmmmm.

ED: Byron, Frank is telling you something.

FRANK: Hmmmmmmmm . . .

SUSPECT: I didn't do it. You guys have got the wrong man. I'm not Byron. My name . . .

FRANK: Hmmmmmmmmmmm.

SUSPECT: Bruce Har . . .

ED: Prove it, Byron. Show me some I.D. Come on, show me. We want to believe you. Show us a driver's license. A credit card. Voter's registration. Anything. Show us. (*A pause*)

SUSPECT: My wallet was lifted. I told you.

FRANK: Shit, Byron!

SUSPECT: It was.

FRANK: Any two-bit killer can walk in here and say, my wallet was lifted.

SUSPECT: Tuesday, on the IRT, uptown side at Canal Street. I was getting a piece of gum when it was lifted. I saw the dip running up the . . .

FRANK: The dip? The dip? Where'd you learn that word? Inside? Where? The Tombs?

SUSPECT: No, no. It's in the Daily News. It's on TV, it's . . .

ED: That's a professional word, Byron. Are you a dip, too?

FRANK: Okay, Byron: last arrest, charge and disposition?

SUSPECT: You've got the wrong man. Why don't you find this Byron?

ED: (*Looks at a notebook*) You make the description. You're Byron.

SUSPECT: Oh, for Christ's sake . . .

ED: Hair, eyes, height, weight, you make it.

SUSPECT: Ten thousand guys look like me!

ED: You can't give me an I.D.

FRANK: You can't account for your movements.

ED: You were picked up a block from the body.

SUSPECT: I was asleep. I told you. Ask the desk clerk. His name's Al.

FRANK: (*Picks up a folder*) Byron, tell me about this yellow sheet.

SUSPECT: I haven't got a yellow sheet.

FRANK: D and D, eight times. Dis con, five times; resisting arrest, five times; assault, five times. Harrassment, eleven times. Soliciting, six times. Loitering for prostitution, four times. Extortion, three times. Attempted bribery, fourteen times.

SUSPECT: I'm not . . .

ED: And don't tell us no convictions. We know what judges are.

FRANK: Byron, you're a crook. I'm shocked that you'd lie about it.

SUSPECT: I'm not Byron. I never assaulted anybody. I'm not a fag.

ED: (*Gets a pint of whiskey from the desk*) Do you drink, Byron? (*He pours some whiskey in a coffee container and puts it on the table*)

SUSPECT: Once in a while. (*His hand goes toward the container. Ed grabs it*)

FRANK: Whiskey?

SUSPECT: When I can afford it.

ED: And when you can't?

SUSPECT: Er, beer.

FRANK: Not wine?

SUSPECT: Beer.

ED: When did you have your last beer?

SUSPECT: Before I went to sleep.

(*Frank gestures to Ed, and Ed hands the container to the Suspect. As he raises it to his mouth, Frank knocks it out of his hand*)

FRANK: Byron, let's take it one more time. Don't flinch. I won't hit you because you spilled my whiskey. I was reaching for a cigarette. See? Don't flinch. It makes Ed nervous. Let's try it again. We know the details get mixed up. You're tired; maybe you had too much wine last night. Trust us, Byron. Our business is details. All we want is a few answers. We're on your side, Byron. We're the law. We don't hate you; the law doesn't hate. Don't look at the puddle on the floor. I won't make you wipe it up. Look at me. Now: you went in there; we know that. What did you do next?

SUSPECT: I wasn't there. Are you deaf?

FRANK: Don't flinch, Byron. It hurts me.

ED: What did you do after you went in there? Did you turn on the light? Tell Frank.

SUSPECT: I wasn't there. I didn't turn on any light. I was home, sleeping. Sleeping!

FRANK: Didn't you take a stocking out of your coat pocket?

SUSPECT: Oh, Christ!

FRANK: You slipped the stocking over your face, isn't that right, Byron? What did you do next?

SUSPECT: I didn't do anything next.

ED: Didn't you take a pair of gloves out of your other pocket . . . (*He checks a file card*) A pair of size eight-and-a-half leatherette gloves, black? What did you do next?

SUSPECT: I don't have any gloves. (*His head falls on his arms*)

FRANK: Byron, pick up your head. Please. Ed. (*Ed lifts the Suspect's head and props it in his hand*)

SUSPECT: I didn't do anything!

FRANK: Goddammit, Byron, how can you sit there and say that? That's not fair. Think of my position. Think of Ed's position. I can't go to the captain and say, "Byron says he didn't do anything."

SUSPECT: I was sleeping. Ask Al.

FRANK: The captain would look me up and down and say, "Frank, don't you know how to question a suspect? A criminal suspect with a yellow sheet a block long; a suspect with no I.D.; a suspect who can't account for his time; a suspect who uses words like dip?" "Frank," he'd say, "don't you know how to get a few simple answers to a few simple questions? Don't you know that much? Don't you like your work, Frank? Do you want to go back on the 'Pussy Posse' and round up the Forty-second street hookers? Shall I turn this one over to Shelley, Frank?" he'd say. Big Shelley. *He* knows how to get answers. That's the captain, Byron. He's not like me or Ed. The captain is not a *patient* man.

ED: What did you do next?

FRANK: Did you gag her?

ED: Did you tie her up?

FRANK: Did you screw her?

SUSPECT: Stop it! Stop it! I'm not Byron. I wasn't there. I was home!

ED: How many times did you hit her?

SUSPECT: I didn't hit . . .

FRANK: Twenty?

SUSPECT: Anybody.

ED: Fifty?

FRANK: How many times?

ED: A hundred?

SUSPECT: None! None! None! (*He slams his fist on the table*)

(*Ed kicks the table out from under the Suspect's arms and he falls to the floor. Frank drags him back to the chair and handcuffs his left wrist to it*)

FRANK: Ed, make a note. (*Ed picks up his notebook*)

Suspect suffering from exhaustion. No, make it fatigue. Suspect suffering from fatigue.

ED. Fatigue. Got it.

FRANK: Eyes watering, breath foul, fingers shaking. Tendency, yeah, tendency, to jump and flinch. Got it?

ED: Tendency to jump and flinch.

FRANK: Inability to give answers. Put it in the report, Ed; the left-hand column. How many times did you hit her?

SUSPECT: Who? Goddammit! *Who?*

FRANK: Who? You hit her; you should know. Her. She. Her.

SUSPECT: I didn't hit anybody!

ED: We know about the hammer.

SUSPECT: What hammer?

FRANK: Wrench. Ed, wrench!

ED: We know about the wrench.

SUSPECT: What wrench?

ED: So you must have hit her.

SUSPECT: You're crazy!

ED: What?

SUSPECT: Nothing.

ED: What did you say?

SUSPECT: Nothing. Nothing.

FRANK: Did I hear right, Byron? Did I hear you call Ed crazy? Did I?

ED: Did you?

FRANK: Did you?

SUSPECT: It—it—it slipped out.

FRANK: You called a sworn officer of the law crazy! Crazy. Why? Did he insult you?

SUSPECT: No.

FRANK: Did he abuse you?

SUSPECT: No.

FRANK: A sworn officer of the law. The law. Crazy. Ed, you want to file charges? (*Ed walks around the Suspect*) I can send for the forms.

ED: What do you think?

FRANK: Did you hear that, Byron? What do you think, Ed says. If it was me, God, if it was me . . . Ed is a prince. If it was me, I'd put you down for assaulting an officer, harassment, dis con, interference and slander. And I'd make it stick. Byron, you're lucky it was Ed. A prince of a partner. Why do you hate him? What did he ever do to you? I guess you hate me, too. I never did anything to you, Byron. I'm just doing my job. I have to get answers.

SUSPECT: It slipped out. I don't hate . . .

ED: I am not crazy.

FRANK: Of course, you're not crazy, Ed. There's only one crazy person in this room, and I don't mean insane. Insane is legal and lawful. I mean crazy. Anybody who calls a sworn officer of the law crazy is crazy. Byron, when was the last time you spoke to a therapist?

SUSPECT: I never spoke . . .

FRANK: Ed, did you *ever* speak to a therapist?

ED: In the Marines. When I enlisted.

FRANK: Did he say you were crazy?

ED: No. No, sir. He said I was well-adjusted. That's the word he used, well-adjusted.

FRANK: Did a therapist ever tell you that, Byron? *Are* you well-adjusted? Does he look well-adjusted to you, Ed?

ED: (*Leans over the Suspect*) His eyes are funny. Look at that, Frank. See the red spots. His mouth is funny, too. See that twist. Remember that nigger we picked up for rape and murder? He had a twist like that. Lemme see your teeth, Byron. Open your mouth, you crazy drunk bastard! (*The Suspect opens his mouth wide*)

FRANK: Ed, I think you've got a point. His tongue is purple. That's a sign.

ED: Wider. Wider. Look at that, Frank.

FRANK: Byron, if you could see your face now. God! It frightens me and I'm not easily frightened. Wider!

ED: What did you do with the wrench?

FRANK: Where did you throw it in the river?

ED: Did you wipe it first?

FRANK: Thirty-sixth Street? Forty-first Street?

SUSPECT: What river? I didn't go near . . .

FRANK: Are you telling us—us—that you did not throw a wrench—or some other hard, heavy instrument, covered with her brains and blood—into the river? Are you telling us that? Us? Us?

SUSPECT: What river?

ED: The Hudson.

SUSPECT: The Hudson? The Hudson? But that's . . .

FRANK: Ed, make a note.

SUSPECT: West. I live . . .

FRANK: Suspect pretends ignorance. Got it, Ed? Suspect pretends ignorance. Pretends he's never heard of the Hudson River. Suspect pretends. Got it?

SUSPECT: I'm not pretending. Don't start . . .

ED: Suspect pretends ignorance.

SUSPECT: I know where the Hudson is. It's west. It's nowhere near where I live. I'm not pretending. I got mixed up.

ED: Suspect pretends ignorance. (*He continues to write while Frank pours himself coffee*)

SUSPECT: Listen! Are you listening to me? My name is not Byron! I didn't hit anybody. I don't know about any wrench. I don't live anyplace near the Hudson and I never go west. I wasn't there. I was sleeping. Did you get that? What are you writing? (*He jumps up. The chair falls. He picks it up and leaps toward Ed but Ed steps around the table. The Suspect stands holding the chair*) I've never been arrested. Maybe I look like this Byron. I look like a lot of guys. If I had one leg or a bent nose or a glass eye, I wouldn't look like a lot of guys. I'm no crook. What did you write? (*Ed backs away*) Let me see! Did you write that I'm pretending? I'm not! Let me see! (*He jumps toward Frank but the chair trips him. He gets up*) Tell him to let me see! It's my right! I'm innocent. I'm a suspect. I haven't been arraigned. I haven't been indicted. Where's my lawyer? Call the Legal Aid

Society. Listen, the Hudson is west. I know where it is. I'm not crazy. I worked on Pier Eighty-eight once. I was a loader, Local Fifty-one. I shaped up. Bananas and melons. I know how to work. I was born in Hoboken. I went to school in Union City. I'm not crazy. I didn't mean to call you crazy. It slipped out. You know that. I was shaky. I'm a shaky guy. I'm fatigued, you wrote it down. You shook me up; what do you expect? You'd be shook up, too. You pick me up in the middle of the night, you book me and tell me I banged some woman over the head with a wrench, and then you keep me here and keep me here and keep me here. What do you expect? You're not crazy. Nobody's crazy. I know you guys are the law. I like the law. I like cops. Every night, I say hello to the guys in the prowl car. Hi, boys, I say. Hi, fella, they say. Ask them. Ask Al. Three-forty-one Bowery. Did you write that down? Did you? Al, the desk man at Three-forty-one Bowery. I said goodnight to him and I went upstairs, fourth floor, second door to the left. I had a cigarette and I went to sleep. Ask Al. (*The phone rings. The Suspect drops the chair. After the second ring, it stops. The Suspect picks up the chair and goes to Ed*) You believe me, don't you? I know you do. Listen, I said goodnight to Al, I had a cigarette and I went to sleep. I was sleeping the whole time she was being killed. That's all. I swear that's all! Did you write that down? Let me see. Let me see.

(*The Suspect grabs for the notebook, but Ed tosses it to Frank. The Suspect jumps toward Frank, but he tosses it to Ed. Both detectives start trotting around the room, tossing the notebook to each other, smiling and laughing as they do so. The Suspect leaps and jumps to intercept it but fails. Finally he falls, breathless. Still laughing, Frank takes the notebook from Ed and, very slowly, puts it in the Suspect's hands. He reads*)

SUSPECT: Suspect pretends ignorance. Suspect dizzy. Suspect confused. Suspect sick. Suspect fatigued. Suspect resentful. Suspect needs help. Suspect wrong man. (*He stops, looks up at them. They nod. He resumes reading*) Suspect wrong man. Very wrong man. Wrong.

(Frank nods and Ed bends down and unlocks the handcuffs. He helps the Suspect up while Frank puts the chair in place)

SUSPECT: Wrong man. (*They help him to the chair. Frank sticks a cigarette in his mouth and lights it*) Wrong man. (*He smiles at them. Ed gives him an ashtray; Frank pours some coffee and puts some whiskey in it. He hands the cup to the Suspect, who sips slowly. Frank nods to Ed. Both smile*)

ED: Byron—you don't mind if I call you that?—I'm going to ask you a few formal questions, in my capacity as a law-enforcement officer. Under the provisions of the constitution of this state, you are free to refuse to reply. However, it is my sworn duty to put these questions to you. Your answers, for your own benefit—and ours—should be clear, short and to the point at hand. If you do not understand a question, inform me and I will repeat it. If you wish to modify an answer, inform me and I will let you. If, after you have answered these formal questions, you wish to sign a statement, you may. Do you have any questions? (*Suspect shakes his head*) Do you want me to repeat anything? (*Suspect shakes his head*) Are you ready? (*Suspect nods. The following is very fast*) Where were you born?

SUSPECT: Hobo . . .

FRANK: When?

SUSPECT: . . . ken. New Jer . . .

ED: What hospital?

SUSPECT: Hey! Hey! Slow . . .

FRANK: What time?

SUSPECT: . . . down! Hudson . . .

ED: Parents married?

FRANK: How long?

SUSPECT: . . . County Hosp . . .

ED: Father's occupation?

FRANK: Mother's maiden name?

ED: Brothers?

FRANK: Sisters?

SUSPECT: He was a . . .

ED: Baptized?
SUSPECT: . . . dentist for . . .
FRANK: What church?
ED: Are you a dentist?
FRANK: Where do you work?
SUSPECT: Mother's name . . .
ED: How long?
SUSPECT: . . . was Windsor.
FRANK: Company name?
SUSPECT: Right now . . .
ED: Boss' name?
SUSPECT: I'm not working . . .
FRANK: Social Security number?
SUSPECT: . . . right now. I'm on . . .
ED: Address?
SUSPECT: . . . welfare. Wel . . .
FRANK: Phone number?
SUSPECT: . . . fare. Wel . . .
ED: Zip code?
FRANK: How many stories?
SUSPECT: Three-forty-one . . .
ED: What street do you face?
SUSPECT: . . . Bowery. The phone . . .
FRANK: How many windows in your room?
SUSPECT: . . . number is Canal . . .
ED: Where'd you get that coat?
FRANK: How much was it?
SUSPECT: This? I got it . . .
ED: Fifty dollars?
FRANK: Twenty-five?
ED: Ten?
SUSPECT: . . . at the Salvation . . .
FRANK: Nothing?
SUSPECT: . . . Army. It . . .
ED: Did you *lift* it?
SUSPECT: . . . was six dollars and . . .

FRANK: Did you lift the pants with it?
ED: Were you in the Army?
FRANK: Where'd you serve?
SUSPECT: I was in . . .
ED: What rank?
FRANK: What discharge?
SUSPECT: . . . the Signal . . .
ED: Did you fight?
SUSPECT: . . . Corps from Nineteen . . .
FRANK: Deal?
ED: Clothes?
FRANK: Cigarettes?
ED: Liquor?
SUSPECT: I got out a . . .
FRANK: Pills?
ED: Guns?
SUSPECT: . . . Specialist Third Cl . . .
FRANK: Did you loot any stores?
ED: Rape any girls?
SUSPECT: My discharge was . . .
ED: Kill any men?
FRANK: Women?
ED: Children?
SUSPECT: . . . honorable, with comm . . .
FRANK: What's that mark on your arm?
ED: You on "smack"?
SUSPECT: . . . endations and . . .
FRANK: "Speed"?
SUSPECT: No! No! I tripped . . .
ED: Where do you "cop"?
FRANK: The Italiano?
ED: The Spic?
SUSPECT: . . . last week on Bleecker . . .
FRANK: What do you pay an ounce?
ED: Four hundred?
FRANK: Three-fifty?

SUSPECT: . . . Street. There was a . . .
ED: Where do you move it?
FRANK: At the high school?
SUSPECT: . . . a trash can cover. I fell . . .
ED: At the Y?
SUSPECT: I don't use any . . .
FRANK: How much cash have you got on you?
SUSPECT: . . . thing. Money? I . . .
ED: Where's your bank?
FRANK: Checking account?
ED: Savings account?
SUSPECT: . . . only have about . . .
FRANK: Safe-deposit box?
ED: What's the manager's name?
FRANK: Did you ever take out a loan?
SUSPECT: . . . four dollars. I don't . . .
ED: Who co-signed?
FRANK: What was it for?
SUSPECT: . . . have a nickle in . . .
ED: A car?
FRANK: A boat?
ED: A house?
SUSPECT: . . . the bank right now. I . . .
FRANK: What'd you do with it?
ED: Horses?
FRANK: Stocks?
SUSPECT: I don't have any mon . . .
ED: Girls?
FRANK: Boys?
SUSPECT: . . . ey. I've been broke for . . .
ED: Where'd you get that ring?
FRANK: Is it part of a set?
SUSPECT: . . . a long time. I was a grad . . .
ED: Who's your fence?
FRANK: What do you "ice" a month?
SUSPECT: . . . uate of Seward Park . . .

ED: You always wear sneakers?
FRANK: Can you climb a wall?
SUSPECT: . . . High School. It's a class . . .
ED: You carry a glass cutter?
SUSPECT: . . . ring of Nineteen fifty . . .
FRANK: Where'd you get that necklace?
ED: Is it gold?
SUSPECT: . . . one. This? It's from . . .
FRANK: Silver?
ED: Platinum?
SUSPECT: . . . my mother. She . . .
FRANK: Was it around her throat?
ED: Did you unhook it?
SUSPECT: . . . gave it to me for my . . .
FRANK: Did you rip it off?
ED: Before?
FRANK: After?
SUSPECT: . . . thirteenth birth . . .
ED: What are those stains on your shirt?
FRANK: Did you throw up?
SUSPECT: . . . day. No. I don't, I don't . . .
ED: Is it vomit?
FRANK: Phlegm?
SUSPECT: . . . remem . . .
ED: Snot?
SUSPECT: . . . ber. I don't . . .
FRANK: Pus?
ED: Wine?
SUSPECT: . . . remember. I don't . . .
FRANK: Blood?
ED: Is it blood?
FRANK: Is it blood?
SUSPECT: Shaving! I cut . . .
ED: When?
SUSPECT: Shave . . .
FRANK: With what?

ED: A straight razor?
FRANK: A safety razor?
SUSPECT: Yesterday. No, the . . .
ED: Where's the cut?
FRANK: How long was it?
ED: How deep was it?
SUSPECT: . . . day before. Look . . .
FRANK: How long did you bleed?
ED: A minute?
FRANK: Two minutes?
SUSPECT: . . . here. Here it . . .
ED: You always shave with your shirt on?
FRANK: What's your blood type?
ED: O?
FRANK: A?
ED: B? (*He starts the cassette recorder*)
SUSPECT: Here, here, look at . . .
FRANK: How much is one and one?
SUSPECT: It only bled . . .
ED: Two and two?
SUSPECT: . . . a few seconds, a . . .
FRANK: Three and three?
SUSPECT: . . . drop, that's all it . . .
ED: Four and four?
SUSPECT: . . . bled. O positive. The . . .
FRANK: Which came first?
ED: The chicken?
SUSPECT: . . . Army tested me . . .
FRANK: Or the egg?
SUSPECT: . . . when I went . . .
ED: The chicken?
FRANK: Or the egg?
SUSPECT: . . . in. Once I got a trans . . .
ED: One and one?
FRANK: Two and two?
SUSPECT: . . . fusion and I got . . .

ED: Three and three?

SUSPECT: . . . sick. One and one . . .

ED: The chicken?

SUSPECT: The chicken and . . . No . . .

FRANK: Or the egg?

SUSPECT: Egg and three. No. Three and . . .

ED: Four and four?

SUSPECT: Four, four, four and . . .

FRANK: Four and four?

ED: The chicken?

FRANK: Or the egg?

ED: Four and four?

SUSPECT: Four are . . .

FRANK: Four and four?

ED: Four and four?

SUSPECT: . . . are, are, are . . .

FRANK: How many *times* did you hit her?

SUSPECT: Eight.

ED: Eight. (*He shuts off the cassette*)

FRANK: Eight.

SUSPECT: Eight. Ha, ha! Four and four are eight.

FRANK: So! You hit her *eight* times. Ed, Byron hit her eight times. What do you think?

ED: It might be right. If he hit her good and hard.

FRANK: Byron, did you hit her good and hard?

SUSPECT: I know that's right.

FRANK: Make up a statement for him.

ED: You want me to type it?

FRANK: Write it out. We can get it typed in the morning. And, Ed, make me a good match. Did you hit her from the right, the left, in front or behind?

SUSPECT: Eight.

FRANK: We know that. Right, left, in front, or behind?

ED: (*Checking file cards*) I gotta push some to make a match.

SUSPECT: Egg.

FRANK: Move it, Ed. I don't want to lose him.

SUSPECT: Chicken.

ED: We got a Smith. A McKittrick; no that was a knife job. A Goldstein; that's a bit old.

FRANK: When?

SUSPECT: No. Egg.

ED: December.

FRANK: Crap! Who else?

ED: An Esposito. She's okay. A Wingate. She's okay, too.

SUSPECT: Tell me what you think. Chicken or egg?

FRANK: Wingate? Last week, right?

ED: Yeah, DOA on Third.

FRANK: Any family?

ED: Nobody listed.

FRANK: I.D.?

ED: Welfare card.

SUSPECT: I say chicken.

FRANK: Make it Windsor.

ED: Aw, come on, Frank, don't shit around!

SUSPECT: Yes, I say . . .

FRANK: (*Rams his handkerchief in the Suspect's mouth*) Make it Windsor!

ED: Goddamn, Frank! (*He writes*)

FRANK: Read it to him.

ED: On the night of August 13th, 1969, at approximately 11:36 P.M., I, Byron . . . (*He looks at the yellow sheet*) Dedson . . .

SUSPECT: (*Pulls the handkerchief from his mouth*) Egg to chicken. Chicken to egg. Ha, ha! Egg . . .

ED: Goddammit, how can I read it to him?

FRANK: (*Puts his hand over Suspect's mouth*) Screw it! Give him a pen.

(*Ed puts a pen in the Suspect's hand, but he throws it on the table. Ed tries again*)

ED: Sign right here, Byron. (*Suspect wriggles*) Hold him still. Sign here, Byron.

FRANK: Byron, you're in the hands of the law. Sign!

ED: Sign, Byron! Hold him.

FRANK: Byron, you gave us the answers. (*He runs the cassette so it plays: "How many times did you hit her?" "Eight."*) You were very good. You did right by the law. Now the law is doing right by you. Sign for the law. Hold the pen. Hold it. (*Suspect throws the pen down. Frank picks it up and slams it on the table. It breaks. He takes his pen and slams it on the table*) Byron, the law has got you. This pen is the instrument of the law. This pad, too. Sign. (*He turns on the fan and moves it close to the Suspect's face*) Byron, this *fan* is the instrument of the law. Sign!

ED: One-hundred and twenty-six miles from here, by road, there's a cell waiting for you, you crook! Look at you, shaking like a wet pile of . . . You can't even hold a pen in your hand! Your nose is dripping, you crooked bastard! Your mouth stinks a mile off!

FRANK: We know you're crooked. The walls know it. Look at those walls. Those are legal walls of a legal room and that's a legal table with a legal pen on it. This is a legal fan. You're *ill*egal! (*Ed moves the fan closer*) You hate the law! You hate Ed and you hate me! You're the enemy! (*He moves the fan closer*)

ED: You no-good, law-hating bastard! When they get you up there, they'll ram you in a cell with a guy nine feet tall with a joint two feet long. The first night, when the lights go out, he'll take his two-foot joint and drill you till you bleed. Then you'll go to a guard and tell him this nine-foot murderer with a two-foot joint spread your cheeks for you. And you know what the guard will say? (*He moves the fan closer*)

FRANK: He'll say, sorry, Byron, tough shit, you law-hating crook! He'll say, *I'm* the law, just like *we're* the law. And because you hate the law, you hate *him*. And he hates you. The wall is the law and the wall hates you. The calendar is the law and the calendar hates you. The pen is the law and the pen hates you. The pad is the law and the pad hates you. The cigarette is the law and the cigarette hates you. The cup is the law and the cup hates you. The fan is the law and the fan hates you. We're the law and we hate you. Everything in here and everything one-hundred and twenty-six miles from here hates you. Everybody and everything in this whole damned world hates you because you hate us and we're the law!

ED: Sign!

FRANK: (*Moves the fan closer*) Sign!

SUSPECT: Chicken, chicken, chicken, chick . . .

ED: Sign!

FRANK: (*Moves the fan closer*) Sign!

SUSPECT: Chicken, chicken, chicken . . .

FRANK: If you sign, Byron . . .

ED: If you sign . . . (*The fan is directly in front of the Suspect's face*) If you sign . . . (*He kicks the cord of the fan and it stops*)

FRANK: We won't hate you!

(*Frank handcuffs the Suspect's left hand to the chair. Ed turns out light over desk. Frank puts pad and pen in front of the Suspect. He and Ed leave. The Suspect rests his head on his arms. After a moment, Ed comes back in, picks up the recorder, plugs the fan back in and rips the day-page off the calendar. He leaves. As the lights begin to dim, the Suspect lifts his head and picks up the pen*)

The Lights Fade

Edgard da Rocha Miranda

AND THE WIND BLOWS

Edgard da Rocha Miranda

A front-rank Brazilian dramatist, Edgard da Rocha Miranda's *And the Wind Blows* is generally considered to be a dramatic classic in the country of its origin. The new shortened version that appears here in print for the first time was made especially for *The Best Short Plays 1972.*

The drama, in its original Portuguese language, first was performed in 1954 in São Paulo, Brazil, where it won the trophy in a national play competition honoring the Fourth Centenary of the City of São Paulo.

In 1957, the English-language version was presented at the Theatre Royal, Stratford, London, under the direction of Joan Littlewood. A dramatic confrontation of the nature of faith, superstition, hope and material progress, *And the Wind Blows* stirred up much praise in the British press. *The Stage* termed it "an outstandingly worthwhile work, both in content and in dramatic style" while L. G. Smith declared in *Plays and Players,* "Edgard da Rocha Miranda has such a powerful command of character and situation that the whole thing bears the stamp of truth; and his dramatic conception transmutes pure truth into pure theatre. If this is not a great play (and I am far from sure that it is not) it is certainly very near to achieving greatness."

The play had its American premiere in 1959 at the Off-Broadway St. Marks Playhouse and once again there was impressive critical endorsement. Brooks Atkinson reported in *The New York Times,* "Even if Brazilian dramas were less rare, *And the Wind Blows* would be worth paying attention to. The characters ring true, their problems are real and the crisis through which they pass is touching. It could hardly be more illuminating." Richard Watts, Jr. of the *New York Post* concurred and found the play to have "a brooding intensity of spirit."

Though born in Rio de Janeiro of Brazilian parents, Edgard da Rocha Miranda was educated in the United States at Choate and Princeton University. After spending several years writing and publishing poetry, he made his debut as a playwright in 1947 with *Memories in Masquerade* at the Gateway Theatre Club, London. That same year, *Not I* was performed in Rio de

Janeiro by Brazil's foremost actress, Cacilda Becker, and, subsequently, was produced in London with Beatrix Thomson at the New Lindsey Theatre.

In 1952, Mr. da Rocha Miranda won the "Sacy," Brazil's equivalent of an "Oscar," for having written the best Brazilian play of the year: *To Where the Land Grows,* produced at the Teatro Brasileiro de Comédia, São Paulo. Since then, he has been represented annually by new works on stages throughout Brazil and on television in all of the nation's larger cities.

Mr. da Rocha Miranda once again was accorded national honors in 1962 when *A Crime of Love,* for which he wrote the screenplay based on his own play, won first prize at the Brazilian Film Festival.

The author, who writes his plays both in Portuguese and English, lives in Rio de Janeiro with his wife, Evangelina, a fashionable jewelry designer and writer of imaginative children's stories.

Characters:

BASTOS

ZECA

DOUTÔ

TONICO

BETO

ALEIXO

SARGENTO

THEREZA

NHÔ JANGO

SANCHA

MONSIGNOR ANDRADA

PADRE MANUEL

MONSIGNOR GUSMÃO

A BOY

OLD MAN

VILLAGERS

Scene:

A street corner in Campina do Monte Alegre, a very small village in the back country of the state of São Paulo, Brazil.

At the left stands the Tendinha do Povo, a whitewashed adobe structure now stained a reddish clay tone and covered by the dust that pervades everything in the village. The Tendinha is a combination grocery-refreshment stand with a door, left, and a small counter, right, behind which are several rows of shelves with cheap merchandise: bottles of beer and cachaça, *a strong Brazilian drink; two wheels of hardened Provolone cheese green with mildew, cans of sausages and other foodstuffs, the labels faded with age and dust; a string of onions dangling from a nail, etc. In front of the Tendinha: two battered iron tables with chairs around them.*

Next to the shop, a sloping, dusty, baked red clay street that leads upstage. To its right, a wooden house of dirty, nondescript color, one window opening on to the street and a door with two front steps. On a string tied across this street, two tattered shirts are drying in the sun.

The time is the mid-1950's, during a serious drought, and the action of the play takes place both in the street and in the main room of Aleixo's house.

Sunday morning.

Before the curtain rises, a few plaintive bars of Villa-Lobos' "Bacchianas Brasileiras" are heard, played on a harmonica. Then, a short, hoarse whistle from a distant railroad train. The harmonica stops abruptly.

As the curtain rises, the train's whistle becomes closer and louder. The people in the street are all turned in the direction of the passing train; all except Doutô, who is slouched in a chair, apparently asleep, under an old, incongruous bowler hat. He is a man of another class and culture, stranded, for some reason, in Campina. Tonico stands in the middle of the street, harmonica in hand. He is seventeen, limps because of a deformed leg; his responses are slow and he stammers.

Bastos, the Portuguese propietor of the Tendinha, leans on the counter. He is short, fat, with a large face and a thick, long moustache. Zeca, a native of the Brazilian backlands with Indian blood, is a slight man of about thirty. He squats against the wall below the counter.

When the roar of the train begins to fade away, like yet another promise unfulfilled, they all turn away from it and go on staring front, longingly. Tonico comes downstage, starts to play his harmonica.

BASTOS: (*Wiping his neck with bar towel*) Hot!

ZECA: Not a cloud . . .

DOUTÔ: (*Shouts; from beneath his hat*) Stop that! Let me sleep.

TONICO: (*Stops playing*) B-b-but why?

DOUTÔ: Why? I'd tell you why if you weren't such a fool, Tonico. Yes, I'd tell you. That sleep is better than consciousness. Death better than life. But better still . . . Oh, well, that is enough wisdom for *Campina do Monte Alegre*. (*Ironically*) Prairie of Happy Hill! He was either a fool or a sadistic son-of-a-bitch who named this cemetery Monte Alegre! Like the one who invented life . . .

(*Pause. The hot, hazy sun shines brutally, flattening out everything, as if crushing all perspective, emptying the world of all meaning. The pall of dust is oppressive on everybody and everything*)

BASTOS: (*Breaking the silence*) Well, I think . . .

DOUTÔ: Portuguese don't think! Not that it makes any difference to think, when you're doomed to live and die in the dust.

TONICO: Maybe it was *alegre* * before?

DOUTÔ: Not before, nor after.

BASTOS: Don't know why I picked *this* place.

DOUTÔ: Nor here, nor anywhere.

BASTOS: But maybe if we had a station?

DOUTÔ: *If! If!* If it rained, we would not have a drought. If man had not been born . . . (*His voice trails off as Beto, a tall, broad shouldered Negro, comes down the street and approaches the Tendinha*)

BETO: Eh, Bastos, got some *cachaça?* (*Bastos doesn't answer*) Make it double, seein' it's Sunday. C'mon, man, make it fast. Throat's dry as a cricket's rasp . . . (*No move from Bastos*) What's th' matter, thought Portuguez like money?

BASTOS: What money?

BETO: Ahh, I'll pay you soon's I wins th' lot'ry.

BASTOS: (*Disgusted*) The lottery!

BETO: Sure! Maybe when the rain wash th' road, peddlers might come through an' I'll get myself a numbah. An' when I wins, I'll pay you ev'ry goddam *centavo*. Don't want no favors from no goddam Portuguez. But I want a drink! (*Bangs on*

* *happy*

counter) Now! (*Bastos quickly pours. Beto gulps it down, then spits*) Devil's dust! Told you t' pour it fast, to beat th' dust to th' glass! Now give me 'nother, to wash it down!

BASTOS: Enough, enough, Negro!

BETO: *Negro!* If Portuguez don't like Negroes, why they go get us from Africa?

BASTOS: To work.

BETO: With no pay! Be damned if I'm gonna work for Portuguez son-of-a-bitch, or for nobody! Where's work got anybody here? Luck's all that counts. If on'y a peddler come 'round an' I could get myself a numbah. (*Then, abruptly, fiercely*) I said 'nother, Portuguez! An' make it double!

(*Bastos hastily pours. Beto drinks*)

BASTOS: At least Portuguese don't make no *woman* work for them.

BETO: That's none of your goddam business! Negroes' free now, *free!* An' I does what I likes, an' don't have to be afraid of no one! (*As he leans over counter, Bastos quickly slips another drink into his hand*) Ahh, see if I don't pay you one o' these days. (*Starts to move away*) Soon's th' rain wash th' dust from the road . . . (*He slips down, his back against the wall*) . . . an' I wins th' big numbah.

BASTOS: (*Half to himself*) And I never give no pregnant woman a lay, neither!

BETO: (*Murmuring drowsily*) An' I'm gonna give Sancha an' th' Negro chile a big house . . . with a roof an' windows . . . (*He now sags completely to the ground, face into the dust; begins to snore*)

BASTOS: The Negro child! He kill them all, before they're born, the ape! He can't lay off his Sancha, not even the last month she's pregnant!

DOUTÔ: (*Cynically*) That is love.

BASTOS: Hm! It's Portuguese loves and takes care of their little ones . . . months before they're born. Never touched my Maria, I didn't, five months, sometimes more, when she was pregnant, no matter how much I wanted to lay her. Sometimes, when

I wanted it bad, I'd go out and spend ten escudos on a whore—yes, sir, *ten* escudos—just not to touch my Maria. That's how Portuguese take care of their little ones.

(*Aleixo comes out of the wooden house. He is about fifty-five, small, nervous, much more sensitive and fragile than the others. His voice is high-pitched, his neck distorted, due to some sort of paralysis, consequently he must turn his whole body around when he speaks to people*)

ALEIXO: Why the hell don't you send for this Portugueza and be done with your cursed dreaming?

BASTOS: Send? How? When I come from Portugal it was to make money, not spend. You know how much the fare cost?

ALEIXO: You stingy *portuga* you've got enough money! (*Indicates the Tendinha*)

BASTOS: That's not money! That's my capital!

ALEIXO: (*Turning away*) Not a cloud, not a cloud in the whole cursed sky! Dust's more'n an inch thick on my turnips.

ZECA: And on my beans. An' just when it looked like we was goin' to have a good crop, for once.

ALEIXO: Why the hell the worst drought had to come this year? I'm a sick man, getting old, too, an' if I don't make money *this* year . . . (*Anxiously*) I got to have a servant—or who's goin' to work for me when I'm old an' without money?

ZECA: You got Thereza.

ALEIXO: But when she marry? Hm, women's all alike, think of nothin' but gettin' married. Ungrateful, that's what she is! Never givin' a damn 'bout nothin' else, not even a sick old uncle who's always took good care of her from the time her people die.

ZECA: If only it'd rain, maybe I'd still save a quarter of my beans . . .

BASTOS: (*Who has been feverishly calculating*) Three thousand six hundred and fifty-three for *each* ticket—and there's the little ones, two of them!

ALEIXO: When a man's sick an' old he deserves rest, with someone to look after him, before he goes to rest all alone in the grave. Someone who maybe cares a bit for him. But who's goin' to care for a sick old man with no money? (*Gazing at the sky*) Ain't it *ever* goin' to rain again?

ZECA: (*Bleakly*) Banhadinho's fast goin' dry.

ALEIXO: An' Banhadinho's always the last water to go.

ZECA: Jeesus!

TONICO: (*Alarmed*) What's goin' to happen t-t-to Nhô Jango?

ALEIXO: Him? What's he got to lose, anyway? He don't plant nothin' to sell.

TONICO: But Figurinha? That calf's all he got left. How he gonna feed Figurinha when . . . ?

ALEIXO: With his silly hopes, that's how! Feed *her* that crap if he wants, 'cause I'm sick to death of it! It's *rain* we need, not crap.

BASTOS: (*Attempting to justify himself*) If I don't save my money, who's going to save it for me? Who's going to give me three thousand six hundred and . . . ?

ALEIXO: Get it down from your dirty shelves!

BASTOS: But that's my *capital!* How am I going to progress, give security to my family without my capital?

ALEIXO: Curse your capital! Curse the weather! Curse the crap and the whole cursed life.

DOUTÔ: (*Yawning*) Amen.

(*Sargento comes down the street. He is twenty, wears old, ragged cotton pants and a torn Brazilian army jacket, a memento of his military service where he earned his nickname. Like the others, with the exception of Bastos and Doutô, he is barefooted. As he enters, the train whistle is heard again and all promptly turn their eyes in its direction. They remain that way, as if it always held a promise, till the sound of the train reaches its climax, then fades away*)

SARGENTO: Why the hell does everybody always turn to that train? Don't you know by now the trains never stop in Campina? Never will?

ALEIXO: Why you come back from the army, then? Why don't you get out of Campina?

SARGENTO: You'd like nothing better, eh? So you could slave Thereza the rest of your life.

ALEIXO: Do *you* have anything better to give her? A tramp that's not good enough to work the land your father leave you!

SARGENTO: You call that land, that lump of baked clay and dust, that requires twice as much rain?

ZECA: I remember, your father, he cropped quite a few bags of cotton just 'fore he die.

SARGENTO: That's where the soil went, what was left of it: in those few bags of cotton! (*A moment*) But I'm not blaming my old man, like he never blamed his. It's just that they didn't know, I s'pose, how to work the land proper, how to revive its fertility. But now with the progress of science—do you know it's phosphate in the land that makes things grow? And if you put it back into the wasted soil . . .

ALEIXO: There you go again. Talk, talk, talk! That's all you're good for: to use words none of us understands, and chasin' things that don't exist. But when it comes to work, you can't even make enough to support yourself, much less a wife!

SARGENTO: I'll take care of her, *real* care, not just keep her alive in a dusty hell! Just as soon as I find that phosphate mine . . .

ALEIXO: Ahh!

SARGENTO: I could take care of the whole damn lot of you, if I wanted to, just as soon as I put phosphate into the soil and . . . (*Aleixo laughs*) Laugh, if you want! But it's in the almanac, right there in black and white: "If you put phosphates back into a wasted soil . . ." (*Aleixo's laughter increases*) Laugh! Laugh! But *I'll* be the one to laugh, the day I find that mine and my pockets bulge with *cruzeiros!* (*As he sticks his hands into his pockets to demonstrate, the material rips apart with a tearing sound, sending Aleixo into even greater laughter*) If you don't shut that dirty old mouth of yours, I'll . . . (*He furiously grabs Aleixo by the shirt collar*)

ALEIXO: Let go of me! Let go of me! God'll punish you if you hurt a . . . a poor sick man! (*Sargento lets go, moves away*)

Why don't you go someplace else and find your damn mine? Someplace where the trains stop?

SARGENTO: I *am* going! But I'll be back! (*Sits, dejectedly*) I'll be back . . .

DOUTÔ: (*Drowsily*) Nor here, nor there. Trains don't stop anywhere, not really, if you know what I mean. But you don't, of course. That's the difference between the cultivated and the ignorant, who have the misery without the meaning. Ah, but that's culture: teaches you the meaning—or rather, that there *is* no meaning. ". . . A tale told by an idiot . . ." A good thing to have, culture. Keeps you from waiting for rain, and for trains, and for phosphates.

BASTOS: (*Emptily*) Maybe if we had a station . . .

SARGENTO: (*Pensively*) If only I could find a mine . . .

DOUTÔ: (*Drifting back to sleep*) *If . . . if . . .*

(*The window of the house opens. Thereza, a pale, fragile girl of seventeen, gazes out into the street. A moment later, Nhô Jango enters. He may be anywhere between fifty and seventy. His face is weather-beaten and he has a graying, scraggly beard. His pants are rolled up to the knees, his shirt and straw hat are in tatters. His step is light and spry as if he walked on a different, more sustaining, level than the heavy dust in which the others drag themselves*)

NHÔ JANGO: Mornin', good mornin', *cumpadre* Zeca! Mornin', Aleixo. Bastos. (*Irritated by his habitual cheerfulness, the others mumble and turn away*)

TONICO: (*Coming forward*) G-g-good mornin', Nhô Jango.

NHÔ JANGO: Ah, good mornin', Tonico, good mornin'. (*Brief pause*) Why's everythin' so quiet, lad? And what you doin' with that harmonica there in your hand? Put it to your lips, lad, this is Sunday. (*Tonico promptly puts the harmonica to his mouth, then suddenly stops and looks over to Doutô: Nhô Jango understands*) Tell you what. Come over to the Banhadinho this evenin' an' you can play for me and Figurinha all your pretty tunes. (*Scratching leg*) Old battle scar itched all night. Guess there'll be a change of weather soon. (*He looks up at the sky; Zeca spits*) Might change soon. I feel . . . good . . .

ALEIXO: You *always* feel good, ain't that what you tell us?

NHÔ JANGO: (*Removes hat*) Thanks to God. But today, I feel 'specially good. Somethin's in the atmosphere.

ALEIXO: *Hotter,* that's what!

TONICO: How's Figurinha?

NHÔ JANGO: Fine, fine. Prettier every day, she is. Her white fur's softer'n silk, 'ceptin' today, she's black with mud 'cause she got a bit too deep in the Banhadinho, where the grass is more tender.

ALEIXO: See if *she* don't drown in the mud, one of these days!

NHÔ JANGO: God, He looks after her. Trouble with you Aleixo, is you never see the good side of things.

ALEIXO: I did—when there was a good side to see. Now everythin's buried beneath this cursed dust!

NHÔ JANGO: Just got yourselves to blame. Before, everything was good and green. God's own country. But when they put up the rails . . . (*The others rise, move about, as if to leave. They have heard this story before. Yet they remain, as though the day's oppressiveness overpowered them and compelled them to stay*) . . . Yes, the people, when they put up the rails, began fig'ring how much money they could make plantin' cotton that was so high an' sendin' it to the city—an' how important Campina would be when there was a station.

BASTOS: (*Wistfully*) Seven years I been here, waiting for the town to progress, for a station . . .

SARGENTO: (*Rising*) That's what I said. The cotton sucked the land, the wrong plowing let it blow away, and the rain was pushed back with all the trees they been cutting. It's ignorance!

NHÔ JANGO: It's the devil! It's the devil puts those needs in people's heads and leads them astray from the good life God give.

DOUTÔ: Who asked him *that?*

NHÔ JANGO: (*As though uninterrupted*) But the needs

God gives—why, if He give the thirst, He also created the water, no?

ALEIXO: But there ain't a cloud . . .

ZECA: Dry smoke all over.

NHÔ JANGO: You'll harvest enough for your needs. An' there's still water to drink.

ZECA: (*Growing alarmed now*) But the Banhadinho's always the last water to go an' it'll soon be dry.

NHÔ JANGO: (*Confidently*) Between now and soon, God will find *some* way of sending help. (*As he continues, Sancha, a mulatto woman, comes down the street. She is about five-months' pregnant and walks listlessly, in a weary voluptuousness. A bandanna is tied around her head. She stops as she sees Beto's face lying sideways in the dust, comes over and turns it up, then goes off*) He always find a way to send help, when people have badly messed up the nature He create. (*Musingly.*) He gotta keep his world goin', I s'pose. (*Then, growing in faith*) Didn't He send His own son once, His own son that die on a cross, to teach people how to go straight again? Think a love's big as that would let His people perish under the dust?

ZECA: (*Trying hard to believe*) You think God *could* send rain?

NHÔ JANGO: Or anythin' else we really need!

ALEIXO: (*Suddenly, grudgingly*) Why don't He then?

NHÔ JANGO: Ask, and see!

ALEIXO: Ahhh! (*Then, half-looking up, almost defiantly*) All right, we ask for rain!

NHÔ JANGO: No, no! Not like you was scoldin' Him! But like you was scoldin' *yourselves.*

ZECA: (*Eagerly*) How we ask?

NHÔ JANGO: (*Appraising them*) You all ready to scold yourselves for trustin' the devil more'n God? (*All nod, except Aleixo*) For messin' up the good life He give? (*Now all nod*) An' ask He forgive you? (*More nods; then, after a deep breath*) The proper way is a procession!

ZECA: *Procession?*

BASTOS: That goin' to help?

NHÔ JANGO: Last time we had a procession here—'fore some of you was even born—why, it rain the *next* day.

DOUTÔ: It is alway that way. One hears of *one* petition which, by mere chance, was answered. Yet nothing about the thousands to which the gods were forever silent.

BASTOS: Very next day, it rained?

NHÔ JANGO: Right! Aleixo was there.

ALEIXO: (*As all turn to him for confirmation*) Well, but it was only a small drought.

NHÔ JANGO: But it rain, didn't it?

ALEIXO: (*Nods, slowly*) That was a long time ago—jus' before they put up the rails—when things was good.

ZECA: Things was *good* then?

ALEIXO: You don't think this village was always the dust hole it is now, do you? Like I said, that was only a small drought, an' soon ev'rythin' was green again. (*Suddenly turning on the others, with unexpected pride*) Why do you think they call it Campina do Monte Alegre?

NHÔ JANGO: God's own country . . .

ALEIXO: (*Reflectively*) Mornin's an' evenin's the air ringing with bells . . .

TONICO: (*Excitedly*) B-b-bells?

ALEIXO: From the church. (*Proudly*) We had a padre those days—acolyte, too, who'd ring the bells six in the mornin', six in the evenin'.

ZECA: (*Fascinated*) Every mornin', every . . . ?

ALEIXO: Mornin's to ask, evenin's to say thanks to God for the good things of that day.

ZECA: *Every* day? I mean, *good* things *every* day?

ALEIXO: (*Nods, deep in the past*) An' no matter if you was up Mandaçaia or 'cross the Varjao, you'd hear the bells, like you was hearing the waters of the Panema streamin' over the rocks of the Salto Grande . . . (*The others listen, enraptured*) An' we had a band. I played the flute, every Sunday. (*Sighs*) My neck was straight those days . . .

ZECA: (*Jumps up, excitedly*) What we waitin' for, then? Let's have a procession!

(*There are excited shouts of "Procession! Let's have a procession! A procession"*)

DOUTÔ: (*Peering from under hat*) Procession, phosphates . . . What's the good? Haven't you got that into your thick heads by now?

ZECA: Aleixo here says things *was* good when . . .

DOUTÔ: Was, will be, but never *is*.

NHÔ JANGO: (*Noting the dampening enthusiasm of the others*) If God give the thirst, why, how can God make the heart of man thirst for somethin' proper if . . . that somethin' don't exist to . . . to fill up the . . .

SARGENTO: (*Comes up to Nhô Jango; quoting excitedly*) "Nature abhors a vacuum." It's in the almanac! But it's something natural—none of this silly God stuff!—like the wind is a kind of rushing in of the air to fill a . . . a low pressure area.

DOUTÔ: And to get people all excited . . . (*Suddenly sniffs the air and points upstage*) Look! The wind! It's starting to blow! (*All turn, anxiously. He leans back, laughs*) And I was just beginning to wonder *what* had got into you corpses! Ha-ha-ha! Atmospheric stimulus, glandular secretion! That's what *hope* is! And it all ends up down the drain!

(*Thereza closes the window. Pause. All now seem a bit dazed*)

ZECA: Aleixo, you said things was . . . ?

ALEIXO: How can I remember, it was so long ago? Now, God's gone away.

NHÔ JANGO: God's always there. It's the people gone 'way from *Him*.

ALEIXO: And the padre's gone.

NHÔ JANGO: When Padre Antonio die, nobody bother 'bout askin' for another. All was too busy plantin' cotton an' thinkin' cotton, even Sundays.

SARGENTO: Who wants a *padre,* anyway?

ALEIXO: (*To Sargento*) How can we have a procession

without a padre, eh, Mr. Know-it-all! Don't your almanac say that?

TONICO: (*To Nhô Jango*) C-c-can we?

NHÔ JANGO: Well, no. (*Then, promptly*) But we might get one.

SARGENTO: Who's got money to get a padre? Try and get one *without* money!

NHÔ JANGO: Eh, lad. Your father brought you up to fear the Lord.

SARGENTO: To fear all right! Like *he* did, when he was dying and begging for the sacraments! But the padre from Angatuba wouldn't come because it was dark and the road was muddy. (*Fiercely*) But it was only because we had no money! (*A moment; reflectively*) And he fighting to stay alive, crying for a padre 'cause he'd been damned on earth, he said, and wanted to be saved in heaven. He was frightened, died in fear, and we buried him in the mud and dark, without salvation. (*Bitterly*) *If* you can pay your way out of hell, it's *money* you need, not a padre! *Money!* (*He rushes off, in a rage*)

DOUTÔ: Only death can get you out of hell.

NHÔ JANGO: God's got nothin' to do with bad padres.

DOUTÔ: God's got nothing to do, period!

NHÔ JANGO: (*Gazing at the flapping clothes on the line*) Change of wind means change of weather.

DOUTÔ: Means a lot of dust.

NHÔ JANGO: But it's a northwester blowin'! Might bring rain in three days!

DOUTÔ: In three day it will stop blowing, that's all, as it's done before. (*Now the spell is definitely broken; all have sunk back into a state of hopelessness*)

ALEIXO: God's forgot us . . .

(*He drags himself away, followed by Zeca. Bastos leans on counter and stares longingly ahead. Sancha, returning, notices Beto snoring, his face fallen back in the dust. She starts toward him, then stops, as if saying, "What's the use?" and continues listlessly up the street*)

TONICO: (*Breaking the oppressive silence*) Has He, Nhô Jango, forgot us?

NHÔ JANGO: Eh? (*After a short pause*) No. Not if you go on trusting Him.

TONICO: You trust God?

NHÔ JANGO: Ay, I do.

TONICO: Y-y-you had a daughter that drown in the Panema, didn't you?

NHÔ JANGO: (*Nods, sadly*) She fell in, the little thing.

TONICO: An' your wife, Nha Joanna, she never come back, did she?

NHÔ JANGO: Ay, the poor woman she got sick in the head when she saw the little thing floating down the river like a piece of washing . . .

TONICO: An' the four cows that give so much milk, they all die, didn't they?

NHÔ JANGO: Ay, when the plague she strike, she strike like lightning.

TONICO: (*Puzzled*) Why, then, you trust God, Nhô Jango?

NHÔ JANGO: 'Cause if you don't, what is there left?

(*Confused, Tonico turns away and slowly goes off. As he does, he begins to play the same plaintive tune on his harmonica, as at the opening of the play*)

DOUTÔ: (*Murmuring*) Let me sleep . . . sleep . . .

NHÔ JANGO: (*Staring at the shirts flapping in the slowly rising wind*) If God give the thirst, He also give the water . . .

The Lights Fade

Scene Two

An hour later.

Sargento is discovered walking downstage, an old, dusty carpetbag in one hand, a spade and pick in the other. He slowly approaches the wooden house, hesitates for a mo-

ment, then resolutely turns away and starts to go as the window is flung open and Thereza appears.

THEREZA: Sargento! (*He stops*) Has something happened?

SARGENTO: You just have to look around!

THEREZA: But I thought you said rain wasn't the most important . . . It was this thing you are going to find in the ground that would save everybody!

SARGENTO: This thing doesn't exist in *this* ground!

THEREZA: (*As he tries to conceal the bag*) What's that? A bag?

SARGENTO: Sure! Sure, it's a bag! (*Comes to window; painfully*) How can I stay any longer? Since I returned from the army, I've been digging like a tractor. But there aren't any phosphates here, and I must go try somewhere else. I must! How can I go on like *this?* (*He pulls out torn, empty pockets; then gazes up and sees the frozen look in her eyes*) Thereza, I didn't mean . . . I didn't know . . . Thereza! Please! Don't look at me like that! (*Silence*) Thereza! Say something, *speak* to me. (*He grabs her hand*) I love you, you know that. But what else can I do? I'd stay, if there was a single chance, I swear I would, Thereza! But life's dead in Campina. Everybody, everything is dying! And I *won't* be buried in the dust like the others! Can't you understand? I'll come back. Soon's I . . .

(*Thereza coughs nervously. Tonico appears, hastens over to Sargento. Too excited to speak, he anxiously pulls at his sleeve*)

SARGENTO: Hey, what's the matter? What happened? (*Tonico still is unable to speak; he begins to shake him*) Speak, boy, come on.

THEREZA: What is it, Tonico?

TONICO: (*Finally*) B-b-b-bells!

SARGENTO: What? (*Tonico frees himself and hastens up the street, unable to control his excitement*)

TONICO: (*Calls out, as he disappears*) B-b-bells! Bells! Bells!

SARGENTO: Worse today than ever, the poor idiot.

THEREZA: (*Sensing something*) But perhaps . . . ?

(*Aleixo rushes on, followed by Zeca. As Aleixo begins to enter the house, Sargento shouts*)

SARGENTO: Say, what the hell's all the commotion about?

ALEIXO: You stop that blasphemin' now, or God'll hear you and punish you! (*He goes in*)

SARGENTO: What in hell's the matter? (*Grabs hold of Zeca*) Tell me!

ZECA: On the main road—a car, big new one, it seems—broke down. Chico Ventura was goin' to Angatuba, and he saw it. An' he come over to tell us.

SARGENTO: What about it?

ZECA: Well, in this big car that break down was . . .

SARGENTO: *Who?*

ZECA: A padre.

THEREZA: (*Strangely*) A padre?

ALEIXO: (*Off*) Hey, where's the harness, Thereza? (*Thereza leaves window*)

SARGENTO: Is that all?

(*Nhô Jango enters, beaming*)

NHÔ JANGO: Well, he's come, hasn't he?

ALEIXO: (*Off*) You there, Nhô?

NHÔ JANGO: Yes! Come on.

ALEIXO: (*Comes out with old mule-cart gear*) I found it. Rat's been chewin' at it.

NHÔ JANGO: Now we go over to get Luis Belmiro's mule. Wouldn't trust the *senhor cura* with no other mule.

ALEIXO: (*Anxiously*) If we don't go quick, Angatuba might grab him!

NHÔ JANGO: (*As they start*) You think God was goin' to send us a padre an' let Angatuba get him?

ALEIXO: N-no . . . (*Then*) But then, how you know He's not sendin' him to Angatuba?

(*They leave, followed by Zeca. Sargento looks after them. Thereza re-appears at window*)

THEREZA: Imagine! A padre in Campina! And just this morning . . .

SARGENTO: A padre! What can you expect from a man in skirts, anyway!

THEREZA: . . . Nhô Jango was saying . . .

SARGENTO: Bullshit! Nothing happens that's not *natural!*

THEREZA: Sargento, couldn't you try digging some more in Campina?

SARGENTO: But . . .

THEREZA: Just a few more days . . .

SARGENTO: (*After a moment*) Well, I sup'ose a few more days . . . (*They look at each other*) If you *really* want me to. (*The shirts on the line are flapping more rapidly in the increasingly rising wind*)

The Lights Fade

Scene Three

Interior of Aleixo's house. An hour or so later.

Thereza is busy fixing up the room as best she can. It contains a very plain rough table and chairs, a low chest with broken glass front, in which a few pieces of cheap and chipped china are seen, against the wall. Back, right, one door leads into Thereza's room, the other into the kitchen. Aleixo presumably sleeps in a dirty hammock which hangs on a peg during daytime. Tonico is seated at the table, deeply absorbed in thought.

THEREZA: (*Passes cloth over table*) There. (*Appraises room, uncertainly*) You think it looks all right for a padre? (*Silence*) Tonico! (*He looks up*) Like it?

TONICO: Oh, yes!

THEREZA: Imagine! A padre in our house! (*More to herself*) I wonder what he'll be like? Very thin, very pale, with kind eyes and . . . Oh, I'd almost forgotten! (*She rushes over to chest, opens lower door, removes a lot of old rags, then takes out a large black wooden crucifix with a Christ in white imitation ivory*) He'll like this! It's proper for a padre. (*Gazing at it*) My mother left it to me. Always hung over her bed. Then she died and her bed was sold and . . . (*She puts rags back, rises slowly, looking fixedly at the crucifix*) I wonder why I never . . . ?

TONICO: (*Calls*) Thereza!

THEREZA: (*With a little start*) Yes, Tonico? (*She hangs the crucifix on the wall*)

TONICO: You think . . . ?

(*A knock on the door. Thereza breathlessly goes to answer it. It is Bastos*)

THEREZA: Oh . . .

BASTOS: (*A bottle of beer in his hand*) Oh what? It's the best beer I got. What you expect, wine? (*Then*) I brought it for the *senhor reverendo*—three and a half *cruzeiros* a bottle.

THEREZA: I'm sure he'll be thirsty. Thank you, Senhor Bastos. God will repay you.

BASTOS: (*Clinging to bottle*) God? (*Shrugs, hands bottle to her*) Well, I suppose since nobody else will . . . (*As compensation*) But there's sure to be a bit of a crowd at the Tendinha today. (*Briskly*) Got to get things ready. (*He goes*)

TONICO: Thereza. You think he'll let me . . . ?

THEREZA: What?

TONICO: R-r-ring the bells—for the procession?

THEREZA: (*Gently*) You're the only musician in Campina, aren't you, Tonico? (*He beams happily; then, to herself*) *A procession!*

(*The lights dim out, and come up again in front of the house. Monsignor Andrada, followed by his secretary, Padre Manuel, enter from the street. Monsignor Andrada is slapping his soutane which is covered with dust. He is middle-aged, tall, fastidious, and has a barely controlled impatience with everybody and everything, including himself. As a result, he often is ironic and sarcastic. Padre Manuel is in his late forties; stout, with a round, ruddy face*)

MONSIGNOR: Confound this dust!

PADRE MANUEL: Indeed annoying, Your Reverence.

MONSIGNOR: Your leaning towards understatement verges on the distortion of the obvious, Padre Manuel.

PADRE MANUEL: Yes, Your Reverence.

MONSIGNOR: Next time you choose a driver for a particularly long journey, on a particularly bad road . . .

PADRE MANUEL: (*Meekly*) But you will agree that I could not have foreseen . . .

MONSIGNOR: (*Interrupts him*) I did not say I expected you to *foresee* anything, Padre Manuel. But since you seem to have two eyes in your head, if not much else, I did expect you to see that both the car and the driver were obviously hardly adequate for a long journey. (*As Padre Manuel is about to protest*) Words will avail us nothing, but I do want you to see to it that he will not sleep as soundly while repairing the automobile as he did while driving it!

PADRE MANUEL: It will be ready at four o'clock, Your Reverence. That is what he said.

MONSIGNOR: (*Looking about*) Where may our saviors be? Did they rescue us from Gobi to land us in Sahara?

PADRE MANUEL: The old man went to unharness the mule.

MONSIGNOR: What's the name of this dreary place?

PADRE MANUEL: I can find out.

MONSIGNOR: Don't bother. (*With a strange feeling*) There is something about it . . .

PADRE MANUEL: Perhaps the fact that there is *nothing* about it.

(*Nhô Jango enters, overhears the last part of the conversation*)

NHÔ JANGO: Oh, it's really God's own country, *senhor cura,* but . . .

MONSIGNOR: (*Turning*) Oh, there you are.

NHÔ JANGO: . . . But without rain . . .

MONSIGNOR: We were waiting. Where do we wash?

NHÔ JANGO: Aleixo will take you in to his place, he'll be comin' soon. As I was sayin', this is really God's own country, but without rain even the best soil won't . . . You see, *senhor cura,* that's why we was so happy when we hear your machine break down.

MONSIGNOR: Indeed?

NHÔ JANGO: Yes, *senhor cura.* All of us. (*Beto snores; Monsignor turns*) That's Beto, *senhor cura,* a good soul, really. Except he have a bigger thirst than most people.

(*Monsignor's eyes continue to wander around: he notices Thereza and Tonico peering out the door; Sancha staring from the street, an urchin slinking against the wall of the Tendinha, staring from under his wide-brimmed hat*)

MONSIGNOR: Why does everybody look at me so strangely?

NHÔ JANGO: Oh, that's because they're all like thunderstruck, you comin' so sudden-like, just after I been talkin' . . .

MONSIGNOR: I fail to see that *that* should be so strange.

NHÔ JANGO: Oh, not strange, *senhor cura,* but you see, since I knew you was comin' . . .

MONSIGNOR: Did *you* help the termites build that ant-hill we skidded into by the roadside?

NHÔ JANGO: It was God.

MONSIGNOR: (*Shortly*) It was only a bad driver.

NHÔ JANGO: Oh, it doesn't make any difference *who* God chooses to carry out His will, so long as . . .

MONSIGNOR: (*Sharply*) So long as I get a chance to wash. Please!

NHÔ JANGO: Sure, sure, just as soon as Aleixo comes. But —well, I might as well say it right now—as the *senhor cura* can see for himself, we need rain pretty bad and since we won't have no rain without a procession—(*Monsignor is growing impatient*) —an' no procession without a . . .

PADRE MANUEL: Just a minute! Didn't you hear His Reverence say he wanted to wash?

NHÔ JANGO: Oh, well, s'pose Aleixo won't mind if I take you in. But if you just let me tell you 'bout the procession . . .

PADRE MANUEL: Not *now.* Later. Come back at . . . five o'clock. (*He and Monsignor exchange a knowing look*)

NHÔ JANGO: Five o'clock is fine.

PADRE MANUEL: Now where's this house?

NHÔ JANGO: (*Points*) Here.

MONSIGNOR: (*Sighing*) Why didn't you say so before?

NHÔ JANGO: (*Simply*) Because the *senhor cura* didn't ask.

MONSIGNOR: (*Testily*) Oh, will you stop calling me *senhor cura!* (*He vigorously slaps the dust off his soutane as he turns to Padre Manuel*) It is all *your* fault! (*Padre Manuel winces. They enter house*)

NHÔ JANGO: (*Calls*) Therezinha! Take good care of the *senhor cu . . .* (*Checks himself*) Take good care of him!

(*Tonico slips out the door, gaping back excitedly. Aleixo emerges just as Monsignor disappears; apparently he's been watching around the corner*)

NHÔ JANGO: Aleixo! What happen to you, anyway?

ALEIXO: (*With feigned casualness*) Why, nothin', I just . . . (*Quickly turns his attention to Sargento, who has just entered*) You still here? Hm—thought you didn't believe in padres?

SARGENTO: I don't!

(*Bastos comes from the Tendinha with a tin of sausages*)

BASTOS: Here they are. Twenty-two *cruzeiros* and fifty *centavos* the can.

NHÔ JANGO: (*Taking tin*) Fine, umm. It's a long time I tasted one of these.

BASTOS: Well, is it . . . God goin' to pay me for these, too?

NHÔ JANGO: Nobody can pay you more, Bastos!

ALEIXO: Wait an' see—after the procession an' the rain.

SARGENTO: (*Contemptuously*) Procession! Rain! You won't get anything out of that black-skirt if you squeeze him in a cane-mill! He's like *all* the rest of them, drier than all the fields of Campina! (*He leaves*)

BASTOS: What he mean? (*Laughing*) It's the procession—not *he* gonna piss out the rain!

NHÔ JANGO: It would be a good thing if everybody started watchin' their language, from now on.

ALEIXO: You are right, Nhô Jango.

NHÔ JANGO: (*Holds out tin to Aleixo*) Here, take this in.

ALEIXO: Me? (*Refusing tin*) Why *me?* I'm even movin' out, so's he can sleep in my hammock.

NHÔ JANGO: It's *your* house all the same. Take it, it won't burn you. (*Notices the terror in Aleixo's eyes*) Say, what's the matter? You look like you seen the devil himself!

BETO: (*Awakens*) Whaat? The devil? I was dreamin' of the evil one jus' now, an' so clear I could almost hear 'im speak! (*He looks around, warily*)

ALEIXO: A padre's arrived, you black fool! God's sent him for a procession an' the rain.

BETO: Christ! Luck's turnin' fo' Campina, now if I could get myself a lot'ry numbah. (*Suddenly; rising*) But how you know it was God send him an' not . . . ?

NHÔ JANGO: Only God sends help. The devil, he sends temptation. Now go along, Aleixo.

ALEIXO: (*Reluctantly takes tin*) A little later. (*Moving off*) Got to see those turnips first.

BASTOS: He's scared, that's what.

BETO: Who scared?

BASTOS: (*Points to Aleixo*) Him! (*Aleixo stops*) 'Cause he was blaspheming.

ALEIXO: (*Trembling*) That's a lie, Bastos! I never in my life done anythin' so wicked!

BASTOS: You always do, and this morning, too!

NHÔ JANGO: (*Looks him straight in the eye; kindly*) You sorry you been blaspheming against the good Lord? (*Aleixo nods, contritely*) Then you got nothin' to worry 'bout, for God forgive as quick as a bat out of hell! (*Aleixo is relieved*) They say He's even more pleased when one sinner repents than I-don't-know-how-many righteous ones.

ALEIXO: Pleased? (*His expression changes*) He is pleased with *me?*

NHÔ JANGO: If you're *really* sorry.

ALEIXO: But how can I know? How can I know when He *has* forgiven me?

NHÔ JANGO: When you're carryin' a hundred-pound sack o' beans on your back, you know when you unload it, don't you? (*Aleixo seems to understand. Nhô Jango starts*) Got to be goin' now. Figurinha must be hungry, then she get mad at me.

BASTOS: Better fix some sandwiches. People's sure to be comin' soon. (*Rubbing his hands as he disappears behind counter*) God pays more . . .

NHÔ JANGO: (*Turns back to Aleixo*) And you take those sausages in for the *senhor cura!* I'll be back to see him at five. (*Remembers*) But don't call him *senhor cura*. He don't like titles. (*He leaves*)

BETO: (*Starts; looks at house, musingly*) God, he send help . . . (*He disappears*)

DOUTÔ: (*From beneath the hat*) Hope! A false start into a blind alley . . .

(*Doutô sighs wearily, resumes his sleep. Aleixo slowly crosses to house, stops, feels his neck, then leaves the tin of sausages at door, gingerly knocks and hastens off. Tonico, who eagerly has been watching everything, is about to put the harmonica to his lips when he realizes that Doutô is present. Then, in a gesture of defiance to the sleeping Doutô, he starts to play the same tune but with a very lively rhythm as:*)

The Lights Fade

Scene Four

Inside the house. It is four o'clock. Monsignor is pacing the room. Padre Manuel watches him from a corner.

MONSIGNOR: (*Stops, consults watch*) It is now four-*seventeen!* (*Continues pacing*) Four hours, yet it seems more like *forty*, waiting in this outlandish place!

PADRE MANUEL: I can well understand Your Reverence's impatience. Eh . . . would Monsignor perhaps like to take a short stroll through the village?

MONSIGNOR: (*Stops*) Stroll? Among these people who look at me as if I were a ghost, crossing themselves, talking in mysterious whispers as I go by? Even behind closed windows, I feel eyes riveted on me like . . . Why, the air here is thicker with superstition than it is with dust. And the sooner we get out of here, the better! (*Resumes pacing*) What *could* be keeping that imbecile?

PADRE MANUEL: He should be here any minute now. (*Goes to window, looks out, sees nothing*) Any minute . . .

MONSIGNOR: I heard you the first time, Padre Manuel. I would say that a quarter of an hour's allowance would still be within reason. (*Again consults watch*) But twenty-one minutes—and not a sign, not a sign of that imbecile!

PADRE MANUEL: I can't imagine what's happened. He said it couldn't possibly take him more than five hours to fix it—and that punctually at four, he would be here and blow the horn for us.

MONSIGNOR: Do you hear a horn, Padre Manuel? (*Padre Manuel shakes his head*) Why don't you go and find *out* then?

PADRE MANUEL: Yes, Your Reverence. (*He goes quickly. Monsignor's pacing increases in tempo*)

MONSIGNOR: It's incredible! (*He raps on table as he passes it*) Incredible!

(*Thereza walks quietly in from the kitchen. She is hesitant and uncertain, Monsignor not being quite what she had expected*)

THEREZA: (*Faintly*) Did you call me?

MONSIGNOR: (*With a little start*) Oh—it's you. (*Uneasily*) Why do you look at me that way, child? (*Before she can reply*) No, I did not call you. (*She begins to go quietly*) What appalling silence! (*She stops*) Aren't there ever any normal sounds in this place?

THEREZA: (*Hesitantly*) It's mostly like this all the time. Except when the train passes three times, sometimes four, a day.

MONSIGNOR: (*With sudden interest*) Train? You mean there is a train? And I could get out of Campina, if the car . . . ?

THEREZA: No one can get out of Campina, not on the

train, 'cause there's no station. (*Monsignor sinks desolately on to a chair*) At first, when I'd hear the train coming, I'd stop my work and listen, as if it was going to bring me something, or maybe take me away somewhere. (*A moment*) But it never brought me anything, and I've never gone anywhere.

MONSIGNOR: (*Turns to her*) Your mother and father, don't *they* bring you things?

THEREZA: They died a long time ago.

MONSIGNOR: Oh? (*Pause*) You should be married. Have someone to look after you.

THEREZA: He has no money.

MONSIGNOR: Surely, your relatives, then . . .

THEREZA: Uncle Aleixo's all I've got. And he's not well.

MONSIGNOR: (*Rising; uneasily*) You must not be impatient. I am certain he will take you places, bring you things, when he is well.

THEREZA: He'll never get well. His neck hasn't moved, not for twenty years, 'cause of a stroke one day, in his cotton field. The year he planted most, too, when suddenly the sky turned black and rained down hailstones. It destroyed his cotton and he cursed and cursed, as he sometimes does, and turned and spit at the sky—and when he wanted to turn back, he couldn't any more. Some say it was because of a bad cold, others thought it was God's punishment.

MONSIGNOR: A heretic, evidently. That's what he is!

THEREZA: Oh, he's not, *senhor padre!* If it wasn't for him, I . . . (*A moment*) True, he never could give me very much for things have been mostly bad, like they say, since I was born.

(*Monsignor is disturbed, moves away; stops as he notices the crucifix*)

MONSIGNOR: Who does *this* belong to? (*He goes on staring, with a strange fascination*)

THEREZA: Oh, my mother. She left it to me. You like it?

MONSIGNOR: Eh? Like? Why, only an artist with a supreme sense of sadistic morbidity, and a pathological leaning toward suffering, could have carved such a . . .

THEREZA: (*Approaching it; entranced*) Yes, only one

who's suffered very much could do it. It was in the drawer such a long time. (*She holds Monsignor's eyes in a strange, reluctant fascination*) Then, when I heard you were coming, I took it out . . . and if you hadn't come, I would never have known how beautiful it really is. (*Very close now*) You're right, only someone who's suffered . . . (*She touches it*) Those long nails, stuck in the soft white skin . . . (*Coughs, nervously*)

MONSIGNOR: Stop it, will you? For goodness' sake, stop it!

THEREZA: I can't. I . . . I'm sorry. I've always had this cough. But I'll get well. I feel much better already, since God sent you.

MONSIGNOR: Don't *you* start that now!

THEREZA: (*Looks at him seriously for a second, then smiles*) Oh, you don't frighten me any more. At first, when you came, I . . . But now I know you and you don't frighten me any more, putting on the "jaguar's skin." (*Suddenly grabs his hand*) *You* haven't got any spots, see? (*Caresses his hand*) Your *real* skin's soft and white, like . . . (*She looks up at the crucifix, then impulsively leans over and kisses Monsignor's hand*)

MONSIGNOR: (*Snatching hand away*) What's come over you, child?

THEREZA: (*Bursting into tears, though happy*) Nothing . . . nothing. (*She rushes into kitchen. Monsignor stands motionless, gazing at his hand. Nhô Jango comes in*)

NHÔ JANGO: Good afternoon, *senhor cu* . . . Here I am.

MONSIGNOR: (*Still dazed*) Hm?

NHÔ JANGO: Like you told me—five o'clock.

MONSIGNOR: Five? (*He consults watch; frowns*)

NHÔ JANGO: To talk 'bout the procession.

MONSIGNOR: What procession?

NHÔ JANGO: For the rain, like I said outside, and seein' we haven't got a padre, we come ask you to head it for us.

MONSIGNOR: (*Peremptorily, though not unkind*) Me? Impossible! (*Nhô Jango's smile begins to fade*) I regret very much —perhaps under different circumstances—(*Stiffening*) I am going straight to São Paulo for an important meeting.

NHÔ JANGO: But what could be more important . . . ?

MONSIGNOR: Allow *me* to be the judge of that.

NHÔ JANGO: But if God send you . . .

MONSIGNOR: I forbid you to mention that nonsense again, do you hear me?

NHÔ JANGO: Yes, *senhor padre,* but since you said yourself you was going to São Paulo . . .

MONSIGNOR: I *am* going!

NHÔ JANGO: . . . And we needin' a padre, an' Campina not even on the main road, but here you are.

MONSIGNOR: How many times do I have to tell you that I am here simply because of a bad driver? That's all it *is,* to anyone with a sane mind! But you people! Who *are* you to presume to know, with such impertinent assurance, what is the will of God?

NHÔ JANGO: The men of Campina, they're not bad, really. Even if they don't exac'ly look like lambs. They've had some rough times, *senhor padre,* believe me (*Promptly*) Not that it wasn't their fault, mind you, leaving God and following the devil. But one day, when they look around and saw all that was left of the devil's promise was dust, they become frightened—especially since they did not know how to return to God. If the *senhor padre* only knew how miserable it's been for them . . . (*The whistle from the passing train is heard. Monsignor is silent. As the whistle fades away, Nhô Jango continues*) Now, they *really* want to return to God—and God must be ready to take 'em back . . . or He wouldn't have sent you for the procession.

MONSIGNOR: (*After a moment*) But—I have to go to São Paulo . . . (*Then, in a sudden change of tone*) Anyway, this is none of my business—a curate's job—and what's more, I refuse to become involved with small town superstition! (*Padre Manuel enters. Monsignor quickly turns to him*) Oh, finally! I thought you were never returning. Come on, let us go! (*He moves to door*)

PADRE MANUEL: Your Reverence. Please!

MONSIGNOR: (*Stops, turns*) What is it now?

PADRE MANUEL: It's . . . it's the car. It's not quite ready.

NHÔ JANGO: You see, *senhor cura,* when God has something in mind . . .

MONSIGNOR: (*Brusquely*) There seems to be a *conspiracy* to keep me here! But I am going straight to São Paulo, even if it is in a hearse!

NHÔ JANGO: But, *senhor cura* . . .

MONSIGNOR: (*With finality*) No! And don't call me *senhor cura!* (*He holds open the door for Nhô Jango*) *Goodbye!* (*Nhô Jango, baffled, bows slightly and leaves*)

PADRE MANUEL: (*Quickly*) It's only a *short* delay, Your Reverence. It *will* be ready in just one hour. Definitely. I . . . I am terribly sorry about all this, Your Reverence, but you *will* admit, it was not *my* fault.

MONSIGNOR: (*Snapping*) Perhaps *mine?*

PADRE MANUEL: (*Meekly*) The driver is quite upset to know how—eh—displeased Your Reverence is.

MONSIGNOR: The inept driver is also an inept mechanic!

PADRE MANUEL: It's really not his fault, for the shock caused the engine to . . .

MONSIGNOR: (*Turning on Padre Manuel*) I don't suppose it's the engine's fault, either, since it was the manufacturer . . .

PADRE MANUEL: Well—I was about to say . . .

MONSIGNOR: Don't! Don't! I know what you were about to say: It's not the manufacturer's fault, either, it's . . . it's . . . (*Turning away*) Good gracious! How much longer do I have to put up with this concerted conspiracy of incompetence, presumption and superstition? How long am I compelled to wait in this arid, desolate place, and listen to rural simpletons' and hysterical girls' prophecy as to *why* I came here—why I am *still* here! (*More to himself*) As if there weren't enough discernible, *plausible,* reasons for everyone to see! (*Turns*) *Everyone,* do you hear me, Padre Manuel? So don't *you* come and say to me it's *God's will!!*

PADRE MANUEL: (*Startled*) I? But I never . . .

MONSIGNOR: (*With mounting impatience and exasperation*) Oh, please, Padre Manuel, please stop talking! Please leave me alone! (*Padre Manuel leaves. Monsignor begins to pace the room*) Are the limits of my endurance to stretch to—infinity?

(*As he dramatically flings open his arms, he finds himself standing before the crucifix. He holds that position for a moment, then, suddenly, falls to his knees in a surge of repentance and shame. He buries his face in his hands and starts to recite The Lord's Prayer. A few seconds later, the door is cautiously opened and Aleixo peers in. A shaft of the hazy setting sun shoots through the half-open door and falls upon Monsignor, in the middle of his prayer*)

MONSIGNOR: (*Praying*) ". . . and forgive us our trespasses as we forgive those . . ."

(*His voice trails off. Aleixo is transfixed. Then slowly, like a branch turning up to the sun, his distorted neck straightens. He is still staring at Monsignor when suddenly he begins to realize what has happened. Cautiously, he raises one hand to his neck, then the other, twists it to left, to right, then rushes out, dazed with joy*)

ALEIXO: (*Shouting*) I'm forgiven! I'm . . . ! Miracle! *A miracle!*

The Lights Quickly Fade

Scene Five

The street. Fifteen minutes later. A small group has gathered around Aleixo, just in front of the Tendinha, in amazement. Beto is moving Aleixo's neck from one side to the other.

BETO: (*Incredulously*) Turnin' all right!

ALEIXO: Ouch! that's enough. It never turned *all* the way! What d'you think I am, an owl?

BASTOS: *Cristo!* Never saw nothing like it, even back in Portugal! God has come back to Campina!

ALEIXO: I sure can tell you that!

TONICO: (*Thrilled*) T-t-tell us how, again!

ALEIXO: (*Delighted, as the others gape at him*) Well, as I said before, I came back after five, 'spectin' Nhô Jango'd be there already, I was that scared of goin' in alone. An' when I poked my head in, I saw *him,* in front of the cross Thereza hung up, an' with a cloud like of thin smoke around him—like it was liftin' him up in the air—(*Impressively*) An' he said, "I forgive you, Aleixo . . . your terrible sins" and all of a sudden, my neck started straightin' up to him like the sack had slipped off my back.

BETO: *Smoke?* You don' say that before!

ALEIXO: Smoke, it was.

(*Nhô Jango enters*)

BETO: (*Aghast*) It's th' devil! I tell you it's th' devil done it! That's how *he* come! With smoke!

NHÔ JANGO: Shame on you, Beto! This is no *macumba.** (*Then, gently*) He's a padre of the church, eh? An' the church is God's, ain't she?

BETO: (*Echoing*) Church is God's . . .

NHÔ JANGO: And the devil don't cure; he make people sick.

ALEIXO: It's only God cures, all right!

BETO: Then it was the Lawd 'imself? Right here?

(*He slowly looks around, then lets out a shout of joy, impulsively grabs hold of Aleixo and dances around with him, as the others look on and laugh happily. Sargento comes down the street, stops and watches them*)

NHÔ JANGO: You know what God has given us? The biggest He do—a miracle!

ALL: (*Joyously*) Miracle! A miracle!

NHÔ JANGO: Now, time we go say thank you to the *cura.*

ALL: To the *cura!* To the *cura!*

NHÔ JANGO: (*Appraising them*) Wait! Better get more people, make it more proper.

* *voodoo rites*

BETO: I go get Sancha! (*Beaming*) Luck is turnin' all right! (*Goes*)

BASTOS: I'll tell Zeca.

NHÔ JANGO: Everybody call somebody!

(*They all hasten off. Sargento rushes to Thereza's closed window, calls softly*)

SARGENTO: Thereza! Thereza! (*Doutô saunters in*) Thereza!

DOUTÔ: Captain Phosphate! Don't tell me *you* got the miracle jitters, too?

SARGENTO: Oh, go to hell!

DOUTÔ: I thought you were a little less stupid than the rest of them.

SARGENTO: What makes you think you're so clever? Just because you're a doctor?

DOUTÔ: So the black-skirt *has* charmed you! My, my, my! That means that *everybody* in Campina has the miracle jitters. Everybody except myself, of course.

SARGENTO: Well, Aleixo's cured, isn't he?

DOUTÔ: As any psychoneurotic can be cured, provided he gets the right doses of suggestion at the right moment. That crooked neck was only the result of a conversion neurosis. The creation, out of a psychic conflict, of a somatic symptom without underlying organic pathology. That's all he had.

SARGENTO: But . . . all the rest of them?

DOUTÔ: They're stupid.

SARGENTO: It's not what they think, it's what it's *done* to them!

DOUTÔ: (*Cold diagnosis*) An extra shot into the bloodstream from the adrenal glands. Temporarily bracing.

SARGENTO: If you'd seen the look in their eyes . . .

DOUTÔ: Wait and see what happens to that look as soon as they find out the truth. (*Seriously*) Think he is a fool to get mixed up with *this?* Wait 'til he hears about this, he'll be bellowing to the four winds that it was *not* a miracle.

SARGENTO: But he can't! I mean . . .

DOUTÔ: You don't know *what* you mean. (*After a mo-*

ment) No sense getting all worked up, lad, for there is no point, no meaning to anything. Except perhaps in the sheer wickedness of a malignant principle to beat you continuously. And there is only *one* way of beating it: to stare coldly at the sky with all the lucidity of the brain and say, "You will not fool *me,* because I *know*. I know I cannot win!" That is the *only* way to save dignity. (*Forces a yawn*) Guess I'll take a nap now. (*Starts, turns*) And *you* need some Urodonal. A good diuretic that will take care of the excessive adrenalin in your blood!

(*He goes. Sargento stands motionless for a second, then dejectedly starts up the street. Suddenly, he hears laughter from a short distance away, and stops, confused. As the laughter increases, he turns impulsively and dashes across to Aleixo's house and enters. The lights come up immediately inside. Monsignor is seated at the table, his head resting on his hand*)

SARGENTO: (*As he bursts in*) Listen here, if you think . . .

MONSIGNOR: (*Quitely*) There is no one in.

SARGENTO: I . . . I . . .

MONSIGNOR: No one, I said.

SARGENTO: (*Aroused*) Do you think you're too grand to . . . (*Controlling himself, with great effort*) Listen, mister, I never liked padres!

MONSIGNOR: Indeed?

SARGENTO: But I didn't come here to quarrel. It's to talk to you about . . .

MONSIGNOR: Please! I can *not* stay for the procession. (*He rises, turns away*)

SARGENTO: It's not that! It's the other thing. (*Coming closer*) You see, ever since you arrived . . .

MONSIGNOR: (*Wearily*) How many times do I have to say that it was only a natural accident?

SARGENTO: But the people, they think it was God. (*Before Monsignor can protest*) Oh, I don't believe that, either, but I do believe that maybe you *can* do a lot for everybody. (*Quickly*) In a scientific-like way, I mean.

MONSIGNOR: What *are* you talking about?

SARGENTO: Well, it's this strange effect you've had.

MONSIGNOR: There is *nothing* strange.

SARGENTO: You wouldn't say that, mister, not if you'd seen them this morning, worse today than ever. Then Nhô Jango came 'round, telling the stories no one ever listens to, but somehow, they listened today. And when he said he knew God would . . .

MONSIGNOR: (*Nearly shouts*) No one can presume to know what is in the mind of God! No one who is in his right mind!

SARGENTO: (*Undeterred*) Then *you* arrived.

MONSIGNOR: No matter what Nhô Jango or anybody else says, God does not *speak* to anyone! (*He begins to pace, very restless; then suddenly stops, passes hand over eyes, changes tone, very quietly*) Listen, let me tell you a story, a story which the events of today have recalled more clearly to mind. It took place in a small village in the back country of São Paulo, too, but to the south, and there was a drought at the time. One day, a boy of thirteen was on his way to school, and already late, when he saw something glittering in the sun—it was a little lambary * thrashing desperately in the mud of a drying pond—and as he watched, he thought he heard a voice—God's voice—whisper to him, "Throw it back into the water! Throw it back into the water." (*A moment*) Served him right for his stupidity! Do you know what happened? He arrived late for class, covered with mud, and when he explained, the teacher thrashed him for lying and the entire class laughed at him. (*Pause*) Do you think I would be fool enough to be deluded again?

SARGENTO: It happened to you, then? (*Monsignor turns away*) And you mean, you've heard it again?

MONSIGNOR: (*Quickly*) No, no. No! I haven't heard *anything!* Anything, except the nonsense you have all been . . .

SARGENTO: Nonsense? But if it's cured . . .

MONSIGNOR: Who?

SARGENTO: Aleixo. The one with the twisted neck. You've cured him and . . .

* *a small fish*

MONSIGNOR: I? But if I haven't seen anybody.

SARGENTO: But he saw you while you were praying, and when you said something about forgiving his terrible sins, he got well.

MONSIGNOR: *I* said . . . ? But that's ridiculous! (*Suddenly realizing*) Oh. (*Whispers*) "Forgive us . . . our trespasses." That's it! I was praying!

SARGENTO: He says it's a *miracle!*

MONSIGNOR: (*Horrified*) *What?* No, no, he mustn't say such a thing! He can't! These things often happen. It's only suggestion, and he can just as easily revert to his former condition.

SARGENTO: It's not only that. It's what it's done to *all* of them!

MONSIGNOR: You don't mean they *all* know?

SARGENTO: (*Enthusiastically*) And they're joyous! Never been so happy, as though they *all* were cured.

MONSIGNOR: My God! I knew something like this was bound to happen. (*Determinedly*) I must straighten this out, at once! (*He goes to door*)

SARGENTO: No! You can't do that!

MONSIGNOR: They *must* know it was *not* a miracle!

SARGENTO: Do you know *what* it was?

MONSIGNOR: A mistake!

SARGENTO: How could it be, if . . . ? Why, it's just as though it had suddenly brought them everything they've wanted. You've put *life* back into them.

MONSIGNOR: I didn't do anything! It's all hysteria!

SARGENTO: Look, I don't know anything 'bout miracles—nor about all this mystic stuff. But I know *life*. I'm a farmer, and I know life when I see it! And I seen it today, return to poor dead faces, just as sure as I've seen green shoots come back after rain, on the face of a burnt pasture!

MONSIGNOR: But it's not a miracle! It's not a miracle!

SARGENTO: Damn it, man! Why do you bother so much with names? Miracle! God! Hell! Something wonderful's been shoved right into your hands, and you're pushing it away, just because you don't know its name! Use it, damn it, so long as it works!

MONSIGNOR: You're mad! Utterly mad! No matter what it has done to them, do you think I'm going to let them go on believing that . . . Why, sooner or later, they are bound to find out it was not a miracle and then . . .

SARGENTO: In the meantime, you'll be keeping them alive!

MONSIGNOR: What about the church? If later it is known that it was not a miracle, and that a padre . . . No! No!

SARGENTO: Please, mister, they've been defeated, disillusioned, too often, they're near the end of their rope—(*Pause. Monsignor's face reveals the contradictory forces within himself. Sargento notices the crucifix, walks hesitantly to it*) Why, I think I would even . . . (*As he begins to kneel before the cross, Monsignor suddenly cries out*)

MONSIGNOR: No, no, no! This is absurd! Absurd!

SARGENTO: (*Turning; flaring up*) Damn you! What good are padres if you don't speed the dying or help the living? Damn the whole damned lot of you!

MONSIGNOR: You dare talk like that to a priest of God?

SARGENTO: So *that's* what God's for? To hide behind when you're in trouble? But when His *people* are in trouble, when He shoves a job right into your hands, you cross your arms and sit back, because you're afraid of the risks, afraid others will laugh at you, afraid . . . ! (*He goes up to the crucifix, shouts*) I don't believe in God! But from what I've heard, He was not afraid, whoever He was! And a man that takes refuge behind skirts doesn't have the right to call himself His servant! (*He snatches crucifix from wall*)

MONSIGNOR: (*Shaken*) You put that cross back in its place! (*Sargento looks defiantly at him*) I said put that cross in its place!

(*Outside, the people are coming down the street to offer their thanks for the "miracle." Thereza rushes into the house with a jug of water*)

THEREZA: (*Reverently*) Oh, *senhor padre!* I've just heard!

The miracle! It's so wonderful! (*Finally sees Sargento*) Sargento! What are you doing with that cross? Did it fall? Here, let me put it back . . . (*She takes the crucifix from him. Monsignor follows it with his eyes, as if they were glued to it. As she passes Monsignor, she notices this, stops*) It *is* beautiful. (*An idea*) If my mother'd been alive, after what you've done for us, I know she would . . . (*Pressing it into his hand*) Take it! It's yours!

(*Monsignor holds it at arm's length, transfixed, as the people suddenly burst into the room and, seeing him with the crucifix in his hand, they all kneel down, as he goes on staring at it, as if in a trance*)

The Lights Fade

Scene Six

The following day.

Beto is whistling while vigorously sweeping the street in front of the Tendinha. Thereza and Sargento are seated on the doorsteps of the house, talking inaudibly. After a moment, Bastos opens the window over counter.

BASTOS: (*Surprised*) All finished?

BETO: (*Puts broom aside*) An' now I'm goin' over to the Banhadinho an' feed Figurinha. I promised Nhô Jango I'd give 'im a hand, he bein' so busy arrangin' for the procession.

BASTOS: It's Monday, already. People be arrivin' soon. (*Lightly*) You sure work hard, when you work.

BETO: What's the use of workin' when it don't get you no place? But now luck's turnin' our way, since th' Lawd come 'round.

BASTOS: Imagine how close He must have been, to help the *senhor reverendo* untwist that neck of Aleixo's after twenty years. Here, have a drink, Beto.

BETO: No. (*Smiles*) Goin' to save ev'ry *centavo* now fo' th' Negro chile. You don't think I'm goin' to sit waitin' for that lot'ry while Sancha's belly's blowin' up like a balloon, do you?

BASTOS: Oh, just one.

BETO: Say, you tryin' to get back th' money you pay me for cleanin' up?

BASTOS: (*Grandly*) On the house!

BETO: (*Touched*) Bastos, you're really a white man with Negro's soul. But no drink, thanks. Got a chile to think of.

BASTOS: Well, thought maybe one drink. To celebrate for our children that's coming soon.

BETO: You don't mean you goin' to send fo' the kids, from Portugal?

BASTOS: Where else? Not from Africa! (*Beto slaps his back, laughing. Bastos laughs, happy at his new decision. Doutô enters, stops as he hears the laughter; goes and silently sits down in his usual chair*) Ah, good morning, Doutô! (*Doutô looks sideways at him, surprised at the unusual greeting. A flute and an accordian are heard a short distance away, off-key, but playing merrily*) Say, old Aleixo's not losing no time.

BETO: Now we'll have a band Sundays, an' dances!

BASTOS: It's their first practice. Go and see.

BETO: (*Now conscious of responsibility*) I got to go feed Figurinha first. (*He leaves*)

BASTOS: (*Calls*) Beer, as usual, eh, Doutô?

(*Doutô does not reply. Bastos shrugs, continues his work behind counter. The music rises in the wind. Doutô turns his face to it, stares strangely. Then, suddenly he turns brusquely away from it and rubs his face*)

DOUTÔ: Ahhh . . . (*Rises*) Guess I'll take some Urodonal myself.

(*He goes. A moment later, Monsignor comes down the the street, followed by Tonico. Monsignor has changed con-*

siderably; the inner restlessness is now gone. Sargento promptly rises, awkwardly stands away from the door. Thereza also rises)

MONSIGNOR: Thank you, Tonico. And come back as soon as you have had your supper.

TONICO: Yes, *senhor padre.* (*Goes*)

MONSIGNOR: Good evening.

THEREZA: Good evening, *senhor padre.*

SARGENTO: Good evening . . . *senhor.*

MONSIGNOR: Any luck today with those—phosphates?

SARGENTO: Well, no. But I'll find 'em yet.

MONSIGNOR: You *will.* (*Sargento's eyes brighten. Monsignor goes in*)

THEREZA: (*Concerned*) Don't you think he looks tired?

SARGENTO: I s'pose visiting sick people from morning to night . . .

THEREZA: He's such a good man. (*Then, touching his hand*) If only *he* could . . .

SARGENTO: (*Shrugs*) Oh, well, since people got to be married by a padre . . .

(*Thereza smiles happily as she goes into the house. Sargento gazes after her for a moment, then hastens in the direction of the music. The lights fade on the street and come up immediately in the house. Monsignor is sitting at the table, his breviary in hand. Thereza comes in from kitchen with a tin tray containing a pot of coffee and a small cup*)

THEREZA: Here's your coffee, *senhor padre.* (*She places it on table*)

MONSIGNOR: Oh, thank you, my child. Ummm, it smells good. (*Thereza smiles, pleased. He sips. Leans back, tired but contented. He pauses a moment, then speaks warmly, reflectively*) You know, this is like holidays when I was a boy.

THEREZA: Oh, but you've been working so hard.

MONSIGNOR: I used to work very hard, too, then. Climbing trees, jumping fences, swimming . . . (*Smiles*) . . . and occasionally getting a black eye. You think that's not hard work? (*Thereza laughs*) You know, it is good to be with people again.

THEREZA: You must see many in a big city.

MONSIGNOR: No, I don't. Mine is one of those jobs where one sees more paper than people.

THEREZA: (*After a moment*) Will you *have* to go after the procession?

MONSIGNOR: After? Well . . . Oh, let us think of after—afterwards! (*They both laugh. An automobile horn is heard*)

THEREZA: What's that?

MONSIGNOR: (*Sitting up*) Do cars sometimes come into Campina?

THEREZA: Rarely. It's more than three miles off the main road.

MONSIGNOR: Oh, well, it's really none of our business, we are not traffic inspectors, are we, Thereza? Here, will you pour me some more coffee?

THEREZA: (*Pours, accidentally spills some on his soutane*) Oh, I'm sorry!

MONSIGNOR: That's all right, Thereza. It won't show on the black-cloth. (*Padre Manuel enters, flustered*) What a surprise, Padre Manuel. I was not expecting you so soon.

PADRE MANUEL: I had to return immediately. It's most urgent, Your Reverence!

MONSIGNOR: Oh, Thereza, I wonder if you would go and see if supper is ready. I *am* hungry.

(*Thereza smiles faintly, goes*)

MONSIGNOR: (*Lightly*) You should not forget that discretion is a precious virtue, Padre Manuel, even if you did seem to have forgotten it in São Paulo.

PADRE MANUEL: Oh, but Your Reverence, I told the Bishop exactly what you asked me to and everything was quite all right: Dom Camara thought it most natural that you should have wanted to rest here a few days before going to São Paulo. After all, he knows only too well of Your Reverence's nervous condition. He even said they would postpone the council meeting a few days, and for Your Reverence not to leave before you felt quite well—and sent his greetings, too, when . . . when . . . (*Tremulously*) Oh, but it wasn't my fault, really!

MONSIGNOR: What happened?

PADRE MANUEL: The driver. Yes, Your Reverence, this time it was only the driver! (*He produces a folded newspaper*)

MONSIGNOR: What is that? You don't mean . . . ? (*He slowly takes the newspaper*)

PADRE MANUEL: If it hadn't been for *that,* this thing would not have been more than a local matter, as Your Reverence had hoped for. But you know the practice in São Paulo; the evening tabloids awarding prizes for the best amateur scoop? You just phone and . . . (*As Monsignor turns the pages*) No, Your Reverence. Front Page.

MONSIGNOR: What? (*Reads, aghast*) "Miracle in Small Village" . . . (*Slowly lowers newspaper*) It's not possible!

PADRE MANUEL: The situation is extremely delicate, as Your Reverence will no doubt realize. This newspaper has an enormous circulation and a thing like this, as Dom Camara says, is bound to entail . . . eh . . . very definite commitments on the part of those concerned. (*Promptly*) Those were the Bishop's own words. (*The kitchen door half opens. Thereza is about to come out, stops, stands in doorway, unseen*) It is really most unfortunate, so the sooner you leave . . .

MONSIGNOR: But—I have promised them a procession!

PADRE MANUEL: That is out of the question! I'm afraid Your Reverence hasn't quite realized the gravity . . . Dom Camara considers the situation so serious that, well, unless Monsignor consents to leave immediately, he feels compelled to transmit his orders . . .

MONSIGNOR: (*Jumping up*) Orders? (*Thereza withdraws into kitchen and quietly closes door*)

PADRE MANUEL: The situation is most pressing, especially in view of the fact that . . .

(*Nhô Jango peers in through the front door, then steps in*)

NHÔ JANGO: Good evenin', *senhor padre.* (*To Padre Man-*

uel) I see you're back for the procession. (*Then, sensing something*) I hope I'm not interruptin'?

PADRE MANUEL: You most certainly are!

MONSIGNOR: You are *not* interrupting. What can I do for you, Nhô Jango?

NHÔ JANGO: (*A bit surprised*) Why, I come like you told me to—to set the day an' time for the procession.

PADRE MANUEL: But Your Reverence!

MONSIGNOR: Padre Manuel, would you mind letting *me* handle this? (*To Nhô Jango*) Now about this procession. (*With an effort*) Do you think we could have it . . . perhaps some other time?

NHÔ JANGO: Some other . . . ? You mean a day or two later? (*He gazes anxiously at Monsignor*)

MONSIGNOR: (*Hesitantly*) Well . . . (*A moment*) Maybe very soon, then? Tomorrow, early tomorrow morning?

NHÔ JANGO: Well, if the *senhor padre* really wants it tomorrow. But we was fig'rin' the day after.

PADRE MANUEL: But that's . . . (*Monsignor gives him a severe look. He sinks into a chair*)

NHÔ JANGO: You see, there'll be people comin' from the 'piahy banks, others way out from the Aterradinho, an' they wouldn't get here before day after . . . An' there's the tall candles. Chico Luz, he gone over to Angatuba to get 'em an' he won't be back 'fore tomorrow evenin'. It's us men folk carry them, the tall candles, I mean, at the back of the procession. (*As he describes the procession, he seems to see it passing before him*) The women go in the middle, the rosaries 'round their hands, prayin' out loud. An' the bells begin to ring. An' the children go in front, carryin' the little common candles. Then the oldest one in Campina that can still walk—it'll be Geraldo Rufino seein' old Caicó's near dyin'—he carry the standard of the Sacred Heart of Jesus, with two men beside him, for guard of honor. (*Impressively*) An' way in front goes the *senhor padre,* all dressed in the white silk robe that Maria Protozio's mendin' specially. An' the procession goes 'round the nearest fields, as far as Carlos Cantidio's place, an' from there it starts to come back slowly. Then ev'ryone begins singin' out loud all the way into church. And when they get there, ev'rybody kneel down an' shut up while the *senhor padre* take the standard from Geraldo Rufino an' carry it all the way up to the altar. An' the bells, they will be ringin' up in the tower, to thank the good Lord for what He want to give us . . . (*Monsignor is deeply moved; after a moment*) But, of course, it's the *senhor padre* that sets the day.

MONSIGNOR: (*Quietly*) The day is set. Day after tomorrow. (*Padre Manuel turns to him, silently pleading*) I think we really *should* have the tall candles.

PADRE MANUEL: Please, Your Reverence! (*Monsignor gives him a severe look. Nhô Jango feels something is wrong. He takes a good look at Monsignor*)

NHÔ JANGO: Excuse me, are you feelin' well?

PADRE MANUEL: His Reverence is ill! He's already had one heart attack and if he becomes worried . . .

NHÔ JANGO: (*Distressed*) Oh, *senhor cura!*

MONSIGNOR: Nonsense. That was years ago. I am better than ever now. Anything else, Nhô Jango?

NHÔ JANGO: No, thank you.

MONSIGNOR: (*Shaking hands*) Goodbye, then.

NHÔ JANGO: Goodbye. An' God bless you. (*He leaves*)

PADRE MANUEL: Monsignor Andrada, if you'd only let me explain to you the whole situation . . .

MONSIGNOR: (*Not listening*) Do you know, Padre, I have the strange impression that most of my life I was another person, as if I had been dreaming—and now've just awakened.

PADRE MANUEL: (*Carefully*) Has Your Reverence considered that perhaps it's the other way 'round?

(*The wind is howling outside*)

MONSIGNOR: (*Absorbed in thought*) I feel that there are two planes of life, really, and the one we call reality is only the one we have chosen to live, the one we *thought* was the easiest.

PADRE MANUEL: (*Warily, but relentlessly*) Monsignor. It is quite understandable you should be so moved. As a high administrator Your Reverence has not been exposed to all this misery and suffering, which is quite common, really. And having a kind heart . . .

MONSIGNOR: Do *you* think so?

PADRE MANUEL: (*Sincerely*) Certainly. Still you must not forget that Monsignor is placing himself and the church in a very difficult position.

MONSIGNOR: Have you thought of the very difficult position in which these people find themselves, even if it be—quite common?

PADRE MANUEL: But that is the sad lot of this life. And if God has meant it this way . . .

MONSIGNOR: No! God could *not* have meant life to be such a failure!

PADRE MANUEL: I suppose it's men who've made it this way, then.

MONSIGNOR: Then it is high time men should start making it *His* way, to the image *He* had in mind. Think of the power He has given us: to kill or to give birth—to disfigure the face of the earth or to perform miracles every day!

PADRE MANUEL: As to *that,* Your Reverence, the Bishop instructed me to tell you that, before you leave, you are to make a public statement to Campina saying that the mi . . . that it was *not* a miracle.

MONSIGNOR: (*Astonished*) He told you that? (*Padre Manuel nods, worried*) No, no, *no!*

PADRE MANUEL: But if Monsignor himself doesn't believe it to have been a miracle . . . ?

MONSIGNOR: What difference does it make *what* you call it? (*Recalling*) "I know life when I see it," Sargento said. *That* is what matters! The life that faith brought back, washing the dust off their hearts! (*Moves away*) "He that believeth unto Me, out of his innermost being shall flow torrents of living waters . . ." (*Turns to Padre Manuel*) Doesn't the Bishop know that? It is Scripture.

PADRE MANUEL: I suppose the Bishop does, but will the committee of reporters know it?

MONSIGNOR: What are you talking about?

PADRE MANUEL: The newspaper has organized a committee of reporters to investigate. (*Picks up newspaper, reads*) "Living up to our principle, we will spare no effort or sacrifice to give our readers the benefits of *truth*." (*Puts newspaper down*)

MONSIGNOR: Truth? The world does not want truth. It's blood they want! It's the dream—the life that has emerged out of the dusty plane they call reality that they want. To nose out, to laugh at, to trample back into the dust! They trample down life in the name of truth, as if both were not ultimately the same thing! (*He is exultant, but Padre Manuel is only concerned with the immediate; consults watch, urgently*)

PADRE MANUEL: There is no time to lose, Your Reverence! The church *must* define its position clearly *before* the reporters arrive tomorrow.

MONSIGNOR: Let them come. I will be here to meet them!

PADRE MANUEL: But what are *you* going to say?

MONSIGNOR: I don't know. (*Then, with sudden inspiration*) "Take no thought, how or what you shall speak, for it shall be given you in that same hour, what you shall speak . . ."

PADRE MANUEL: But Monsignor, the Bishop has sent you *formal orders!*

MONSIGNOR: I have *higher* orders!

PADRE MANUEL: How, Your Reverence, how can you be *absolutely* sure? Everything that has happened here is only natural, considering the circumstances. That is what Monsignor himself said, just before being caught up in this . . . this whirlwind of excitement that hasn't permitted Your Reverence a moment to think clearly! Your Reverence has been working like a slave, not sleeping properly, tiring himself to exhaustion. And both your ailing nerves and your emotions have been subject to a tremendous strain by so much misery, such frantic expectations. All this has taken outsized proportions in Monsignor's feverish state of mind, believe me. (*The wind howls, reaching its peak; the door is blown open*) And this exasperating wind! It's enough to drive anyone crazy! (*He slams the door shut, turns, apologetically*) Oh, pardon me, Your Reverence, but I can't help it. I'm becoming a bundle of nerves myself, it's really telling! (*Notices Monsignor's hands trembling*) Why, look at your hands, Monsignor, they are shaking! (*Monsignor lifts up one hand, stares at it*) And wouldn't it be a terrible thing to put the church into . . . such a delicate position . . . expose yourself so openly, and fan any further the expectations of the villagers only to find out in the end that perhaps you had made a mistake?

MONSIGNOR: (*Distantly*) Mistake?

PADRE MANUEL: Think how easily the imagination takes off, and how quickly it drops back!

MONSIGNOR: (*To himself, the awful memories resurging*) The ridicule, the cruel laughter . . . (*As he lowers his trembling hand, it is another man who appears—tired, haggard, haunted*) My God! Could I have exposed these miserable people to . . . such a monstrous disappointment? (*Rises*) To such a colossal lie?

PADRE MANUEL: You mustn't get too excited, Your Reverence. Please sit down. Remember what Doctor Lacerda said. Your heart and your nerves—no strain, no worries.

MONSIGNOR: (*Moves about, desperately*) That first time by the mud pond . . . *was* it a voice? (*The wind gradually is dying away*) Did I *hear* it? Oh, that laughter . . . the children . . . the entire village . . . If I could only . . . (*Suddenly*) But what *is* truth? Do you know? Is it the disenchantment of derision? Is it all that disappoints and frustrates? Or is it . . . ? (*He gazes at his trembling hands*) Is it only the overwrought nerves of an emotional fool? We are *all* fools! Children, journalists, priests! And *how* can fools ever be certain of *anything?* How . . . ? (*He has reached the limit of his physical strength and sinks into a chair*)

PADRE MANUEL: Oh, Monsignor Andrada, you mustn't take it so hard. Everything will be all right again as soon as we leave here. (*Tonico rushes in, stops abruptly as he sees the haggard look on Monsignor's face*) What do you want? (*Tonico just stammers, unable to speak*) Go away, will you? Can't you see His Reverence is not well?

MONSIGNOR: (*With an effort*) What is it, Tonico?

TONICO: It's . . . it's old Caicó.

MONSIGNOR: Oh? (*Then*) Do you think we could . . . go a little later?

TONICO: They say he waiting for you 'fore he die.

MONSIGNOR: (*Rises, wearily*) Let us go then. (*He gets his hat*)

PADRE MANUEL: But, Your Reverence! It's very urgent!

MONSIGNOR: So are the sacraments for a dying man! (*Monsignor and Tonico go, leaving Padre Manuel in a state*)

The Lights Fade

Scene Seven

That night. A faint light from an oil lamp on the Tendinha's counter sends eerie shadows across the faces of Bastos, Beto and Zeca, who are silently awaiting Monsignor's return, alternately looking up the street and curiously at Thereza, who stands nervously by the door.

BASTOS: (*After a moment*) He's taking a long time . . .

ZECA: Those Caicós is as stubborn to die as they is to live.

BASTOS: (*Crosses to Thereza*) What's the matter, feeling sick? (*She shakes her head*) Quarrel with Sargento? (*Same*) Then why are you . . . ?

THEREZA: (*Suddenly cries out*) Leave me alone! Leave me alone!

BASTOS: (*Surprised*) Say, I didn't do nothing.

THEREZA: Neither did I! Neither did I! I swear! But I couldn't help hearing, I just couldn't help it!

(*Beto and Zeca cross to them. Aleixo enters*)

BASTOS: Hearing?

THEREZA: They were saying . . .

ALEIXO: Who was saying what?

THEREZA: The Monsignor—and the other one.

ALEIXO: (*Uneasily*) *What* was they saying?

THEREZA: (*Dazed*) I don't know. Something about going away. And they were angry.

ZECA: (*Anxiously*) Angry?

THEREZA: (*Nods*) He said, "The sooner you go." And something about "Orders. Orders. Orders!"

ZECA: *Who* said that?

THEREZA: Padre Manuel.

ZECA: You sure?

ALEIXO: Are you? (*Thereza nods*) My God! (*Then, slowly*) They want to take him away!

BETO: Who want to take 'im away?

BASTOS: You think it could be the other one who . . . ?

ZECA: *Before* the procession?

BETO: He can't!

THEREZA: (*Bursts into tears*) It's all my fault! My fault! Oh, God, please don't punish me, by taking him away! Please! (*She rushes into the house. The others remain silent for a moment, extremely worried and baffled*)

ALEIXO: But *why?* Why they'd want to take him away?

NHÔ JANGO: (*Enters*) Good evenin', everybody.

ZECA: (*Musingly*) Think he'll stay?

NHÔ JANGO: God never leaves. It's people that . . .

BETO: He means the *senhor cura*. For th' procession.

NHÔ JANGO: Didn't I tell you it was all set? You people sure don't deserve all that God give you, never trusting Him . . .

BASTOS: But Thereza, she heard them talking 'bout him going.

NHÔ JANGO: Going? (*Then*) Well, I suppose some day he'll have to go, and we'll sure miss him.

ALEIXO: *Before* the procession!

NHÔ JANGO: Haven't I told you . . . ?

ALEIXO: But . . .

NHÔ JANGO: And what the *senhor cura* say he do, he do.

BETO: Even if the other say fo' him to go?

NHÔ JANGO: (*As they turn expectantly to him*) The other one was there when he looked at me and said: day after tomorrow. Yes, he looked at me . . . (*Reflectively*) He looked . . . not quite himself, come to think of it . . .

BETO: It's the other one's fault, come upset 'im. Damn him!

ZECA: That fat-faced bastard!

NHÔ JANGO: (*Pensively*) . . . Not quite himself, he didn't. (*Then*) Oh, well, he's tired, that's all. He *must* be, after all the work he's been doin'.

BASTOS: That's what I say! He's just tired.

ALEIXO: And you think he'll stay?

ZECA: Didn't you hear Nhô Jango?

BETO: Then he won't let us down?

NHÔ JANGO: 'Course he won't. (*Pause*) Maybe that's what's troubling him, though.

BETO: What?

NHÔ JANGO: That he's *got* to go, and we're keepin' him here.

BASTOS: He should know *himself* if he got to go. He's a padre of God, isn't he?

ZECA: The other one's a padre of God, too, no?

BASTOS: But with no purple sash like him!

ZECA: Yes, but *he* just come from the city.

BETO: (*Recalling*) "Orders," Thereza said. "Orders!"

ALEIXO: (*Bewildered*) What you aimin' at? What's all this mean? (*He looks imploringly at each of them*) Won't someone tell me what's this all *mean?*

(*They are very concerned now and instinctively turn to Nhô Jango who is lost in deep thought*)

ZECA: Jeesus, I wish he'd come back . . .

BASTOS: And tell us . . .

ALEIXO: (*With growing anxiety*) It's gettin' late! Why don't he come back? We gotta know . . . We gotta know what's this all about.

(*Their faces now are all turned to the street. The lights go down, and when they come up again it is dawn. They have remained there all night. Suddenly, Monsignor appears at the end of the street. Exceptionally tired and preoccupied, he doesn't notice the little group*)

ZECA: (*Starts*) Here he comes!

(*They scramble to their feet and go up to meet him. Monsignor just nods to them, proceeds to the house and goes in. They stare at the closed door, then turn to each other*)

ZECA: Jeesus, he looked worried!

BETO: Didn't even speak to us!

BASTOS: Maybe he's angry. Maybe . . . (*Baffled*) I don't know.

ALEIXO: Why didn't you ask him? We waited all night . . .

BETO: Why didn't *you?*

ALEIXO: Me? I . . . I don't know. He looked so peculiar, I . . .

BASTOS: Death pale, he was.

ZECA: (*Suddenly*) There *is* something wrong! (*All turn promptly to him*)

BASTOS: What's wrong?

BETO: You mean . . . ? (*A tense pause*)

ALEIXO: C'mon, say what you mean, for God's sake, man!

ZECA: Eh . . . (*Vainly struggles to put the feeling into words*) Ah, I don't know what it is. But I know *something's* wrong!

(*The others follow his eyes as he looks toward the house, then down at Nhô Jango who remains deep in thought. The lights dim and come up in the house. Monsignor enters and sits, exhausted. Padre Manuel is asleep in a chair*)

MONSIGNOR: (*After a moment; quietly*) Good morning, Padre Manuel.

PADRE MANUEL: (*Awakens, with a little start*) Oh, good morning, Monsignor. Did Your Reverence sleep well? (*Notices his exhaustion*) But Monsignor! You haven't slept at all! You must be very, *very* tired. I waited up for you till after two and I must have fallen asleep.

MONSIGNOR: Evidently.

PADRE MANUEL: (*Concerned*) Would Your Reverence like to rest a bit? (*Monsignor shakes his head slowly*) I will get you some black coffee, then.

MONSIGNOR: No, thank you. (*Meditatively*) They served me coffee all night, with little flour cakes. They didn't know what to do, they were so pleased I could be there at his last moments. He died like a candle, a tall candle. "I'm not afraid to die," he said, "now that God's back in Campina, and He will take care of my family." (*A moment*) Then he said, "Only I didn't want to die just yet, now that things are picking up so good in Campina!"

PADRE MANUEL: (*Polite, but firm*) Monsignor is very tired. And must not strain his emotions, or his heart. (*He gently draws him to the corner chair*) Now I will let Your Reverence rest a good hour before we leave for São Paulo.

(*Monsignor does not answer; he has permitted Padre Manuel to take over. The lights go down in the house, come up on the street. The men are staring at the door*)

NHÔ JANGO: (*Reaches a decision*) I think we got to let him go!

ALL: Go? Him? Before the procession?

NHÔ JANGO: If the church want him to . . .

BETO: Ain't they got plenty padres in the city?

NHÔ JANGO: Church is God's. She know best.

ZECA: You said what he say he do, he do.

NHÔ JANGO: Ay, that's why we must tell 'im to go. Poor man, that's why he was lookin' so broken up. We sure put him in a tough spot, and after all he done for us.

BETO: But th' procession?

ZECA: How we goin' to have rain without . . . ?

NHÔ JANGO: Well, there's still water to drink—and even if it takes another few weeks to rain, you'll still harvest enough for your needs. (*A sudden thought*) Hasn't all Campina been happy since we got the miracle? (*All agree*) And if we don't get the procession, we *still* got the miracle, don't we?

ZECA: Yes, but if I could sell some of that crop of beans, too . . .

ALEIXO: And turnips . . .

NHÔ JANGO: There's no room in a man's heart for God and for more beans than he can eat. (*Suddenly*) Would you like the miracle to disappear?

ZECA: What?

ALEIXO: But *how* can the miracle disappear?

NHÔ JANGO: Dunno. But if you're *that* set on beans or turnips, or anything else, *that* will sure crowd God way out of your hearts, just like it done before. An' if God goes, the miracle goes, too, I sup'ose, for I never heard of no miracle without God.

(*The train whistle is heard. They silently exchange looks*)

ZECA: Jeesus!

BETO: (*Sadly*) Guess Nhô Jango's right. We don't want to lose th' miracle.

NHÔ JANGO: Let's go tell him.

ZECA: (*A last attempt*) We can't *tell* 'im to go. Wouldn't be polite, would it? We just say to him he can go, if he wants.

NHÔ JANGO: You can't fool God, *cumpadre*. He's listenin' to your heart. Come on.

(*They trudge across the street behind Nhô Jango. He mounts steps, pauses uncertainly, then knocks. Lights up in the house. Monsignor is in exactly the same position. Padre Manuel is closing the suitcase. He comes and opens door slightly*)

PADRE MANUEL: Oh, it's you. His Reverence can't see anyone.

NHÔ JANGO: Please, *senhor padre*. It's very important.

PADRE MANUEL: (*Peremptorily*) He is not well.

NHÔ JANGO: But it's very important what we got to say.

PADRE MANUEL: We? (*Looks out, sees the others*) Wait a minute. (*As he turns to fetch him, Monsignor appears at the door*)

NHÔ JANGO: Good mornin', *senhor cura.* I mean . . .

PADRE MANUEL: Ssshh! Don't interrupt! His Reverence has a communication to make.

MONSIGNOR: (*In a hollow voice, staring ahead*) The church has sent me an order to communicate to the people of Campina that . . . that . . .

NHÔ JANGO: *Senhor padre,* you don't have to say it, we already know it. God bless you for being so good to us. But you can go now. That's what we come to tell you. (*For the first time, Monsignor turns his eyes on them, questioningly*) That's right, *senhor padre.* You can go since the church she want you.

MONSIGNOR: You are telling me to leave . . . ?

ZECA: Not *tellin'* you . . .

NHÔ JANGO: We know you *gotta* leave.

MONSIGNOR: . . . Before the procession?

NHÔ JANGO: You see, *senhor padre,* looks like God's already forgive us, by givin' us a miracle. An' we don't want Him to get mad with us again, maybe go 'way, if He thinks we wantin' too much, keepin' you when you gotta go. So ev'rybody here have decided we keep the miracle, an' God, with us.

MONSIGNOR: You mean, you are willing to give up the *procession?* To exchange rain for . . . ? (*Pause; then, almost exalted by their enormous sacrifice and need for God, he raises his eyes to heaven*) It is *we* who make a lie of Thy promises. It is *we* who forsake Thee in forsaking our neighbors! (*With exultant determination*) I shall remain here! To fulfill Thy promise, Oh God, to give them torrents—torrents of living waters for their great thirst for Thee!

(*A huge shout of joy comes from the men while, inside, Padre Manuel sinks into a chair*)

The Lights Fade

Scene Eight

Wednesday, the morning of the procession.

In the darkness, we hear children singing the last verses of the hymn, "We Want God Who Is Our Life, We Want

God Who Is Our Love," presumably in front of the church, warming up as they wait for the start of the procession.

When the lights come up, Campina is bustling with activity. Bastos is straightening his merchandise. Beto stands on a small ladder gluing paper flags to a string that stretches across from the Tendinha to Aleixo's house. In his excitement to complete it, he drops a large pair of scissors to the ground. Tonico rushes in, rag in hand.

TONICO: (*Excitedly*) The bells! I've f-f-finished cleaning them!

(*Aleixo briskly enters with an armful of large fireworks which he holds with difficulty. Tonico stops, gapes at them*)

ALEIXO: Get out of my way, Tonico. Can't you see I'm in a hurry? (*Tonico steps aside. Aleixo turns, calls*) Hey, Zeca! Where are you?

ZECA: (*Rushes in, his face hidden behind a bundle of fireworks*) Here I am! Say, is the church still far?

ALEIXO: We're nearly there. Come on, let's go. (*They hurry out, followed by Tonico*)

BETO: (*Again drops scissors*) Don't know why my hands is tremblin' so. Maybe it's th' water I been drinkin'!

(*Sargento passes through, carefully carrying a clean shirt in one hand, a basin of water in the other, as a boy comes running in from the opposite direction and almost bumps into him*)

SARGENTO: Look out where you're goin', boy! (*Goes*)

BOY: (*Calls to Bastos*) The procession, *senhor,* where she start from?

BASTOS: The church. Down the street and turn right.

BOY: (*Going*) *'brigado!*

BETO: (*A final touch*) There. (*Stepping down*) Now I go feed Figurinha.

(*Monsignor Gusmão, very brisk and determined, enters. He stops, looks rapidly around, frowns as he sees the paper flags. Padre Manuel follows, breathlessly*)

MONSIGNOR GUSMÃO: Where *is* this house?

PADRE MANUEL: Right here, Your Reverence.

(*Bastos and Beto look intently at them*)

BASTOS: (*Calls*) Ay, *senhor padre!* (*Padre Manuel turns*) He's come for the procession, too? (*Monsignor Gusmão turns and scowls*)

PADRE MANUEL: (*Huffily*) Ssshh!

(*Monsignor Gusmão and Padre Manuel go into the house. An old man passes through with a bunch of lollipops for sale*)

BETO: (*Impulsively*) I'll start off your day, Bastos. (*Bastos turns, surprised*) Here, and I'll pay fo' it. (*Tosses coin on counter*)

BASTOS: But I thought . . . ?

BETO: Doutô say Portuguez don't think! (*Then*) Just a little one, eh?

BASTOS: (*Just realizing it*) Say, the wind's stopped.

BETO: An' not a cloud.

BASTOS: Ah, but this time we don't need clouds. It's the procession going to bring the rain.

BETO: Bastos! You think . . . ? (*He stops*)

BASTOS: What?

BETO: (*Quickly*) Oh, nothin'. Give me that drink, will you? (*As Bastos pours; uneasily*) You think he should 'ave stayed?

BASTOS: You mean he should have *gone,* when they call him?

BETO: When the church call 'im, we said he could go, didn't we? An' we'd keep th' miracle.

BASTOS: But *he* said he'd stay, and bring torrents of rain.

BETO: (*Confused*) Yes, but if th' church is God's—like Nhô Jango say—how can th' church she want 'im to go and God He want 'im to stay?

BASTOS: What you mean?

BETO: (*Gulps down his drink; then, darkly*) 'Ceptin' it *wasn't* God . . . wasn't God all th' time but . . .

(*Doutô has come in, unnoticed*)

DOUTÔ: Nor God, nor the devil. Think *they* would get mixed up with anything down here? (*Laughs*)

BASTOS: (*Very worried*) There's a new padre come from the city, Doutô. Purple sash, too. Seemed angry.

DOUTÔ: Purple sash, eh? (*Then*) Yes, nobody can help corpses. But you *can* leave them alone. It stinks less that way. (*Pause*) That's what *he* should have done.

BASTOS: He gave us a miracle, didn't he?

DOUTÔ: (*Cynically*) "The Lord giveth and the Lord taketh away . . ." Silly game to play, if you have any dignity. (*Sits*) Bastos, give me a cupful of methylic alcohol—that's *cachaça* in Greek.

BASTOS: (*Surprised*) Beer, you mean?

DOUTÔ: *Cachaça!* Double. I know what I mean! Think I'm a fool like the rest of you? (*Gulps drink down*) Another double, Bastos.

BASTOS: Think you should, Doutô?

DOUTÔ: I *know* I should! I know everything, Bastos, too much. (*Belches*) I have culture, which puts me at the top of the ladder. And I can see everything. Void above, void below. And the next step, from the top of the ladder, logically, is to jump into the void, the one below, of course, seeing there's a law that pulls you down—and none that I know of that lifts you up, except the wind, maybe, for a few days. (*Laughs painfully*)

BETO: (*Moves to him*) You laughin' at us?

DOUTÔ: The only laugh is on oneself! (*Belches*) Preserves dignity. (*Pause*) Look! The wind! It has stopped, of course. (*He sinks his head onto the table and laughs, a smothered sob of one who does not know how to cry. Beto and Bastos stare at him uneasily. Thereza enters*)

THEREZA: (*Anxiously*) Where is Sargento? Isn't he here?

BASTOS: No. What's happened.

THEREZA: (*Going*) Nothing. Nothing.

BETO: I got to go feed Figurinha. Promised Nhô Jango. (*He starts to go, stops, impulsively returns to counter*) First, give me 'nother, Bastos. A small double.

(*Bastos pours. Sancha enters, carrying clean, folded garments*)

BETO: Hey, Sancha! (*She stops, smiles, as he puts arm around her*) You the prettiest *mulatta* I ever seen! (*He holds her tightly*)

SANCHA: Please! Got to take this to th' church.

BETO: (*Kissing her neck*) Ah, there's plenty time. (*Paws her breasts*) First give me a little kiss! (*He hugs her tighter, his face close to hers*)

SANCHA: (*Smells his breath*) You been drinkin' again, you good-for-nothin' nigger! (*She struggles to break away*)

BETO: Drink or no drink, you're my woman an' I can kiss you when I likes. I can lay you when I . . . (*In the struggle, the garments fall to the ground*)

SANCHA: (*Distressed*) The padre's clothes, for the procession! Look what you done! (*She picks up garments, attempts to brush off the dust; ominously*) Mean bad luck, lettin' padre's clothes fall on th' ground! (*She goes off*)

BETO: Ahh, dammit, I ain't no superstitious slave! (*Goes*)

BASTOS: (*Putting bottle away*) Will you keep an eye on things, Doutô, while I wash up for the . . . ? (*Sees Doutô is asleep*) Oh, never mind. (*He disappears*)

DOUTÔ: (*Stirs; hazily*) Celebrate. Celebrate . . . before it's too late. (*He reaches out for drink; spills it*) Why is it *always* too late, mother? (*Pathetically*) Mother, where are you? (*Gets up, looks around, swaying*) Where did they send you when they brought me to life? (*Bitterly*) Life! Why didn't they send *me* instead, blundering fools! What do doctors know? *No one* knows! There is nothing to know. (*Wearily*) Nothing but high pressure and low pressure. Where are you? They say mothers have the answer. (*Desperately*) Then tell me, where does it all end up? *Where?* (*He sees Thereza walking past; softly*) So you *have* come back, to give me the answer! (*He goes to her, as if in a trance*)

THEREZA: What answer, Doutô?

DOUTÔ: A beautiful answer! It *must* be beautiful from one so beautiful . . . (*He kneels down and embraces her legs, reverently*)

THEREZA: Let me go! Please let me go!

DOUTÔ: Don't go! Don't! Not before you tell me!

(*Sargento enters*)

SARGENTO: What the devil . . .

THEREZA: Sargento! Help!

(*Sargento tears Doutô away. He lunges back*)

DOUTÔ: Don't go before you tell me! (*For an answer, he gets a powerful blow from Sargento which sends him sprawling face forward onto the ground*)

THEREZA: (*Bursts into tears*) Oh, Sargento, I'm afraid!

SARGENTO: (*Consolingly*) Don't worry! He can't hurt you now.

THEREZA: I'm afraid! (*She rushes into the house, sobbing*)

BASTOS: (*Returns*) What's happened? (*Sees Doutô*) I told him not to drink *cachaça!*

(*He pours water on Doutô's head. Doutô sits up, painfully, face covered with dust, then slowly rises, wiping blood off his mouth*)

SARGENTO: If you try to touch her again, I'll . . .

DOUTÔ: (*Stares vacantly*) There *is* no answer. (*He drags himself away with a pathetic attempt to preserve some of his dignity. Bastos shakes his head, sadly, and goes behind counter*)

SARGENTO: (*Uneasily*) I—I'd better change my shirt.

(*He leaves as Nhô Jango enters with several very long candles in his arms, followed by Tonico*)

NHÔ JANGO: (*Excitedly*) They've come!

BASTOS: Just those?

NHÔ JANGO: No. Have already given out the others. (*Happily*) You should see the crowd in front of the church!

TONICO: Can I—I go to the bells now?

NHÔ JANGO: In a minute, Tonico. Go and call Doutô. Then, as soon as the *senhor cura* come out the door you can go.

(*Tonico leaves. Nhô Jango hands candle to Bastos*) Here, this is yours. And this is for Beto. (*Remembering*) Did he go feed Figurinha?

BASTOS: Think so.

NHÔ JANGO: Ah, I always knew Beto was a good man. (*Hands him the other candles*) Here, Bastos, take these. May be some latecomers. (*He straightens his tattered jacket, removes straw hat*) Now I go to call the *senhor cura.*

BASTOS: (*Holding him back*) Don't!

NHÔ JANGO: (*Curiously*) Why not? Eh?

(*Aleixo and Zeca enter*)

ALEIXO: We've already taken the fireworks to the church!

NHÔ JANGO: (*To Bastos*) What's the matter? Come on, out with it, man!

BASTOS: Don't go in there!

ALEIXO: What's wrong?

BASTOS: Another padre has come from the city. Purple sash, too. And angry! They're all in there now. (*Nhô Jango slowly turns toward the house*)

ALEIXO: Maybe he come for the procession? (*Silence; then, fearfully*) What's goin' to happen?

NHÔ JANGO: (*Holding candle firmly; meditatively*) Wait . . . An' trust God.

ALEIXO: (*Revolting*) We goin' to wait while in there . . . ? (*Then, emptily*) *Wait!* Old age *won't* wait. (*All seem to take the same positions as in the first scene, as if they now were awakening from a dream, sinking back into despair*)

BASTOS: Seven years I been waiting.

ZECA: Jeesus.

ALEIXO: Wait.

BASTOS: Seven years. And just when it looked like . . .

ZECA: (*Cries out*) Jeesus Christ!

(*The train whistle is heard; they all turn in its direction. The spell is broken by Tonico, who rushes in, terrified*)

TONICO: D-d-d-Doutô! Doutô!

BASTOS: Can't you see he's not here, idiot!

TONICO: Dead!

BASTOS: Doutô? (*Incredulously*) But just now . . .

ZECA: Jeesus!

BASTOS: (*As Sargento appears*) Bet I know who kill him!

TONICO: Sleep! Sleep kill him! Told Lasinho he wanted to sleep quick. Took medicine. And he die.

ALEIXO: (*Shudders*) Killed himself!

ZECA: On the day of the procession!

ALEIXO: It's a bad omen!

SARGENTO: Stupid peasants, that's what you all are! It's *idiotic* to be superstitious! (*He sits, wipes sweat off face with shirt sleeve*)

ALEIXO: (*With sudden rage*) Why didn't he go 'way like we told 'im?

BASTOS: (*Nods*) He should've gone, when the church call him.

ALEIXO: Curse him!

NHÔ JANGO: (*Quietly*) Wait. An' trust God.

(*Beto comes rushing in, stops abruptly when he sees Nhô Jango*)

BETO: (*Breathlessly*) 'Twasn't my fault! I swear 'twasn't my fault! (*Nhô Jango looks at him strangely*) Don't look at me that way, Nhô Jango! I went there, jus' like I promise, soon's I finish fixin' the flags. (*He catches Bastos' sharp look*) Why you lookin' at me like that, Portuguez? No white man could 'ave done no better! (*Bastos continues to stare*) I know what you're thinkin', Portuguez son-of-a-bitch! An' if you open your goddamn mouth, I'll . . . (*As he goes menacingly toward Bastos, Nhô Jango grabs hold of him*)

NHÔ JANGO: (*Forebodingly*) What you tryin' to tell me?

BETO: 'Twasn't my fault . . . (*Imploringly*) What could I do, tell me? What could I do? When I got to Banhadinho, jus' her eyes was starin' out of th' black mud!

(*Silence; then Nhô Jango begins to go, shakily, holding on to the long candle for support*)

NHÔ JANGO: (*Desolately*) Mustn't let the crows get the

little creature. God, He must 'ave loved her, too. And now He took her with Him . . .

(*He disappears. An awful pause. Suddenly, Tonico bursts into sobs*)

BETO: Shut up! Shut up, I tell you! (*Tonico moves away, crouches in a corner. Beto storms over to counter*) Double *cachaça!* Quick! (*Bastos pours nervously. Beto snatches the glass, gulps it down*) 'Nother double! (*Banging fist on counter*) Fast, Portuguez son-of-a-bitch, to beat th' dust!

BASTOS: (*Shoves the bottle at him*) Take the whole bottle! Take *all* the goddamn bottles! My business is screwed up anyway!

BETO: Don't yell at me, Portuguez son-of-a-bitch! I'm not afraid of nobody! Of nobody! You, God, or the devil! (*He pounds his fist on the counter as:*)

The Lights Quickly Fade

Scene Nine

(*Inside the house. Monsignor has just finished his account. Monsignor Gusmão seems deeply impressed.*

MONSIGNOR GUSMÃO: (*Slowly*) It is a fantastic story, like a dream. (*Rises*) Yes, a perfect setting to induce all sorts of strange feelings, I admit. (*Kindly*) Still, I feel confident you are well aware of the urgent necessity to make a public clarification of the occurrence.

PADRE MANUEL: The reporters might arrive at any moment now.

MONSIGNOR GUSMÃO: And the church *must* take a definite stand. (*Monsignor remains silent; a note of reproach in his tone*) Have you quite realized to what point your obstinacy has already involved the church?

MONSIGNOR: (*Quietly*) And have you realized to what

point I have involved *them?* (*Rises*) Oh, I know I am wrong. I *must* be wrong if the church thinks differently. I have said that a thousand times to myself. Do you think I was not aware of the consequences, of the enormous dangers?

MONSIGNOR GUSMÃO: Well, I am glad you seem to be . . .

MONSIGNOR: (*Interrupting*) Yet, if you had only felt that dark . . . that irresistible urge.

MONIGNOR GUSMÃO: Andrada, you have extenuating circumstances in your defense, circumstances that would have taxed even a temperament less imaginative and emotional, less subject to . . . eh . . . reveries. (*Monsignor turns suddenly to him*) Do you know it was I who asked the Bishop to be sent here, as soon as I heard what had happened? (*Places hand on Monsignor's shoulder*) Because an old friend, to whom you had confided so much, would be better qualified to help you.

PADRE MANUEL: His Reverence *does* need help. He is not well.

MONSIGNOR GUSMÃO: (*Confronting him, yet kindly*) You have not forgotten that once before you had an analogous false impression?

MONSIGNOR: It was *I* who made it false.

MONSIGNOR GUSMÃO: But remember what happened because you believed . . . ?

MONSIGNOR: Because I failed to keep on believing, to keep on acting on that belief, I turned truth into a lie! I stood in the way of the light and kept others in the dark!

MONSIGNOR GUSMÃO: But you were wrong!

MONSIGNOR: Wrong? No. No. *This* time . . . (*Offstage, very low at first, then quickly rising, the children's voices again are heard, singing the hymn*) . . . even if I'm afraid, terribly afraid, I will go to the end, for how can I go against *this?* (His *hand unconsciously clutches his heart; then, raising his eyes*) I know Thou wilt not forsake me . . . if I do not fail Thee again!

MONSIGNOR GUSMÃO: Wake up, Andrada! For God's sake, wake up! This is utterly mad! You have no right to let yourself go like that, to work yourself up into an hysteria that will sweep *everybody* in its frenzy! Can't you see what's happening to you? Listen, Andrada, this . . . delusion of divine calling has its roots in the repression of a very natural impulse. Yes, *natural.* But because the consequences were, let us say, disastrous when you first acted upon it, you repressed it from then on, thinking it was an emotional weakness. And when the deeply repressed impulse surged violently to the surface, finding favorable terrain, it swept you with it.

PADRE MANUEL: Yes—yes.

MONSIGNOR GUSMÃO: And you only felt it to be of supernatural origin because you had repressed it too deeply—because, by continuously refusing to admit this "weakness," your conscious mind did not know it for what it always was: a devastating compassion. (*Padre Manuel nods assentingly*)

MONSIGNOR: (*After a moment; an enormous realization slowly emerging*) Compassion was the voice of God?

MONSIGNOR GUSMÃO: That is all it was!

MONSIGNOR: (*With rising excitement*) Then I did . . . Then I will go on hearing it!

MONSIGNOR GUSMÃO: But it was only something *natural,* Andrada.

MONSIGNOR: (*As if a revelation were suddenly unfolding*) Yet, the Creator . . . *how* else could He work? I mean, it is only logical to expect Him to write His designs into the natural tendencies He gave His creatures! Why do you think man was made to feel compassion? To indulge in a meaningless sentimentality? No, no! It *has* a purpose, but it is up to us to follow His designs, using the means He has given us. (*Walks about, with the joy of one who has found a rich new meaning to The Great Spirit of Life*) We are part of the universe. The wind blew, the blood stirred, life awakened. Compassion is God! Love is God, and faith . . . *and* the wind! God, the source of life gushing forth in a generous invitation to make us drink of Him and so quench the thirst that consumes us. All that impels us toward the preservation of this precious thing called "life" is God, trying to rescue us from the devastation of doubt, leading us away from the false ideals that frustrate us . . . raising us above the dust . . . and death. *That* is the miracle! But it is always up to us to go along with God or to remain behind.

MONSIGNOR GUSMÃO: All right! Tell it to *them!* Explain to them what you have said to me—what the miracle was.

MONSIGNOR: Explain? But they would not understand.

MONSIGNOR GUSMÃO: (*Urgently*) Andrada! Every second is precious now. You *must* tell them!

MONSIGNOR: But how could they understand? How could . . . ? Oh, what irony that men should need a false miracle in order to know the *real* one. I can't tell them that!

MONSIGNOR GUSMÃO: Andrada, you know that the punishment for a priest who disobeys is . . .

MONSIGNOR: I know I have to be punished!

MONSIGNOR GUSMÃO: Then, can't you see that even your sacrifice will have been in vain? (*Monsignor turns to him*) Yes! For if you refuse, *I* will have to tell them. *I* will have to deny the miracle!

MONSIGNOR: (*Suddenly staggers, in pain; then, passionately*) If there is a way . . . deign, in Thy mercy, to make them understand . . .

(*Outside, Beto smashes a bottle against the wall of the house. Monsignor Gusmão goes to window*)

PADRE MANUEL: (*Frightened*) Your Reverence, don't you think we had better leave before . . . ?

MONSIGNOR GUSMÃO: Come on, Andrada. They don't *deserve* your sacrifice. Tell them!

MONSIGNOR: (*Turns slowly to crucifix on wall*) One whose feet I am unworthy to touch and who was clean of *any* blame, sacrificed himself for people less deserving than these. (*A horn blows outside*)

PADRE MANUEL: My God, it's the reporters!

MONSIGNOR GUSMÃO: (*Turns*) I am terribly sorry, Andrada. (*He hastens out as the lights come up on the street*) People of Campina! Hear me, all of you! I have an important communication to make. (*All gather closer to him*) Dom

Camara, Bishop of São Paulo, has ordered me to tell you that there is no reason to believe that the cure which took place here was a miracle.

MONSIGNOR: (*Rushes out, shouting*) No! No! Don't listen to him! Don't listen to him!!

MONSIGNOR GUSMÃO: (*Attempting to restrain him*) Andrada, have you gone mad?

(*As Monsignor tries to free himself, Beto suddenly screams out*)

BETO: It's th' devil, I tell you! It's th' devil!

(*He dashes toward Monsignor Andrada as others shout: "Out with him! Out with the devil!" Beto grabs Monsignor by the throat and begins to shake him, violently. Monsignor screams. Beto lets go. Monsignor staggers forward, gasping for breath, then sinks to the ground*)

PADRE MANUEL: (*Rushing to him*) Oh, Monsignor, Monsignor! (*To Monsignor Gusmão, who also has rushed forward*) It's his heart! (*The people gather around the stricken Monsignor, stunned, crushed by sorrow and perplexity*)

NHÔ JANGO: Oh, *senhor cura! Senhor cura!*

(*Padre Manuel takes Monsignor's pulse, then desolately looks up to Monsignor Gusmão, shaking his head. As Monsignor Gusmão begins to give him the last rites, all kneel around Monsignor Andrada*)

NHÔ JANGO: (*Quietly weeping*) Oh, *senhor cura,* don't leave us now . . . please don't leave us now!

MONSIGNOR GUSMÃO: (*Rises, slowly*) Padre Manuel, have the body taken to the—church.

(*Padre Manuel rises and motions to the men around him. They lift the body of Monsignor Andrada and begin to carry it out, preceded by Monsignor Gusmão, and closely followed by Nhô Jango and the rest of the people, all with bent heads and stooped shoulders, like a sad, bitter parody of the longed-for procession. Suddenly, the bells of the little church start to ring. All stop and look up. The men carrying the body turn to Nhô Jango, as if silently ques-*

tioning him. At the same moment, the children's choir begins to sing. Nhô Jango does the same, motioning for the others to join in. Weakly, at first, but in gradually rising volume, everybody takes up the song, as they walk out toward the church. But now their heads are uplifted, their shoulders squared, and their ears and hearts filled with the sound of bells—"like the waters of the Panema streaming over the rocks of the Salto Grande")

Curtain

Stanley Richards

Within the comparatively short span of four years, Stanley Richards has become one of our leading editors and play anthologists, earning rare encomiums from the nation's press and the admiration of a multitude of devoted readers.

Mr. Richards has edited the following anthologies and series: *The Best Short Plays 1972; The Best Short Plays 1971; The Best Short Plays 1970; The Best Short Plays 1969; The Best Short Plays 1968; Best Mystery and Suspense Plays of the Modern Theatre; Best Plays of the Sixties* (the latter two, *Fireside Theatre-Literary Guild* selections); *Best Short Plays of the World Theater: 1958–1967; Modern Short Comedies from Broadway and London;* and *Canada on Stage.*

An established playwright as well, he has written twenty-five plays, twelve of which (including *Through A Glass, Darkly; Tunnel of Love; August Heat; Sun Deck; O Distant Land;* and *District of Columbia*) originally were published in earlier volumes of *The Best One-Act Plays* and *The Best Short Plays* annuals. His television play *Mr. Bell's Creation* holds a record: it has had more live television productions (both here and abroad) than any other play.

Journey to Bahia, which he adapted from a prize-winning Brazilian play and film, *O Pagador de Promessas,* premiered at The Berkshire Playhouse, Massachusetts, and later was produced in Washington, D.C. under the auspices of the Brazilian Ambassador and the Brazilian American Cultural Institute. The play also had a successful engagement at the Off-Broadway Henry Street Playhouse and is currently in the 1972 repertory season of the New York Theatre of the Americas.

Mr. Richards' plays have been translated for production and publication abroad into Portuguese, Afrikaans, Dutch, Tagalog, French, German, Korean, Spanish and Italian.

In addition, he has been the New York theatre critic for *Players Magazine* and a frequent contributor to *Playbill, Theatre Arts, Writer's Digest, Writer's Yearbook, The Theatre, Actors' Equity Magazine,* and *The Dramatists Guild Quarterly.*

As an American Theatre specialist, Mr. Richards has been

awarded three successive grants by the United States Department of State's International Cultural Exchange Program to teach playwriting and directing in Chile and Brazil. He taught playwriting in Canada for over ten years and in 1966 was appointed Visiting Professor of Drama at the University of Guelph, Ontario. He has produced and directed plays and has lectured extensively on theatre at universities in the United States, Canada and South America.

Mr. Richards, a New York City resident, is now at work on a collection of *Great Musicals of the American Theatre;* the second volume of *Best Mystery and Suspense Plays of the Modern Theatre; Best Short Plays of the World Theatre: 1968–1973;* and *The Best Short Plays 1973.*